CONNECTIONS

CONNECTIONS

JACKIE WEIN

ARPress
45 Dan Road Suite 5
Canton MA 02021

Hotline: 1(888) 821-0229
Fax: 1(508) 545-7580

Ordering Information:

Quantity sales. Special discounts are available on quantity purchases by corporations, associations, and others. For details, contact the publisher at the address above.

Printed in the United States of America.

ISBN-13:   Softcover   979-8-89330-366-7
                eBook   979-8-89330-367-4

Library of Congress Control Number: 2024900495

For the animals

ONE

MEMORIAL DAY

Chapter 1

When Rosa pulled up her living room blinds, it was officially morning on 83rd Street. She used the bottom of her housedress to clear a spot in the blurry window and pressed her eyes right up against the glass to squint at the world. "Eh, Princess, Wally is up too." She spoke to the Poodle standing in front of her, her paws resting up on the sill, even though she was still an inch too short to see out. To the fuzzy shadow of the roving super hosing the sidewalk, Rosa kicked her heels together and spat drily, "Achtung."

She patted her bun and rearranged a hairpin so it held her long, thick gray hair tighter. Rosa always put her hair up as soon as she got out of bed. Even before she put on her girdle.

"Okay, bambina, you ready? Rosa's thinking maybe she needs her jacket." She stuffed a wad of paper towels under her arm, the side of her heavy breast holding it firm. She went to the hallway, picked up the little roll of pooper-scooper bags, and pulled her tweed sweater off the rack that served as a closet in the old apartment. Her niece had knitted the sweater and sent it from Italy, maybe eighteen years ago. No, it was twenty-one, she remembered, because it was for her fiftieth birthday. It was what Rosa called her "dog sweater." It was too warm to wear under a coat in the winter and too hot to throw over her shoulders in the summer. It was perfect for walking the dog, early mornings and late evenings in spring and fall, to saunter up to Lexington Avenue or maybe over to Gracie Mansion for a stroll by the river.

Who else but the mayor would have a house—not a brownstone or converted garage or a loft, but a real eighteenth-century goddamn country house—with a yard so big it was a public park, in the middle of the busiest, most crowded city in the world? "Just goes to show." Rosa wasn't sure what, but it must show something. She showed them.

When her beloved Princess II had died, she had refused to let the vet have her body. To be flung into a pile with a lot of other dead animals and burned? Like garbage in an incinerator? Not her baby! The pet cemetery in Connecticut was a fortune. Besides, how would she get there to visit?

So Rosa borrowed a shovel from the janitor down the block. Then she borrowed the janitor. And while she kept a lookout, Hector dug a small grave in back of a bench in Carl Schurz Park behind the mayor's mansion in the busiest city in the world. When it was done, Rosa opened her straw tote and removed the precious little body. She pulled the plastic bag back and kissed the tiny eyelids and the tiny nose, which now felt spongy against her lips. Then she wrapped her tightly and placed her in the hole. She stood back, trying to hide Hector as he filled in the dirt. When he was finished, Rosa looked around until she found a long rectangular rock under a tree. She put it on the top, hoping nobody would notice the fresh earth. She didn't need a marker to know where Princess was. She would be forever where she loved to walk and play and smell the river breeze. And Rosa could come here as often as she wanted to sit on the bench in front of the tomb and silently talk to her.

"You and me, we have some-a wine now," she had said to Hector.

"Come on." She wiped her cheeks with the back of her hands and gratefully pulled Hector back to her apartment. She prayed nobody would wonder what he was doing with a shovel in the middle of the spring and arrest him. She could see the headline of the *Daily News*: SPADE SLAYER SEDUCED SEXY OLD BROAD. Which was why Rosa decided it was better to keep the brown paper bag over the bottom of the shovel and carry it herself, like a newly bought broom.

Whenever people complained about City Hall or New York City politics, Rosa smirked to herself and thought of Princess lying peacefully in the mayor's backyard.

"Let's get dressed, little girl." She took the red rhinestone collar off the next hook and, as she bent to put it on Princess III, something cracked in her spine. Straightening up and reaching for her back, as if she could realign it with her hand twisted behind her, Rosa mumbled to herself. She was the only person who could say "oy vey" with an Italian accent.

Chapter 2

Eileen Hargan reached to the edge of the sink for support as she hoisted herself out of the tub. The rim seemed to get higher every time she took a bath. She dropped the lid and sat on the toilet seat for a minute. The water had been too hot; it left her weak and drained.

The floor creaked somewhere in the apartment, and her bowels immediately twisted in fear. Another sound, closer, as an old slat of wood cringed under a weight. The door blocked her view of the hallway. She could easily touch its edge, open an inch, and pull it in. But she didn't want to see what was lurking there. "Fibber?" she whispered tentatively.

Instead of her past flashing before her, Eileen's future engulfed her. She imagined the police breaking in, finding her body crumpled on the tile floor, blood spattered on the walls. Her neck was paralyzed, but her eyes swiveled to her robe hanging on the back of the door. She saw it sway slightly as the door moved almost imperceptibly. Her chest pounded from the weight of breaths she could not exhale. She wanted to get her robe, cover herself, so that when they found her, she wouldn't be naked. The official photographer's flashbulb went off in her brain, capturing the wrinkles on her cheeks, the pleating of skin between her breasts, the circle of shiny scalp showing through her thinning hair, and the blue veins bulging on her thighs and ankles. But she couldn't move, couldn't get it. They'd call her nephew. Maybe Danny would come before they took her away. See her naked body. Turn away in revulsion.

The door squeaked on its rusty hinge. She stared at the widening space, waiting for the face that would appear. The face of the monster. The bogeyman. She caught a movement down lower, and a black-and-white head peered around the door. "Fibber McGee, you little bastard." Relieved and refreshed, Eileen stood up, shoved her partial plate in her mouth—grateful nobody saw it laying on the sink—and then put on her robe. "And you know I don't let little boys in the bathroom with me. What am I going to do with you?" He was too low to see in the medicine chest mirror, so she turned around to give him an exasperated look.

"Naughty boy." She bent down and squeezed him.

Chapter 3

Eyes by themselves are not particularly fascinating. Or even beautiful. Even though we like to romanticize their loveliness, or their depth, or their meaning. Because we want to believe that we can look through them, or past them, to the soul. If you removed fifty of them and put them in a bowl of water, they probably wouldn't look much different than floating marbles.

Clifford Marcus's eyes worked. They moved, they dilated, they blinked. If his vision were tested, he would probably be able to read the last line of the chart. His eyes—which were almost the color of the sea—gave just the right touch of blue to accent his pale complexion. But they did not perceive much. And even though Dr. Michelle Kravitz knew it was biologically impossible, she could actually see the emptiness behind them. While she was looking at him through the one-way mirror, the blue faded to a dull gray.

She watched him, with his arms crossed, holding his elbows as he rocked back and forth on the floor. She pulled the wall shade down over the glass, stalling with the cord before she turned to face Jessica Marcus. "I think it's worth a try. I don't know anything else to suggest at this point."

She wanted to remain professional—she was professional—but, she thought, there are times when you had to do what you had to do. She came around from behind her desk, pulling the extra side chair with her. She sat next to the pretty blonde woman she'd been seeing for two years and took both her hands. "I don't want to keep leading you on when there's no hope. At least, none that I can offer. There's just no point in your coming here, week after week, when we can't help him."

"I know." Jessica took a tissue out of her pocket and wiped her nose. "I know you did everything you could."

"He's not any better now than when we started. I know it sounds so… final. Cruel. But unless you institutionalize him…" She held up her hand. "I know—never. But unless you do that, I just don't know enough—we don't know enough here at the Center—to do anything for him. That's why I'm suggesting it."

"I'll talk to my husband tonight. So this is…good-bye."

"No, I'm not turning you out. I want to talk to you again. And Clifford. I want to see him from time to time. I'd like to keep in touch. After all we've been through together, I feel we're friends." Michelle smiled warmly and squeezed the other woman's hands.

"We are. You've been a wonderful friend. To Clifford and to us. Don't think we don't appreciate all you've tried to do. I don't mean to sound ungrateful, but I feel so…discouraged."

"Of course you do. Look, you've been doing this for nine years. Taking him from one doctor to the other, putting him through tests and more tests. Trying different meds. Hoping; being disappointed. There might not be any treatment for neurologically impaired children that will help your child. It's time you tried to accept the fact that it might never change, never be different. And get on with your life. I know that sounds harsh, but you've got to try."

They stood up together, and Jessica bent slightly to give the petite doctor a quick hug.

"If you ever feel like talking or need to unload, I'll be here. I want you to think about this as an alternative, something you can do on your own. And I want to hear how it works out."

Jessica walked through the door and gently pulled her son to his feet. She left without looking back.

Chapter 4

Jason Ruderman shuddered when he heard a jingle in the hallway as someone shook a key ring. He tightened his hold on Sabrina, rubbing his naked legs against her under the blanket. A thrust of metal into the lock, a jamming sound. A pause; more jangling. An indistinguishable curse. After almost a year here, you'd think Chris would be able to pick out the right key the first time. Sabrina lifted her head to listen. When the door finally opened and then closed quietly, she jumped out of bed and went into the living room.

Jason strained to hear the murmuring, to figure out what kind of mood Chris was in. Not that it mattered. He wasn't going to take this anymore; he would just put his foot down. The minute the bedroom door opened, Jason would say, *"Look, I hope you had fun tonight, but as long as you're living here with me, you can't do that anymore. You'll have to choose between me and your freedom."* He would not allow himself to be intimated.

There was a thud as cushions hit the floor. So Chris was going to sleep on the convertible again. Jason stretched out his arm, wishing Sabrina would come back so he could hold her. He wanted to hold someone, wanted to be held. Why did he do it, knowing how much Chris hated him for it? Knowing, even as he was begging Chris not to go out, how much he would be resented. His words, squeezed out between clenched teeth, had been tinny. They sounded shrill, even to him, stretched thin like pulled taffy. "Chris, please don't leave me, not tonight." As he pleaded, he knew Chris would stay out even later, maybe not come home at all.

Jason had lain in bed all evening, trembling, imagining Chris with someone else. Not so much making love as just being with someone, holding someone, when he needed to be held so badly. He had turned Chris away, he thought as he choked back a sob. "Sabrina," he whispered in the dark, wishing she would come back. Maybe she didn't want to be with him either. Jason curled his knees under his chin and chewed his bottom lip, sniffling to keep his nose from running onto the pillow.

Chapter 5

Her father was probably a Golden Retriever; about all that could be said for her mother was that she was a bitch, with possibly some Beagle or Terrier in her. Which would account for the caramel-colored spots on her back—more like sandy islands in a sea of white foam—matted now with dirt and grime. If anybody could trace her lineage back far enough, they'd surely find some Collie and some Irish Setter relatives. She was, with the thirteen pounds that had fallen off her ribs, forty-seven pounds. Her long face showed more aristocracy than the finest pedigree, and when she stood attentively, her tail swirled like a plume of feathers, higher than her head. All the pride of her strength and will showed in her bearing. She could afford to be arrogant, because she had survived.

She had been born in Vermont in the fall—one of three thousand puppies and kittens born every hour in the United States—and her long, thick fur was good protection during those first cold months of her life. Her mother taught her and her littermates how to squeeze under fences to find back porches and look for food scraps. When she was three months old, she knocked over a pail in back of a ski lodge and got caught stealing the garbage. But the manager liked her and started feeding her regularly. The first time it snowed, he fixed up a place for her in the garage. He called her Kid.

When the weather got warmer and the ice and snow melted, he closed up the house. "Wish I could take you with me, Kid, but I don't even know where I'm going. Just heading west. But if you're around when I get back next season, I'll see ya." He slammed the trunk and without turning around yelled, "So long, Kid," got into his car, and drove off. Kid ran down the road barking, calling to the car. But it didn't stop and after a while, she couldn't even see it anymore.

With a dim sense of loss, she roamed the countryside searching for something she did not know. Even if she had found her mother, she would no longer remember her. She returned to the lodge several times. She scratched at the garage door and tried to jump up to look in the kitchen window. But the lack of sound and movement within made the only house she had ever known uninviting.

Toward the middle of summer, when the heat sucked all the moisture out of her body and made her paws weak from her weight, she lay in the grass, letting the blades cool her belly while she dozed. When she woke, her ears stood straight up; she tilted her head toward the distance. The talking and giggling noises floating in the air meant people. Nearing them, the need for play and for companionship filled her young being and with renewed energy, she followed the ribbons of sounds.

They gave her water and food and affection. When the sun was setting and the picnic things were being packed away, the eight-year-old girl and six-year-old boy whined, "Can we take her home with us, please?" Their mother and father walked off toward a tree. It took them less than three minutes to decide. The man checked her neck for a collar, so he could notify the local SPCA In case someone was looking for her, and put her into the car. It was her first ride, but she didn't pay attention because she was so busy cuddling with the two children. By the time they arrived in Connecticut, they had voted on her name: Beauty. Once she got used to it, ever after the word meant "belonging" to her.

It was the happiest two years she'd ever know. She quickly learned the rules of living with people, took over the house and yard, and became one of the family. She ate well, played well, and loved totally.

The divorce changed everything. Although she couldn't understand the conversations and arguments, Beauty could feel the tension, the sadness that separated them all from each other. In the end, it was hard enough uprooting the children every six months in order to keep them together, spending half a year with each parent. But it wouldn't be fair to the dog. Besides, who could manage alone with two kids and an animal? The dog would surely be lonely if she stayed with the one who didn't have custody and who would then be tied down because of her.

So for her own good, they gave her away. They'd never have put her out or sent her to the pound. They were decent people; they went to the trouble of asking around, and then they put an ad in the local paper, describing her carefully as a "lovable mx br, affectionate, gd watchdog." They posted it on Craigslist. But unfortunately, nobody bothered to describe the man who came to look at her. No matter how much Beauty cried and clung to their legs, and the children wailed and pleaded, the strange man took her away. He brought her to an appliance outlet in White Plains, where she would protect the store from holdups during the day and intruders during the night. Because she yelped and tried so desperately to get out the door when it was open, he kept her on a long rope during the day and for the first weeks at night.

Sometimes she finished all her water by Saturday night and had to wait until he opened up at noon on Sunday for a drink. Sometimes he forgot to leave extra food over the weekend. The only conversation he had with her was to say, "Damn mutt, can't you shit on the paper?" For five months, she suffered from hunger, thirst, unpredictable beatings, and unbearable loneliness. Until the day she saw him carrying a heavy television set out to his van after hours. He couldn't set it down and pick it up again to close the door, so he left it open. Kid-Beauty-Damn Mutt watched from behind a washing machine until she saw him bend over the TV to secure it to the floor of the van. Then she bolted. "You damn mutt, come back here!" he yelled. Then he continued to maneuver the TV.

As she ran, her lean body streaking through the trees behind the parkway, her legs stiff from disuse, she knew what was far worse than her nostrils straining for the scent of food, worse than the dryness of her throat and the thickness of her tongue: captivity. So for nearly six months, she ran, mostly for the joy of it, scrounging, finding little-populated parks and woods to roam in. Sometimes, when she was tempted to nuzzle up against a person or catch a child's ball in a playground—when the need to touch living things pulled at her—she remembered what happened the last time. Some primal instinct for stealth kept her alive. And free.

Chapter 6

Men who didn't know her liked to tell Louise Sidway, in a suggestive tone, that she looked like she'd been around. "Around, over, under, and through but never Sidway," she'd answer. The fact was that she had been, and she wore her experience like a battle scar…a permit to be hostile. When she walked, her slightly hunched shoulders squared off her five-foot-eight frame, dragging her heavy hips and thighs down to a squat shape. Her lower jaw was perpetually thrust out in a defiant scowl. The makeup she wore to soften her harsh features only accentuated the geometric shape of her face. Her brick-red hair, bluntly cut to cover her ears, was like a copper helmet.

She couldn't help her masculine appearance, but most of her militant personality was part of an act. At thirty-one, she had given up ever finding anyone for whom she would stop playing the role. Her overbearing nature was a turn-off. Which suited her fine because then she didn't have to put up with any sexy talk, social pressure, or insensitive lovemaking. It suited her fine—*most of the time*. She had no family, few friends, and scarce pleasures. Louise Sidway felt it was all the city's fault and dreamed of the day when she could afford to go back to Maryland…and buy a small farm.

Until then, the only real joy she had was from Honda. As she turned the corner of 88th Street, she started to walk faster. She checked her watch, knowing that even if she hadn't been right on time, he'd be at the window, looking for her. She waved to him as she approached the staircase to the entrance. She saw him crane his neck to make sure it was really her. As she got closer to the building and farther from his peripheral view, he turned away excitedly to go to the front door. When she unlocked the inside door downstairs, she called up, "Hey, you big lug, I'm coming. Mommy's coming home." Waiting for her was unbearable, so she talked to him all the way up the three double-flights.

Chapter 7

Eileen Hargan neatly entered the amount of the dividend in her little ledger book, squeezing two zeroes in the cents column. More quarterly stock checks would probably be coming in this week, but she didn't want to leave this one lying around to be misplaced or lost or stolen. Not that she had ever misplaced or lost anything in her life. She made out a deposit slip and then put it on the small shelf in the hallway, on top of the envelope for Con Edison. She sat down at the mahogany secretary she loved because of all its little drawers, slots, and cubicles, took a lined pad, and meticulously planned her itinerary.

First, Chase, so she wouldn't have to carry the check around, and then over to the customer service center to pay the gas bill. She wasn't cheap, but why give the post office an extra forty-nine cents when her feet were quite capable of bringing her and her payment to their office? Besides, she liked to watch them type her account number into the computer and in a second read everything about her history with them for the past fifty years. The clerks were usually patient when they answered her questions about how the machine worked, probably as glad to break up their boredom with conversation as she was when she started it.

When she'd gone back to visit the school where she had taught for forty-three years and seen that they had all their records on computer, she regretted not being able to start all over again. She shook her head in disbelief to discover eleven- and twelve-year-olds were required to learn about chips and bytes and disks and programming. And that they *understood* and spoke this new language of computer science, which was so foreign to her. It was a completely different world out there, and she wished she could come back in about a hundred years just to see what was going on. Even for one hour.

The radio had predicted a beautiful day, so she'd take Fibber McGee with her. He slowed her down to a stroll, giving her an excuse to stop and nod at doormen and workmen in the neighborhood. Afterward, she'd bring him home, have lunch, and go to Associated for skim milk. Well, excuse me, Morton Williams. Why they would change the supermarket name to such a stupid one, she didn't know, and she'd always call it Associated. In her flowery scrawl, she added "Call Dr. Pomalee" to the end of the list.

Now that it was almost spring, she wanted to be sure Mr. McGee got started on the heartworm pills early, just to be sure. Maybe they could give her an appointment for this week.

She printed "Things to Do Today" on the first line, bent the bottom half of the page up, rubbed the crease, and neatly tore it off. She pulled the list from the clear plastic binding, put the empty scrap of paper under the last sheet, and then placed the pad and pen in their proper niches. She hung her list on the refrigerator door with a scrambled-egg magnet and went to get her Boston Terrier's leash.

Chapter 8

Rosa hooked the leash handle over the mini-picket fence imprisoning a puny tree. "Now, just sit there like a good girl," she said needlessly. She picked up the broom she'd left leaning against the stairs and started to sweep the sidewalk. If she waited for that Wally Schilder to do it, the dirt would get washed away by the snow, and this was only April. There used to be a time people took pride in their houses, even if they didn't own them. When Marliese Vilmer was the landlord, everything was kept ship-shape. Rosa missed her so much. Just when she had been improving, just when there was a big breakthrough in her therapy and it looked like she'd actually speak again, she'd had another stroke.

The brownstones Marliese had owned were sold to some real estate company. They hired a superintendent who lived in an apartment across the street from Rosa and who was supposed to service their buildings on 82nd and 83rd Streets. He had it too easy. Taking care of all the small apartments on the block wasn't really a full-time job. Daily, Wally Schilder picked up the garbage, made sure the boilers (which were held together with Scotch tape) gave heat and hot water, and then disappeared for the rest of the day. In an emergency, if you were lucky, Mrs. Schilder came to the door, said her husband was out, and then slammed it in your face. For this, the Schilders got free rent, free gas and electric, free telephone service (although they never answered their phone), and free cable. It infuriated Rosa. She watched Wally some mornings, going out with a toolbox. She long suspected he picked up extra money on another block, doing odd jobs for other landlords. Ones that owned one or two row houses and didn't have the money—

or, more important, the space—for a live-in super. Some day, when she was more ambitious, she would follow him and see what he was up to. She was grateful for Hector, the full-time super of the high-rise on the corner. He was always willing to help her when he had time. Change the light bulb in the ceiling, unclog the kitchen sink drain. Put in a new fuse.

In the meantime, she had to look at this view from her window. If she wanted it clean, she'd have to do it herself. "You resting, little girl?" Rosa asked as she swept the dirt toward the curb. Yes, this was a different world. A different Princess. Thank God for her.

She always vowed she'd only do the three squares right in front. But as she saw Mr. Browning come out a few doors away, she inched up to the next building. Rosa enjoyed being out there, talking to all the neighbors, having everyone call to her. Not that she needed an excuse, but sweeping was a good one for socializing.

Chapter 9

Lenny wanted to walk away. Or run. Pretend he wasn't married to Jessica, wasn't the father of a son like Clifford. If only he had enough nerve to just pack his bag. They'd find him, of course. Make him come back. Money was one thing. Maybe if he agreed to pay not only child support but alimony, whatever, maybe then they'd let him off the hook. He could write a check once a month or once a week. Cut the ties. The responsibility. If only he could do that. But they'd keep pulling him back, tugging at him, pointing their accusing fingers at him. The only way to do it was to go far away, change his name, his identity, start all over again, where they *couldn't* find him. Give up his business, his relatives, old friends. Stay out of touch; pretend to be dead. Some men could do it—*did* do it—but Lenny Marcus knew he wasn't one of them.

He closed the *Post*, picked up his iPad, and opened the app for the *New York Times*. He glanced at the woman he had married fifteen years ago. He tried to remember how he used to feel. He still loved her. But she looked at least ten years older than thirty-eight, especially her eyes, where tiny lines drew a fan at their edges. She was still beautiful, he supposed, but she just looked so tired to him. Or maybe he was tired of looking at her. He wondered if she ever dreamed about escaping too. If life was such that nobody would think her terrible or a bad mother, he wondered if she would do it.

With a twinge of guilt, he knew he added to her burden. Because she was no longer able to share it with him—her efforts, her hopes, her devotion. And that must make it all the harder for her to bear, doing it alone. The few times she had started to complain or just to talk about Clifford in the past three, maybe four years, he had cut her off with a reminder that he felt the best place for Clifford was a special home or boarding school. So they didn't discuss it anymore, because neither of them would give in, and Jessica sensed that any comment about her frustration or the futility would open up the subject again.

"Haven't you got enough work to do around here, taking care of him?" He thumbed the Menu button to get out of the Times and pointed his iPad in Clifford's direction before snapping the cover closed and putting it on the table.

"It won't be that much work. Especially if we get an older one who's housebroken."

"Who's going to walk it three or four times a day? You? You're going to get all dressed in the wintertime and go out in the cold with a dog? Before you fix breakfast?"

"If I don't mind, why should you? I'm not asking you to help or take it out."

"But it's still a big imposition. Having another helpless thing around… Oh, God, Jessica, I'm sorry." Lenny put his head in his hands and rubbed his forehead, as if the rubbing would erase the hurt, calling their child a thing.

"Listen, it's okay." Jessica came over and sat next to her husband, pulling his hands away from his face. "Even with old people it seems to work. There was something on TV last week. About bringing puppies and kittens into a nursing home once a week. The people looked forward to it. People who hadn't spoken to anyone or participated in anything for years. The pictures were so touching—elderly women holding out their arms for them. Their faces just lit up as they held them in their laps or stroked them."

"It's different, Jess. They're old, not sick. Not mentally incapable."

"Some of them are. Some of them are senile. Or have Alzheimer's. They find the patients feel more comfortable, more open and communicative. And they're doing some wonderful experiments with autistic children." Jessica spoke faster in her enthusiasm to convince him. "And what Clifford has is a lot like autism. There were a few cases that when they got a dog in the house, for the first time the child actually *responded*. Reacted to another living thing. Even Dr. Kravitz said it's worth—"

"Jessica"—Lenny took his hand from her lap and touched her soft blonde curls—"enough. You're the one who's doing everything. If you want to try it, well, okay. I suppose I could even take the late shift for walking."

"Oh, Len." She threw her arms around him. Just as her weight sagged against his chest, a frightened wail from Clifford's room made her jump up and go to her son.

Chapter 10

Jason clicked the shutter of his mental camera to save the scene of the sanitation truck pulling alongside one of its pails, with a bag lady bent deep into it. A burly garbage man grabbed the metal rim in his gloved hands and, for a minute, Jason thought the woman was going to jump inside for a ride to the jaws at the back of the truck.

He turned onto Columbus Avenue, consciously inhaling the scent of spring, along with the aroma of toasting rolls and perking coffee. He stopped in a hamburger place for breakfast, skimming the News as he sipped his coffee. The clatter of the thick cups and plates behind the counter, the sizzle of bacon on the grill, the squeal of brakes outside, the rumble of cars dipping into the huge pothole on the corner—all soothed Jason's nerves. He loved the West Side and was sorry he hadn't moved here years ago instead of only last summer.

Back in the 30s, it was the place to live in Manhattan, even though the Depression had changed it all. Most of the comfortable middle class had moved out of the area or jumped out of its windows, but he remembered hearing stories about his family's seven-room apartment overlooking the Hudson. By the time they moved to Long Island "to give the children a better place to grow up," changes had already taken place. Then they had grass and trees and beaches and parks, and his three older sisters considered the suburbs their realm. In the Jewish American Ruderman castle, there were only princesses. But Jason had felt deprived, because he longed for the noise, the traffic, the broken sidewalks, the blinking traffic lights, the commotion of the city.

When he was old enough, the great thrill on a Saturday night, while his sisters were dancing at a country club or a party, was to go downtown. To watch the couples strolling on Broadway, all dressed up, on their way to a theater or restaurant. To join them, pretending he was going somewhere too. When it got late, he'd go into one of the arcades or suck the foam off a beer at the all-night Grant's on 42nd Street, electrified with excitement. Or take the subway down to the Village, pocket his tie, open his collar, and mingle with the Bohemians—later, the hippies—terrified someone would recognize him and tell his father. It was different then, a time when it was safe to walk the streets and ride the trains.

When his sisters married and moved to better suburbs, his parents bought a small place in Florida, a novel thing to do at the time. It was only natural for him to move to the city where his roots were planted when he got out of college. In those days, the only place to live was the East Side. The glorious old buildings on the West Side were falling apart, bulging with the poor, the rent-controlled, and the Puerto Ricans swarming into New York. The plaster fell, the gilt trim peeled, the walls cracked, the bathtubs still stood on clawed feet, sometimes in the kitchen, and upper-middle-class people didn't want to live with the cockroaches—or with the Spanish.

So like everyone else, Jason looked for an apartment in the other direction. Although he was lucky to find something in a pre-war on 52nd Street off Second Avenue, in all the years he would end up living there, he never really thought of it as home. Turtle Bay was only a geographic area to him, never a neighborhood. Surrounded by commercial buildings and people who came there at nine to go to a job and left at five, he considered them all transients. Then he moved north to the 80s, which felt more like a community.

Jason had managed a photo shop on 39th Street for eighteen years. When the lease was up for renewal and the rent practically tripled, the owner decided to pack it in and retire, leaving Jason in a panic. It was Chris who convinced him to use his savings to open his own place. It was Chris who decided that Columbus or Broadway would be perfect and went with him to check out locations. And actually found an old camera store for sale. It was Chris who figured out that he'd have enough money to carry the store for seven months without taking in a cent.

Of course, it helped to know that if worse came to worst, Chris could at least pay the rent. Just in case the business didn't work. But it did work, had been working, for two and a half years. He would never get rich, but the store was certainly providing enough of an income for him to be comfortable. And even he realized that no matter how much money he would ever have, he'd never be secure. That was Jason Ruderman's nature.

Chris was an editor but also did a lot of writing at home. After he moved in, they were cramped, with his desk set up in the corner area of the living room, where the clacking of the keyboard interfered with the television sound, and the television sound interfered with the clacking. When they decided to get a bigger place—after all, it seemed like they were going to stay together—Jason thought he'd just look on the West Side. So during the post-lunch lulls in the store, he walked up and down the side streets, talking to people and doormen to learn what was available. Chris didn't care one way or the other because of his job's flexible hours and said it was more important for Jason to live and work on the same side of town when he had to worry about staying open late and working on Saturdays.

Jason knew he was going to live there as soon as the super unlocked the door. The ceilings were almost twelve feet high, some had beams. Intricate moldings on the walls; long, unnecessary hallways; thick doors with transoms; a square eat-in kitchen (a true luxury in Manhattan); an almost six-foot-long, high-rimmed tub—it all sent shivers of elation through him. It was only a one-bedroom, but as he quickly redecorated the rooms while the super tapped his foot, he knew it wouldn't matter. It was twice the size of the apartment they were in now, and the dining alcove between the kitchen and living room, well-defined by beams, could be closed off to make a study for Chris.

The building was not just a reminder of an elegant past but had adapted nicely to current housing needs and the requirements of the new middle class. The block itself was being transformed as little by little, the old multiple-dwelling brownstones were bought by individuals and renovated to their former grandeur as one-family houses. The larger buildings were being spruced up, their lobbies refurbished, doormen reinstated. There were scaffolds all over, promising pointing of bricks, new windows.

Chris had also fallen in love with it on sight, so they wasted no time bribing the agent with three thousand dollars, the super with one thousand, and signing a two-year lease. Jason was buoyed by his flair for decorating and by Chris's admiration of his creativity.

Even Sabrina had adjusted well to the move. He thought that at seven, she would be nervous and jumpy in new surroundings, especially since everybody kept insisting that Yorkies were high-strung. But she must have felt their pleasure, their comfort in being there, because she immediately seemed at peace and at home. After sniffing along all the baseboards and woodwork like a vacuum, she found a place behind the French doors in the living room where the sun spotlighted a patch of the hardwood floor for most of the morning. She claimed it as hers, so Chris put her pillow there. They were both sure that's where she stayed all the time they were out. While they were home, she followed either one or the other around, always staying a little closer to Jason. Nothing made her happier than when they were home together, sitting on the couch or lying in bed, where she could snuggle between them.

When Jason only worked on the West Side and left at the end of the day, he felt like a stranger, a visitor. But now, he belonged. In fact, everything seemed to be perfect for Jason Ruderman—his business, his home, his dog. Except for one thing. From the minute they moved in, his relationship with Chris started to fall apart.

Chapter 11

Kid-Beauty-Damn Mutt was lying at the trunk of a tree in the Botanical Gardens near a seldom-used path. A woman who walked very slowly, leaning on a stick, sat on a bench in front of her. She felt safe because this woman had sat there many days, knowing she was behind her. Sometimes she talked to her, her voice tiny and small but soothing. She always carried a small plastic bag inside her pocketbook. She would open it, smooth out a napkin or square of paper towel next to her, unwrap a sandwich, and eat her lunch. The dog's nose twitched, her mouth salivated, yet her basic fear of bondage kept her back. One day, the old lady finished eating and gently slipped the remains through the large slat in the back of the bench. Kid-Beauty-Damn Mutt crawled in the grass, grabbed the baloney and the bread and then darted back to the tree, keeping her eyes on the woman, who pretended not to notice.

After that, the leftovers got bigger, and the woman would divide her sandwich, leaving half of it on the bench. The dog stopped running, walked right up and ate, sitting in front of the woman. She finally let the old lady rub her head, massage her neck, or scratch her ears, which brought peaceful memories of being loved back to her. Now, feeling secure in her presence, she crept under the bench, its seat cutting the heat of the sun from her back, and slept. A sound or a smell or a disturbance in the air startled her awake. Her eyes opened on two legs in front of her snout. She looked up through the slats, just as a young man grabbed the woman's purse off her lap, turned on his sneakers, and ran. She screamed. It took a few seconds for the dog to scramble out, because she could not stand to her full height under the bench. By then, the boy was several yards away. She leapt onto his back without once touching the ground. Her weight, sprung from such a distance, knocked him down, and she barked against his ear, baring her teeth, racing around him in close circles. The old lady screamed again. The dog picked up the purse, her eyetooth puncturing the vinyl, and carried it back to her, dropping it at her feet.

The old woman fell to her knees, sobbing into the dog's neck, and hugged her. It was sort of an unspoken agreement that they would go home together. The woman didn't have much income besides her Social Security, but she shared whatever she had. She wanted to call the dog Protector or Lifesaver or Savior but thought it would be too embarrassing to both of them. When she looked into her warm, loving eyes, she said softly, "You're my little heroine, aren't you. Heroine. Roine. Roine, that's it." She filled out the application for a license, because she didn't want anybody to take her dog away because she hadn't obeyed the law, and spelled it as Rowan to make it easier for the people who processed the papers to pronounce it.

The old lady didn't play too much, but it didn't matter. Because Rowan was no longer a puppy; she had matured into an intelligent, warm companion. They answered a want in each other that made them inseparable for a little over a year. Until one afternoon when Rowan nudged the woman's back with her paw to remind her to feed her and licked her ear and saw there was no flutter of an eyelid. She knew, with her distant wolf and coyote ancestors' instinct for the way of life, that the old lady was no more. She sat beside her bed and howled her grief through the night.

By sunrise, several neighbors had called the police. When the super unlocked the door to let them in, Rowan was lying on top of her. But they took her anyway. She followed the stretcher to the street and after they slid it into the back of the ambulance and she tried to jump in, they slammed the doors. Someone said, "What about the dog?" And someone else said, "Aw, someone will take it in."

Rowan knew it was useless to try to follow the woman. Forlorn, she ran through the streets, whimpering. After two months, she joined a pack of vicious dogs that plagued the Bronx, and became as mean as they were. Eventually, her twisted front paw, hurt in a fight, slowed her down. So she was the only one of the pack picked up by Animal Care & Control when they ran out of an abandoned building.

Now, at five years old, she had lived a lifetime. Slightly lame and filthy dirty, Kid-Beauty-Damn Mutt-Rowan still showed an arrogance and spirit as she stood in her metal cage, her head slightly stooped because of its ceiling. Doomed to die in thirteen hours.

Chapter 12

Rosa sipped her glass of red wine, wishing she could go across the hall for a chat like she used to. She shook her head sadly, trying to get Marliese Vilmer out of her mind. She thought about her a lot. Today, Marliese crept into Rosa's thoughts constantly. But Rosa didn't want to face her or think about what happened to her.

"Wonder how Marliese is, bambina." She stroked Princess and considered calling Martin. But she wouldn't know what to say, how to ask if she was still alive. Rosa used to speak to Marliese's son regularly during the time she was in the hospital.

One day Martin told her he'd be coming over the weekend and would see her in person. When she heard them arrive—Martin and his wife and their son—she went across the hall. When she realized what they were doing, she frantically yelled from the doorway, "What she gonna do when she com-a home?"

"I'm afraid my mother-in-law won't be coming home." Marliese's daughter-in-law, with her platinum hair and long fingernails with very white moons, dismissed Rosa. But Martin sat her down and patted her shoulder. "We know how good you've been to Mother, especially since she got sick. You were her dearest friend. Still are. I know it hurts you. It hurts us too. To have to do it." He spoke to her as if she were a child. Or senile. "But she's worse, much worse, than after the first one, and the doctor says there's no way she can come home. The rehab center can't do anything more for her. She'll be going into a nursing home this week."

Rosa stayed and watched them go through the closets, move the knickknacks, examine the silver. She saw a balled-up cardigan on the floor and automatically picked it up. She gently folded the sleeves back, bent it in half, and put it on top of a pile of clothes. "This she's gonna need in the winter."

"That pile is for the Salvation Army."

"What? You mean you give all-a this stuff away?" Rosa's stomach churned.

Martin and his wife looked knowingly at one another. "Of course, you can go through it and anything you want, anything that fits, you're welcome to." The woman's voice reminded Rosa of diet soda. It seemed sweet. Until the artificial sugar went down and left a bitter aftertaste.

There was noise; greetings. She knew it was Marliese's sister from Arizona. That must be her husband and her two sons. Then Martin's daughter and son-in-law came. She'd be the one who had the baby. Marliese had never seen her great-grandchild, and Rosa knew she kept hoping they would bring the baby to her. "When the weather gets warmer," they said. Then, when the weather got warmer, they said, "Wait 'til it gets a little cooler out."

They were all polite when they said hello to Rosa. "Oh, I remember you from when I was a little kid." Or "You still have that funny little dog?"

Dully, Rosa sat down on the couch, a smile frozen on her lips.

"What the hell is this supposed to be?"

"Why did Grandma keep this, do you suppose?"

"Put that on the give-away pile."

"Who do you think will give us a bigger tax write-off—the Salvation Army or Goodwill?"

"This is disgusting. Can you imagine keeping it all these years?"

"Oh, let's just throw these out; I'd be too embarrassed to donate them to charity."

"Do we have another carton for garbage?"

"Who wants this table? Barbara, maybe you could stick it somewhere in your basement."

Every sentence jabbed at Rosa's heart as she listened to and watched a lifetime of mementos being discarded, while the descendants of a wonderful lady threw her heritage—and their own—into the garbage. It didn't matter what country it was; these possessions were from another world, from a childhood and a family long gone. They were part of Marliese Vilmer. Rosa shuddered to see how they were sorted out so impersonally. Oh, they didn't put the cut crystal from the great-grandmother in the donation pile. They weren't stupid. But the faded, frayed photograph of a nameless ancestor? That they put into the big black plastic bag.

Rosa had gone home, shaking. *It could just as easily be Italy as Germany*, she thought. Then she lovingly touched the few meager reminders of her own childhood, wondering what would happen to them when she died. Who would go through her things and look in her drawers? Hold up her old-fashioned corset and laugh, asking, "Would you believe the old girl still wore something like this?" She didn't have anything worth money, no jewels or antiques like Marliese had. Her sister wouldn't come from Italy. All these years, she'd never come. Why would she come when Rosa died?

But that's the way it was. Like across the hall—Marliese Vilmer's whole family together in her home for the first time. So many times she had wished for a visitor, some company. She would have been so very pleased to have them all gathered under her roof. If only she could be there too, to enjoy them.

Later, when Rosa had heard the shuffling of cartons and bags being dragged over the tile floor to the front door, she got into bed, clutching Princess to her chest. Princess was the only thing in Rosa's life worth anything. A chill shuddered through Rosa as she wondered what would happen to Princess if she died. Who would take care of her dog?

Now, thinking back to that day, remembering her friend and her own anxiety, a melancholy sadness overcame her. A teardrop fell into her glass, as it had turned out that Princess had died. Rosa had thought very carefully before getting another dog, knowing that at her age, she would probably die long before the dog did. She picked up her little love and rocked her. Guilt flooded her in anticipation of leaving her an orphan. What would she do without her? Would she be sent to some family and cry and howl all day, wanting her mama, wondering where she was? Would they put her in a cold cage at the Humane Society or the ASPCA, where she would cower, petrified, hating Rosa for abandoning her?

Now that Marliese wouldn't be able to take care of her dog as she had promised, Rosa thought of writing to her sister, asking her to take the dog. Going on an airplane, in cargo? To a strange country? It would probably smell funny to a dog. No. Besides, her sister might not even be alive then. But no matter where she went or how wonderful the people were, Princess would not be happy. The only thing was to have her put to sleep so she wouldn't mourn for Rosa.

Suppose she had a heart attack in her sleep? Or worse, a stroke, like Marliese, and didn't die? Nobody would find her for days. Poor Princess. Rosa couldn't bear the thought. She knew it was the only kind thing to do. She would write down instructions and leave them somewhere where they'd be found. But what would she instruct? Take her dog to the vet and have her put to sleep? She should do a will, even though there was hardly anything to leave to a niece and nephew in another country. But she should do it, for Princess's sake. Her fear for Princess and her fear for herself burned in her eyes. And Rosa whimpered to herself in Italian.

Chapter 13

Louise Sidway stuck her thumb under the leather to adjust her shoulder-strap bag. She didn't realize how tired she was until she climbed the two flights of subway stairs onto the sidewalk and counted the long crosstown blocks she'd have to walk from Lexington Avenue. She decided to stay on 86th Street, which seemed shorter because of store windows she could glance into and the crowds she'd have to pass through. Her feet hurt, her back ached, and she wished she could get home and just undress and relax. But she couldn't because of Honda.

As she approached the last landing in her building, his whimpering turned to yelping. "Sh-h-h, you want to get us thrown out?" she called, knowing he would only cry louder at the sound of her voice and that the neighbors would complain anyway. When people asked her why she chose such an unusual name, she casually answered that it had been the name of a Japanese lover she once had. That always shut them up. The truth was he reminded her of a motorcycle. She smiled as she unlocked the door and braced herself for the streamlined mass of black, with the chrome-colored triangle on his forehead, that would jump on her. His front paws rested on her shoulders.

"I know you're part Labrador, but nobody ever told me you're part horse too," she teased him. Following their ritual, Honda turned, raced to the bedroom, and stood on her bed to wait for her. She dropped her bag and followed him, collapsing with tiredness. She held him tightly against her, one hand kneading the thick fur of his neck. She kissed his face. "Hey, you gorgeous fella. I missed you."

After resting like that for a few minutes, cooing and stroking, she jumped up. "Come on, kid. If we don't go out now, the old lady's not going to make it." She hated using a choke collar on him, but he had once tugged so hard that he had come right out of his leather collar and almost gotten hit by a car. It was for his own protection. Louise gulped at the thought of something happening to him.

She'd been living in Manhattan only a year when her parents were killed by an exploding gas heater. Although Honda was really her dog, she had left him behind when she moved to New York. He was still young enough to adjust in a new home, where he'd have a long future. But his mournful eyes added to her grief. She couldn't explain his loss of two people to him. How could she, when she didn't understand it herself? He stayed close to her for the two weeks she was back in Maryland. She sobbed into his chest, screamed her anger at God into his ear, and held on to him for support. He was her only link to her past, the only living connection between her and her parents.

She rented a car so she could take him back with her and kept her sanity by talking to him for the five-hour drive. She had to move, because the landlady had a fit when she saw the dog. Still, she would have given up anything she had for him; she still would, because she loved him more than anything else she had.

Whenever she brought a man home, Honda always acted as chaperone. Some of her dates resented him; some would ask her to lock him up because they were afraid to kiss her in front of him; some were jealous. Honda stared at them with wary eyes, daring them to touch her. Except for rare occasions, she was relieved when they left. She'd cuddle up with Honda and tell him he was still the only man in her life. Her therapist once told her she deliberately used the dog as an excuse to get rid of the guys. She figured her dog was worth ten guys. She was bored with the therapist anyway, so she stopped going.

A cab turned the corner of York Avenue without slowing down, its horn blaring. They both jumped backward. It reminded Louise of the man who had told her, "It's cruel of you to keep such a big dog in an apartment. He belongs in the country." The guy was a schmuck. But Louise had felt terribly guilty in the beginning. Then she decided people belong in the country too; cities are not natural places to live.

But dogs don't have any more choice of circumstances than human beings do. Ask Honda which he'd rather have—a loving home in New York with her, or his freedom in the country with someone else.

"You'd rather be with me, right, Champ?" she asked him now. He was the only thing that really mattered in her life. If anybody ever tried to hurt him, she thought she'd kill for him. In fact, once, when she was very lonely and very depressed, she had…Jesus, she didn't want to think about that. She turned her head away, as if Honda could see her shame, and roughly yanked him towards the curb.

Chapter 14

"Something wrong?"

"No, sorry," Jason answered Suzanne, his sales clerk. "What did you say?"

"I told that guy you'd have to help him. The lens is mounted wrong, and he can't get it off the camera. I was afraid of breaking it. Here. I'll finish the lab receipts."

"Thanks." Jason went to help the customer, realizing how distracted he'd been. He knew he had been pouting all morning. First, he tried being indignant, but he couldn't maintain his anger when his chest was swollen with heartache. He wanted to come right out and say what he felt. But he was afraid Chris would just snicker in that demeaning way and walk out. Then where would he be? The very thought tore him apart. Even now, in anticipation of the threat, he wanted to cry, plead, and say, "I know you're pissed off because I've been acting stupid. But it's only because I need you so much."

He knew that would be the end for sure. Chris hated that kind of needing, that helplessness, accusing Jason of leaning too hard, like a drunk against a lamppost. The more he recognized the truth of it, the more Jason wanted to crawl into Chris's arms, admit he was weak, and beg forgiveness. Then have Chris stroke him and hold him, like a baby.

"That's okay." He waved his hand in dismissal as the man took his wallet out. "No charge."

Jason had always considered himself a fairly independent, self-sufficient person. Until he'd met Chris. Then he realized all his previous affairs had been casual ones. It was easy to be strong when you didn't care that much. With Chris, his insides boiled and his doubts and reservations melted, flowed right out of him. All the poetry and songs he'd ever heard equated love with giving. But it wasn't until he was forty-nine years old that Jason Ruderman fell so in love with someone that he unconsciously and naturally gave of himself.

Now he was scared that he was going to smother Chris. He only held on so tightly because he was afraid of losing him.

He had to stop acting this way. He would stop. Right away. Chris had given him so much. Confidence in himself, what he was, who he was. He'd taught Jason to believe in himself. Even opening the shop had been Chris's doing. And if it ended this very second, Jason would be a better person for the relationship. Because loving had given him freedom—from himself and his own fears. He owed Chris at least as much—freedom.

Gratitude and affection surged through him. Filled with tenderness and warmth, he nodded to Suzanne as he went into the small sanctuary of his darkroom. He turned the knob once beyond its stop, and the red bulb switched on over the door. Even though he didn't use it for that purpose anymore, since the computerized self-serve kiosks took over the picture business, he occasionally developed special photographs. And he relished the privacy of the dark, inhaling the smell of the chemicals as if it was an aphrodisiac. He took out his cell phone and dialed Chris's number. It went right to voicemail, so he tried his direct line.

"Christopher Barrett's office," his secretary answered, and Jason's ribs tightened over his heart.

Chapter 15

The stark gray walls made Clifford think this was another institution where white-coated people would attach wires or machines to him or pretty ladies would ask questions. When they went to the desk, he heard his parents speaking, but the words droned in his brain. Beyond the waiting people and the desks, there was a long counter with animals on it. People were signing papers and carrying big cartons with holes in them. There was barking, mewing, and yelping. Clifford didn't understand what was happening, but apprehension made him hold tight when his father took his hand and followed a fat girl down a narrow hallway toward two doors.

Clifford needed to follow the same routine every day. Exactly. He wanted to be told what he was going to do, when he was going to do it, where he was going to go. This was all different.

Clifford didn't read or watch television or listen to stories read to him, so he couldn't fear the usual monsters, villains, dragons, or bogeymen that haunted childhood nightmares. But the shapeless, formless demons his solitary soul created, the fiendish horrors his mind invented, clutched him from within and rooted him to the floor with terror.

Lenny pulled him, but he was paralyzed. Jessica knelt down and said "It's okay, darling, this is going to be fun. You're going to have a friend. It's okay. Mommy and Daddy aren't going to let anything hurt you."

He stiffened as she put her arms around him to reassure him. Over his head, Lenny Marcus gave his wife a defeated look that said her idea was a flop before it took off.

Frustrated but determined, Jessica put her hands under Clifford's armpits and tugged him straight. She hoisted him right off the floor, waited until her husband held open the first door, and then set him down on the other side of the threshold.

About two dozen cages decorated the sterile room. The traffic whooshing down FDR Drive right outside seemed to make the animals jumpy. It made Clifford uneasy too. Maybe the cars were a reminder there was life—and freedom—beyond this building.

The room was air conditioned and heated, so the temperature was always comfortable. The cages were large enough for a dog to stand to its full height, unless the larger ones were already occupied and a newcomer couldn't get the right size. The crisscross of metal helped to circulate the air and make it easier to clean. But the rods cut into the pads of the feet and left temporary ridges in bellies and sides. Smaller paws sometime slipped between them. The smell of disinfectant was testament to the fact that they were clean, as antiseptic as the walls and floors. The animals were imprisoned in agonizing and desolate misery.

Most of the dogs had at one time been part of someone, even though some of them were picked up as puppies born of strays. The craving for touch, the sound of voices, which, to many, still meant caring, was as horrible as the pain of their abandonment. The boredom, the isolation, the fear, the unnatural enclosure were worse than prison. At least there was a reason for prison. But the pathetic dogs did not deserve any punishment; their only crime was not belonging. They did not understand.

Clifford did not understand either. He only felt a wrench and a twisting of his little heart.

Their need to relate to people, to express their affection, to make contact, caused a commotion every time someone came into the room, even a familiar attendant. It was not like an orphanage where the children know one of them will be chosen and so must try to get attention. It was only the requirement of companionship that caused the furor.

The moaning and yelping echoed in Jessica's eardrums, and she was surprised at herself, because she thought she didn't have any pity left for anyone except Clifford. She was filled with sorrow and guilt because she couldn't free them all or take them all home. Lenny glanced at her and saw her pain. "Look at it this way. We're going to save one. One is better than none." He knew what she was feeling because he felt the same way.

"I know, but it's horrible."

"Look." His chin motioned for her to watch Clifford, whose head was turning in every direction.

"Aren't they nice, honey? Do you want to keep one? You can have any one you like, and we'll take him with us, okay?" Even though he didn't say anything, Jessica thought her words registered. She was so used to his nonresponsiveness that she could detect the slightest difference in him…a faster blink, an extra swallow.

The smaller dogs jumped on hind legs, leaning against the metal, poking their black noses through the openings. Some of the bigger ones stood and howled or hit the cage with a paw, as if beckoning to them. For the first time in his life, Clifford felt something—excitement. His father guided him up the aisle. "Look, son, look at this cute little puppy. Do you like him?"

Clifford put his hand up to the cage, and the puppy squealed, licking him. The wet tongue tickled his palm. He smiled. Lenny and Jessica nudged one another with their eyes. They were thrilled. Clifford never smiled. They didn't dare break the spell, their hope.

Kid-Beauty-Damn Mutt-Rowan watched the three of them. She waited, motionless. When they came closer, she looked at the smallest one and sensed the distrust that made him withdrawn. She stood then, regal in her stillness, not making a sound, not moving. Except for the white plume of tail that spun in circles behind her.

Clifford stopped in front of her, and his empty blue eyes met her dark black ones. There was a brief moment, as though time stood still, when they both saw the same solitude and loneliness, recognizing themselves in each other.

Clifford turned to his mother and pointed to the cage. "Kola."

When he was younger, he had a koala bear that he slept with and cuddled. In an attempt to make him have the same contact with people that he had with the stuffed toy, the psychiatrist of the moment suggested Jessica take it away from him and make him transfer that need to humans. Clifford hardly spoke so he never said anything about its loss or a replacement. But occasionally, when he wanted to be held, he lifted his arms and said, "Kola." The word was a translation of the only affection he had ever shown for anything. The toy had been gone five years; Clifford hadn't used the word in two.

"I thought we agreed a puppy would be better. To make sure it would adjust to him," Lenny whispered.

"What do you want me to do? Do you realize he spoke, Len? He must really want it. Let's just see what happens." Jessica turned to her son. "Clifford, darling, do you want to look here…come on, honey. See this one. He's just a little baby. He wants to be picked up. Do you want to hold him?"

Clifford followed his mother and stopped with her in front of each cage. Then he walked back and stood in front of the part Retriever, part Beagle, part Terrier, part Collie, part Setter, the caramel-spotted, graceful animal, née Kid-Beauty-Damn Mutt-Rowan. He squeezed his hand through the hole. The dog sat down and nuzzled her snout against the small fingers. And whined.

The Marcuses nodded to the woman who had been watching from the door. She opened the cage and let the dog out. She tumbled over herself and them, trying to get to Clifford. Standing on her hind legs, she was as tall as he was. She dug her front paws into his shoulders and started to lick his eyes and cheeks and chin.

Lenny automatically went to support the boy, thinking he would be knocked over. Jessica put her hands out, ready to enclose him when he became afraid of the animal's closeness and ran back to her. Lenny stood behind, waiting. Jessica squatted in front, waiting. Clifford put his arms around the dog and pressed his face into her thick neck.

Jessica blotted a tear on her face, and Lenny took a long swipe at his nose. "Come on, Kola. Let's go home."

Chapter 16

E ileen cursed as the driver stepped on the brake and sent the standing passengers skidding into one another. The traffic on Third Avenue was practically at a standstill. She knew it would move faster as soon as they passed the bridge entrance on 59th Street. She looked at her watch again and mumbled to herself. The young girl sitting in front of Eileen lifted a bud out of her ear and raised an eyebrow, thinking Eileen had said something to her. She looked away guiltily, afraid an acknowledgment would require her to offer her seat. Eileen realized that and stared at the girl's head. Young people today were like that. Maybe it was because she didn't look that old. Hah, you old bat, she told herself. Who're you kidding?

Eileen bent slightly so she could look out the window. She couldn't see the sky, but she knew from the shadows on the glass and concrete that dusk would soon start to settle on the city. Frantically, she searched the street past the driver's head and saw that the confusion of cars and trucks and cabs thinned out a few blocks away. She had nobody to blame but herself. Everybody yelled at her to take cabs. The last time she went to the doctor, Danny had said, "Even if it's the middle of the afternoon, you could splurge. At your age, why do you have to be bothered waiting in line, climbing up those high steps, standing all the way, and then walking from a bus stop? Take a taxi, dammit." Easy for him to say, easy for her friends. What did they know about her situation?

Her friend Patsy had announced one day, "Don't kid me, Eileen Hargan. You've got piles stashed away. What with your Social Security and your teacher's pension…and I almost forgot the money your father left you."

"It wasn't very much, even forty years ago."

"Maybe not, but I bet you still have every penny of it."

"Wouldn't you like to know. Everybody counts everybody else's money.

But nobody really knows how much it costs somebody else to live."

"How much it costs to be insecure, don't you mean?"

"Never mind. Besides, I was brought up to save for a rainy day."

"You have enough money saved for the next flood! You can gild your own luxury ark and last forty years on what you've got."

"Mind your own business, Patsy McQuinlan." Eileen had said it jokingly, but she was angry. Everybody thought she had a lot of money put away. What's a lot, when you never know what you're going to need it for? Patsy McQuinlan had five children and thirteen grandchildren. Eileen Hargan had nobody except her nephew Danny. Suppose she got sick. She wouldn't go to one of those state-owned homes. No way. She'd go to a private place to live out the rest of her life. She had to be damned sure she could afford to do it. And if that happened, what would she do about Fibber? She'd keep the apartment and have somebody come in to live with him. No, the poor little thing would absolutely die without her. He wouldn't understand where she'd gone. There was no place that would take her with him, that was for sure. Didn't matter. Her mother used to say, "Don't look on anybody else's plate or in anybody else's bank account." It wasn't anybody's business if she wanted to live like this. She didn't deprive herself of anything she really wanted. But she'd never, ever do this again and go down to Judy Boylan's, unless she left there by two or three o'clock at the latest. Every other Thursday, Judy came uptown for tea and an afternoon of what they called "girlie talk." When she left, she always said, "Maybe you'll come by me next time, huh?" And Eileen always answered, "Maybe." Then, when they'd talk, Eileen'd remind Judy, "You know how I hate to leave Fibber McGee if I don't have to." Last time, Judy said to her, "Oh, I've been listening to that stupid excuse for years. You've become a little old lady, know that? Never go out, never get dressed…in real clothes.

You go as far as the supermarket and the bank and come right home. That nephew of yours, heart of gold, begs you to go for a weekend, a week, even a day. He'll pick you up and bring you back, with Fibber, and you never go. You're just shriveling up in that apartment, and it has nothing to do with your damn dog!"

So Eileen went to visit Judy Boylan down on 13th Street, where she'd lived for the past forty-seven years. Just to prove Judy was wrong. Eileen had to admit she hadn't minded so much. It was an excursion for her. She put on a pretty dress, and shoes with little stubby heels. As a last thought, she even wore her black spring hat and carried white gloves. Then she noticed she was the only person on the bus with gloves, so she folded them and put them in her pocketbook. No, it wasn't so bad, unless she thought of Fibber, and then a longing for him stabbed her. She knew he'd be okay alone. He always was when she went out to do errands. But she didn't like to stay away so long. She missed him. But she also realized she was apprehensive about other things more than about him.

Now, as she gratefully stepped through the back doors of the bus someone held open for her and started toward home, the block between Third and Second, it began—the anxiety that fluttered in her chest, tickling her ribs. It was still light enough outside, but things happened even in broad daylight. The fear that someone would break in when she was out and would be there waiting for her when she returned was unbearable. As she walked down the pretty tree-lined streets with the well-kept brownstones wedged between large buildings, it all looked so harmless and peaceful. But hurrying along, Eileen imagined sitting on the toilet…a grotesque man lunging at her from behind the shower curtain. She pictured him hiding in the bedroom closet, waiting and watching out of a narrow slit while she got undressed, and then he would charge out and attack her. Or he would be under the couch when she sat on it to watch television and would grab her ankles and pull her by her feet, looking up her bathrobe, between her legs. However he got her, he would do terrible, perverted things to her. But he probably wouldn't have to kill her. Because she would choke to death on her own terror.

When she was rational, she asked herself why Fibber wouldn't bark to warn her. But she had the answer all ready. He would be drugged, of course. Part of her fear concerned her beloved little Boston Terrier helplessly watching her being murdered, too lethargic to come to her rescue. Her body might lie there for days or weeks before somebody found her, before Danny might be worried and drive into the city. Poor Fibber would starve to death by then or die of a broken heart.

As she climbed the steps to the front door, Eileen braced herself. If he wasn't already inside, she knew what happened to old ladies. She thrust the key into the inside lobby door, picturing a hulking black man sneaking in behind her…waiting until she was at her own apartment, waiting until he heard the click of her lock, waiting until she opened the door. And then he would be behind her, pushing her inside, a knife against her back. He would tie her up to a kitchen chair and gag her. She would watch him ransacking her things, waiting for him to come back to rape her, to do unmentionable things, and—finally—mutilate her body with his knife.

Her heart thumped; her arms broke out in goose pimples. She wanted to turn around and check behind her, but the hairs on the back of her neck weighed her down with such a heaviness that she couldn't swivel her head. Her bladder was full.

She unlocked the apartment and rushed inside, dropping her bag on the floor. She slammed the door quickly, bolting it before it had closed tight, so that she had to open it and close it again. Fibber, alive and crying his delight, jumped on her. His stump of a tail moved back and forth like a scolding finger. Eileen bent to hug him. With one arm, she clutched him tightly; with the other, she crossed herself. She wailed a Hail Mary in gratitude for her safety, and wet her pants.

Chapter 17

Chris lit a cigarette, drew on it deeply, and blew in Jason's face playfully.

"Thanks a whole lot," Jason said, coughing.

"Don't let her bother you."

"Oh, I wasn't even thinking about her," Jason said. He picked up the piece of paper on the night table, read it again silently, and then recited it aloud in a low voice. "'And Adam said, This is now bone of my bones, and flesh of my flesh: she shall be called Woman.' Genesis chapter two, verse twenty-three."

"Wait 'til she gets to the New Testament. We'll be in for a lot of 'ye sinners.'"

"First we have to go through all the 'thou shalt nots.'"

"How about, 'Thou shalt not fuck around with us, Mrs. Pedersen'?"

Jason laughed.

"Seriously, does it bother you?"

"Not in the way you think. Maybe a couple of years ago it would've bothered me. Now I'm just angry."

"Don't waste your energy being angry at her. She's not worth it."

"I know. All the more reason I can't get over her audacity. Thinking she's better than we are, than I am. Thinking she has the right to judge. The nerve."

Nettie Pedersen lived on the top floor, probably so she could be closer to God. There would have been a saintliness, a holiness to her devotion and worship, if it weren't for two things: One, she ordained herself as the Almighty's interpreter and spokesman; and, two, she was married to a drunk.

She had been overheard commenting to neighbors about two gays having moved into the building. People shrugged, as if to say "so what?" In this day and age, who cared? She made a formal complaint to the landlord about renting to homosexuals. That was before same-sex marriage became a reality. He patiently explained that they both had signed the lease and besides, the law allowed two people of any kind to cohabit. He politely told her that as long as there were no wild parties, drug-related crimes, or loud music, she should mind her own business.

She then tried to have Jason and Chris evicted on the basis that pets weren't allowed. They weren't, in most New York City rentals. But since this was an old building with some elderly rent-controlled tenants who had animals but no lease, and since the landlord himself had a German Shepherd, he didn't care. He patiently told her, in so many words, that as long as the dog didn't bark all night or shit in the lobby, she should mind her own business.

Nettie Pedersen was so sure of her righteousness that she did all these things out in the open and even put copies of her letters under their door. When it was obvious that her campaign was getting nowhere, she started leaving Bible quotes for them—anonymously.

"Before I knew you, I would've been…bothered," Jason admitted. "Ashamed that people knew. But not anymore."

"Good." Chris put his arm around Jason and blew a smoke ring up to the ceiling. "I know you've changed. I'm glad you see it in yourself."

"You know I do. See all the good things in myself that you've brought out. I'll always be grateful to you."

"They were there all along, Jason, only you just didn't see them yourself."

"I feel good about myself. Even good about being able to look her in the eye and not cringe. I know who I am, and guess what? I like myself, generally speaking. I'm proud that you like me too. You know what's wonderful? All my life, I felt so humiliated, so afraid someone would find out. Now, I'm not ashamed anymore. I feel free, because I can be myself. I'm me and people will either like me or not like me. I don't have to please them. I don't have to please anyone except myself. And you, of course." He pinched Chris's cheek. "Oh, my God, and of course, you too." He nuzzled Sabrina who was lying flat on her stomach between them, listening.

"I don't want to hurt anyone or cause anyone pain. But what I'm doing couldn't hurt anyone, unless it's me. No, that's not true. I suppose it could hurt my family, but it shouldn't. As close as I am to them, I never could face telling them. But now I know I'm going to. I want to. Once I do, I think they'll even like me better because they'll understand me so much better. And they'll still love me…I'm sure of it. Once they know about you, I think they'll be glad for me, glad that I'm happy. And I *am* happy." Jason leaned on his elbow and stroked the thin hedge that started on Chris's chest and wound up in the shrubbery around his groin.

Whether it was the sudden huskiness of Jason's voice or the deep breath as Chris inhaled the smoke and pleasure, Sabrina sensed the lust, the sensuality, and leaped off to hide under the bed. Chris stubbed out his cigarette and slid down from the headboard.

Jason flicked his tongue lightly over Chris's nipples. When they hardened, his head went back and forth, his lips sucking one, then the other. As if his flat breasts were connected to his groin, their tautness pulled his penis straight up so it dug into Jason's belly. His own cock responded by springing to stiffness. He moved all the way down, his legs straight out, his tongue wriggling down and around, leaving glossy spots of wetness, until he got lower, and the coarseness of the pubic hair numbed his face. He kept crawling backward until his knees were off the bed and able to bend. Gently, his hands pulled Chris's thighs farther apart. His tongue licked the underside of his testicles, lightly circling, darting into the corrugated grooves of skin, moving up the center, lingering at the spot between his balls and prick, and then fluttering beneath the long, rigid organ, measuring its length in liquid inches, reaching the tip, blowing softly with his breath, retracing it back underneath as it twitched and pulsated from his teasing. It throbbed, and Chris moaned while Jason did it again. He reached the tip, curled his tongue, glided it back and forth across the slit, and then moved it back down along the top of the petrified muscle.

Chris's shoulders sank deeper, his buttocks lifted up to thrust into Jason's mouth, his hands reaching for Jason's head, pulling it down. "Oh God," he groaned. Jason moved up, his knees straddling Chris, his torso raised so he could bring his mouth down hard over the stiff prick, deep and hard, his nose pressed into the softness of Chris's belly. His lips held on tight as his head bobbed up and down, almost off, then down all the way, back and forth, up and down.

"Let me do you too," Chris whispered, trying to sit up, trying to reach under Jason's chest. Jason quickly put his hand where his mouth was, never losing a beat of the frenzied rhythm. "I want to make you feel good. That's making *me* feel good. I don't want you to do anything except enjoy it."

"I am, I am. Christ, Jason, I'm going to explode. It's terrific. You're terrific." His words came out in short staccato pants, and Jason stopped talking and used his mouth again, more intensely, heaving his weight in time to Chris's tremors until the body beneath him jerked, and the penis inside his mouth swelled, stilled, and burst in a great rush of hot syrup. Chris wailed a wordless prayer and collapsed, turning to rubber.

Jason lay with his head buried in his lover's stomach. "You *are* bones of my bones and flesh of my flesh."

The bed stopped thumping, the sex smell came, and the tone of voices gentled. Sabrina peeked out and knew it was over. She jumped up, wagging her tail.

Chris's fingers played with Jason's thick curls, kneaded his scalp. "I love you, Jason. That was wonderful." Then he moved his hand to pet Sabrina.

"It was for me too. And you know what?"

"What?"

He bellowed up to the ceiling, "Eat your heart out, Nettie Pedersen."

Chapter 18

W ith the phone tucked in the pocket between her neck and shoulder, Jessica was able to talk while she dunked her nylon underwear in Woolite in the kitchen sink. "We can't get over it. It's not even a slow progression. It's like one minute he was half-dead, in a coma. The next, he's alive and kicking, as if nothing happened. As if all the years before now never happened."

"I'm thrilled. What else can I say? I'm just…well, thrilled." Michelle Kravitz's excitement matched Jessica's.

"It's not only that he's *talking*. That in itself would be a miracle. But he's so *animated*, so enthused. All of a sudden, he wants to know everything. He's going through a stage most kids go through when they're two and three, asking questions and stuff. It's like he has to catch up on all those years he missed."

Michelle's voice rose so much with her enthusiasm that Jessica had to move the receiver away from her ear. "I told you they're doing it in many places. People volunteer with their pets or they get a local shelter to bring the homeless ones to people confined in institutions. It's wonderful therapy for the disabled, for the emotionally disturbed, and especially for old people. They react; even the most withdrawn people reach out. And returning veterans suffering from PTSD, from nightmares and the stress of war, are comforted. The animals' affection, their acceptance, bring out the best in a lot of people. Even here in the city, the ASPCA-run Pet Assisted Therapy program has been very successful".

"I might look into it," Jessica said.

"What for?"

"Well, I'd like to help someone else. This has been so fabulous, and I think I'd feel terrific seeing results like that, giving someone new life. It's wonderful; it's exciting. Will you come and see the change in Clifford?"

Michelle's voice boomed. "Of course I will."

"Even if they let me bring the dog over there, it wouldn't be the same as in our own place. I want you to see for yourself, watch him talk and cuddle and *play*. Like a normal kid."

"I promise I will. I'll stop by one night next week on my way home. Is that okay with you?"

"Yes, yes. Try to let me know the day before. I want Lenny to be here, so he can thank you too, so he can see your reaction. I can't wait."

Jessica rinsed out the plastic pail she used to wash the floors. She put her underwear in it so it wouldn't drip all over and went to the bathroom to hang it in the tub. Afterward, with the empty pail swinging over her arm, she stopped in the living room archway. Clifford lay on his side, facing the TV. Kola was lying on her side next to him, her back against him—with her tail straight, she was longer than he was. Clifford's arm was folded to pillow his head; his other was around her, stroking her massive chest. They looked like two lovers holding each other in the night. Jessica swallowed the lump in her throat. "Whacha doing?"

"Nothing."

"Should I turn the TV off?"

"No, I'm watching. I'm just lying here, watching."

"Don't forget we have to go out in a little while. Our appointment's at one."

"I won't. But you said they already examined her before we got her."

"I know, but we want to make sure. Anyway, we should have our own vet, one who knows her, just in case she gets sick or anything. Besides, you heard what the lady said: it's almost time to start the heartworm medicine for the summer." Jessica impulsively put the pail down on the wooden floor in the hallway and then knelt beside them on the rug. "Anyway, we're not going to let anything happen to this pretty girl, are we?" She put her face in the thick breast. The thudding of Kola's tail echoed through Jessica's face to her ears, in time to the beating of her own heart.

They all shifted until Jessica was on her back, with the dog's head on one shoulder, her son's on the other, and her arms around each of them. "I love you, Mommy," Clifford whispered. Jessica turned her head so he wouldn't notice the tear, which fell onto Kola's snout. Her tongue stretched up to lick it off and then reached for Jessica's cheeks.

Chapter 19

Dr. Michelle Kravitz sniffled to cut the burning in her nose. She wished she could take some of the credit. Wished a modern medical discovery or treatment had cured Clifford Marcus, instead of a scroungy mutt. Realizing the intangible bond between boy and dog—a bond that couldn't be tested or analyzed or controlled by any scientific method—made her pause in respect and awe of the things she didn't understand, the things beyond her and her own private world.

It had been so long since she reflected on such things or had an abstract question, an emotional response. A light flickered in her dark soul. There was still love in the world. People still fell into it. Even a hopeless little boy and a sad, unwanted dog could feel its impact.

Michelle went to the window. She wanted to open it, but it was sealed, like all the windows in the building. But she could see the breeze ruffling the leaves on the trees below; she almost could feel its breath on her face, almost smell the sweetness of the flowers recently planted in the three-by-four-foot gardens on the sidewalk. She almost could feel lonely. Sad. The light flared in her and blinked. It was called hope. And she was overwhelmed—and grateful—to know that she still had any.

Chapter 20

A few young boys hung over the railing on the top floor, looking down on their heads as they climbed up. One of them threw or spit a wad of gum into the stairwell. It just missed Louise's hair. *"No me joda,"* Louise yelled without looking up. A few giggles overhead assured her she had used the right expression to say "Don't fuck around with me." The boys were laughing at the culprit, not at her. At the next landing, she ventured an upward glance, and they stepped back a little. "Hey!" she said loudly and gruffly. It was a greeting.

"Hallo," only one of them answered. They were probably about ten or eleven years old. Any older, and she'd be petrified they'd have switchblades or ten gang members behind them. They probably did anyway. But they were still young enough to be just a little afraid of her and of their parents. She followed Yolanda Santiago up the last flight, deliberately exaggerating her panting for the boys' entertainment. They laughed when she pretended to collapse, out of breath. She ruffled two heads as she went by, waiting for Yolanda to unlock her door.

"Elena!" The shrillness of Yolanda's voice made it a shriek. A girl of about nine came running to kiss her. "Hi, Mommy."

"Say hello to the lady, Elena. This is Señorita Sidway from the Welfare." When the girl saw Louise, she swayed slightly, swinging her hands behind her back. "Come on, say hello. Hey, you want her think I don't teach you no manners?" Elena shyly played with her skirt.

"Hello, Elena." Louise casually dropped her hand on the girl's shoulders. "I hear a lot about you, about how you help your mother with the twins and everything. Where's your brother and sister?"

"They went to the store with Señora Sanchez," she mumbled behind Yolanda.

"Gee, you're real pretty." Louise felt obligated to compliment her.

Elena tilted her head in a little laugh, trying to bury herself in her mother. She *was* pretty. Her long hair was in a neat ponytail. Pulled straight back, it left a few dark threads at her temples, which trailed loosely along her jawbone. She was so serious. Louise wondered how she would look with that thick hair in a short, stylish cut, bouncing with body. She'd turn into a real beauty. Unless she got pregnant during puberty or ran away from home at thirteen with some pimp. Louise saw girls like Elena, with four kids by the time they were twenty or twenty-two. They might start out trying to be good mothers, but alone, with no money, how could they cope? She hoped that wouldn't happen to Elena.

Her mother must've been pretty once too. Yolanda was still attractive but haggard and worn-looking. Who wouldn't be? After her twins were born six years ago, her husband ran back to Puerto Rico. Then her mother ran *from* Puerto Rico to suffer the last year's ravages of cancer, living with her daughter. The husband stayed in Puerto Rico, then came back, and then left again. Yolanda never knew when he closed the door if it was for the last time.

Now that Louise saw where Yolanda actually lived, she felt even more compassion for the woman. To live in a dump like this, to have to hold your nose to get past the stench of urine and garbage in the hallway, to practically seal your door against invading armies of roaches, to have so few possessions and all of them faded, bare, mismatched, although clean and comfortable…Yolanda had evidently trained her children well, too. Louise noticed the neat piles of books and crayons on the table, which must serve as dining/cocktail/kitchen table. And desk. Good for her. Louise Sidway was determined to help Yolanda Santiago.

Louise remained where she was, examining the contents of the apartment, trying to figure out what had brought her here. This was a far cry from the great criminologist she had intended to be. When her friends were daydreaming about becoming models or actresses, Louise Sidway imagined herself a warden at a maximum security prison. Her innovative procedures and trusting rules would revolutionize the national penal system. She would be loved by the inmates, adored by the staff, revered by the whole country.

When she arrived in New York, full of her own importance and with her master's degree in sociology, she had to take the civil service exam like everyone else. It was just her luck—that year the penitentiaries were full, not only of prisoners but of employees. And she felt overqualified to enroll in the Correctional Services Training Academy. So she accepted the next best thing offered to someone with her credentials. She planned to work only temporarily as a case worker for the Department of Family Assistance and Disability and Children and Family Services, which was how the Welfare Department had glamorized its name. But as she became more involved, Louise realized she'd probably never leave.

In the beginning, she wouldn't admit that she enjoyed the power— the power of deciding who would get what. Who was entitled. The power of having people squirm before her, trying to please her so she'd sign the right papers. When she got into it with her therapist, she finally understood that it was more her need for power than her desire to reorganize the nation's correctional facilities that had made her go in for criminology.

Louise came back quickly from her ego trip. With the steady stream of pathetic people she interviewed, her feeling of authority eventually wore off. She got no pleasure from being in command of poverty-stricken women trying to feed hungry babies or from controlling ambitious, willing men whose lack of education or language kept them unemployed. The thrill was gone. Instead, she got through her heavy caseload each day, trying not to care, trying not to get involved. She learned how to process the people like file numbers. She was good at objectivity, which was why she soon was promoted to a supervisor.

Every once in a while, somebody got to her. A lot of cases were referred to her. On the occasions when she immediately had an affinity for someone, it screwed up all her remoteness. Or she'd have an instant rapport with a person about whom she'd think, *There but for the grace of*

God go I. Which is what happened with Yolanda Santiago. And Louise pulled in a few favors to get Yolanda in the back-to-work program of the Human Resources Administration without going to the end of the waiting list.

As Louise walked around Yolanda's living room, lost in her own reflection, she absently patted the plastic cross hanging over the couch and thought, *So much for my dreams of running a prison.* What had happened to Yolanda Santiago's dreams? Louise couldn't make them come true, but she could at least help Yolanda to dream.

Chapter 21

Fibber McGee was too old to jump up, but he whined and pawed Eileen's knee until she picked him up and sat him in her lap. Even though she held him tightly, his whole body vibrated. The pounding of his heart, loud and fast, pulsated through his bones, the echo thudding against Eileen's palm.

She leaned closer to him, squeezing, and whispered behind his ear, "Don't worry, I'm not going to let him hurt you. It's okay, darling." She swayed slightly on the pew-like seat, chanting "Sh-sh-sh" like "Ah-ah-baby." She wasn't at all self-conscious of her conversation because no embarrassment would prevent her from soothing her love. Besides, she wasn't the only one. There was a whole cult sitting here, acknowledging one another's presence with nods, commiserating with smiles at the next one trying to calm her animal. It could have been a London park, with nannies sitting on benches, rocking their carriage handles up and down. Instead of a veterinarian's waiting room.

"Look over there, Mr. McGee. There, there, calm down. Can you believe that woman talking into a carrier, to a cat? Anybody who would talk to a cat is crazy, don't you think? That's a good boy; take it easy." She kissed the top of his head and tried to intimidate the cat woman by staring at her. Then she giggled softly. "What would people think about my explaining to my dog about the nutty woman talking to her cat? Eh, Fibber, don't you think that's funny? Well, it won't be long now, and then we'll go home and have a nice nap."

It was incredible how they knew. But they all did. As soon as Eileen started walking toward 74th and York, Fibber pulled back and tried to turn around. No matter how she varied the route—one block over, one block down, two over, three down—he could tell. Other times, when she walked in that direction, he was perfectly content to trot along with her, safe and happy. How he could tell that on this particular day, on this particular walk, they were on their way to the vet's, she didn't know. Even the first time, before animals had a chance to get poked or jabbed or prodded, they were all scared. It seemed to Eileen, from all her waiting-room observations, that the bigger the dogs, the more petrified they acted. There was a Doberman mix in the neighborhood who bullied every other dog he met on the street. She had seen him in Dr. Pomalee's waiting room once, hiding under the bench, whimpering like a sissy.

Eileen was always apprehensive coming here, anticipating being told the end was near (as if Fibber would change from his playful, still frisky self to advanced senility overnight) or that he had some dread disease. Eileen had nightmares about that. She knew she would be able to cope with her own illness a lot better than with his. In her case, she'd be able to understand; she'd be able to treat whatever it was or at least hope. If it were Fibber, the only solution might be to put him to sleep. She couldn't even think about that; she could only pray that if the time came, God would give her enough strength to do what was best for him. Her main concern was with who would take care of Fibber if she became incapacitated. Danny was a good, sweet, devoted nephew, but he would never love Fibber the way he needed to be loved. The way he was used to being loved. Danny's idea of a dog was a four-legged thing you had to feed and walk and occasionally pet, in exchange for an automatic household alarm system.

She was glad the receptionist interrupted her rambling worries by calling her turn. Fibber was practically comatose, once she got him up on the table. A young attendant had to help her lift him, because he was trying so desperately to get out of the room.

Dr. Pomalee was abrupt. The only reason Eileen went to him was that he was kind to the patients themselves, and he was within walking distance. "Still giving him the aminophylline?" he asked from under Fibber's tail.

Eileen winced out loud as he squeezed the anal glands to check them. It evidently didn't hurt the dog as much as it hurt her, because he gave only a half-hearted yelp compared to her loud gasp.

"Yes, Doctor." She covered the dog with her body to hold him down, while the doctor walked around to the head of the table. "Do you think there's any change?"

"Let's see." He picked up the folder with her name on it. And Fibber's. Fibber McGee Hargan. Like a school record. Or report card. "We did a cardiogram last October. There's no way to tell without doing another one, but I don't think it's necessary right now. I think we'll wait 'til it's a year."

Eileen wondered if she should insist. Even though it was expensive, you couldn't take a chance when it came to health. She'd never forgive herself if anything happened to Fibber because she didn't give him the test. That's why she came for checkups regularly, every six months. Her doctor would be pleased if she treated her own body so conscientiously.

"Sounds good. Very good." He pulled the stethoscope out of his ears and playfully caressed Fibber's ear. "For an old man, you're okay." While he studied the chart, Fibber's paws slid back and forth on the steel table, trying to get off. "It's okay; let him down. I'd say he's in very good health for eleven. But I want you to keep him on the pills. They help his breathing and take the strain off the heart." He made some notations while Eileen sighed with relief.

"Oh, if it's all the same to you," she said, "could you give me a prescription? I go to this discount—"

"Sure."

There was no point in paying top price for the pills just because he had them right here when she could get a senior-citizen discount from the drugstore. Eileen Hargan felt absolutely justified in sending the receipt to her supplemental insurance company with her others. It would be different if she sent Dr. Pomalee's bill to Medicare. That would really be cheating. Besides, she was afraid she would lose all her benefits if they ever found out.

Chapter 22

Laurie Jensen passed the bill to Eileen Hargan. Then she typed something into the computer, put the printout in the folder, and stacked it on Stacy's desk to be re-filed. She pointed to the sign over the desk to remind Ms. Hargan that it was called Manhattan Veterinary Associates, Inc. Some of the older patients still wrote "Hospital" and then either had to void their checks or correct them. "You know, we take MasterCard and VISA if you want to charge the visit."

"No, no. I don't like running up bills. Is there anything you can't charge these days?"

Laurie waited patiently while the woman entered the check on her stub. Actually, this was a nice break in her day; the girl who usually relieved Stacy was out sick, so she was filling in. She didn't often get to come downstairs and talk to the patients. She remembered Ms. Hargan from the first week she started working here. Laurie had changed in the past ten years; the business had changed. But Ms. Hargan looked exactly the same. Pert and petite, her snow-white hair was crisp and bouncy, except for the scalp shining through on top. Even her dog looked the same, although he had been only a puppy back then.

"It's gone up, hasn't it?" Ms. Hargan asked.

"No, I think it was sixty-five dollars the last time you were here too." Laurie leaned over to check the screen to make sure she was right. "And don't forget we have to add the heartworm pills. Enough for the season."

It was hard for some of the elderly patients to pay. Laurie felt guilty for not mentioning that if it was really a hardship, they would accept less. If she *did* tell Ms. Hargan, though, it might embarrass the old woman. God, she was wearing a dress that had to be thirty years old. Although she was trim and neat and her clothes fit her body perfectly, Laurie thought she probably hadn't bought anything new in decades.

It wasn't a standard procedure, but they did it for some of the long-time patients, and Eileen Hargan had been with them for a long time. Dr. Pomalee hadn't been in practice very long then. *He's changed too,* Laurie thought. He seemed to have shrunk a little from the six-foot-four height that had awed her in the beginning. His hairline had definitely receded. But two wives later, he was still as handsome as ever.

When Laurie first met him, he had just bought the brownstone, lived above the office, and rented out the top two floors. He was delighted to learn she had just gotten her certification after finishing her two-year veterinary technician course at La Guardia and was waiting for her state license. He hired her on the spot. She assisted him in surgery, gave the medicated baths, answered the phone, administered injections, kept the appointment book, ordered the supplies, fed the boarders, and balanced the books. And in her spare time, she cleaned out the cages. She had come a long way, baby. She and Dr. Pomalee both had.

He recently had taken in two associates and had an architect redesign the building. He moved his living quarters up to the fourth floor. The basement was converted to "guest rooms" for boarding. The first floor had the waiting room and six examination rooms—three for Dr. Pomalee and his other doctors; three for "holding" the next patient. Sometimes it was like musical rooms. The second floor contained operating and X-ray rooms. The third was clerical and storage. The staff had increased to thirteen, with attendants and techs. Laurie Jensen was now a vice president of the corporation, and she ran the office.

It had become a very large business, as had the whole industry; theirs was only one of the about twenty-two thousand veterinary hospitals in the United States. Laurie Jensen knew this and many more statistics. She had been accumulating them for years.

Chapter 23

The odors from the open back door of a Hungarian restaurant, mingling with the scent of newspaper ink, the sour stench coming from a dark doorway, and just-baked bagels, were as sweet to Jason as the honeysuckle-jasmine scent floating through a romantic novel.

As the papers were thrown from the truck onto the sidewalk, he moved closer, with all the other people who had been loitering on the corner, waiting for the Sunday *Times*. Three teenage boys quickly wrapped the main section around the bulk of the paper, which they had been collating all afternoon. Jason called it the "Saturday night outdoor factory," which had an assembly line on many street corners in Manhattan. Not as many as there used to be, with so many people getting digital editions of the *Times*. Jason thought there was something very unsatisfying about swiping the pages on an iPad or turning them with a mouse on a laptop, as well as having a subscription and getting the Book Review and the Arts & Leisure section a day early. Of course, nothing changed from Saturday morning to Sunday morning in literature or on Broadway, but it was always a pleasant surprise to open the sections and relish the contents on the day they were meant to be read.

He gave the head guy a ten, watched him put the *News* inside the *Times*, and then held out his arm for the wad of papers and his change. He started down Amsterdam Avenue, pulling Sabrina closer to him. No, there was nothing as relaxing as spreading the sections out on the table Sunday morning and reading them one at a time with a second mug of coffee.

The traffic never eased in New York, and Jason wondered how he could be expected to curb his dog when the cars and busses squeezed their tires so closely against the pavement. A giggle came to his throat, like a little burp, as a perverse thought crossed his mind. One curbed dog to go. Squash! The leash tugged back, and he stopped and watched Sabrina squat on the sidewalk. While she was urinating, Sabrina looked up at him guiltily. He had not given her enough lead to go into the street. He very softly said, "Good girl," knowing that she would hear his whispered approval and be grateful for it. She knew every inflection of his voice, every gesture of his body, every mood of his soul. For she loved him. If only Chris had one-tenth the sensitivity or cared or expressed one-tenth of the feeling that Sabrina did! There must really be something wrong with him. Even when things were going well, Jason was not satisfied. He should go for help. It wasn't normal. Chris was right about one thing, though…Jason made himself miserable. Why couldn't he just take things for what they were? Be satisfied, even glad to have as much as he did? And accept Chris as he was—for what he was.

He looked dully at the throngs of people strolling along, enjoying the perfect spring night, and he was angry at himself that he couldn't find pleasure in it too. That he couldn't enjoy closing up his shop after a busy day. Couldn't go home and eat his dinner alone, or take a walk for the papers, or put his feet up and watch television, without thinking about Chris all the time. But the other people walking hand in hand or arm in arm just made him feel lonelier.

He could understand that Chris didn't care if people wondered what he was, or commented, or speculated. Or even if they thought they knew. He could even understand that he didn't want to show up at a business or literary function with Jason and make them actually sure. Not the people he worked for or with. Not his precious writers. But Jason could not understand why Chris would go any place that they couldn't be together, especially on a weekend. Jason would never do that. He wouldn't have gone, because he would rather stay home and do nothing with Chris than go to the finest, most exciting affair without him. If Chris would rather do something else, be with other people, then he couldn't possibly love Jason enough or as much as ... As *much as what?* Jason asked himself. *As much as I want him to.*

That Chris had a whole other life that he couldn't or wouldn't share with him was what made Jason feel so rejected and alone. Even though Jason kept wishing and hoping, deep down he knew that Chris would never be what he wanted. Which is why he was always disappointed. Why he always had that sense of loss…for what was not.

A blaring radio from a car slowing at the traffic light jolted Jason out of his preoccupation. He shifted the weight of the papers to his other arm, switched the leash, and hurried around the corner, away from the crowds and lights and smells.

Chapter 24

The letter came on Tuesday. The thick Macy's sale catalog was rolled up tight, wedging the envelopes inside the mailbox. Eileen scraped her hand trying to get everything out. She sucked the blood from her index finger and had to juggle the handles of the plastic grocery bag and her pocketbook and the mail before starting up to the second floor.

"Hello-o-o, Mama's little boy," she sang out, trying to get the key in the lock. She could hear Fibber moaning with excitement, his snout at the crack of the door, not quite whining, not quite yelping, not quite able to bear the few seconds between hearing her footsteps and being in her arms.

Once inside, she dropped everything on the floor and stooped so Mr. McGee could stand on his hind legs and hold her shoulders with his front paws—the way he used to play or fight with other dogs when he was younger and friskier. She rubbed her face against his and massaged the little indentation under his ear.

When he calmed down, she brought her things into the small, neat kitchen. Once the groceries were put away, she looked through the mail, taking everything out of the envelopes and sorting the contents into two piles—her Con Edison and Verizon telephone bills and an interest check in one; junk (including one corporate annual report and two letters to stockholders), two catalogs, and the Macy's flyer in the other. She left the important things on her desk to attend to, the rest on top of the TV for later.

It wasn't until 5:30 that she saw it. She had taken a short nap, cuddled tight with Mr. McGee. She woke up, washed her face, paid the two bills, got the chicken ready, and went for her afternoon walk with Fibber. When she returned, she changed into her slippers and brunch coat, put the chicken in the oven, and sat down in her club chair. She didn't know if the sigh came from the worn spring in the seat or from the worn bones inside her. It was too early to watch the six o'clock news, so she started reading the junk. She read every word of the solicitations, the political statements, the ads. Then she reached for the white-sale booklet. The letter was about a third of the way through the booklet, between ads for mattress pads and pillows. Sometimes the mailman accidentally stuck envelopes in the folds of magazines when he jammed them down into the box.

The kitchen timer beeped and the smoke alarm wailed, but Eileen couldn't stand up. Much less think of eating.

Chapter 25

Princess stopped in mid-gait. Her body stiffened, her spine arched. Proud and alert, her ears reached for a sound, her front leg bent, poised like a ballerina's above the sidewalk. Then her paws tapped a melody on the pavement, springing back in time to an exciting rhythm only she could hear.

Rosa shielded her eye against the sun. "Eh, bambina, someone a-coming?" She walked toward the river, squinting to see what had aroused the dog. Princess strutted, her stump of a tail straight and high, undulating like a bustle.

Rosa's arthritic knees became rejuvenated as she pranced next to her girl, anticipating some excitement. "Oh-ho, I see who it is." She held tight as Princess tugged at the leash. "There come your boyfriend, eh, bambina? No wonder you look so pretty. There he is—Mr. McGee." As the dogs approached each other, Princess stopped, her head high, waiting for Fibber to get closer.

Rosa liked the little black-and-white dog and had known his mistress for years—at least two dogs ago for each of them. She silently snapped her fingers, resisting the urge to call Princess "Molly." Ah, how she used to love to listen *to Fibber McGee and Molly* on the radio. *You could live in the same neighborhood for years and years and not know anyone, unless you have a dog.* That's what Rosa always said. *You go out walking; you meet the same people at the same time every day.* Then, when you see them in the supermarket or in the cleaners or a local restaurant without their animals, you feel kind of funny and shy. Like you have nothing to talk about, no reason to say hello to half a couple. "Hello, handsome." Rosa petted Fibber's head and then brushed her fingers behind her back. She was glad Princess's fur wasn't like Fibber's—the long, straight hair always felt dirty to her. "Hello." She smiled at Eileen Hargan. "How you been?"

"Fine." Eileen had to clench her teeth to keep from crying. Her cheeks rippled.

"Haven't seen you for a while."

"Oh, well, you know how it is in the cold. Run out to the curb, to the tree, run back. Now that it's getting warmer…"

"You okay?"

"Yes." Eileen clutched her bag tighter to her wrist, protecting her secret. She swung around and almost lost her balance as Fibber McGee made a circle around Princess, touching noses, smelling her tail. Maybe she should tell this Rosa lady. She knew everything, everybody. She'd know what to do. She'd know how awful a thing it was. No, the letter said not to tell anyone. But it wasn't like the police. She heard that Rosa was a busybody, always talking. Not that Eileen Hargan personally ever heard her say anything bad about anyone, but…No, she couldn't take a chance.

"Did you see that little puppy down the street? The black one?" Rosa asked.

"What? No."

"You know, the little Lhasa that died? Or Shih Tzu. I cannot tell; they all looks the same to me. The black one that was always a-sweeping the sidewalk with her long hair?"

"Yes, yes, I remember it."

"With the nice lady with the blonde hair. *That* one?"

"Ah, yes."

"Well, she say she never have another dog. Don't we all say that?" Rosa smiled at Princess to prove her point. "Well, she just did it like that. Went to the ASPCA one day last week and got a puppy. Cutest thing, it is. She say she miss her dog so much; she's so lonesome, she had to do it." Rosa raised her hand to make an arc of the leash and walked around the two dogs, holding it over the other woman's head—a dog walkers' sidewalk minuet, without the music. Eileen started walking at the same time, and the leashes became more entwined. Rosa dropped hers for a second to untangle the mess, and when she slipped her fingers back inside the handle, Eileen Hargan was already two doors away, pulling Fibber McGee. "Sorry! I'm late," Eileen called over her shoulder. "I have to run. Now, Fibber, I said 'come'!" She pulled harshly.

Princess strained to follow, and Rosa scooped her up in her arms. "No, baby, he's going home now. What could be bothering her? Come, we go for a nice walk. You meet someone else. Honest."

All the way to the next corner, Princess kept turning her head around to catch a glimpse of the retreating Terrier. Rosa turned with her. And she noticed that Eileen Hargan wouldn't even let him lift his leg without yanking him hard. "Something bad is bothering that lady," she told Princess confidentially.

Chapter 26

The gray rooftops of Jackson Heights always depressed Laurie. The Flushing train rumbled above Queens; the squat apartment buildings were grotesque shadows in the twilight. The train jerked as it grabbed the tracks and then grated along the steel where it bent into a crescent. Laurie pressed against the back-door window, the spot she took every night, to catch the momentary profile of Manhattan against the royal blue sky. Then the last car swung around the curve after the others, obliterating the view.

Her nipples flattened against the cold glass. Feeling desolate, she shuddered. Leaving the city was like leaving home. For all its dirt and noise and crime and indifference, it still held a glamour 'and awe for Laurie, and she wished she could afford to live in its heart.

The grinding of the wheels on the track jangled her nerves and lulled them at the same time. When the noise changed at a certain point, when the sound of metal on metal became shrill, like a dentist's drill hitting a high tone, it signaled the approach of her station. She was tired by the time she got to Elmhurst, but she decided to walk two extra blocks to Woodhaven Boulevard to the liquor store. The liter of Merlot was just the treat she deserved after the busy day she'd had. She held the bottle by its neck through the bag while she unlocked her door, slipped inside, double-locked the door, and hooked the chain. Then she set the bottle on the catch-all table in the foyer/dining area/ guest room/den/hallway and bent to stroke the two heads nuzzling against her legs.

"Okay, okay, you want your dinner, huh?" Laurie never thought she'd get used to a cat, much less two cats. She was a dog person. But there was no way she could take care of a dog by herself or have that kind of commitment to come right home every night, walk it, clean up after it, and never be able to go away. Other people who lived alone had dogs and did take vacations. But Laurie knew herself well enough to know she would never be able to do it.

She used to laugh at people who told her that she actually had to own a cat to appreciate what wonderful pets they make. When she'd say that cats were too independent and not affectionate enough, the answer invariably was, "But that's what's beautiful about them." Luckily, her two were affectionate—and needy. And a lot easier to care for than dogs. All she did know at first was that she didn't think these two cats should die, and that's what would have happened to them if she hadn't adopted them.

She'd read that three to four million dogs and cats were euthanized in shelters every year. *Maybe there are actually more cats out there*, she thought, as she'd also read that there were an estimated seventy million strays, *but since cats are able to survive better than dogs on their own, they just don't get caught.*

That wasn't the case with Felix. Laurie had found him one day when she was opening up the office. Or rather, he had found her. A perfect tuxedo specimen—formal, black, a white shirt where the lapels would split, and four white spats. She put some food out for him, and after the first few times, he just followed her inside and refused to move out. He would roam around the waiting room, harassing the crated and leashed animals, until Dr. Pomalee insisted that he be caged—or sent to a shelter. They had put him in a corner of the room, so he could watch the comings and goings.

Laurie had to take care of him because the night attendants grumbled about doing it. They only had from four in the afternoon until midnight to care for the sick boarders—checking IVs, taking temperatures, giving drugs, feeding, walking ambulatory dogs, cleaning cages—and they complained about having to come upstairs to feed a lone cat. It was a natural progression, from moving him up to her office, where he had some freedom to walk around on the third floor, to feeling sorry for his being cooped up and alone all night, to taking him home. And now she was a full-fledged cat person, loving their antics, their companionship, and their adoration of her.

She slipped off her shoes in the kitchen, opened the bottle of wine, felt behind the tall glasses in the dish closet for one with a stem—wine didn't taste as good in a water glass—and poured some wine. Then she ground some vitamins into the canned cat food, glancing out of the corner of her eye at Felix and Oscar, sitting near her feet, watching her intently. Oscar had been acquired the same way, only taken home immediately. Not just because Dr. Pomalee said they couldn't house strays but because all the cat people she knew told her she had to have two, so they could keep each other company. To Laurie, her breed was pedigreed alley cat, even though Dr. Pomalee said the cat was a Domestic Shorthair. She had named the cat Oscar—it didn't matter that she was a female—after about a month, when it became obvious that she was a slob, scattering food pellets and litter on the floor and allowing Felix to set the house rules. Laurie thought calling a girl Oscar added spunk to the cat's already spunky nature.

Laurie started fixing the other bowl. "You'll never be human…like a dog," she said as she put their meals on the floor. Smiling at her silliness, she added, "But I guess I love you anyhow."

For someone who had never had an affinity for cats, they had grown on her quickly, and now she couldn't imagine her life without them. But two was the absolute limit, she reminded herself every time another stray wandered into her life—like the current apricot-splattered calico that was currently in residence in her office. If she didn't find a home for it within a week, she would be sentenced to the ASPCA.

Laurie hurried through her own leftover barbecue chicken dinner, put on her velour robe, even though it was a warm night, and poured another glass of wine. She brought her pillow from the bedroom, picked some cat hair off a spot on the couch, and set the wine glass on the cocktail table. Then, with a tingle of excitement, she opened her laptop.

Chapter 27

Louise leaned against the wall so she could slip her right shoe off. She rotated her ankle a few times and flexed her toes. She noticed that the blister on her little toe had broken, leaving blood matted to her stocking. She squeezed her foot back into the pump, grimacing as the leather rubbed against her raw skin.

If the commissioner of Human Resources had not passed the word along that he expected good representation from each department, and if her superior didn't have a daughter who was graduating from NYU tonight, Louise would not be here, wearing heels too high to walk in and a silk dress too hot to breathe in.

It didn't matter that the press was there. That a lot of local politicians felt it important enough to be there. That the Honorable Wallace Cooker was going to announce the new program and his plan to seek federal funding for it. It didn't matter what the excuse was for attending. Everyone was on the make. From her invisible blind in the corner, she observed the prey. And the hunters. All of the women seemed elegantly put together. Casual perfection. *If I cared,* Louise told herself, *I'd feel like a wallflower. No, a wall-weed.* But who cared? The men looked like a bunch of straightlaced, pompous assholes anyway.

The smoke drifting toward the vent over her head—from people who had snuck outside to grab a cigarette—made her eyes tear. She thought she'd faint from the heat and the press of people. Waiters mingled, holding their trays high over heads, and slowed down to lower their goodies. Louise smirked at the way some people never seemed to interrupt their conversations or break their gazes but had developed an extra sense that allowed them to feel or smell a passing tray. While still talking or still looking at someone, they could stick a hand out and get something. Like a lizard with one of those long tongues that darts out to grab an unsuspecting bug. Then there were those who did stop talking, making loud exclamations of surprise as if Santa Claus had just dropped from the chimney, and who studied each hors d'oeuvre, biting daintily into at least three of them while ignoring the waiter patiently standing by.

Watching, Louise realized she was starving. She headed for a small group circling a waiter. Louise's normal pose was shoulders pushed slightly forward, elbows bent at waist level. Even standing almost still, she seemed to be revved up and in motion. She looked like a jockey racing for the finish line…without the horse under him. In tailored suits and her frequently worn jeans, it didn't matter too much. But the two-piece pastel dress she was wearing did nothing to soften her harsh appearance. In fact, the contrast only exaggerated the brusqueness of her bearing.

"Okay, okay, let's stop hoarding the horse"—she laughed at their expressions before adding—"der-ves." She pushed her arm in between the bodies, picked a caviar on toasted cocktail bread, and stuffed it into her mouth in one bite. The people politely made an opening for her to join them.

Introductions weren't necessary, since they were all strangers anyway. The others slowly drifted off, leaving Louise with cheese spread filling her mouth and a cocktail frank and a tuna cracker in the flat of her hand. She had put her glass down on the rim of a planter somewhere and knew it would be easier to get a new drink than to find the old one. She waited at the bar for a Scotch on the rocks with a splash of water and a twist. Then she sipped some of it off the top as she turned around. "Whoops," she apologized to the chest she bumped into.

"It's okay. You come here often?"

Louise grunted a smile at the lame joke. "Not if I can help it. I hate these things."

"Doesn't everybody?" He clinked his glass against hers. "Let's drink to that."

"To what?" Her glass acknowledged his.

"To discontinuing all cocktail parties." He stuck his hand out. "Ken Hollis."

"Hi, Ken Hollis. Louise Sidway." She let him pump her hand. "What are you doing here? I mean, how did you get invited?"

"I'm a consultant to the mayor. On social services and welfare and things."

"Oh."

Ken Hollis translated the one syllable into "big deal."

"What do you do when you're not 'consulting' with the mayor?" she asked flippantly.

"I teach. Sociology. At Hunter. And what about you? How come you were invited?"

"Me? Oh, I'm the commissioner's daughter." She bent her head into her glass and walked away, sipping, leaving Ken Hollis's eyes searching the large room for the commissioner.

Locating him and confirming to himself what he originally thought, he looked for Louise. When he sighted her across the room, he realized she had been watching him. His brows bunched into a question mark. He looked toward the commissioner and then back at Louise. She laughed and waved, nodding her head and turning in the direction of the commissioner, who was charcoal black.

Chapter 28

"It's just another form of harassment. Trying to get us out so they can raise the rent."

"They can't get you out—especially you; you're a senior citizen. Just calm down. They can't touch you." Everyone at the meeting seemed to be talking at the same time.

"Well, *I* think it's the greatest thing that could've happened. It will mean security for all of us."

"Look who's talking. Sure, you can afford it. What about the rest of us? I live alone. I don't have two salaries coming in."

"The first thing is, we shouldn't let animals in this building if it goes co-op. They cause a mess, and we'll have the right to—"

"Oh, c'mon, lady, don't be ridiculous, talking about what we'll do *after*—"

"Quiet, please! Can we have some quiet?" The dentist who lived on the first floor and called the meeting used his fist as a gavel. The only response he got was a sore hand.

A deep voice shouted above the others. "What about the big shots? They're only interested in buying at the insider's price and then selling to make a profit."

"That's called flipping it over."

"Who cares what it's called? I call it greed. They're not interested in how it affects their neighbors. Or the building. They just want to make money."

"Whatever you think the landlord is up to, he'll get his way!" Jason yelled before he had a chance to plan it. Although his volume was not as loud as some of the other voices, the sureness of his voice created a momentary lull.

Relieved, and still rubbing his hand, the dentist pointed to Jason. "Go on; finish."

"Well, whatever motives you think they might have or whatever results they're trying to achieve, it seems to me they'll get their way if we keep this up. They're counting on our acting like this. Divided. They know we can't get together and make any decision."

"He's right."

There was a chorus of "yeah, yeah."

"Sh-h-h! Let the guy talk."

Jason tried to curl his feet under the grade-school chair. There was no room to cross his legs. Even straight out, his right knee rubbed under the armrest. The classroom was too small for all the tenants who showed up, but at least the school let them have it for the night. He shifted his whole body so he was sitting sideway, which was slightly uncomfortable because everyone was looking at him. Or *to* him.

"Would you like to come up here and talk?" The dentist gestured, hoping to be helpful.

"No, that's all right. I only think we shouldn't let them get their way. We have to have an *orderly* meeting. It might sound dumb, but we should do it as parliamentary procedure. We're in a classroom. We should try to remember how it's done."

"Yeah. Let's elect a chairman," someone called out.

"No, you're supposed to first have nominations," a voice demanded from the back of the room. And then the momentary order ended.

"Maybe we should do it by floor instead."

"Well, *he* seems to know what he's talking about. Why don't we just make him the chairman?"

"You can't pick somebody like that!"

"Why not? You want it official? Okay, I nominate…what's your name?"

"Ruderman, Jason Ruderman. But look, I'm not interested in being—"

"I nominate Jason Ruderman as chairman. All those in favor say aye."

"No, no, you have to have someone second it first."

"Okay, I second the motion."

"Me too."

"Now we can vote. All those in favor, raise your hands."

"Shouldn't we have an alternative, like in politics? Aren't you supposed to have a few candidates?"

All the disagreement and shouting before anything was even organized was a bad omen to Jason.

"Come on; let's get it over with or we'll be here all night. If we like him, fine. You got somebody better, nominate him."

"I didn't say I didn't like him. It's okay with me, I just thought—"

"Sit down, will you? And this was a stupid time to call a meeting. Seven o'clock."

"I second that. Next time, let's make it either six o'clock or eight."

"Six o'clock is too early. I don't get home until six thirty."

"This is ridiculous. And somebody is supposed to be taking minutes so they can write them up later."

"Minutes? It's going to be more like 'hours,' the way things are going."

A chorus of voices called out more arguments.

"I nominate my neighbor, who's an outstanding citizen and very good at getting things done: Nettie Pedersen."

"Who'd she say? I didn't hear."

"Nettie Pedersen."

"Who the hell is that?"

"The busybody on the tenth floor. The one with the chignon."

"Sh-h-h-h. She'll hear you."

"Who cares? She's a pain. Always putting memos in the lobby, going around asking people to sign petitions about the stupidest things. The way the garbage is picked up. Getting rid of dogs. Having the super fired. What's a chignon?"

"I don't want to buy; some of you do. I think we should find out from these two people what their position is. Whose side they're on. Before we vote."

"Good point, good point."

Nettie Pedersen stood up, patted her bun (as if one hair had ever dared come loose from it), and said, "I think most of us here are in the same position—rent-stabilized tenants, having a difficult enough time making ends meet. Those of us who can manage are trying to put away something for our old age, since there might not be enough Social Security for us." Her accusatory tone was meant for the senior citizens who were collecting it, using it all up.

Nettie Pedersen was not unattractive. In fact, she looked younger than she probably was. Her eyes were black and hard, like small agates set in their sockets. Her figure was bland, neither too heavy nor too thin, too tall nor too short. In fact, she was a totally nondescript person. Until she opened her mouth to talk. Then her overbearing self-righteousness animated her. "Even if they offer the apartments at very low prices, who could afford them? You have to figure a monthly mortgage payment, *plus* the maintenance, which will probably be more than the rent we're paying now." A few murmurs were heard, and she nodded to her supporters. "I think we have to do everything we can to stop it. Keep the building a rental. At least that way, there's only so much they can raise us every year."

Several people commented their agreement. "Yeah, I'm all for that."

"Right, we can't let it go through."

"You got my vote, lady."

Jason felt like a giant in his Lilliputian chair, but he refused to stand like a schoolteacher in front of the blackboard, like the Pedersen woman. "I must tell you honestly that I don't know *what* I want to do," he said, and before anyone could moan about his indecision, he added, "We don't have enough facts to make any kind of sound decision. I might tend to feel one way now, but I could change my mind when I talk to some knowledgeable people. I think that goes for all of us. And you senior citizens who are so nervous about your fixed incomes and being able to afford the maintenance, if you read the red herring, you would see that no matter what kind of plan we end up with, *you* cannot be evicted. Ever. So you have nothing to worry about. I think our first priority is to get organized and have a really strong tenants' group. Then we get an attorney to represent us. Once we decide the pros and cons, we can either fight the conversion so we *don't* go co-op or try to get the best deal possible, if we do. The most important thing is… whatever we do, we should do it together. After all, we're all on the same side. We want to keep our homes. Keep living here."

A few people clapped hesitantly. Then more joined in. As they looked toward Jason, he shuffled his legs under the desk.

"Fucking faggot," Nettie Pedersen hissed between her teeth.

Chapter 29

It seemed familiar. The Pine-Sol disinfectant, the flap of starched jackets against starched pants, the steady peeling of crepe soles off the waxed floors. The background din of howls and whines and yelps and moans. Kola couldn't recognize the place. She didn't have to. It reminded her of the other place. Her senses were sharpened by fear, and the sounds and smells were exaggerated. The soft hairs that made her fur so smooth stiffened into quills, pricking inward, piercing her skin. Her tongue ached from swallowing to try to force saliva into her throat. The saliva that bubbled around her mouth and hung from her tongue. Her instinct to run away and to be free hurled her against the door.

Then the small arms were around her middle, the light body on her back. And even though they were much too weak to restrain her, the strength of the little boy's love hugged her. "Don't worry, Kola. I'm not going to let them hurt you. Ever. And I'm not going to leave you here. You gotta come home with me after."

She let Clifford lead her back to the bench where Jessica was sitting, the woman's arm reaching for both of them. She sat between the boy's legs. Rather than prison bars, Kola knew they would shelter her.

"Oh, what a sweetheart you are." Clifford instinctively held Kola tighter, but he smiled at the lady who had just come into the waiting room. "Aren't you a honey," she said to Kola who knew, without being touched, that the lady was not speaking to Clifford or to his mother but to her, in a warm, friendly way. Kola stood, her tail arched in a plume behind her. When the woman saw the welcome reaction, she went over to Kola. "Wanna know who thinks you're gorgeous, huh? Well, we glamour girls have to stick together."

Jessica bent her head to hide her smile. Because Laurie Epstein was probably the most unglamorous person she had ever seen. Her features were bland, and her brown eyes looked huge in the expanse of forehead because she didn't seem to have any eyebrows. Her cheeks were dented with tiny reminders of old pimples.

Kola's tail made furious circles in the air. Clifford pretended to walk to the front door, knowing, hoping, that she would bound after him.

Understanding the jealous maneuver, Laurie went on talking directly to the dog. "Yes, I know you're a sweetheart and you like this attention, but you only have eyes for your little master, right?" Squatting, she turned and said to Clifford, "She's just beautiful. What's her name?"

He stared back, without speaking. Jessica's heart pleaded with him not to snap back to his old self. It was the first time she remembered seeing him act threatened—before this, he didn't care enough about anything to feel threatened. "Kola," Jessica said for him.

"Like in Coca?" Laurie spoke directly to Clifford, even though the answer had come from his mother. "What a nice name. I bet you thought of it." Laurie talked to him as if the conversation was between the two of them.

He nodded his head.

"I think it's very clever," Laurie said.

"She's *my* dog," Clifford insisted.

Jessica exhaled.

"Oh, I could tell that right away," Laurie agreed, continuing to stroke the dog's head. "Soon as I walked in."

"You could?" Clifford came closer.

"Of course. Just the way she was sitting close to you, there was no question you're her owner. She's probably a lucky dog to have you. I know you take good care of her."

"Me too. I'm lucky." He squatted right beside her. "She's the best dog in the whole world. And she's my best friend." He put his hands on her possessively but let Laurie keep on petting her.

"Well, then, I'd say you're both very lucky, aren't you?" Laurie said. "Have you brought her here before?"

"No, we only got her a few weeks ago."

"Well, have you answered all the questions yet?" She looked toward the top of the receptionist's head, visible in the open glass window.

"No."

Stacy lifted her head and whined, "I was just going to call them in, as soon as I got finished here."

"Just asking, just asking," Laurie said. "Want me to do it for you? I'm back early."

"Thanks."

"Okay." She reached for Clifford's hand. "Now, what's your name?"

"Clifford," he said, hiding his hand behind his back as Laurie reached for it.

"Come on, Clifford. We'll go take some information from you. Or maybe it would be better for you to sit out here with Kola and keep her calm, and I'll talk to your mom."

"Okay?" he asked his mother.

Jessica nodded and followed Laurie inside. She couldn't remember why she had thought Laurie was unattractive. And yes, she did have eyebrows, although they were very light. Her warmth toward Kola and her kind looks toward the other patients softened her face. With a new hairdo, some eyebrow pencil to frame her eyes, shadow, and a makeup base with good coverage, she'd be beautiful. Well, maybe not exactly beautiful. But certainly striking.

When Laurie finished taking what short case history there was, she went back to the waiting room to say goodbye to the little boy and to give the dog one last pat. She dropped the form on Stacy's desk, thought better of it, and took it with her upstairs. She wanted to add her own observation of Jessica Marcus's miracle to the computer.

Chapter 30

They hadn't bothered to cut letters or words out of the newspaper, like they did on TV or in the movies. Maybe because they knew Eileen would never show it to the police or to anyone. Her instinct had been to call Danny, but she was afraid he would screw it up—take the note to the FBI or worse, try to find the perpetrators himself. Yet she was afraid *not* to call him. She didn't know what to do.

The instructions had been simple enough. Go to D'Agastino's on 80th and York. Buy anything. Ask for a brown paper bag; if they didn't have any, then take the plastic. Place 10,000 dollars in tens and twenties, fold over the top of the bag. Wrap it around the bills as tight as possible. Scotch tape the flap. Make sure D'AG BAG is on the outside. At 10:30 on Friday morning, go to Gristede's on 86th and First, take a basket, and walk down a few aisles. Examine some items, like a head of lettuce or tomatoes. Act naturally, compare prices, check the weight. Put the items in the cart, stroll around, get a roll of towels or a package of toilet paper, and put all the items on top of the brown bag. Go to the pet supplies, leave the cart in front of the dog biscuits, start examining different products on the shelves. Take one or two items in your hand to look at the labels, and make your way up the aisle. Pick up a package of rawhide chews, go to the express lane, and pay for it. Don't look back at the cart while you're shopping. If somebody happens to be in the aisle and tells you that you forgot your cart, say thank you, put your hand on the cart handle, and continue looking around the dog food until that person is gone. Check out, go home, and wait.

Or never see Fibber McGee again.

Eileen didn't know if she could call it a ransom note…*before* a kidnapping had taken place. She pondered the question for the rest of the day, as if that would make the difference as to whether or not she had to pay it.

It wasn't a joke. When she read the first few sentences, she thought somebody was playing a game. Who would expect her to have 10,000 dollars? And what would she have that would be worth a fortune to her? Nothing, except her little love.

Eileen didn't have to take her notebook out and turn to the columns to know exactly how much cash she had. She had five CDs, four for 10,000 dollars; one for 15,000. She used the interest to supplement her Social Security and her Board of Education pension. And that was barely enough. Occasionally, she thought about not renewing one of them, so she could keep 10,000 dollars handy in a savings account for when she absolutely had to have extra money for something. But suppose she lived another twenty years? Even at age seventy-three, another twenty years was feasible. Fifty-five thousand dollars wouldn't last as long as she would, especially with inflation. And now, the thought of just taking almost a quarter of it and giving it away…she shuddered.

She thought of all the times she'd done without, because she didn't want to break up the even amount. A vacation, maybe. (That was before she had Fibber, when she was younger and would have enjoyed a cruise or a week in a resort.) A new winter coat. Re-covering the couch. And each time she thought about doing something, she decided she'd feel better not doing it but knowing the money was in the bank.

Now…

Of course, she'd probably die with every cent intact, and Danny would get it. That was fine with her. It made her feel good to know how grateful he would be. Although she wouldn't be around to see it. But what about Charlene? She'd end up spending it on new clothes, or redecorating, or tennis lessons, the way she was doing now. There was always the possibility that Danny would leave her. Oh God, if only that boy would come to his senses. At fifty-seven, he wasn't really a boy anymore. And they had been married almost twenty-five years.

But then if they did get a divorce, Charlene would sue him for alimony and get half of Eileen's money anyway. The money she had so diligently put away every single week for her entire life. Painstakingly. Dollar by dollar in an envelope, traded in for tens, each hundred deposited. Every thousand reached, a triumph. No matter how hard it was. Of course it wasn't so hard years ago when she lived with her parents and her expenses were low. It was easy to save then.

Her skin crawled as she imagined Charlene showing off a fur or a piece of jewelry. It would kill her. But how could it kill her if she were already dead? Unconsciously, she smiled at her stupidity and reached out for Mr. McGee. As she squeezed the back of his neck affectionately, she realized the money didn't matter. Nothing mattered, except her little boy. She would die if anybody touched him. Took him away. Or if they ever considered... no, that was just to scare her.

She was sure. Who would hurt an innocent little animal? They were just trying to show her they meant it. She would do anything, spend anything, to save him.

It could have been worse. They could have made it 50,000 dollars. Or 100,000. Thank God, they didn't. Then she would have to think about selling some of the stock too. She had every share her father had left her. Never touched it—since 1977! She knew her sister had had to sell most of hers over the years. That was different; she had a mortgage; she had a child to bring up and put through school. There was almost nothing left when she died.

But suppose she got sick? They'd put her in a public hospital in a ward and let her waste away if she couldn't afford to pay. If she had a stroke or a heart attack, they could send her to one of those state-run nursing homes. Just leave her there in a bed, with festering sores and dirty sheets. Until she died. No, she had to keep that money for her old age. Danny would probably laugh and say, "When do you think you'll reach old age if you're seventy-three now?"

Chapter 31

Chris held his glass up and tilted it until the light made a shimmering asterisk in the crystal. The red wine dazzled like a star ruby.

"And then they took the vote, and except for a couple of the old cronies who wanted *her*, it was almost unanimous."

Chris laughed and took a sip of wine. "I don't think I've ever seen you this excited."

"It's not that I'm excited," Jason said, sounding apologetic, "but it just made me so mad, the way everyone was screaming. They needed someone to get it organized. Already, in one night, I got a committee together and floor captains elected. I mean, I think it's a challenge, don't you? We shouldn't run around without knowing what's going on. I got the names of two lawyers who specialize in tenants' rights, and two others who handle conversions. I'm going to start calling tomorrow to see if we can get one of them to meet with the committee. If this building does go, I think it might be a great opportunity. To own a piece of real estate in the middle of Manhattan would be a nice thing to fall back on. But it might not necessarily be the best thing for us, for this building."

"Good for you." Chris nodded his drink toward Jason in an imaginary toast.

"Well, it's just that…hey, look, I'll be damned if I'm going to let a bunch of schmucks who live in this building make decisions like that for me, for us. Or let a nut like that Pedersen woman get involved."

"It's going to be a lot of work, not to mention money."

"Oh, I know. We talked about money briefly. I told them by the next meeting, we'd try to have some kind of plan worked out for how much it will cost, like for attorneys' fees, and how we'll prorate it with the senior citizens and everything. We're going to have a committee meeting on Thursday to do some preliminary planning."

"Thursday? I thought we were going out for dinner on Thursday."

"Oh, I forgot. Well, listen, we'll go another night, okay? If I have to get the four members together at one convenient time, it will take a lot of e-mails back and forth. As long as they already agreed, I'd rather not change it. Boy, I wish you had been there. You'll have to come to the next meeting, Chris."

"I wouldn't miss it for anything." He stretched and yawned widely. "I'm tired. Almost ready to turn in?"

"Naw." Jason looked at his watch. "I'm too wound up. Maybe I'll go get some air." He got up and walked to the coat tree in the hall, where a peg had been added halfway down for Sabrina's coat, packed away now, and another, which they called the hitching post, for her leash. "Want to go for a little spin, once around the block, baby?" he asked as he put her collar on. He came back into the living room to squeeze Chris's shoulder. "I'll be back in a few minutes."

Chris started twisting his glass again. "Okay," he said, concentrating on the kaleidoscopic lights.

Chapter 32

Louise bent her head at an angle to better read the graffiti. The lights momentarily went off, and the noise seemed louder in the dark, the screeching echoing off the walls of the tunnel. The overhead fans blew the hot, dusty air around, and she felt stuck to the plastic seat. The lights came on, illuminating the filth and the empty soda can rolling on the floor. It was like a game you tilt in your hand to get the metal ball through a maze and into a hole. The can started, skidded, turned, and rolled backward. Then it stopped, balanced itself, and went forward with the train. All the passengers watched it, like spectators at a sporting match.

The girl swung her legs back and forth under the seat in time to a silent song in her ears. Louise waited for her to turn her head and then smiled reassuringly at her. "We're gonna have fun."

"What?"

"Fun!" Louise shouted over the grinding wheels. "Two stops," she mouthed, and held up her fingers. The little girl nervously rolled the handles of the plastic Duane Reade shopping bag tighter in her lap. If they did this more often, Louise thought, she'd get her a little overnight bag. She could probably pick one up at a street fair for six or seven dollars. Christ, even Barbie dolls had suitcases. And maybe a new pair of sandals to replace the worn ones she was kicking under the seat now, as if she were on a swing. Louise was looking forward to it. She hoped Elena was too. Not that the Upper East Side was the country or even the suburbs, but it was a vacation from the squalor of the ghetto. A chance for a young girl to be away from her family, to feel grown up

"

and see new things. Have a real holiday on a holiday. Maybe Louise would take her to Chinatown for supper. Or the South Street Seaport. Then she could stop back to walk Honda before going to a movie or possibly a walk on Fifth Avenue. It would be nice at this time of year.

Louise saw Elena eye the token booth, the modern tiles, and the clean signs at the 86th Street express stop. As she guided the girl to the subway stairs to the street, mentally planning the weekend's itinerary, she felt like Auntie Mame. And Louise beamed.

Chapter 33

Laurie stretched lavishly, arched her back, and massaged the base of her spine with her hands, enjoying the relief in knowing that tomorrow was Memorial Day, and this particular Sunday was the middle of a three-day weekend. It was only 7:30 in the morning, and she had the whole day ahead of her, plus another. She luxuriated in her laziness, until Felix jumped from the windowsill onto her chest, swiping her once across the face and whining—demanding—to be fed.

She went into the kitchen, opened a can of cat food, divided it into two bowls, and put them on the floor. She added some water to the kettle and sat down at the shelf that swung down on its hinge to make a table. She toyed with the idea of calling her old friend Joan to ask her over. She could probably be here by nine. After catching up for an hour or two, though, what would they do all day? Or she could call her great-aunt Corinne, wait for an invitation to Sunday dinner, take the bus to the railroad station, and join the closest family she had in New York—maybe the world. Because she would probably never see her parents again. She'd never call them, that was for sure. And after all this time, it looked like her mother would never defy her father and get in touch with her. She shrugged her thoughts away before they invaded her mood.

She could go to Queens Center and do some shopping. She certainly needed summer clothes. The thought of trying on bathing suits made her cringe. Then again, when was she going to go to the beach? On the other hand, she could just go out and get the papers, come back, get undressed, and lounge around all day—reading, napping, watching TV. She sure could use the rest.

The last three or four months were terrible, she thought as she stirred the freeze-dried instant coffee through the boiling water. She held her cup with both hands, tilting it toward the fluorescent light, smiling widely to see if she could see her teeth in the vague outline of her face in the black liquid. She remembered how apprehensive she'd been of the new software program when it first arrived. Maybe it was her generation, or her sex, or just a personality flaw that she was so intimidated by electronics. It was probably because it was foreign to her and that she didn't understand anything about it. After the hands-on instruction in the class she'd attended for three days, she'd been able to approach it a little more boldly. Now, she was expert at it. She was no longer intimidated, just respectful of it and awed by its capacity. She treated it almost reverently. Each time she used it, she discovered some new function to try. If she ever finished figuring everything out, feeding it data, and applying all that she learned to operating it, they would be some team!

But the amount of data she wanted to give it was overwhelming, and she was too busy most days to worry about it. God knew when she'd find the time to enter all the statistics. Maybe once she didn't have to convert all the files to the new system anymore…It seemed it would never be finished. With a mental snap of fingers, Laurie carried her mug into the bedroom, put on a pair of slacks, and sipped her coffee between applying eye shadow and mascara. Dressed, she took her bag and went to the front door, where Oscar and Felix were waiting for her, waiting to peek into the hallway when it opened. They knew her better than she knew herself. Oscar twisted her head away when Laurie tried to pat her. "Bye, guys. Just pretend it's a regular workday." She double-locked them in and, with a twinge of excitement, headed toward the subway.

Third Avenue was wall-to-wall people strolling in their shorts and tank tops and flip-flops, stopping and examining the wares. Vendors on both sides of the street in white open-sided tents hawked socks and T-shirts and cell-phone accessories and reading glasses and silver jewelry. Laurie joined the crowds for the first big street fair of the season, determined not to spend any money on junk.

By 1:00, the sun was strong, the crowds dense…and all those publications were calling to her to cull the facts and enter them into her computer. Painful images of abused animals assaulted her brain and coiled around her lungs, squeezing the breath out of her. Compelled, she headed home to her laptop.

Chapter 34

Donna Griffen had been "on the floor" at Chase for a week. She liked talking to the customers, advising them which kinds of accounts to open, how and when to invest their money, and explaining statements and notices to them. She felt a little like a schoolteacher, especially now, as she walked from her desk to the other side of the bank, her heels echoing on the marble, and waited to be buzzed into the inner sanctum. The eyes of the pupils—people tapping their feet on the snaking tellers' line and the people crossing and uncrossing their legs in the chairs, looking up to her to come back to help them—watched her intently.

And help is what she wanted to do. Which was why she had been very uncomfortable about the old lady who was trying to withdraw her CD early. Donna had checked the woman's bank history and saw that she hardly ever withdrew *anything* from her money market account; that made Donna more suspicious. When she had patiently explained to the woman that she would lose the equivalent of a month's interest, the clear blue eyes had studied the vaulted ceiling and refused to meet hers. Donna was sure the petite elderly lady was in the process of being ripped off. Swindled.

As she stood behind the teller's counter now, on the pretext of looking at the account on the computer, Donna kept her eye on the woman and dialed the manager. "It's just that she's an old woman, and you know that notice we got from the police department? Well, I think somebody's waiting for her outside for that money."

"Okay. Stall her as long as you can while I call the police."

"Thanks," she said. She grabbed a handful of forms and walked back to her desk, her heart thumping in time to her heels. "Well, it seems that you're the first depositor in this branch to withdraw a certificate of deposit early, so I had to call the main branch to find out which of these have to be filled out." She thumbed through the forms, reading some, entering information on others.

Mr. Bass, the bank manager, dialed the Nineteenth Precinct. He was kept on hold for five minutes, as the operator constantly clicked on and said, "Ringing," as if he couldn't hear the extension ringing himself. Finally, someone in the detective squad picked up. Although the detective thought it was very wise of him to call, he told Mr. Bass that they were investigating four robberies, and no one was left on duty except him—and he couldn't get away. But he thought there was a senior citizens' bunco squad that handled cases of fraud against the elderly. He didn't have the number, he told Bass, but Headquarters might be able to help.

After getting a run-around and being transferred from department to department, Leonard Bass decided the hell with it. He nodded to Donna to go ahead. After all, it was the woman's money; if she was stupid enough to withdraw it all, it was none of his business. Citizens not going to the aid of a crime victim was one thing. Demanding that a person be a victim and *be* helped against his wishes was another. And not his problem.

Donna slid a form over to the woman at the side of her desk. She pointed with a long pale-blue nail. "Just sign here," she said. Then she took it back to the tellers' counter, had the money withdrawn, and the account closed. She watched the teller feed the bills into the counter and then brought the cash to the frail-looking woman and counted them again, in front of her. She watched the woman count the bills too. She lost her place halfway through, started again, and then stuffed them into the tote bag she had been hugging to her chest.

"They *what?*" she said to Mr. Bass as soon as the woman had walked through the revolving door. "I assumed you told me it was all right because someone was going to wait for her outside. You know, to see what she was going to do with it. Or where she was going."

"Look, there are three customers waiting." He motioned toward the chairs. "I think we've spent enough time on this one account…and lost money in the bargain."

"But…" It was too late. Mr. Bass had walked away.

Donna waited until lunch. Rather than use her own extension and take a chance on being overheard, she brought her memo pad with the account number, name, and address to the lobby, and she called the mayor's office from her cell phone. She hoped it wasn't too late.

Chapter 35

A jogger left the path around the reservoir and, without breaking stride, ran toward the grassy knoll, the sweat rolling off his face and arms, the muscles in his neck bulging against his skin. Jason couldn't understand how people could get pleasure out of what he considered unnatural abuse to the body. Jason, pleased at the confirmation, watched the man drop onto his stomach in the grass, gasping for breath. Jason shook his head in amazement when the jogger visibly forced his arms into pillars and started doing push-ups.

Jason hadn't realized he had come so far, but the early morning walk was invigorating after a sleepless night. Even Sabrina was excited at their outing and pulled at him from ahead. A squirrel darted across the path in front of them and, like a puppy, Sabrina tried to gallop after it. She was panting now. Jason picked her up with one hand and stroked her head to calm her down. "What do you think you are, a young chick?" he asked as he looked for an empty spot on a bench. He found one and automatically brushed at the rotted wood and wiped his hand on his jeans before sitting down. Sabrina was content to sit in his lap, erect and alert, watching the goings-on. Sometimes she seemed too ladylike and dainty to even put her paws on the ground.

"Allo, allo, remember me?" The voice came from behind Jason. Sabrina jumped off his lap, and he held the leash tighter as he turned around to look. He saw a large back bent over with an arm reaching under Jason's bench. He felt Sabrina tugging excitedly on her leash; if she were any bigger, she would have dragged him under the bench.

Jason stood up, just as the woman did. "Ah," she said, squinting at him. "Ah, now I remember you face." When she smiled, a gold tooth in the back of her mouth winked at him. "I see the dog. I was a-walking back there"—she turned to point to a concrete path behind the trees—"and I look over and I see this little girl." She bent down to continue the conversation with Sabrina, who was standing on her hind legs, clawing at the woman's shins, begging to be picked up. "And I say to myself…that look like the dog who live by First Avenue. I try to look over, but your back…I can't tell for sure who you are. Until you just turn around. But you…you I remember right away." She picked up the Yorkie and held her in one arm like a baby, stroking Sabrina's long fur out of her eyes. "I don't see you no more. What happened to you?"

"Oh, I don't live there anymore. I moved over to West End almost a year ago." Although the woman didn't really look familiar to Jason, her loud voice and heavy accent reminded him of someone or someplace. He slapped his cheek as it dawned on him. "Oh, you! Now I know who you are. The Poodle lady!"

"Yes, that's a-me." Rosa felt better now that he remembered her and seemed glad to see her.

"Oh, don't tell me…" Jason lowered his voice sadly and looked to the ground where the dog should have been with its mistress.

She understood what he thought. "Oh no, Princess, she fine. But I have to take the bus over here, where I have to go. Too far for me to walk. Too far for Princess. We're just two old ladies, you know." To prove it, she pressed her chest with a fist to push her breath in and out loudly. Still holding her hand there, she walked around to the front of the bench and sat down. "Not like this little girl," she grunted, gruffly clutching Sabrina to her bosom. "My doctor, he near Fifth, so I see the trees and decide I sit for a while before I go home. It's-a beautiful here. Like the country in the middle of the city."

"Hey, tell me what's happening in the old neighborhood," Jason said. "I miss everyone."

Walking a dog, meeting other dog walkers, chatting to neighbors, and swapping pet stories was as close as most New Yorkers would ever get to a backyard fence to gossip over. And Rosa knew every dog and owner within a five-block radius of 83rd Street. Excited to be the source of information, she lifted Sabrina into her lap and started bringing Jason up-to-date on his old neighborhood.

Chapter 36

When the phone rang, Ken Hollis jumped out of the chair and zipped up his beige cardigan with the brown suede pocket flaps and elbow patches. He stuck out his hand. "I gotta be going anyway." Although it was cool today with a beautiful breeze, it was too warm at this time of year for a sweater.

The phone rang again. Bernie Petris also stood, took the hand offered to him, and shook it. "Thanks an awful lot for coming in. I hope we can work something out."

"I know we will." He looked at the phone ringing the third time. "G'head. Answer it. I'll be in touch." As he opened the door, he heard Bernie's fingers snapping several times, and he turned around.

Bernie waved him back, even as he spoke into the phone. "I understand what you're saying, miss, and I think you're right, but I…I know there is. As a matter of fact, we're trying to organize something now, but with all the red tape and then the city…Hey, wait a minute. Let me put a guy on here who would be interested. We were just having a meeting on this very thing, and we're trying to get a committee started or something just like you're asking for. But he's an expert on this type of thing. Hold on a minute." Bernie put his hand over the receiver as he held it out. "Speak of the devil. Gal at a bank in Yorkville had an elderly woman withdraw a lot of money this morning. She's sure somebody's ripping her off. Why don't you talk to her? You never know."

"Hello, my name's Ken Hollis. I'm a consultant to the mayor, and I've been working on crimes against the elderly. We're trying to set up a special task force, but I want you to understand that I probably can't do a thing right now. Might take months before we get it going." With that, Ken Hollis sat down and unzipped his sweater, ready to listen.

Chapter 37

Rain strumming the air conditioner lulled Laurie. Cars steadily swooshing on the wet street, water slapping rhythmically against the bricks, massaged her nerves. She kept the blinds up, the window open a few inches, and the lights off so she could lie on her bed and enjoy the music of the storm. Even though it was afternoon, it was ominously dark outside.

Sunday was her only day to catch up with herself, and she didn't feel at all guilty for not finishing her chores yesterday or for going to the office instead of cleaning and doing the laundry. But she missed taking care of herself last weekend, and she promised herself last night, as she shut off the alarm, that she would relax today. She had slept until ten, made bacon and eggs without worrying about the cholesterol, and perked real coffee without worrying about the caffeine. In jeans and a T-shirt, without a bra, she wrapped herself in a plastic slicker and went to the supermarket. She didn't feel like taking her shopping cart in the rain, so she bought only as much cat food and litter as she could carry. Returning with the papers, which she kept dry under her slicker, she put her nightgown back on and curled up on the couch with another cup of coffee and the *News*. Later, she dusted and vacuumed the cat hairs off the upholstery.

Afterward, she chose to do a little spring cleaning on her body rather than on the kitchen and bathroom. So she gave herself a facial and a pedicure, tweezed her eyebrows, and shaved her legs. It seemed like a very long time since she'd had a day like this all to herself, without any obligations or commitments, and it was delicious. Now that the new system was almost "live," after all the long and hard hours she had put in, she felt good about goofing off. A little vacation—she felt she was entitled to it.

Felix, who was lying with her after her nap, stretched, with his front paw flicking her cheek. She squeezed him and then rolled him off her chest into the crook of her arm. By the end of June, they'd be all set. "And then," she whispered into Felix's ear, "just wait and see Dr. Pomalee's reaction when I invite him to a complete demonstration." She stroked his head with two fingers.

Lightning bolted across the sky, momentarily illuminating the room. In the flash, she saw the green eyes open on the dresser and then close quickly, just before Oscar streaked through the air, landing on top of her for protection. "Maybe I'll give the computer information about myself. My money and things. And it can figure out how I should budget myself. Or my love life; that would be even better."

Felix hissed at her as she unconsciously wound his fur tightly around her finger. "I wonder," she mused, "if computers can laugh."

Chapter 38

Kola's back legs bicycled furiously; high-pitched yelps forced her mouth open; strenuous gasps made her chest heave up and down. In her nightmare, she could not recreate the cold, the hunger, the lost-ness; she could not picture the man who kicked her or the truck that drove away and left her. She couldn't imagine the grief of her old woman dying. She couldn't feel the metal rungs denting her snout or her paws pushing against a cage trying to get out. She couldn't hear the clamor of animals in the kennel howling at the scent of death just beyond the steel door.

Kola couldn't remember the specific feelings or faces. But they all came together in shadows of giant monsters and terrifying evils swooping in and out of focus. Just as a demon descended, its outline moving to define its shape, just as hundreds of tentacles of fear reached down for her, held her still, her eyelids fluttered, straining to open.

It was dark and quiet. Her breath moaned through her ribs in a soft cry. She swiveled her head enough to see the gentle face emerging from the mound under the blanket. She inched upward until her back was pressed into the boy's back. She lay motionless for a long time, her head bent in an awkward angle, just looking at him, her eyes melting with all the love and possessiveness and gratitude of her being. Then she rolled on her spine, her belly exposed, her four paws folded over her, in a primal wolverine gesture of subordination.

Chapter 39

The light touched the tips of the buildings in the distance like a copper wand, lifting the veil of darkness hovering over them. At 6:40, more than an hour later than usual, Louise had already done eight blocks—three more to go in one direction and then head back—which would be her morning mile. It was something between a jog and a brisk walk with an energetic dog that helped her work up a sweat, and now that she'd been doing it for a few months, she felt trimmer and firmer, although she worried that her thighs and buttocks were going to become more muscular and make her look even heavier. Only during the last few weeks had she felt the sense of freedom that came with turning the clocks ahead and being outside when it was light. In the winter she didn't like walking at that hour—she was usually out by 5:30—which seemed like the middle of the night.

People who knew thought she was crazy, that it was unsafe to be on the streets that early. But she knew better. The city might not be fully awake, but there were plenty of bodies out there. If she walked anywhere near Lexington, there were a lot of people, mostly men, who scattered in different directions from the express stop on 86th Street on their way… somewhere. Private sanitation trucks picked up garbage from stores and fast-food places. Oriental grocers cut up melons and fresh fruits and doled out portions into plastic boxes. Two-way radios squawked unintelligibly from identical cars waiting by the curb for a call, the drivers either sleeping or doubled up in the front seat, playing gin. Sidewalk breakfast vendors unhitched their wagons from the cars that brought them and brewed their first urn of coffee. Bundles of the

Daily News and the *Post* and the *Times* were tossed out of trucks with clever slogans painted on the sides to wait in front of office buildings for cigar-stand owners to bring them in. Janitors hosed their sidewalks while the doormen stretched awake. Dellwood drivers stacked cases of milk outside all-night markets. East Indians unlocked their newspaper kiosks on every other corner.

Regardless, Louise had her big, fierce watchdog with her.

The sound of metal gates rolling up, garbage grinding, things hitting the sidewalk were like a cock-a-doodle-doo to Louise. The only thing that interrupted the music and her gait was Honda stopping every once in a while to bark at some homeless person curled in a doorway.

She felt invigorated and even though she was late—according to her regular schedule; early for everyone else's—she needed a cup of coffee, an extra jolt of caffeine. She needed it before her shower, with her T-shirt matted to her skin, her hair stuck to her scalp with perspiration, and her armpits sticky with deodorant and sweat. She needed it sitting at a counter, mingling with taxi drivers and construction workers on their way to a job. She was afraid to tie up Honda, not that anyone would dare approach her big killer, but she couldn't relax with him howling outside, tethered to a hydrant or a pole. She'd drop him off first and go right back out.

Ken Hollis grabbed his suit jacket as it started to slide on to the seat. He made a hook of two fingers, hung it out, and then laid it over the back of the seat, keeping his eyes straight ahead. What a great morning! With the temperature a pleasant 72 degrees, he didn't bother with the air conditioner. He was more comfortable driving with his elbow resting in the open window anyway. At seventy-one miles, the Long Island Expressway was not even that long, especially on its most heavily traveled segment, but normally, by measuring speed in feet per hour rather than miles, it took forever to get into the city. Or out of it. One hundred fifty thousand cars travel over it daily, but, as many commuters would swear, 149,000 of them always decided to drive on it at precisely the same time.

Taking the car at all had been a spur-of-the-moment decision, and now that he was whizzing along as if he were on a country road, he was glad he'd made it. He had agreed to meet Donna Griffen before the bank opened so she could feel free to talk to him. Actually, that was easier for him too, since it was all so unofficial. But when he started thinking about taking the subway uptown to the coffee shop on 85th Street she'd mentioned, then going all the way down to City Hall for a meeting, getting back uptown for an evening class he was teaching, and finally going back to Penn Station, he thought the hell with it. He'd rather sit in bumper-to-bumper traffic, worrying about the car overheating and paying through the nose for a garage. He never expected to be driving along at 45 miles an hour. He might do this more often. Even though it would be more convenient to park near Hunter so he'd have the car close by, the rates would be much cheaper in Yorkville. And if his luck held out, he might even find a spot on the street up here.

It made all the difference, leaving before seven—unless he considered that leaving an hour early to avoid the traffic would give him an hour to kill when he got there. He could always pick up a paper and have a pre-breakfast cup of coffee. As a matter of fact, the topic of conversation at many a social gathering in his area was always how backed up the traffic was on the LIE. Someone would brag, trying to win the most-harrowing-drive contest, "Would you believe it took me an hour and a half to go for a twenty-minute ride?" But then, there was always someone else who occasionally had to go somewhere in the middle of the night, probably between 12:30 and 5:00 a.m., and would boast, "It only took me twenty minutes to do what usually takes me an hour and a half." The truth was that since construction first started on the Long Island Expressway in 1954, nobody ever took a twenty-minute drive on it in twenty minutes. In broad daylight.

Ken hadn't noticed that the lights were all out. It was just something that he knew was there. And the next minute it wasn't, and he didn't know when the change had taken place. When he first started, he began counting the lights, nodding his head as he passed them, like an animator flipping life into cartoon characters. He made it to fourteen and never realized that he had stopped counting and that they were all off now. Ken read that in 1975, when the city had to cut back, they had taken out almost 500 of the lights on the Expressway, leaving a total of 1,220 in operation, with every other one lit. With an astronomical time switch that automatically adjusted to sunrise and sunset, a backup photoelectric control was added so the light of day would strike the on and off switches. They were well prepared for a power failure.

Ah, I spoke too soon, Ken thought about the traffic moving, as his lane slowed and a line of red brake lights punctured the gray dawn. He felt in the console caddy for the E-Z Pass and clicked it onto the windshield.

He fiddled with the radio knob to get rid of the static and heard "hazy, hot and humid, with the highs reaching near ninety. Alternate side of the street parking is in effect today." The cars ahead of him came to a standstill and then slowly fanned out toward the seven toll booths. When he saw two uniformed attendants crossing the plaza, about to open the additional booth for the morning rush, he stepped lightly on the gas pedal and swerved the steering wheel. His left arm was stretched outside, his hand bracing the roof of the car and his fingers tapping the fiberglass impatiently. He waited, watching three men in bright orange vests set up bright orange cones to add a new path into the Midtown Tunnel, leaving only one in the opposite direction.

"Sure, we have mechanical wonders to let nature control our machinery," he complained to nobody, "but they still haven't been able to figure out how to squeeze nine lanes into three." Ken leaned to the right and looked in the rearview mirror. He put his hand through his hair and unconsciously pulled on the curls, like he'd done when he was a kid, trying to straighten them. He used to worry that people would think he was a sissy because of his curly hair, that they'd think he had it permed. And the blond made it worse; he was sure everybody thought he had it done in his mother's beauty parlor. But it didn't bother him at all anymore. Then again, he had the small bald spot on the back of his head to bother him these days.

He examined his reflection and thought that now, with the gray coming in, it made his hair look gravelly. Rough. It went well with his dark skin tone.

It was wonderful to reach the age of thirty-four and not give a damn what anybody thought of you. *There's nothing that attaining maturity can't heal.* Ken smirked and then added out loud. "That, and twelve thousand dollars' worth of therapy."

Louise scraped off some of the cream cheese with a knife. She'd asked for a "shmear" and got what looked like half a pound. She probably would have eaten it all if she hadn't been feeling so virtuous about the extra ten blocks she did after dropping Honda home. She licked her upper lip while she was smoothing out the cheese, admiring the well-done, toasted everything-bagel in her hand. She opened her mouth and bit down hard, savoring the crunchy noise.

"Well, well, well. So this is where the movers and shakers dine out!" Ken Hollis said as he slid onto the stool two seats from her.

Louise's teeth stuck in the thick dough; the bagel sprang like a seesaw onto her face, leaving a glob of cream cheese hanging from the tip of her nose. Even though she meant to turn the other way to hide, she was so startled that she looked Ken Hollis right in the face. For a second, unable to chew, she couldn't recall where she'd seen those deep brown eyes before.

He stopped laughing when the counter man put a heavy mug in front of him while holding the glass pot in a question mark. "Got any decaf?" Ken asked, adding, "I'll have a toasted English with it." He watched the man change pots for the one with the orange lid and pour his coffee, which gave Louise a chance to swallow the piece of bagel, not thoroughly chewed, and wipe her face with a napkin. Although she was now neater, she was sure she smelled and could have kicked herself for not showering and dressing. But if it bothered him, that was *his* problem.

"Come here often?" She grinned, acknowledging that she remembered him and his line and that yes, she was a mess. "No. As a matter of fact, this is the first time."

"I didn't realize you lived in this neighborhood."

"I don't. I drove in from the Island." He looked at his watch. "I'm supposed to meet someone here for breakfast, and I'm real early. Do you live around here?"

"Nah. I just put on this disguise when I go slumming. You know, the sweaty old clothes, the dirty sneakers. So nobody will recognize me."

"I don't blame you. Your father—the commissioner—must be very careful so nobody kidnaps you."

They both laughed.

"Actually, I live practically around the corner, on 88th Street. I jog every morning. Well, not quite jog; more like brisk walking. I take my dog with me so he gets his exercise too. I brought him home, and I was just dying for a cup of coffee." Louise didn't know why she was explaining or why she cared. He wasn't good looking. Not with that long crooked nose. And he was much too thin for somebody so tall. She hated thin men. Even sitting, he looked lanky. Skinny, with curly hair. The only nice thing about him was his voice.

"This is a real treat for me," Ken said. "A good old-fashioned coffee shop. A good old-fashioned Greek coffee shop. I thought they'd all gone the way of the candy store."

"There are still a lot of coffee shops left."

He shook his head. "Not downtown. They're all salad bars now. Serve yourself. I hate that for lunch."

"You don't like salads?"

"Yeah, *with* my meal, not *as* a meal. I don't find them very filling. Besides, I don't like serving myself and sitting at a cramped table with strangers."

"Come to think of it, you're right," Louise agreed. "But around here, maybe since this is so residential, there are still a few of them left."

Ken swept his arm at the cracked vinyl booths, the worn Formica tables and broken tiles on the floor, and smudges of hardened grease on the grill. "You can't get this in a salad bar. Even in the suburbs, the diners have all gotten so ritzy. You need a reservation, or you have to stand on line for a table. You know, sometimes you just feel like having bacon and eggs for lunch or grilled cheese or a real hamburger and French fries, not the kind that comes from McDonald's."

"You have something against pasta too?" she asked.

"You mean cold noodles in weird shapes and colors?"

Louise did her imitation of the old spaghetti-sauce commercial: "Dat's-a pasta. Basta with the pasta!"

Although it was all very logical to progress from talking about lunches to talking about dinners to making a date to have one together, Louise didn't understand later how it actually happened. Or why, as she was vigorously washing herself in the shower, she was singing.

Chapter 40

At 10:30, Chris Bartlett hopped into a cab to go home to pick up the manuscript he needed for the monthly editorial meeting. It had been easy to forget about it since he hadn't had a chance to sit at his desk last night. Or the night before. Or the night before that. Jason needed to use the computer to write a letter to the tenants; then he had to write a letter to the committee members; then he had to write a letter to some local churches and schools to see about borrowing an auditorium for the next meeting. Jason was so busy these days that he probably hadn't even noticed when Chris left last night to go to a movie by himself. He definitely hadn't noticed when he'd come home.

Chris closed his eyes to the wind as the taxi sped through the Transverse in Central Park. Emerging on the West Side, the traffic stood still. It was already 84 degrees with 75-percent humidity, and Chris could feel the perspiration start at the back of his neck and trickle under his collar. He'd have to change his shirt when he got home. After the light turned green twice and they didn't move an inch, Chris jumped out to dash the last few blocks on foot.

Rosa brushed Princess with a baby brush. The fur on her back was so thin that her pink skin was exposed. Growths the size of pimples dotted her little body and even though the vet had told her they were normal at her age, especially in Poodles, Rosa was afraid of hurting her. The brushing didn't help her hair, her skin, or her circulation. It didn't do anything except give Rosa a chance to continue the loving, affectionate ritual that she'd started when Princess was a puppy. "Then, bambina, when we done, Mama gonna go out for a while. Go visit the chiropodist. He look at my bunion and maybe fix-a my feet so we go for a nice long walk. You like that, huh? Oops, he called a podiatrist now."

Clifford refused to go to camp. Besides, he no longer fit into the special education classes for special-needs students. He was going to start regular school in September, but it was too early to have him thrown into a normal group for an extended period over the summer. So, as Jessica had promised her husband, she escorted him to the 4Cs, which Dr. Kravitz had recommended, every Monday, Wednesday, and Friday morning. The Comprehensive Children's Counseling Center had a summer preteen group program that seemed to help Clifford interact with kids his own age. Then she went home to study for the Graduate Record Examinations. She was determined to get into graduate school and get her master's degree. Step one was to take the GREs. For the first time since Clifford was born, she had some options, some choices to make. She could actually leave home and have a real job. And she knew what she wanted to do. Something with animal therapy for people.

Laurie could see her reflection in the computer screen. Her hands were arched over the keyboard, like a pianist's, her fingers moving fluently as she arranged the facts into a new composition. The light tapping of her fingertips on the letters, the clicking of the keys making contact with their mechanical brain, the liquid rhythm…it flowed through her like a concerto. She watched her bare nails superimposed on the white-on-black data input and decided a manicure with bright red polish would be dazzling. The pain swelled in her heart; the music surged in her mind. She played beautifully.

Eileen knew something was wrong. She'd felt it as soon as she woke up. Leaving the supermarket after making what the TV shows called "the drop-off," rushing, not daring to look, she had been too fast, too nervous for the automatic exit door. She walked into it with such force that her glasses fell off. In her hurry to pick them up and get out of there, she stepped on the left lens, smashing it with her own foot. She'd been afraid to leave the apartment since that day, afraid to leave Fibber alone, afraid to stay there with him. But she couldn't see. She finally brought her glasses to Cohen's yesterday for repair. Walking to Third Avenue, she kept looking behind her, to her side, out of the corners of her eyes, wondering if the messenger on his bike, or the Con Ed guy drilling on the corner, or the black deliveryman in the undershirt was one of them, was the one after her and her Fibber.

Now, coming back from Cohen's, her old glasses in the new case they'd been nice enough to give her, she knew something was wrong when she saw the landlady peeking out at her from behind her first-floor window. Her hands shook as she jabbed the key into the front door. Once inside, the old woman opened her door and said she had found the envelope under the front door, without a stamp on it. Eileen recognized the block printing. Even if she hadn't, she would have known it was from them.

She pressed it between her thumb and index finger. The softness felt like a packet of tissues or a wadded-up cloth. Or something. When she put her thumb under the flap and tore half of it open, enough to put her fingers inside, she felt what it was.

The ear fell on the floor. The thud it seemed to make as it bounced gently on the worn rug thundered in Eileen's temple as her pressure soared. Her blood thickened as it froze and got stuck in her veins. Then it thawed, sending the icy liquid racing through her body, leaving a terrible cold under her skin.

Nausea rippled in her stomach and rushed through her ribs. It pushed to her throat, choking her. She strained the muscle under her tongue, trying to hold it back. But she couldn't.

Eileen opened her mouth and threw up all over the little foyer.

Chapter 41

Louise was as dazzled as Elena by the array of real-looking figures that beckoned to the crowds of young girls who swarmed into the American Girl store on Fifth Avenue. The revolving door kept turning more people into the entrance, and if they didn't step out quickly enough, they'd go around for another swing, right outside to 49th Street. The shrill squeals of excitement were contagious, and it seemed everyone was oohing and aahing and touching the dolls at the same time.

Louise and Elena were pushed along to the escalator and were just as eager as everyone else to explore the wonders of the second floor. Louise felt a little guilty for bringing Elena to a place where she could probably never return, never again enjoy an expedition to this wonderland. She promised herself she would buy her one doll and give her a glimpse into a universe of indulgence. But she was taken aback by the prices and by the seemingly unlimited must-have extras available for each personality—because each doll had not only a personality but an entire biography, cultural background, family history, hobbies, and goals. Louise enjoyed seeing Elena's pure joy in holding some of the dolls.

Louise was part of the sisterhood of women watching their daughters and granddaughters and nieces examine the dolls, combing their hair with skinny fingers, trying to decide which one they liked best—and pleading for an extra outfit or shoes or the accompanying book. And once a decision was made, there would be a little cry of "Oh, look at that one. Isn't she more beautiful?" Louise thought Elena would choose one that looked most like her—darker skin, curly black hair. So she was surprised when Elena picked Isabelle, with her long blonde hair and her aspirations to be a dancer—what Elena *wished* she looked like. For herself, Louise would have chosen a brunette with tanned skin and brown eyes.

How could Louise not get Elena an extra outfit for her doll? How could she dress and undress her little friend if she had only one thing to wear? So $134 for Isabelle, $36 for a dress—which was probably more than Yolanda spent on Elena's clothes—another $36 for a makeup kit, and $30 for the accessory bag. Louise's VISA credit card was probably smirking.

Fortunately, she had waited too long to make reservations for lunch, and the café was all booked. She'd take Elena somewhere for a hamburger or a slice of pizza. They certainly didn't have stuff like this doll store when Louise was growing up, but her heart felt full with pleasure as Elena clutched her red shopping bag in one hand and took Louise's hand with her other.

Chapter 42

Rosa opened the washrag, spread it under the cold water, slowly rotating it until it was soaked. Standing at the unfamiliar sink, more like a basin with legs, she looked around the small, old-fashioned kitchen, approving of its tidiness. She couldn't help noticing that the cabinet doors didn't close all the way, as the wood was swollen with years and years of paint. Or that the single work surface was badly pockmarked with nicks and cuts, that the original linoleum had holes large enough in places for the gray concrete to show through. It looked just like her own kitchen, down to the small Kelvinator. She had wanted to use ice cubes, but the trays were so stuck to the tiny freezer compartment that she couldn't get them out. Funny—they both even had the same vintage toaster, the kind with little doors for the bread, from before toasters were pop-ups.

Rosa twisted the cloth tight, squeezing out the water, and wondered why she and Eileen Hargan, neighbors for at least forty years, had never visited one another, never been in one another's apartment. Maybe they could start now. It would be nice to have someone from just down the block stop by, have a glass of Chianti, and talk. As soon as the poor woman was back to herself, Rosa would definitely ask her.

"Now, here, this-a gonna make you feel much better," she soothed as she walked into the living room. She patted Eileen's forehead and cheeks lightly so the cold wouldn't shock her. Then she folded the cloth into a band and held it against her skin. "You feeling a little better now? Good." She didn't wait for an answer. Rosa sat down next to Eileen on the faded chintz couch and put her other arm around her, rocking her slightly.

"You sure that's what he said?" Eileen's words sounded like hiccups through her sobs. "That he couldn't talk because he was in a meeting? Was it himself or his secretary?"

"No, he got on. After I tell the secretary it's about his aunt. But don't-a worry. You know how these big executives are. Always making important deals, at meetings. If I say you sick or in bad trouble, I'm sure he would-a come like that." Rosa tried to click her fingers but her arthritic joints refused to bend. She made the gesture anyway.

"Always telling me he'd do anything for me, that I shouldn't worry—he'll take care of me in my old age. Always promising, her too, and then the first time I ask, just once I need someone, and where is he? He knows Fibber is my whole life. He should understand that it was almost a tragedy. God, I would have died…honest, look what just the thought of it did to me." Eileen took the washrag to wipe her nose.

"Well, the way I explain, maybe it really don't sound too serious. As long as your boy"—Rosa patted Fibber McGee's head—"is still here, alive, with you."

"No, it's not right. What could be worse? I ask you, what?"

"I know. You think I don't know? If something happen to my Princess, I do like you do. Faint. Or die. Or kill somebody. Yes, I would kill anybody who hurt my little bambina. Monsters, that's what they are. Scaring you like that. Where you suppose they get the ear from? Some poor little animal belongs to someone else? It's not fake. Monsters, they are. Don't worry, I stay here with you. We're the same. If your nephew, if he come, he won't understand anyway. About loving you dog so much. It's better he don't come. You see." She stroked Eileen's shoulder.

"Thanks. I'm so glad Miss Schlosser had enough sense to call you when she saw you walking by. But where could it have come from? Some other poor little thing…"

"And its mama crying *her* heart out somewhere."

The buzzer jolted them both like an electric shock. Eileen gasped, her breath caught in her chest.

"You expecting company?" Rosa asked.

"No, no. It's them. It's them," she wailed.

"Don't be silly. Maybe Miss What's-her-name downstairs, she wanna know how you feel?" Rosa insisted on being calm, even though her voice sounded far away to her, traveling the distance over her heartbeats.

"No, she would ring up here, not the downstairs bell. Oh, Fibber, come here, come here, they're going to get you, and us too."

Fibber stopped barking to cock his head at the front door and listen for footsteps.

"I go ask. Where's your box?" Rosa anxiously looked around for an intercom, her legs turning soft as soon as she stood on them.

"Outside the bathroom door. But it doesn't work. You can't talk, only ring back. Oh, no, don't ring them in. Don't let them in."

"Mine neither. Doesn't work. I'll go down and see." The buzzer sounded again, more shrill and more insistent. Rosa scrambled to the old box, originally brass but painted many times to match the different colors over the years. In the dim hallway, the two black buttons poked out of it like bulging eyes and, since she didn't know which was the door release and which was for talking, she pressed them both, alternately, several times. She did that at home too. She became more nervous about somebody leaving before she could buzz the person in fast enough than she was about a stranger ringing.

She hurried to the front door and waited. The slow, heavy footsteps on the stairs kept in time with the thumping of her heart. She raced into the kitchen and came back with a long knife with a serrated blade that she knew would not be good to stab someone with. But feeling more secure, she clutched it to her breast and squeezed her right eye against the peephole. Ken Hollis's warm smile was a sinister sneer in the pinpoint opening.

INDEPENDENCE DAY

Chapter 43

Jason carefully slid the ruler down the paper. His tongue moved back and forth, circling around his lips, as he guided his hand to draw another line down the page. He leaned back and tilted his head at an angle to admire his handiwork. Pleased, he made columns of the headings—FLOOR, APARTMENT, TENANT, TELEPHONE, E-MAIL—trying to center each one in the space he had allotted. He smoothed the paper and slowly started copying the names from the steno pad he used for his notes. He would have preferred to type them in, but it would take much too long. He would have asked Chris, who was a whiz on the computer, but he didn't want anyone's help. He realized it wasn't so much not wanting to share the responsibility as it was guarding his position of president. Protecting his control. Or just possibly, a way to have a secret from Chris, something private that he wasn't a part of.

Something had happened to Jason recently; he felt different. He *was* different. Everything was different. For the first time in his life, he felt whole, complete. He didn't know when it had happened or why; he never noticed a gradual change. One morning he woke up, and he was a different person.

He still loved Chris, actually loved him more intensely. But it wasn't the same pathetic desire to be wanted, to be taken care of. It was an independent attraction. And it made Jason feel good about himself, about Chris, and about their relationship. Made him feel self-sufficient. Mature.

Even sex had changed. He no longer was turned on by the physical strength of Chris's lovemaking. At some point earlier, he'd come to understand that before he met Chris he had found partners—*looked* for partners—who were very dominant, more so than his submissive nature demanded. He liked to be overcome, overtaken. Maybe so he didn't have to admit that he had any choices, that he could say no. It was the easiest cop-out in the world. Pretend to himself that it wasn't his fault. Meeting Chris had changed that, although he was the strong one and Jason the weak. Now, though, he preferred to be equal to Chris, not just give in to him. And now that he *could* say no, he didn't. But it was by choice, not by indecision. And it was better like that. *He* was better. *Who knows?* he thought. *I might even become the stronger one if this keeps up.*

Jason stroked a piece of scrap paper with his fine felt-tip marker to make sure the ink was flowing smoothly. Then he carefully printed TENANT ASSOCIATION on the tab of a manila folder and filed his chart away.

Chapter 44

Michelle Kravitz peeled the paper off her straw and methodically rolled it up as she listened. Although she sympathized with Jessica—she wanted to feel as rotten as Jessica did—she knew that in the recesses of her mind, she was gloating. She imagined the fuzzy gray coils of her brain slithering into smirks—a proper scientific image for a psychotherapist! She quickly concentrated on smoothing out the strip of paper, pressing it back and forth with her fingers, pursing her lips to prevent a smile from forming.

"Do you blame me?" Jessica Marcus didn't wait for an answer. "I mean, what more can I do? It just isn't fair. All the years of sacrificing. Don't get me wrong; it's not that I considered I was sacrificing, because I did it willingly. I did it because I love Clifford. And now it's finally finished. Or so I thought. He's a real person. He doesn't need me twenty-four hours a day. I can have a life of my own. And what happens? Waaah!" She exaggerated a wail.

The woman in the next booth turned around to see where the noise was coming from and caught Michelle's eye disapprovingly, as if they were teenagers laughing over ice cream sodas and boys, instead of adults having a serious conversation over their Cobb salads. Michelle wanted to stick her tongue out at the woman. God, she was feeling bitchy today. Maybe because she was so disappointed herself.

"It's unbelievable." Michelle pushed her plate out of the way. She moved her glass closer and sucked her iced tea through the plastic straw. It gave her time to think of something to say, other than *"At least you didn't have to struggle. You always had a husband to support you, pay the rent. It's not my fault that you had to stay home and take care of your son. I never had any choices to make, because I've always had to work to earn my own living. And I've come a long way, baby. On my own, with no help.* " But of course she bit her tongue over the words.

Folding the wrapper tighter and smaller, Michelle felt herself sliding back into her professional mold. "Maybe you can try looking at it as a new challenge, instead of a defeat. I mean, anyone who could overcome all the obstacles you did—"

"But they were all beyond my control. That's it, I think. I did what I could do, what I had to do. I didn't have to decide anything. I just wanted Clifford to be normal, to get better."

"You're not giving yourself enough credit, are you? You've told me often enough how your husband never gave you any moral support, how you had to do everything practically in spite of him. Well, that's heavy decision making as far as I'm concerned, going against your husband's opinions."

"It *sounds* good but believe me, it was easy. Maybe because I was so determined. For Clifford's sake. So what do you think I oughta do?"

"Well…"

"And please don't give me that crap that you can't advise me. I'm not a patient, remember? I never was." Jessica's voice softened. "Tell me as a friend."

"Okay." Michelle unrolled the hard little wad and ripped it into tiny pieces onto her plate. "Let me read the letter again…friend."

Chapter 45

"A billion? That's an incredible amount. Are you sure?"

"Nah, it could be fifty million. Or five million. What's the difference? Whatever it is, it's sickening. Maybe it was a hundred million. That's it. God knows what they do to them."

"Oh, I don't want to know." Eileen covered her eyes with her hands, as if that would stop her from hearing.

"You *should* know. How it's ever gonna stop if nobody does anything? If they don't even listen?"

"Maybe this isn't the best time to discuss it," Ken Hollis coaxed Rosa.

"When the time? When they all dead?" Her accent became thicker as her anger soared, and she sputtered her words. "Tortured. Maimed. For what? So's some woman can put gunk in her hair, or they teach some college jerks that you pound a monkey's skull with a hammer, it gets headaches?!"

"Don't—please don't," Eileen wailed. "I can't think about my poor baby, about what could happen to him."

Rosa squinted at her as she shook her finger. "You *should* think about what coulda happen. Why you think they're doing this? What you think they want him for?"

"What? What are you suggesting?"

"Suggesting? I'm not suggesting. I'm telling." Still shaking her finger at Eileen Hargan, Rosa turned to Ken Hollis.

"They gonna take this poor lady's dog, the love of her life, and they gonna sell him to a laboratory, that's what."

Eileen threw her head back against the couch with a moan that sounded like it started in her knees.

"And torture him," Rosa added maliciously.

Ken pulled himself out of the dainty chair. It reminded him of dollhouse furniture. Just like Eileen Hargan reminded him of a doll, with her translucent white skin and neat white hair, illuminated by the button eyes. So shiny, so blue, like colored glass. He knew she was made hard, like porcelain. And just as breakable. He towered over the two of them on the couch and gently touched Eileen's shoulder. "Come on, now, you've got to do this. Not only for your Fibber McGee's sake but for all your friends." He patted Rosa with his other hand. "And their animals and all the people you don't even know who love their pets as much as you do. Well, almost as much. C'mon now, it's the only way."

Oh, God, why hasn't Danny come? Why isn't he here to help? But this Mr. Hollis was so nice. He seemed sincere and warm. He didn't try to humor Eileen by pretending he was a great dog lover or make fun of her for being so worried. No, he could probably be trusted. Why couldn't her nephew be like him? "Oh, I don't know. I don't know. I suppose."

"You listen to him. You gotta tell. Or nobody's safe anymore."

Eileen Hargan blew her nose loudly and then went into her bedroom. She returned and handed Ken four envelopes. "And that." She pointed to the one Rosa had carried up and left on the little table by the door. "Okay, you stop them." She sat down next to Ken Hollis and tapped her knee, signaling for Mr. McGee to sit in her lap.

Chapter 46

Felix meowed from the top of the toilet tank.

"Sure, easy for you to say," Laurie teased him. "You don't have to change the litter."

He watched her rake the pebbles, leaving smooth tracks in the box. He jerked his head as she swung the seat up, close to him, to shake the plastic shovel over the bowl before returning it to the corner caddy meant for the toilet brush. "And that's the thanks I get for coming back early, huh? For bringing my stuff home to work here. Keep you company." She washed her hands and shook the water at him. He tried to claw it. He waited, alert and anxious. She laughed as she sprinkled him again and again. He was sitting on the edge of the tank, his right paw reaching toward the sink, trying to catch the spray. "You're so dumb." Laurie opened her folded fingers over his head. "Dumb, dumb, dumb. You haven't caught it yet, have you? Why don't you give up?" Oscar followed the trail of her playful voice into the bathroom and joined the fun.

"Okay, guys, gang up on me, right? Well, I'm gonna get you." She took a hand towel and swiped at them both with it, daring them to catch it, as she dangled it every which way, just out of their reach. A dog would have grabbed it and had a serious tug of war. But Laurie was beginning to enjoy feline grace and agility more and more, as well as the indifference that she had laughingly told Stacy was good for humility—hers, not the cats'.

When the game was finally over, Laurie felt good about playing with them, about playing herself. They were still wound up and chased one another for a while, until Felix curled up on the couch, ready for a nap.

Laurie cleared a space on the dinette table, emptied the manila envelope, and spread out all the brochures and reports and pamphlets and newsletters she'd been collecting from all the humane societies, and wildlife coalitions, and animals' rights committees, and conservation groups, and animal-protection organizations. Then she took her highlighter and made angry red slashes across the facts she would enter into the computer.

Chapter 47

The uptown express on the Lexington Avenue line ground into the Brooklyn Bridge station. The rush-hour crowds, anxious to get home, pushed each other to make sure they got on before the doors closed.

From the narrow, twisted alleys that the rays of the sun never reach to the broad cobblestone plaza of the Seaport, from the judicial aura hovering over the courthouses and state office buildings to the clamor of people examining exotic vegetables and slimy fish on the streets of Chinatown, from the new boutiques and shopping avenues to the smell of money and power on Wall Street to the smell of souvlaki and frankfurters steaming in sidewalk carts, from the bleat of the Staten Island ferry to the splash of water against wood pilings, from the vendors selling their watches and T-shirts to the new glass and steel monuments shadowing them, Lower Manhattan throbbed with its own pulse.

Before she had plunged into the darkness of the underground, Louise stopped for a second to look up at the skyline. The setting sun glinted red on the new World Trade Center and bounced a rosy glow on window glass and building cement angled to catch its reflection. Her heart lifted with her eyes. She wondered how something so astonishing could seem so ordinary. Then she allowed herself to be pushed down the stairs with the mob.

The wave of people rolled to the sway of the train. The air conditioning turned clammy perspiration to ice, freezing the odors of bodies pressed close. Louise leaned her weight against her taut right arm in the stirrup and thought about buying a bottle of bourbon on her way home. Just in case.

Chapter 48

Jason slapped water in his armpits and lathered them. He rubbed the foam onto his chest and stuck his belly out so the water would hit it. He wanted to get an early start this morning so he could take care of the paperwork and finish up by the time Suzanne came in. Then at least he could make the meeting at Roosevelt Hospital and be back in time to close the store. He didn't know how he got invited to join an organization like SAVE. It was a joke that they said they heard he was active in tenants' rights. Didn't they realize it was only in his own building? And what did tenants' rights have to do with AIDS anyway? Or gay rights, for that matter? He didn't want to get caught up in another cause. Especially this one, which seemed far removed from his life. Well, there was no harm in going once.

It did seem worthwhile—Support for AIDS Victims Everywhere— matching up volunteers to neighborhood sufferers. But why was it necessary, with AIDS so much on the decline today that it was practically nonexistent? If you could call 50,000 new cases a year "nonexistent." And with HIV under control. If you could call the 34 million people worldwide with AIDS under control. Well, the guy said even though it started as an AIDS thing, it was more for cancer patients undergoing debilitating radiation or chemo treatment. It was performing normal, everyday functions for those too sick to handle them but not sick enough to be bedridden. Walk a dog, pick up a package at the post office, get a suit from the dry cleaners, do a load of laundry, pick up the person from chemo or radiation. He certainly didn't have to commit himself to anything with them or to spending any time organizing and recruiting, as they suggested. He didn't have any time, for God's sake. But it was the dog part that got him. He knew how he would feel if he was sick and not able to take care of Sabrina. It reminded him of POWARS—Pet Owners With AIDS Resource Sources—once a very strong organization but disbanded fifteen or sixteen years ago for lack of need.

A draft hit his back as the bathroom door opened. The curtain slid across the rod. He whirled his head around just as Chris lifted his foot over the rim of the tub. Chris stepped in, reached across Jason to get the bar of soap from its pocket in the wall, and then stroked Jason's back with it. The soap thudded as it fell to the floor. Chris's fingers played with Jason's slippery skin, gently rubbing his shoulders, massaging, sliding to his buttocks, kneading…his finger tracing the crack where his cheeks split, finding the hole, lingering at the opening, retracing its route. Jason's breath stopped in his chest.

Weak from the steam and the desire rising in his lungs, Jason leaned forward and braced his arms against the tile under the showerhead, the water hitting him low on his back. He heard the squeak of Chris's knees rubbing the porcelain a second before he pulled his cheeks apart, hard, and tickled his anus with his tongue. Jason flattened his palms on the faucets, his weight against his arms. His muscles made shiny ripples under his skin. Then Chris's fingers jabbed inside him and pushed his insides out in a jet of white syrup that hit the wall. It hung on the tile. Then slowly slid down to the drain.

Chapter 49

Lenny hesitated at his front door, methodically cracking his knuckles one by one. He could turn around and go right back downstairs, and…and what? He really had nowhere else to go except home. But it didn't feel like home anymore. Not home like his parents' house was, even after all these years. Not the warmth of a family sitting around a fire, the poppa reading the paper, the mama knitting, and all the children doing their homework or napping or laughing at comic books. Who was he kidding? His family never owned a fireplace in their lives. His mother didn't knit or crochet. And the children never got along well enough to be in one room doing anything together except fighting. Yet the memories were warm. Or maybe it was the longing for that childhood, or the loss of his own youth, or going back to a time before responsibility and pain and problems.

As the elevator door quietly closed behind him, a sense of hopelessness overwhelmed him. As if his last route for escape was gone. But deep down, he knew better. There never was any escape. Not for people like Leonard Marcus, whose stability and values forced them to endure. To suffer their obligations. Until they died. Or cracked.

Chapter 50

Laurie followed the cursor across her screen, her fingers trying to keep in time to the bouncing ball. She didn't break her rhythm as she glanced at her watch. Since they changed the procedure and no longer allowed the attendant to relieve Stacy, Laurie actually felt better. If she didn't have an excuse to come downstairs every day, she probably wouldn't even stop for lunch. Yesterday had been a disaster. But you'd think when she lost track of the time and didn't come right down after Stacy buzzed her that somebody would have called her to ask where she was. Instead of sitting there until Dr. Pomalee came back with Dr. Stevens, and the patients were piled up. It was so crowded and so noisy that two people paced outside in the street with their large dogs to avoid a ferocious confrontation in the waiting room. But that was precisely why she took charge now. The kids who worked there summers and part-time during school months—even those who wanted to go in for veterinary medicine—didn't have the smarts to handle the reception desk or schedule appointments. Except maybe Rick. He was good. But he had too many other responsibilities since the other attendant quit.

At 11:55, she exited the program. The main menu came back to the screen with the prompts she needed. She patted the top of her machine in approval. She was just as amazed as she had been the first week that all the information would be filed away. She carried the pile of rabies and distemper reminders she had printed in their self-mailers and went down to the front desk.

"How's it going?" she asked as she fanned out the morning's chart folders to get an idea of who had been treated so far. "Busy?"

"Not too bad." Stacy swiveled her chair around to face Laurie. "Except the damn phone hasn't stopped ringing. Mrs. Lefkowitz came in for diarrhea and no sooner did she get here than Bruno shit all over the floor. She ran outside for him to finish, but of course I couldn't find Rick, so I got stuck cleaning it up. It was loose. Like water. Yuck."

"That's show biz, huh?" Laurie winked absently.

"There's more. A first-timer came in with the cutest little puppy. She just adopted it from the Humane Society. Wanted to check her out. The little thing was so scared, she made a puddle, not five minutes after I cleaned up the other mess."

"Oh, well, at least you worked up an appetite for lunch."

"Funny you should say that. I was just thinking how I lost it completely."

"Force yourself."

Stacy leaned over and stretched her lips in the small mirror taped over her desk just under the reception window. "And most important"—her words were distorted through her open mouth as she applied gloss—"if Dr. Michaels calls from the AMC, get a number and find out when he can be reached. I left three messages for him. Dr. Haberkorn needs to talk to him."

Laurie ran her finger down the appointment book, wanting to see how much time she'd have before the first afternoon arrival. "Mmm, nobody's due 'til 12:30."

"Right, but Dr. Stevens is off this afternoon, and Dr. Pomalee said he'd be back about 1:00."

"Okay," Laurie said.

"And Mrs. Bassetti called. She wants to come in to pick up some more Lasix for Princess's heart. I left it on top of the film, so you don't have to go hunting for it."

"Thanks. Enjoy," Laurie called as Stacy whipped the long handle of her bag over her shoulder like a lasso.

Chapter 51

Princess hung from the large breast, her belly pressed against the soft flesh, her back paws dangling straight, unable to swing close to her midriff. She rested her head on Rosa's shoulder, her face turned in to her neck. She was unable to see her mistress's eyes, but she felt them warming her, just as she felt the security of the hand that cradled her little back and would not let her fall.

Rosa walked back and forth, humming an Italian lullaby, as if rocking a baby. She stroked her head. "Who's Mama's little girl?" she sang. She made a hole between two of the slats in the old wooden blinds and closed one eye to peek out. "Who would do such a thing? Dio, it's terrible. Terrible. Thank heaven, Fibber McGee, you little friend, he's okay." Rosa tilted her head lightly against Princess's, her hair on the dog's fur.

Without disturbing a muscle, Rosa walked to her easy chair and carefully backed into the seat. Sitting, she swayed her buttocks slightly in the cushion to soothe Princess, who was already asleep. "What I would do if something happen-a you, bambina." She tightened her hold. "I die if you die. You hear?" She nuzzled her face, and Princess opened her eyes. Rosa shifted her to her lap and caressed her body, so frail, so tender where her fur had thinned.

"But worse, much worse—ah, I cannot even-a think—what would happen to you, my precious, if I die. My heart, it breaks to think about my poor little baby crying for me, wondering where I am. Like if those men do something terrible and take you away. You crying, looking for your mama, waiting for me to come get you. Oh Dio, Dio mio," Rosa wailed and hugged her Princess tight. Then, making an effort to be more rational and because she could not even conceive of such a notion, she thought about her will. Maybe she should change it. After all, even though she indicated that Princess should be sent to Italy to her sister, would they send her poor baby there? How could she ride in the plane by herself? In a crate? And maybe Josie wouldn't be so loving, even though she promised. Or maybe she'd be too old or too sick. Or dead too. And now that it looked like Marliese would not be coming back, what would she do?

Rosa gently put Princess on the floor before she stood up and suddenly decided to ask Eileen Hargan if she would take care of Princess if she should die. She patted her bun, put on deep-red lipstick, and picked up her black pocketbook. "You stay home and mind the house. Mama gonna pick up you pills." Rosa double-locked the door. Her chest hurt from the fear. And she looked up at the high, dark ceiling in the hallway and silently reminded God that He had to let Princess die first.

Chapter 52

The plastic crackled as Clifford pressed the ridges of the zipper down to close the bag. He liked the popping sound it made. He pulled the two halves apart, took the peaches out, smoothed it flat on the table, and locked the tracks together again.

"I'll be right there, honey. Got all your stuff?" Jessica asked from the bedroom.

"Yes, Mom." He put the fruit back, zipped the bag for the last time, and stuck it in his backpack. "Have a nice day." Clifford squeezed Kola good-bye, lingering over the hug. "You be good and 'fore you know it, I'll be home." His voice was a husky whisper. He raised it to call "Ready."

"Coming, sweetie." Jessica hurried to the front door, held the green canvas bag behind Clifford so he could put his arms in the straps, patted Kola reassuringly, and said, "You be careful now. Be back soon." As the elevator stopped in the lobby, she asked Clifford, "Got everything?"

"Why'd you say that? 'Be careful.'"

"I don't know. Just an expression."

"Not for a dog. You don't tell a dog, be careful. What's she got to be careful about anyway?"

"I said it was just something I said. It didn't mean anything." The guilt crept into Jessica's answer. "Today's the pool day, huh?"

"Yes, but it's silly to say that to an animal. As if she has to look both ways before crossing. Or not talk to strangers. Or sumpthing!"

"All right. I didn't mean it. You want me to go home and say I'm sorry to Kola?" She nudged his arm apologetically as they crossed 68th Street.

As soon as she dropped Clifford off, waiting on the sidewalk to make sure he went inside the Center, Jessica headed toward the bus stop on Lexington. Her fingers played inside her pocket, nervously polishing her keys. Lenny could not make a decision like this for her or without her. It affected her life more than it affected his anyway. What right did he have to say it was his money because he worked for it? She worked just as hard providing a home and being a wife and mother. Maybe harder. And him sitting all day, adding up columns, calculating numbers, reading ledgers. Where were his priorities? If they didn't pay up, and they actually took Kola—kidnapped her as they threatened— Clifford might regress to his other self. And where would that leave her? Back to being a slave. She couldn't risk it. Even if it meant not going to graduate school, she had to use the money. Clifford's health should be their first priority.

And where did he get off saying she wasn't *allowed* to write out a check on their money market account, that she could only use the checking account?! It was a helluva lot of money. But you couldn't put a value on Kola. Or on what she had done for their lost little boy, unlocking his mind, freeing him, when all the treatments and therapies and all the doctors hadn't been able to. Fifteen thousand dollars was cheap when you looked at it like that.

As soon as Merrill Lynch cashed the check for her, she'd put the money in a pillow case like they said and toss it in dryer number four in the Laundromat on 83rd Street, between First and York. Jesus, suppose somebody had a week's load of wash in there? What if the money fell out of the pillow case? Jessica had visions of an audience standing in front of the machine, staring in its porthole, hypnotically watching the bills spin dry. Maybe she should staple it closed. Which pillow case should she use? Any one she chose would ruin a set of linens. Maybe

Clifford's Batman one, instead of breaking up her king-size pair. No, he'd be upset. God, here she was giving away a chunk of their savings and worrying about losing a twenty-dollar pillow case.

Chapter 53

Laurie swore she'd never do social media. She had opened a Facebook account a few years ago but never posted anything on it, never searched for a "friend," and never responded to anyone looking for her. Not that too many people were trying to find her. Now, however, to take a break from the depressing statistics she was reading and inputting, she went to Facebook—and then had to look for the password she had used so long ago to open the account.

Who cared what someone had for breakfast, for God's sake, or what movie they went to or how they liked a restaurant? Why would anyone be interested? It was like reading someone's boring diary. She didn't understand what the appeal was, how some people felt compelled to write every single day about what was going on in their lives, which was nothing, and search other people's pages to see what they were doing and eating and feeling. Such a waste. She had no idea how to tweet or blog or do any of those other things. And she didn't want to know.

She wanted to scream at them all, "There are poor animals out there being killed and tortured, and you're writing about the jeans you bought!"

Chapter 54

Eileen rehearsed her excuse over and over before calling Judy Boylan. In the eleven years since they had retired and their bimonthly Thursday afternoon get-together had become a ritual, Eileen had never canceled. She knew it would have to be something terrible—worse than just not feeling well—to be believable. But under the circumstances, she couldn't face gabbing and gossiping.

She dialed the number but hung up before it started to ring. She paced in front of the phone, went to the bathroom, dialed again, and hung up a second time. Fibber watched her and then asked to go out. "Now, now, you don't have to go. You just want my undivided attention," she reprimanded him absentmindedly. "Later." Unaccustomed to Eileen's preoccupation, he slunk into the bedroom.

She drank a glass of water, called again, and finally waited for Judy to pick up.

"It's Fibber; he's sick," Eileen said breathlessly, crossing her fingers behind her back and praying that just this one time, a lie would not come true. "I have to take him to the doctor."

"I could wait for you to come back," Judy offered

"No, no, he can't squeeze me in 'til after lunch, and I don't know how long I'll be. And I'm so upset, I wouldn't want to make any plans, in case it's something bad. No, I wouldn't be very good company."

"Why, Eileen Hargan, what makes you think you're good company anyway?" A hearty laugh followed the question. "It's fine; we'll do it next week. Call me when you get back to let me know how he is."

Eileen thought she probably wouldn't be up to it next week either. What could she say then? Now she'd have a whole week to worry about that! Thank God, in another few weeks, Judy would be going off for the summer, as she did almost from the day she had started teaching. She'd rent a villa for July and August—in Spain or Italy or Greece— where she said you could live like a millionaire. Then Eileen wouldn't have to think about her or their date, at least until after Labor Day.

She went to reassure Fibber McGee, who was curled up on her bed, licking himself. Eileen gasped when she caught him. "Naughty, naughty!" She shook her finger at him, trying not to look at the tip of the slimy red thing poking out of its furry sheath. "Shame on you, Mr. McGee. You're much too old for that."

Chapter 55

The corner of 181st Street and St. Nicholas Avenue was crowded with makeshift counters selling books for a dollar, velvet-covered trays displaying gaudy jewelry, and pillars of crates and cartons, the open ones on top spilling summer fruit. On an impulse, Yolanda stopped to examine the small cones of flowers poking out of pails of water on the sidewalk. She tugged at the wrapping paper of a bouquet of daisies to compare the freshness with another bunch. The vendor yelled at her, "Don't you touch. You show me what you like, I give."

"All right, all right, don't get excited." She pointed to another bunch. "That one, with the pink carnations in it. How much?"

"Same's all of them. Five dollars, lady. Why you don't take two together?"

"No. One's fine. Thank you."

"You take two, I give you both for eight dollars."

"No, really." She watched him wrap the wet stems in another piece of paper and take out a huge wad of bills to give her change of a ten. She grabbed the singles and ran as she saw the M3 bus coming. It would probably take her an extra half hour to get down to 84th Street, transfer to the 86th Street crosstown, and then get back to the hospital, but she had a two-hour break before her second shift.

She went to the back of the bus and sat at the edge of the seat, awkwardly holding the flowers away from her. The paper was already soggy. She'd just put them in front of the door. Ms. Sidway wouldn't be home at this hour anyway. She wished she had some paper in her bag so she could leave a note, but this would be a nice surprise. Then she'd call tonight to tell her she had left them. To say thank you.

Yolanda Santiago was a strong, determined woman. But without Louise Sidway, she didn't think she'd have been able to get through the past year—her husband leaving. For good. She wouldn't have cared so much if she weren't so afraid for the kids. She could handle Elena. At least for now. She was a good girl but was depressed about her father. And the little ones would be okay. They were too young to understand. But it was Ricky who worried her. He had been hard enough to control when Ricardo lived with them. With Ricardo gone, she was sure her son would run off with one of the gangs, get into big trouble, and quit school.

Then Louise came into their lives. And funny how things worked out, because Yolanda wasn't even going to apply for assistance. If she hadn't, the two women never would have met. The way Louise just stepped in and sort of took over, talking to Ricky like she was, as she called it, his "Dutch aunt" gave him an incentive to stay in school. And this part-time job she got for him was great. Of course, the job had been after school and only a few hours a week. Plus Saturdays.

But now, during the summer, nobody was more surprised than Yolanda when Ricky got up by himself every morning, as soon as the alarm went off, and never complained about not being able to hang out with his friends. In fact, he seemed to like working. He seemed to take his responsibilities very seriously. She only prayed her little Ricky would make it through his last year of high school and graduate next June. God, she was proud of him. And when he used his own money to buy Elena that skirt, Yolanda almost burst with pride. And gratitude.

She was making a decent living. Of course, arranging food on trays and delivering them to patients wasn't the most exciting job in the world, but Mount Sinai was such a big hospital, she could always apply for something else, once she proved how good she was. At least that's what Louise had said. And being able to work extra shifts like today, doing dinner too, gave her a chance to make extra money. Señora Sanchez, who watched the children for her, was so glad to have an adopted family to take care of, so glad to be around children again since hers were still in Colombia, that it didn't matter how long Yolanda was gone.

In fact, one of these days, Yolanda decided, she might even suggest that the señora move in with them. It would be cheaper for her and certainly cheaper for Yolanda. She probably never would, though. If Louise got the señora approved as an authorized day-care provider, then the state would start paying her. But all in all, things were working out. There was finally a light at the end of the tunnel. God was watching out for Yolanda. And so was a tough-looking, loud-talking redhead.

Chapter 56

Ken Hollis was just the right size for the wing chair. He was a little taller than Louise's father, so his shoulders reached higher into the back. Even though Louise had had it recovered in a more modern fabric, she could still see its fancy brocade upholstery as it was in the living room in Maryland. Facing the fireplace, its textured back toward the archway entrance, her father's body was invisible from behind, and the room looked empty. Only a corkscrew of pipe smoke hovering above the chair gave him away.

Every time she walked into the apartment, the chair pulled her eyes toward it. The gray dotted with small wine-colored circles fit into the rest of the room, with her parents' massive breakfront and her burgundy convertible sofa. It fit, but it seemed out of place, out of time. Maybe because her father was no longer there. But now, with Ken Hollis sitting in it, sipping a Jack Daniel's, it once again looked comfortable. Part of a life, of a family.

She could see Ken from the tiny kitchen, where she was opening the cabinets, looking for the peanuts and her mother's little sterling silver bowl to put them in. She had been prepared to invite him up the other night after dinner. She had dusted and left the cocktail napkins and the glasses out. Scrubbed the bathroom sink. But it ended up being so late, because they had sat and talked for ages over their coffee, that she hadn't asked him. And he never suggested it. It hadn't even bothered her. He walked her to her apartment, waited until she unlocked the inside door, and then gave her a little salute before going to the garage to pick up his car for what she knew was going to be a long drive home.

It didn't bother her because she knew he'd be back. Not this soon, maybe, but she just knew that she would see him again. That she was as comfortable with him as…well, as he was in the wing chair. No hassle, no funny business, no rehearsing what she'd say to get rid of him.

Now, though, when she hadn't expected to hear from him so quickly, when her hair was really frizzed up from the humidity, her makeup melted off, and her shirt stained from lunch, he calls her at work to ask if she wants to go for a hamburger!

As Honda watched her put a coaster on the end table, his brows wrinkled, pleating the silver arrow in his forehead. His body was spread flat in front of the chair, his head resting on the ottoman between the thick rubber-maze soles of Ken Hollis's Avias. Louise wanted to be pleased that Honda liked him. She was pleased, but resentment momentarily narrowed her lips. As soon as she sat down on the couch, holding her Chablis, Honda sighed audibly, turned onto his side, facing her, and closed his eyes.

She took a long, slow swallow, looking at Ken through the distortion of her glass. He seemed to feel at home. So did she. It didn't matter that she was home; it didn't often feel like it to her. Louise leaned back against the cushions and closed her eyes, letting the wine pave her esophagus with a sweet syrup and coat her insides with tenderness. Of course Honda was pleased. He missed her parents also; he missed having a man around. Louise was pleased too. If only Ken wasn't so skinny.

"Thank God." Ken leaned forward to look at the dog. "What?"

"I was getting stiff from not moving my legs. I was afraid to kick him."

"I don't think it would have mattered. He seems to adore you."

"Jealous?"

"Damned right I am. I get up at the crack of dawn to take him out. I rush home to feed him. I can't go away for a weekend. I buy him the most expensive food, give him treats, and even cook for myself once in a while just so he can have leftovers. And how does he show his appreciation? By worshipping a total stranger!"

"You sound just like a Jewish mother. In fact, you sound just like my Jewish mother."

"Does that mean I won't have to convert for you?"

"Yeah. Anyone who can lay the guilt on a dog will make a big hit with my family."

Louise laughed spontaneously. Without making any effort to tone down the volume of her usual guffaw, or to tell a funnier joke, or to soften the loud chortle that would suddenly seem to be the only sound in a room, without even trying, she knew her laugh was a dainty, ladylike trill. Because her heart was giggling.

Chapter 57

Eileen's blue eyes took inventory of 83rd Street as they scanned both sides of the street, east to west and back again. Her head nodded unconsciously in time with her right foot tapping impatiently on the stoop. Fibber McGee whined. Eileen Hargan held on to the concrete banister and let him pull her down the steps. He led her to the next brownstone and circled the scrawny tree in front of it. Now that she couldn't leave him home alone and had to take him with her wherever she went, he was outside more than ever. She wondered how he could possibly have anything left to make. He looked at her for approval as he lifted his leg over the miniature fence and dribbled a few drops. "Good boy, Mr. McGee. That's my little man. Aren't you good?"

Eileen stood on the sidewalk, squinting into the sun. Waiting. She waved to Wally, who was sweeping the sidewalk a few doors up the block. She timed a black delivery boy going into the house across the street with groceries, making mental notes in case she was asked in court exactly how long he was inside—that was assuming they found the hacked-up body and caught him! When he came out not even two minutes later, whistling as he mounted his bike, Eileen shook her head vigorously from side to side to clear her ridiculous thoughts. Too much television. Too much imagination. Too much fear. But after what had happened to her—what almost happened to her—she had every right to suspect everyone. Of everything.

Ah, the postman's cap was outlined in the white haze, his Bermuda shorts exaggerating the geometric angles of his bare legs. The silhouette of his three-legged cart looked like a strange creature from another planet. Eileen walked toward the corner to meet him, silently rehearsing her complaint.

"Morning, miss," the postman called to her as he took his bundle up the steps of number 429 and disappeared inside. Eileen waited at the curb, with Fibber sniffing the ivy surrounding the tree trunks and leaving a few drops at each stop.

"You come later and later each day," Eileen said as he walked out, beginning to talk before the door closed behind him and he started down the steps. "Why, when I first moved here, the postman came at 10:00 every morning. Sharp. And then again at 3:00 in the afternoon."

"Two deliveries a day?" the postman responded in surprise. "How long ago was that?"

"It doesn't matter. The service has been deteriorating for years, while the postage keeps going up. Now here it is, the seventeenth of the month, and my phone bill hasn't come. Or Con Edison. They're always here by the fifteenth. That's when I pay them. That day." She walked along next to him as he pushed the cart. He stopped and went into the next building, and when he came out, she continued the conversation as if he had never left. "I don't like to be late, not even one day. I always pay everything on time. If they shut my phone off, it will be your fault."

"Now, you know they're not going to shut your phone off if you're one day late paying. Or a week late. You know what? They wouldn't even shut it off if you didn't pay at all. Not after all this time." Joe Briney smiled good-naturedly, took the thick rubber band off a bunch of envelopes, and went into the next building.

If it wasn't Eileen, it would have been one of the other old ladies. He supposed they had nothing better to do than wait for each bill to come. When it didn't, they yelled at the mailman. They were all like that. It must be a symptom of age, he thought, like arthritis. He'd have to warn his wife to look out. First time his bones creaked out loud in the morning or he asked why the Verizon bill hadn't come on the appointed day—whichever came first, bones or bills—she'd better put him away.

"That's not the point," Eileen said, as if there had been no interruption. "I just don't want to be late. I like to pay everything when I'm supposed to. Keep my records straight."

"I know. I bet the phone company—and the gas company—wish all their customers were like you, Ms. Hargan. Beautiful out, isn't it?"

"Yes, but it's too hot." Eileen looked up at the sky. "We need some rain."

"Here we are." He took out his stack for her apartment building, and she followed him inside.

"So, you taking the missus to California again this year?" Eileen asked.

"Naw." He fanned out the envelopes and started placing them in the boxes. "Too hectic. I just might stay home and do some stuff around the house—painting, things like that."

"Well, when you do, you'd better tell the other guy—the relief, the temporary helper—to be careful. Or I'm going to go down to 34th Street if I don't get my mail on time." Her wagging finger threatened him. "Or write to Washington!"

"Tell you what: I'll put up a note on the bulletin board to be extra careful about 83rd Street. But don't worry; I'm not going 'til the fall, probably." He passed her an envelope.

For a minute, Eileen's stomach turned queasy. But *they* didn't actually mail anything; they delivered their messages in envelopes for her. No, with the service being what it was, how could anybody rely on the post office if they wanted to send a ransom note or one of those letter bombs she sometimes read about in the papers? "Hmmmph, it's just an ad."

"Well, let's see, we've got some more to get through." It was a good thing Joe Briney was easygoing by nature. Because next, they'd get mad at him for what people sent to them. But this one, she was one of the few who at least gave him a Christmas gift. Talk about inflation! She complained about stamps going up, but she was still giving him the same three dollars—crisp new ones in a money envelope—that she gave him nine years ago when he started this route. *Poor little old lady, he thought. Poor? Hah, probably has a million bucks stashed away or close to it.* He noticed the brokerage statements she got every month. What good did it do her, though, if she had nobody to spend it on…except her raggedy old dog?

Chapter 58

The temperature had hit 88 degrees by 11:00 a.m., and with the heat index at 97, the air was thick. It clung to bodies with a heaviness that weighed people down and sucked their energy. Breathing was exhausting. Like you were inside a cloud. The concrete sidewalks turned sticky and stuck to shoes. The steel and concrete and glass of tall buildings absorbed the sun's rays and intensified their power. The humidity was oppressive.

Lenny Marcus's tie hung out of his seersucker jacket like a mottled tongue. Coming out of the restaurant after lunch into the dense heat had momentarily shocked him. He walked up Madison Avenue quickly, anxious to get back to the office. His body felt as rumpled as his suit. Even the soles of his feet were burning. Maybe he'd stay late and clean up some of the stuff on his desk. At least it would be cool. And there'd be no arguing. He could time it to get home just when dinner was put on the table. And he double-checked his iPhone calendar—this was a Center day for Clifford, so they'd eat about seven, and Jessica would be busy asking about his swimming lessons and crafts. Nuts! He tried to snap his fingers, but they were too wet. The water tower in the building was turned off at 6:00, so there wouldn't be any air conditioning after that. No matter what, he wouldn't go home. Maybe he'd stop somewhere and have a drink.

Rosa rolled the tissue up and down the trough between her breasts where the perspiration had accumulated. She spread her legs and tented her skirt to catch the hot breeze from the floor fan. It was probably cooler outside than in her stuffy apartment. But for the one or two really uncomfortable nights they had had so far, it didn't pay to buy an air conditioner. If she did, she wouldn't even know where to put it—in the bedroom or the living room. And who would put it in for her? She could ask Wally, but she'd have to give him something, at least twenty dollars. She'd manage. What did people do before they had air conditioning? They survived. They went to work, they went about their business, and they never knew any different. But they got spoiled; they expected air conditioning everywhere now. "Right, bambina?" she asked.

Princess struggled to stand, her mouth open, her little body panting hard. She shuffled toward Rosa, strenuously pulling her back paws after her. Poor thing. She should have at least gotten one for her baby. Princess could barely breathe as it was, but the temperature made it such a great effort. Rosa was afraid her heart would just give out. Relieved to have made it halfway across the room, Princess's four legs folded under her, and she collapsed on her side in front of the fan. With a grunt that was part wheeze, part sigh, she closed her eyes. She was so still that Rosa leaned forward and stared at her chest until the faint ripples confirmed that Princess was still alive.

Laurie inserted her flash drive with one hand and removed the plastic lid from her cup of iced tea with the other. She broke a packet of sugar over the tea, replaced the lid, and punctured the slit for her straw. Then she leaned back in her Posturepedic secretarial chair and took a long pull on the cold drink. She carefully set it down on a napkin, as far from the keyboard as she could, and logged in to her computer. When she was prompted for her password, she entered FELIX11. Anybody who knew her well and wanted to break into her files would try her cat's name first. Same with her bank card. But that password had the seven easiest characters for her to remember.

She accessed a Word document from her directory—as long as she was doing it on her lunch hour, it didn't matter. Someday maybe Dr. Pomalee could use her information for the book he was always saying he was going to write. It might even be the inspiration he needed to get started. He'd probably be excited too, when he saw the data she had collected. But she'd save it until it was all finished—if it ever was.

She spelled out ODDCOUPLE to retrieve her protected file and slid her notes and pamphlets closer to her. Adding to the information already in the document, she typed: "Three-and-a-half to four million dogs and cats destroyed every year in US, one animal every three seconds, twenty-four hours a day, 365 days a year. Approximately ten thousand a day." Give or take.

Jason almost caught her in the act. Since he had to go to the meeting right from the store tonight, he went home after the lunch rush to walk Sabrina. As he came into the lobby, the elevator door whooshed on its spring, the arrow above it lit up green, and Nettie Pedersen's face flashed in the round window before the car left its mooring. Jason stuck his tongue out, pushed the button, and then went into the small cubicle to get his mail. There it was, next to the notice about the exterminator coming on the second Tuesday of every month, crudely lettered with a black felt-tip pen:

ROACHES SPREAD DIRT

RATS SPREAD PLAGUE

GAYS SPREAD AIDS

LET'S GET RID OF ALL THE VERMIN IN OUR BUILDING

He ripped the paper down, leaving its corners still Scotch-taped to the wall, crumbled it up, and stuffed it in his pocket. Then he went back to the elevator and rattled the knob as hard as he could, the door banging against its lock. The whirring motor got louder as the car got closer. He pulled the knob again and shouted up the crack, "You stupid bitch."

Chapter 59

Clifford tripped on a rock. As he went down, he flattened his hand to brace his fall, letting the leash slip out of his fingers. "Ma! Ma! Kola!" he screamed at the top of his lungs, not even feeling the rawness where the skin was scraped from his knees and the dirt rubbed into it. His panic was far greater than his injury. His shrieks pierced Jessica's ribs and made her heart jump. She dropped her book on the bench and ran toward her child. As she got closer and saw the streak of fur become a golden-white blur behind some trees, her instinct made her go after the dog rather than her son. She ran in the direction she thought Kola had gone but couldn't catch sight of her. Clifford's cries turned to a wail. Jessica started to cry herself. "God, no, not after all this. She can't run away. Oh, God, don't let her get lost."

It was useless, so she turned around and headed back toward Clifford. He was sitting in the same spot, his arms folded over his head, hiding his face. Two women were trying to console him, not knowing how deep his anguish was. "Clifford, darling." Jessica reached for him. His arms tightened around himself, and Jessica felt such hopelessness, such despair, that she wanted to crawl into the darkness with him. He couldn't—he *couldn't*—go back. Oh, God, don't let him. And the money was all for nothing then. Kola lost and the money too. A wave of thankfulness washed over her as Clifford stood up and came close enough to her for Jessica to wrap her arms around him.

Kola's tail stiffened in the wind she created with her speed. Her legs stretched long, her ears pulled back, her nostrils spread, her head reaching for the currents. She yelped with joy. As she sped past concrete paths and wire garbage pails and metal vending carts and the wheels of baby carriages, toward the open field, she saw the countryside that reminded her of where she'd come from, and she ran faster to get to it.

She emerged from an opening and darted across the moat of traffic that formed an island for the Grand Army Plaza. Then she ran toward the tumult of Fifth Avenue. She stopped abruptly and looked all around. The noise confused her…of horses whinnying in front of their buggies, of the cars and busses, of people stampeding across the street as the light turned. Where was her boy? Why wasn't he on the other side of the leash? He should have been attached to one end of her leather umbilical cord. She was used to the city. But it took a second of utter fear for the transition from her happy fantasy to the lonely world surrounding her.

She turned in tight circles, fast, trying to get her bearings. Then she backed up as far as she could, ignoring the screech of tires and horns as cabs tried to avoid her. She took a running leap onto a metal bench and vaulted over the wall. Back into Central Park. Because Kola knew, without knowing, that the last thing she wanted was freedom.

Chapter 60

The kiss didn't come as a surprise. But her reaction to it did. He'd called yesterday to say he'd be in her neighborhood and would like to take her to dinner. On her way to pick up a salad during her lunch hour, Louise saw a sign and on the spur of the moment, she ducked in the doorway. Following the red arrows up the wall, she climbed a steep flight of stairs. Before she had a chance to catch her breath, a buzzer released the lock, and she walked into the manicure place. Waiting for her turn, listening to the sing-song jabber of Vietnamese, Louise felt guilty. She always swore she would never do this. Or sit under a dryer, or have her eyebrows pulled out. Or her pores squeezed. Well, she'd been meaning to cut her cuticles for weeks anyway, and she was only going to have clear polish put on.

All afternoon, she found herself stretching her arms straight out, spreading her fingers, and admiring her nails. She noticed that she was holding her hands differently, carefully, so she wouldn't chip the polish. Now that her hands looked more dainty, she regarded them with more respect. *Like they say about women*, she thought. Act like a lady, and they'll treat you like a lady.

She wore the same dress she had worn to the cocktail party where she'd met him. She had no choice, because she had no other dress. When he came to pick her up, he greeted Honda warmly, and her big, strong, protective dog slobbered all over him. Ken declined a glass of wine because it was getting late and he'd made a reservation. She liked that. He didn't ask her what she wanted to eat or where. He just confirmed that Sparks would be all right with her. All right? It was perfect. Somehow, she knew he would order her own favorite—a New York strip, medium, with a baked potato. She was relieved Ken suggested a steakhouse rather than a restaurant with unpronounceable French entrées with sauces disguising the meat. Or some healthy piece of fish that swallowed easily, leaving no trace of flavor in her mouth. Louise liked to chew hard.

Back in her apartment now, she waited for her mother's old Pyrex coffeepot to start perking so she could lower the flame. Then she took a long T-shirt into the bathroom with her and changed. Her outfit was all wrinkled and damp from clinging to her skin. So was her bra, so she left it off. She put her dress on a hanger and stuck it on the shower head behind the curtain. She could tell from the muffled lilt of his voice through the door that Ken was asking Honda questions. The response showed Honda was only too happy to answer.

As she came out of the bathroom, Ken pretended not to notice her return and said to the dog, "So whaddya think, boy? You think she likes me?" Honda's thumping tail said he did. "You think she had as good a time as I did?" Honda did. Ken was sitting on the ottoman, holding the dog's large head between his hands, alternately massaging his face and rubbing his ears.

"I've heard of 'love me, love my dog,' but aren't we carrying things a little too far here? Huh, guys?" Louise turned the coffee off. She took out two mismatched mugs, one in the shape of a basset hound whose large ear was the handle, and a white one with the message, "Same Old Shit. Different Day."

Ken followed her. "Need any help?"

"No, thanks." Louise stared at the glass percolator. "My mother's secret to good coffee: let it stand for five minutes before you pour." She turned to face him, and that's when he kissed her. It seemed like the natural thing to happen, there in the tiny kitchen, with enough room for two people only if they stood sideways, with the homey smell of fresh coffee…and the afterglow of a bottle of red wine.

The surprise was not their mouths touching softly, separating while they looked into each other's eyes. It was their slowly coming together after what each had seen of the other's soul, then grabbing one another like magnets. Fluid rushed to Louise's mouth. His tongue softly glided over her gums, above her teeth, behind her teeth, coating the insides of her cheeks, probing her palate, spreading the syrup of their saliva, his and hers mixed together. Lips engulfed lips, sucked the other's, pulled apart but, like putty, stayed attached.

Louise's hips were pressed against the stove, her back rigid, avoiding the hot pot. Her breasts pushed against her shirt, enjoying the gentle friction of the cotton ribbing. She thrust her chest towards his, but he pulled away so they couldn't touch. Her nipples tingled. They reminded her of teeth. You never feel them until you have an awful toothache. She never thought about her nipples; they were just there. Until now, when her whole being seemed rolled up into two tight little brown nubs aching to be touched.

Ken pulled back to look at her. He licked the kiss off his lips and opened his tie. He stared at her breasts, acknowledging that he saw her desire. It made her quiver. She took his hand and led him to the bedroom. Before she had a chance to close the door, Honda darted in, looked at them, and slunk under her bed. It was as if he could smell the sex. The fluid that flowed from her mouth to her groin, liquefying bone and tissue and muscle on its way. The craving that oozed out of her pores. She pulled her shirt over her head, took off her panties, wet from her want, and lay down in the dark. Ken undressed and got into bed beside her. She hoped the weight of the mattress wouldn't crush Honda.

When he touched her, finally, she wanted to scream. Wanted him to jab inside her, hard. She couldn't wait. But he refused to hurry. He wanted to savor the intensity of her excitement. The pain of her longing for him. The tip of his tongue brushed the tips of her breasts. The air hardened the moistness left on her skin, and her nipples swelled more. Her senses were swimming. She spread her legs, and they were sticky from the sap between them. She pulled Ken's shoulders toward her until his body was poised over hers. When their eyes locked, she knew that he took no delight in the anguish of her need, only pleasure in trying to fill it. Her whole body melted from his look.

Just before he thrust himself into her, she felt a moment's betrayal. Because she could hear Honda whimper.

Chapter 61

"I don't want to talk about it anymore. It's final."

"We have to talk about it. At some point, you just might have no choice. All right, you still have one now, but I mean if you weren't able…if you weren't capable of making the decision."

"But that's not the case here. I don't have to cope with that now. And I don't have to talk about it if I don't want to." Eileen's blue eyes, usually bright and clear, darkened. Once again, it was like she was facing junior high school kids committing some prank or catching them giggling behind her back as she wrote on the blackboard. She looked at Danny as she would have the students—stern, uncompromising, and totally in command of her home and her life, as she had been of her classroom.

"Maybe he'd even like it better there," Danny argued. "He'd have more room. And you could take him for long walks where there's grass. God, the poor deprived thing has probably never seen grass."

"Don't you worry about him." Eileen bent down and used both hands to lift Fibber McGee into her lap. "He's perfectly happy. Aren't you, sweetheart?" She squeezed him protectively. She watched Charlene walk around the living room, pretending to stay out of it. Charlene picked up the ceramic Boston Terrier on the top of the knickknack shelves, turned it over, and then replaced it. Eileen wondered what she expected to see—a Lenox china stamp? A Woolworth's price tag? "Besides, it would be perfectly traumatic for him to make a change now."

"Him or you?"

"Both of us."

"Dogs adjust a lot better than you think. He'd get used to it, especially since he'd still be with you."

"You have to promise me one thing," Eileen said as her eyes followed his wife around the room, watching Charlene wrinkle her nose at the oversized papier-mâché pencil laying on the cocktail table. It was very crude to begin with, but the yellow of the hexagonal edges had somehow turned reddish with time. White drippings of Elmer's glue, where she had stuck the broken tip of the lead point back on years ago, covered the top. Still it was one of her favorite things. From a long-ago fifth grader with beautiful blonde braids. "Promise that if… if something ever happens to me, you'll have him put to sleep. I don't want to think about him crying for me."

Charlene and Danny looked at one another and exchanged some message with their eyes. God, Eileen used to hate it when her students would pass a note back and forth and, just as she'd reach for it, rip it to shreds so she couldn't read it. She was always sure they were making fun of her. Just as she could tell these two, although they weren't being malicious, were sharing a secret about her.

"Come on, Aunt Eileen, you know we've been over that. I already promised you. I have no reason to go back on my word. But the point is, if you would come home with us, the chances of something happening to you would be a lot less. At least you'd be safe. Away from these animals in the city, trying to take advantage of an old lady."

Safe, she thought. *What good is safe if I have to stay in that little bedroom upstairs that used to be the baby's room? What would I do with all my furniture? My things? My papers?* She was humiliated that Charlene was here, listening. Eileen wished they hadn't found a spot to park on the street and that Charlene had had to sit in the car, double-parked or in front of a hydrant. It wasn't the same with her here. If Danny had come alone, he'd go home and repeat every single word to Charlene, but Eileen didn't mind that. This was different; it made her squirm. "I know you're only trying to help," she said, "but I just can't."

Charlene walked over to her chair. Looking down at Eileen, she spoke to her husband. Like her mouth was at the back of her head. "Now, honey, we can see Aunt Eileen has made up her mind. She wants to stay here. No matter what's wrong with it, it is home for her." She patted the hand resting on Fibber's back. Then she even patted Fibber.

The dog swiveled his eyes to Charlene without moving his head. Eileen felt the soft vibration of the grumble starting in his chest. That's all she'd need…for Mr. McGee to start growling at Charlene. Then, if she ever absolutely had to move in with them, they wouldn't let him come with her. Or if they did, they'd be cruel to him. She quickly put him on the floor and stood up. "Okay, I'll do this: I'll think about it."

Danny and Charlene knew she wouldn't. They also knew they were dismissed. Class was over. They both kissed her, on opposite cheeks, and left. Frustrated but relieved.

Chapter 62

Ken had trouble with his lecture. His words were about the effects of increasing longevity in urban families, but his thoughts were on Louise. Images of their lovemaking wandered in and out of his mind. He spoke about living longer, but saw her naked body beneath him. He talked about elderly parents filling empty nests, while feeling himself inside her again. He casually walked toward his desk and sat behind it, hoping no one was aware of the desire that was beginning to bulge between his legs.

He rushed through his closing remarks, gave a reading assignment, and dawdled over packing up his papers, until the last summer-school student had gone. He stood up and pulled his trousers away from his body, where his shorts were digging into the swelling. He was relieved to get back to the privacy of his small office. He could not get Louise and what had happened between them out of his mind. Nor did he want to. The telephone interrupted his pleasure.

"Hallo, Mr. Hollis?"

"Yes, who's this?"

"Rosa. Rosa Bassetti. You remember? From Ms. Hargan's apartment. The other day."

"Yes. Hello."

"You know, the lady with the ransom note for her dog, who was so upset, and you come and—"

"I remember, I remember. How could I forget you, Miss Bassetti? What can I do for you?"

"Not for me. For her. Eileen Hargan. I wanna know what you done so far to catch these people. Animals!"

"We're working on it."

"Working how?"

"Well, I've been talking to the local precinct. In fact, we're trying to organize a senior citizens meeting to give advice on some of the swindles going on, to teach you how to protect yourselves."

"Swindle? This isn't a swindle! Like getting one of those poor old ladies to give away her money. Or donate it. Or take out magazine prescriptions. This is a real crime, no? And Ms. Hargan—what if she have a heart attack over it? Then it would be murder. No, a meeting is not enough. No way. We have to get together and do something real—act. You know, Ken—okay I call you Ken?—it's one thing to frighten somebody. A terrible thing, no question. But to threaten a person's animal, a pet that, you know, to lots of us is our child, our little baby, well, that's something different. We gotta stop them before they do it again. Or really do it to someone. You wanna talk? I got some ideas. I help you."

"Well, sure, Miss Bassetti." Ken smiled into the mouthpiece. "We can use all the help we can get."

"Good. I be your private 'I.' I for Italian. Get it?"

Chapter 63

Chris Barrett got home first. He knew once he changed and cooled off, he wouldn't feel like going out again, so he put his things down, turned on the air conditioner, and took Sabrina right out. When he came back, he stuffed his shirt into the duffel bag that was getting full from dirty laundry. Jason hadn't been doing the wash regularly. Jason hadn't been doing anything regularly lately, except getting on Chris's nerves with his newfound causes. Although, Chris had to admit, Jason's commitment added a new dimension to his personality, an enthusiasm and excitement, even an innocence. He realized, deep down, that it was frustration, maybe mixed with a little jealousy at Jason's dedication to something other than Chris that was getting to him. It made Jason very irritating. And at the same time, very appealing.

Chris changed into a pair of shorts and a fishnet shirt and walked into the living room. The apartment had cooled off. He raised the temperature control and went over to his den niche. He unpacked the briefcase he had left by the desk, put the galleys on the chair—tonight's homework—and looked at the mail. He slid the insurance and cable TV bills under the rubber band binding the pile of household bills in the top drawer. They were going to clean up all their paperwork, together, over the long weekend coming up. And paint the kitchen. Chris was looking forward to the four days of working together, enjoying the satisfaction from their physical labor. He was sure Jason was too, especially since he planned to close the store on Saturday. Aside from the theater tickets they had for a Sunday matinee, they were just going to relax and play it by ear. Maybe go downtown to watch the fireworks. Maybe go to the Cloisters. A real mini-vacation in Manhattan.

He threw away the junk mail, lit up a cigarette, and then made two stacks of envelopes—one for Jason and one for himself. Still dreaming of their holiday, with the cigarette hanging from his dry lips, he didn't pay any attention to the crudely printed envelope, misspelled to "J. Roderman."

Chapter 64

Rosa took Princess down to the river. Even though it was much too hot for such a long walk, she needed to go there. Both of them were slowed by arthritic legs and tired hearts. The sun was strong; it seemed to suck the color out of everything. There weren't too many people on 84th between First and East End, the street she chose for her route. She always tried to walk down a different block so she could say hello to old friends in the neighborhood and enjoy a little change of scenery. She already planned to come home across 86th Street and hopefully catch palsied, cranky Mr. Untermeyer sitting on his stoop.

Princess's nostrils started contracting to catch the river smell. *"Dolce, dolce, eh?"* Rosa also wrinkled her nose, and they both perked up once they had sight of the trees, rippled in the haze, and the outline of Gracie Mansion peeking through them. A slight breeze from the water fluttered her hair, and Rosa lifted her head so it could touch her neck. Princess could not know what was special about their tree or that its twisted roots had stretched over the years, like gnarled old fingers, to cover the little grave beneath it, but she galloped toward it. Even though Rosa realized it was only because Princess knew that's where they were headed, she felt it was an omen.

It was a long time since she had buried Princess II here, but Rosa still felt very close to her. It was comforting to sit sideways on the end of the bench beneath the awning of leaves, her toes engraving a cross in the loose dirt behind it. It was a good place to think.

She didn't know exactly where to start in thinking about trying to solve the mystery. It could be anyone. Young, old. Man, woman. She had no ideas. No clues. What should she look for? Who? That young girl across from her, eating a sandwich, with the foil wrapper lying like a napkin in her lap, glinting in the sunlight. Her? Maybe she was sending signals, like they did to ships. Maybe she was telling someone that Rosa could be the next victim. "Ah, the heat, it makes me crazy, bambina," she said aloud, while trying to memorize a description of the suspect—just in case. What she really needed was a camera. She slapped her thighs at the conclusion. "That's what we get, Princess, a camera. A little tiny one like they give for spies. Maybe to hide in a lighter. Your mama, she might have to start smoking."

Chapter 65

"We have to talk."

"What about?"

"Things."

"What things."

"Things going on between us."

"I didn't know there was anything going on between us."

"Maybe that's the problem. That there really isn't anything going on between us anymore."

"What's that supposed to mean?"

"Just what it sounds like." Jessica had promised herself she wouldn't cry, yet here she was, tears hovering over her eyeballs. She blinked; the bubbles broke and leaked out from under her lids. One perfect drop shimmered on her cheek before she wiped it away with the back of her hand. "This is not what I had in mind when I said 'talk.'"

"What *did* you have in mind?" Lenny asked.

"I thought we could sit down and have a real conversation. Talk about our feelings—our feelings about each other."

"I don't have any feelings about it, one way or the other, so I guess there's nothing for me to talk about."

"See, that's the problem. We're just going around in circles. Okay, you don't think there's anything to talk about; I do. So does that mean I'm not allowed to talk because you have nothing to say?"

Lenny looked at her for a moment and then went back into the tiny entrance they pretended was a foyer.

Jessica followed him, watching him methodically and deliberately smooth the sleeves of his seersucker jacket before hanging it in the closet. "That your answer? Huh?"

He went into the bathroom, leaving the door open, and splashed water on his face.

She waited in the doorway. "And you think we have nothing to talk about? A man who comes home and doesn't even have the courtesy to speak to his wife? A man who uses silence as a punishment? And you think I'm the one with a problem?" Jessica's face reddened with anger; she turned away before he could notice.

Kola slithered into the bedroom after her, sat in front of the bed, and put her head in Jessica's lap. Unconsciously, Jessica stroked her, squeezed the fur on the back of her neck, and rubbed her finger over the hard ridge of Kola's brow. Calmed, Jessica bent over until their noses touched. She looked deep into the eyes that were pleading with her to be happy.

"Poor girl, don't worry; nobody's going to abandon you. What would we do without you? We almost found out the day you ran away, didn't we? Thank God someone grabbed your leash. And thank God I had my cell phone number engraved on your collar. You really scared us, girl."

Jessica wrapped her arms around Kola. A long, pink tongue unfolded to lick the traces of salt from Jessica's face.

Chapter 66

Trying to hurry through Penn Station on a Friday night in summer was like trying to do the breast stroke in quicksand. Rush hour started at noon and lasted all night. The throngs milled around, waiting for the boards to post the track numbers. When a departure was announced, a mass of people moved in the direction of the gate, poking their overnight bags and totes and animal carriers and packages into one another and keeping very close so nobody could break into their midst. The mercury in the station always seemed to climb to ninety-nine, no matter what the temperature was outside. The density of the heat, the condensation from body perspiration, the heaviness of the air, and the thickness of the humidity vaporized and hung like balloons suspended from the ceiling.

More people arrived and departed at Penn Station on any given day than lived in Barbados and Iceland combined. More than the entire populations of Kansas City and Albuquerque and Seattle. More than the state of Wyoming.

Friday night is the worst, Ken Hollis thought as he tried to get through the Amtrak waiting room to the Long Island Rail Road, *but when it falls on the eve of July Fourth weekend—a four-day weekend for most people—forget it.* Ken had made the mistake of thinking the station would be cooler than the steaming sidewalks and had entered in the middle of the block, instead of Seventh Avenue. He loosened his tie as he squeezed through the people. He opened the top two buttons of his shirt, which was translucent with sweat. He refolded the suit jacket hanging limply over his arm. The 4:26 to Montauk cleared out hundreds of weekenders destined for the Hamptons, but the hole their departure left filled up instantly.

Penn Station had a thousand "movements" a day. Although the official terminology referred to trains, not bowels, it seemed to Ken that their rumblings on the loops and curls of track beneath the city could be likened to a huge monster's digestive tract, to swallowing and then eliminating the population. The LIRR alone scheduled 735 commuter trains a day, and all it took was one ten-minute delay or one cancellation to start a rash of bad jokes on the Internet and a series of protests in the newspaper.

Ken went into one of the crowded bar joints, hoping for a cold beer, but he couldn't get near enough to the bar to order one. He left and walked as close to the center of the waiting room as he could, so he'd have an equal chance of making it to a track on either side. He was anxious for tomorrow morning. He'd leave home early—there shouldn't be anybody going into the city—pick her up at nine. He'd probably run into heavy traffic going back out, but it just would have been too hectic to try it tonight. Especially with the dog. He knew she wouldn't want to leave him with anybody or board him and probably would have turned Ken down if he hadn't invited Honda. But the truth was, he was just as excited about showing Honda a good time and letting him run around as he was about having Louise there.

He wanted to make love to her again. Slowly this time. Caringly. In his bed. After spending the day with her. He surprised himself, wanting her there in his house. Thinking of her now, as sluggish as he felt, with the sweat dripping inside his clothes, there was a throbbing in his groin. He moved his jacket in front of him. The garbled voice announcing the 4:37 to Bethpage jolted him out of his reverie. As he was carried along to Track 7 by the stampeding herd, he had a smile on his face.

Chapter 67

Fibber McGee lay down on the sidewalk and refused to budge. His head was pillowed on his front paws straight in front of him, and if it weren't for his stump of a tail wobbling behind him, he would have appeared dead or overcome with heat prostration. Eileen tried to pull him to a standing position, but he stubbornly hugged the concrete. She peered into the distance to see the object of his attention. Princess was prancing toward them at the end of her leash, with Rosa Bassetti panting for breath behind her. As they neared, Mr. McGee stood, gracefully paralyzed in anticipation. They faced each other on hind legs. Then, almost bowing an invitation to her, he danced around her. Princess preened at his courting.

Rosa's bones groaned as she bent to pet him. He ignored her. "So, you see your boyfriend, bambina. He make your day? Wouldn't it be nice," she continued to Eileen, "if we—I mean, people—could get so happy from so little. So…how you comin' along?"

"Fine, I'm fine now. Really. Even my nephew says that since I paid them, they won't be back. Won't bother me anymore."

"We hope. Did you think anymore about if it could be anyone you know?"

"No. How could I ever figure out who it could be? Fibber, now you stop that, you hear?" She tugged him away from Princess's rear. "You all ready for the noise this weekend?"

"Nah. I give my Princess some aspirin at night. Like tranquilizers they are. They start setting off firecrackers, the poor thing she goes crazy from the noise. They ought to have a law against them."

"They do, you know. But nobody pays attention. So what are you doing to celebrate?"

"Me? Just like any other day to me. Same as New Year's Eve. Or my birthday. You?"

"Oh, I'm not doing anything. My nephew invited me for the whole weekend. I could go for a week, if I wanted. Or forever. But…well, I don't like to go too far. I like staying in my own house. Sleeping in my own bed. Don't we, Mr. McGee?"

"Me, too. Hey, why you don't come? I open a nice bottle of Chianti. We have a little chicken. I even take out my flag—from when I become a citizen—and we drink to America. To independence. Come on, say yes." Rosa was buoyant at the idea of an impromptu party. "Do it for him." She nodded toward the dog. "He deserves a holiday too. I make something special, some stew, for our little sweethearts."

"Well, I don't know…"

"Sure you know. We have a good time. I go shopping now. You come—when? Five, five-thirty?"

"Okay," Eileen said with a laugh. It might be fun for a change. She hadn't been out of the house for dinner in ages. "I'll bring dessert."

"Good, good, I get busy now." As Rosa hurried down the street, she warned her dog under her breath, "You don't get too excited now. You too old to be Princess McGee."

Laurie felt foolish lying on a beach towel in the grass in shorts and a tank top, when so many people were walking by wearing their street clothes. But in another two hours, there wouldn't be room for one more sunbather in Forest Park. She was determined to get some color, and to Relax—with a capital R. After only twenty minutes here, she was fidgety. She knew she'd never last the two hours she had promised herself. She watched the joggers on the path in front of her and silently asked how people could be running in weather like this. And in nylon workout outfits too! She sat up and spread the *Times* in front of her, smoothing out each page as she turned it. It was an uncomfortable position, with nothing to lean on. Besides, she couldn't read with her sunglasses, because the prescription was for distance, and couldn't see without them because of the glare. She closed the paper, folded it in half, and tucked it back in her tote bag. She rubbed her hands together but the suntan lotion spread the black stain of newsprint.

It was 10:20—an hour and forty minutes to go. She wondered what Dr. Pomalee was doing this weekend. He'd be picking up his kids, but would he conveniently run into his ex-wife? Would he come back into the city at the end of the day (silly), or stay in the guest room (most likely)? His children were too old to be picked up; they probably had their own plans with their friends anyway. So maybe he'd just visit for a while. And stay for dinner. Or maybe they wouldn't be home at all, and he wouldn't even go because there'd be nothing for him to do, nobody to see. So he'd stop in the office and check on some of the animals. Especially since they had two post-ops.

Now 10:25—an hour and thirty-five minutes left. No matter what, she absolutely was not going to the office until Wednesday, July 5th. She was totally underpaid for a forty-hour workweek and if she counted all the extra time she put in, she probably wouldn't even be making minimum wage. Well, it was her own fault. It's not as if Dr. Pomalee asked her to come in. She did it on her own time. He had no idea how much time she spent there. Or did he?

Of course, it would be nice and quiet, a good time to make a big dent in her data input. All those statistics would take forever at this rate. It was so much easier to work on the desktop and then put her work on a flash drive and bring it home to her laptop. And this would be a perfect time to bring the stray home; the subway would be empty. If Dr. Pomalee went to the office at all, it would be late in the day. But she'd never know because she wouldn't be there to find out!

Only 10:30. An hour and a half more.

Even with the windows wide open, the apartment smelled from paint. So did Jason. He didn't mind that so much, but the turpentine fumes and its residue stinging his arms made the inside of his stomach itchy. "I'm gonna jump in the shower now, okay?"

"Okay, that's it. Finished. What d'ya think?" Chris cocked his head in the doorway and studied their handiwork. "Think it's too much?"

Jason came up behind him, playfully, tiredly, and dug his chin into Chris's shoulder. "Only for people who don't like sex in the kitchen."

"Come on, really."

"I think once we put the knickknacks back and hang the baskets on the walls, it'll look great. Maybe we shouldn't have done the refrigerator, though."

"Well, it would've looked terrible if we had left it white." Chris backed up far enough to stand next to Jason, draping his arm loosely around Jason's neck. "It kinda grows on you."

"So does mold."

"Be serious."

"I am. I'm going to go soak in the shower, put on a pair of white ducks, and then, know what I'd like? I'd like to take a walk in the fresh air, even if it is steamy, go sit outdoors at an open café, and have a nice dinner, a few drinks. I'd like to not think about having to wash all the dishes and glasses and pots tomorrow and put everything away. And not talk about the letter, okay?"

"Okay by me."

"Good." Jason took off his T-shirt as he headed toward the bathroom. He caught a glimpse of a wet, black nose sticking out from under the couch. "I hope you're damned grateful, Sabrina!" he yelled.

"For what?"

He knew Chris would ask, and he was ready with an answer. "That dogs are color blind!" His shirt snapped as he swiped it at the air.

Chapter 68

Louise blotted the lettuce with a paper towel after she took it out of the spinner. She could see the deck beyond the living room. The kitchen with its pass-through counter was a perfect blind for…She caught herself before she finished the thought. It was sheer habit to think of it as a blind, as hunter and prey. She didn't feel that way at all. In fact, she was actually comfortable. She put the lettuce leaves in a plastic bag to crisp them and put it on the top shelf, slightly rearranging the milk and soda bottles. As she cut the tomatoes on a little round wooden board, she tried to recall the times when she had been passionate with somebody. Or sexy. There had been quite a few, she supposed. But she couldn't remember ever being *comfortable* with somebody. This was a new experience. And a much more fulfilling one.

The sudden movement of Ken's backing up as a flame shot up from the charcoal jarred her. He waved his long barbecue fork, like a saber, knowing she was watching. "Okay!" he shouted. "It's okay. Everything's under control. Just means we have a great fire going." He reassured Louise and then the rest of his audience, resting under the chaise lounge. Louise could hear Honda's contented sigh. It was all so natural. She was natural. It was very strange. Strange and beautiful. It made her feel beautiful. She smiled at her face in the toaster as she diced the onions.

Ken pushed the briquettes around a little more. Then, satisfied, he sat in his chair, his dangling left hand grabbing clumps of fur. The dog loved it and tried to catch his fingers. Ken wanted to be with her, but he wanted more to sit here alone and be aware of her presence nearby. He liked the kitchen sounds she made…crockery scraping crockery, the metallic jangle of silverware, a faucet squeaking as she turned it on and off, and the broken hum of a barely familiar melody, keeping in time to her slicing and chopping.

"Do you have a salad server?" she yelled out to him.

He stoked the fire before he went back inside. "Why? Aren't you going to serve it?" She opened her mouth to laugh, and he gave her a loud, affectionate kiss. "It's on the top shelf."

"I saw the bowl; I meant a fork-and-spoon kind of server."

"Oh. Well, I got that too!" He went to the sideboard in the dining area and brought back sterling silver tongs. Slightly blackened.

"Nice. Let me guess. They were a wedding present and when you split, your wife got the house and car, and you settled for the silver."

"Not even close. There were no wedding presents, and there was no wife. I told you that."

"I know, but I didn't believe you. I thought I'd catch you just now."

"Did you really think I'd lie? Why would I do that?"

"It's not that I thought you lied. I just can't believe a nice-looking, smart, all-together guy could have escaped all this time."

"Maybe that's how I stayed so 'all together,'" he teased her.

"Well, you're not all that terrific, you know!"

"No?"

"You have one very major fault that I can see."

"Oh, yes, what's that?" he dared her.

"You're a menace"—Louise patty-caked her hands against him— "who has to be watched carefully…or else you'll burn the whole neighborhood down."

"OhmyGod!" The words came out in a rush as Ken whirled around to face her view and then ran outside to fan the black smoke rising from the barbecue. When he finished, she was standing next to him, a glass of red wine in her outstretched hand. "Thanks," he said. "I could use that. Let's sit a few minutes before I bring the steaks out. It's so beautiful at this time of day."

"It sure is." The sun had set, leaving a spectrum of coral to deep red on the horizon, each shade flowing into the next, as if the hues were dripping and not just puffs of colored cloud floating past one another. "Is it always this spectacular?"

"Probably. I don't always notice. Actually, I arranged it."

"You arranged it?"

"Uh-huh. I ordered a special showing for tonight. To impress you." He smiled that benevolent, big-daddy smile that stopped her breath in her chest. He could be serious without being serious. That's what she liked about him. He could say something, without requiring an answer, an embarrassed response from her. That's what put her at ease, she decided.

As soon as they sat on the glider, Honda tried to squeeze between them.

"C'mon, you big baby, you're too huge to be a lap dog," she reprimanded him and at the same time boosted him up. "Do you mind?" she asked Ken sheepishly.

"I mind that he's trying to horn in on my time. Jealous, aren't you?" He gave Honda his hand and started roughhousing with him.

The color disappeared from the sky, but it was still light out. They sat in silence, enjoying the silence in the last of the sunset. Ken put the steaks on the grill, the meat hissing as the flames seared it. Louise's skin was hot from the sunburn she'd gotten and from the wine. She rocked dreamily while Ken watched the meat, whistling softly.

When she had tiptoed into the kitchen for some instant coffee this morning, he was already waiting for her. It was his idea to take Honda to the beach before anyone got there. They ran in the sand, towards the sunrise. The water curled into little waves, dappled with silver in the new light, and then gurgled into the quiet. Louise watched the ocean, thinking that it probably didn't look any different from its first day. She wondered how many people since the beginning of time had stood on the edge of a continent like she was, and pondered the vastness of the universe and the smallness of themselves.

After their full day yesterday, between the ride out, and their sightseeing by car because she was afraid to leave Honda alone in Ken's house ("Who knows what he would do in a strange place?" she had argued), and a spur-of-the-moment pizza brought in, nothing had happened. At first, Louise had been glad. She always thought the second time was awkward. Trying to make it as good as the first time and usually finding out it wasn't. Or realizing that the first time really wasn't as good as you imagined it to be. Nothing happening was a relief to her. No pressure to try to match her eagerness of the first night or to enjoy it. But now, feeling as mellow as the wine she was sipping, she started to want him.

She had blurted out that he was so "together," but appraising him as he tended their dinner, she knew it was true. He was independent, in control of his life and a lot of other people's lives, yet he didn't seem to have a need to display his power. That was appealing to someone who was as strong as Louise and used to being leaned on. She had a sudden urge to be inside his arms, protected, soothed. She wanted to tell him all about her life, her hurts, and give herself completely up to him. She wanted to confess that she wasn't as strong as she pretended, nor as emotionally competent. She wanted to be a little girl in her daddy's lap. Thinking back on past lovers, it occurred to her that the best times—maybe the only times—for sex had been when she opened herself up enough to let a little of herself out. But just as she let someone peek at her inside, she closed up even tighter than before, withdrawing for long periods into her dark moods. Louise knew she was vulnerable. She also knew that she could trust Ken Hollis with her very being.

Her insides loosened. Everything fluttered in her belly. Organs and muscles and nerves detached themselves and then rushed together, twisting into a sinewy knot. Its rhythmic contractions in her belly made her weak.

Chapter 69

The quiet was eerie. Even the steady whiz of traffic that always hummed into Laurie's window from Queens Boulevard had slowed to a slight buzz. A fluff of cloud crept into her, the emptiness fluttering like a wing in her chest. She was so alone.

Three thousand puppies and kittens are born every hour in the United States, 70,000 a day, keeping the animal population at somewhere close to 200 million. Laurie slashed the sentences with a red highlighter so she could add those numbers to her list of statistics. There are between 70 and 80 million canines, 80 to 90 million felines, and more than 50 million feral cats. Close to 60 percent of American households have pets; at last count, cats outnumbered dogs in popularity for the first time.

Laurie slid the magazine next to her computer and started copying the figures. As she typed, the yellow numerals popped up on the screen, one at a time like mechanical ducks in a shooting gallery.

Lenny Marcus didn't realize that most restaurants wouldn't be open. A lot of them were closed on summer weekends; of those that weren't, many of them started their vacation during the holidays. He was disappointed to find signs on the doors of the first three he went to, and he ended up eating a much more expensive dinner than he'd planned. Even though it wasn't very good, he savored every bite, knowing how much it would cost. It didn't take much for Jessica to spend; why shouldn't he?

He walked slowly back to his hotel. Looking all the way down Lexington Avenue from the 50s, Manhattan was like a ghost town. There was hardly any traffic, any people. It seemed spooky. He went to his room. The blast of cold as he opened the door chilled his perspiration. The dial on the air conditioner was missing, and there was no way to change the temperature setting. He put on the television and scrolled up and down the guide to see what was on. Nothing much. The reception wasn't even as good as home.

"Ah, the stories I could tell you," Rosa said.

"Better than the ones you already have?" Eileen asked. "Another couple these"—Rosa waved her glass—"I can. So you never missed it. Being married?"

"Naw. I wish—it would have been very nice if I'd been born maybe fifty years later. You know, to be young and single today, to have that freedom we didn't have. That would be nice."

"Oh, you're a devil, aren't you? I thought I was the naughty one. I was seventeen and a new bride when I came over. My Gianni was a good man. But strict. Old-fashioned like all the men in my life. Like my father, my uncle. But I didn't know any different. I was a good wife. 'Specially when he got sick. I waited on him after the first heart attack. Took good care of him. Soon as he went back to work—the doctor, he said the best thing was to go back to work—boom, another heart attack. Who would expect him to die so young? I was lonely, you know, not used to being alone. Didn't have anyone here. And having to support myself. People talked about widows then, you know. So I gave them something to talk about!" Eileen giggled. "Now don't go telling people what I told you tonight," Rosa warned.

"'Course not. You either. That's our secret. But you would miss the excitement. Today, I mean. Not having to hide. Not being afraid of getting caught. It wouldn't be as much fun, don't you think?"

"You're right. Definitely."

Buoyed, Eileen went on. "Like there was this time…Oh, I shouldn't tell you this at all, but I'm having so much fun. I stayed in a hotel with this man. Think of how daring that was in my day. Our day."

"Oy, I wouldn't think you would. Me, yes, but a nice lady like you?"

"See how old-fashioned you are? Still thinking nice ladies don't do it?"

Their laughter filled the little apartment and stretched into long chuckles while they both remembered their own long-ago escapades.

"So what happen?" Rosa asked. "When?"

"When you stayed at the hotel?"

"Oh, yes. Well, we were on a high floor. I was going to sneak out before him in the morning, so nobody would see us together. Him being married and all." Rosa's head bobbed up and down in anticipation, encouraging Eileen to embellish a little. "So there I was on the thirty-seventh floor"—she added about ten floors to the story—"standing in the hallway, about to push the elevator button. And I got so scared…I just imagined the doors opening and my father standing there, looking at me. I tried to think of all sorts of excuses why I would be in a hotel at seven o'clock in the morning."

"But what would *he* have been doing there at seven o'clock?"

"That never occurred to me. You know how it was. You were just so scared of getting caught. It didn't mean you were rational. I just froze, petrified that he would see me. So I found the exit door, and I walked down thirty-seven flights!"

"No!"

"Wait. That's not the best part. All the way down, I'm thinking, what if the door is locked and I can't get back out? And I'm trapped in the staircase for days. Weeks. Well, that didn't happen. Instead, I was so relieved that the door opened, I pushed it hard and practically fell into the middle of the lobby. Filled with businessmen standing around. Before breakfast. It was a convention, no less!"

The happy ripples of laughter from two old ladies drifted out the window into the hot night.

The clamor of glasses clinking, animated conversation, and waiters rattling trays gave the place a festive aura. The same celebrating was going on at beach houses and country cabins from the Berkshires to Amagansett, on wooden decks and brick patios, near the ocean or in the woods or at the mountains. But these people, the ones left in town, had their city to themselves, sitting under umbrellas on their sidewalk verandas, watching New York parade by. The clang of the manhole cover bouncing as cars rode over it, the belch of fumes from the Columbus Avenue bus leaving its corner stop, the faint smell of garbage and urine permeating the smell of their food, the flashing of traffic lights and headlights and neon lights…the commotion and odor and noise and harsh illumination just added to the party mood. It was a holiday, after all.

Jason tipped back in his plastic chair, rattling the heavy metal chain that ran around its legs and through the base of the table. He looked at Christopher, whose profile next to him accentuated the angular cheeks that dominated his stubby nose. He knew Chris would be upset that in the glow of the artificial candle, Jason could see his scalp shining through his thinning hair. Jason thudded down in the chair and as he came forward, he squeezed Chris's knee under the table.

Louise's toenails excited him. They weren't polished, so he could see how white the tips were. How smooth and unblemished the skin between them was, the skin they protected. The brown leather thong holding her foot to her sandal looked vulgar against her delicate flesh. He blinked away his incredible desire to hold her ankle and slip his tongue between her toes, sliding his saliva from one tiny cleft to the next. He was mesmerized by her feet. He looked away, but the image was frozen in his brain. As if he had pressed the PAUSE button. Ken closed his eyes and hit PLAY.

She was lying on her back, naked under the sheet tented over her bent knees. Her feet were flat on the bed, close together. He lay before her, leaning on his forearms. He licked her big toe, traced its cuticle, slightly tickled it around the edges. Her toes flexed and splayed. He thrust his tongue between the first two. It folded lengthwise to squeeze into the tight pocket. He moved it back and forth and then darted it between the next two and the next, at last savoring the narrowest slit between the end two. Her feet moved apart to escape the torment, revealing the long avenue leading up to their source, her source. He clamped his hands around her ankles, wanting to crawl between them, yet not daring to even look.

As he repeated his devotions to the other foot, his penis throbbed with fullness beneath him. He moved up to relieve the pressure, bracing himself on his elbows. Then slowly, relishing his own agony as much as hers, his tongue felt its way up her legs, retreated, and started again, wetter, faster. When it reached her still-bent knees, he slapped his hands under them, pulled himself to a crouch over her, and firmly but gently pushed them apart as far as they could go.

He swept the sheet away and allowed himself to look. Lying down, she was soft to the eyes. Her face and shoulders and legs, tinted pink from the rays of the sun, added swirls of luminescence to the paleness of her body. Bronze freckles spotted the parts of her that had been exposed to the air. But there, between her chest and the crease where her thighs met her torso, was the creamiest, most beautiful skin he had ever seen. Skin he had glimpsed through the nail of her big toe. The unadorned, unpretentious toenail that hinted of her unpretentious personality. Its plainness and naturalness expressed simplicity akin to innocence to him. It aroused him.

The thickness in her breasts rolled to their sides as her chest rose and fell heavily with her breathing. Her nipples trembled in their center, conscious of his stare. Even though she was tall, almost as tall as he was, her low buttocks and wide hips pulled her height down, and she always appeared shorter than she was. Lying on her back, with her behind sunk into the mattress, she was long.

He was still knelt before her folded legs; he gently rested his palms on her knees and continued his inventory of her. She watched him watch her, and it seemed that whatever his sight focused on burned from the touch of his eyes. Her saliva evaporated from the heat; she could not swallow. He could not turn away from her. He scrutinized every inch of her, unable to contain his lust, unwilling to let it go. His gaze lingered over the russet swatch of velvet concealing the opening to her soul. He thought the skin stretched over his bulging penis would tear. He parted her knees and looked. A tremor opened the mouth between her thighs; a little tongue quivered inside. Her lips suckled. Dizzy with desire, he descended upon her.

Louise sat on the edge of the chaise, facing him. Ken's eyes were closed. She wiggled her toes and self-consciously pulled her feet under the chair before she spoke. She noticed he had been looking at them. She was sorry she hadn't gone all the way and gotten a pedicure. Or it wouldn't have killed her to have polished her toenails herself. God, she was so stupid sometimes. "It's been such a lovely evening," she said.

She thought she startled him out of a dream. Because when he tried to answer, his voice cracked.

Chapter 70

Yolanda fanned herself on the fire escape. The backs of her thighs stuck to the vinyl of the folding chair, and she shifted her buttocks to pry herself off carefully, like peeling a Band-Aid from sore skin. She tugged her shorts down. Four stories above the sidewalk she had a box seat view of 187th Street. The stoops in both directions were colored with women in bright shirts and pull-on pants, gossiping on the steps. Near the corner bodega, a group of older men kibitzed over three checker games, the players teamed against each other across wooden crates. An open fire hydrant gushed over children in bathing suits; a little kid held his hand over the valve, and they squealed as the water squirted in all directions. Teenage boys played ball in the street and girls, pretending an interest in the score, cheered them on, combing their hair and massaging their lips to spread the gloss. Then they turned to take selfies with the boys behind them. Toward the avenue, some tough guys leaned on the cyclone fence surrounding an empty lot, leather vests flapping on their bare chests as they strutted in front of one another, smoking and cursing.

"Please, Mama, please," Elena's voice whined from inside. "No."

"But why not?"

"*Porque.*"

"Because, why?"

"Porque. Because I said."

"But, Mama—"

"*Suficiente!*" Yolanda slapped her hands on her thighs. When she stood the sweat dribbled down to her knees. She raised her leg to climb back inside the window. Straddling the sill, she yelled, "Go downstairs and play, you wanna do something. Or take the twins outside and watch them."

"But I wanted to ta-alk." Elena's voice broke the word into two syllables.

"Then go talk to Señora Sanchez. I'll let you go over there."

"Ma, that's not the same. I see her every day. That's no fun."

"Fun? Poor Elena. Life is not supposed to be fun." Yolanda stepped into the living room and opened her arms to her daughter. Of course life should be fun for a nine-year-old. God knows, she'd have a long enough time of hard work and responsibility. "Okay, you can call her. It's just I don't want to bother Ms. Sidway. She's been very good to us, you hear? We don't want to be a pain. And just 'cause Ricky got us a new phone don't mean it's for talking."

"What else is a phone for, Mama?" Elena giggled.

"You know what I mean. It's for important talking. And emergencies. Not for…I can't think of the word in English. Just don't annoy her, okay?"

"I won't, Ma. She said I could call her whenever I wanted to."

"Maybe she didn't mean on a Sunday night. G'won, before I change my mind." Yolanda slapped the girl's behind affectionately.

Chapter 71

Sabrina had been with Jason through his roughest and happiest years—his loneliness, his courtship, his adjustment to living with someone, passing his fiftieth birthday, taking the plunge to open a business, moving to the West Side. There were many times he considered leaving Chris or severing their relationship, fearing that his lover was a temporary pleasure in his life, knowing Sabrina was a permanent fixture. He didn't think about it often but when he did, there was no question in Jason's mind how much Sabrina meant to him. How much he needed her. Probably more than she needed him. There were periods in his life when her acceptance of him was the only thing preventing him from total self-destruction, when her love saved him from drowning in the dark depressions into which he sometimes sank. He would do anything in his power for her, so it would not have occurred to him not to pay the ransom—it was not one of his choices. Even when Chris tried to convince Jason to call the police, he didn't suggest not paying, because Chris loved Sabrina too. Still, Chris thought they should try to catch the culprit. And save the money. Jason would not consider it.

"I still think Nettie Pedersen had something to do with it," Chris said, rolling his eyes to the ceiling.

Jason re-counted the bills. "Nah. Too obvious. She'd be the first suspect; she'd have to realize that. Anti-gay, anti-animal, and no doubt anti-Semite. Probably why she at least nods to you."

"Uh-uh. Guilt by association. She hates me as much as she hates you."

"Well, I'm glad she doesn't play favorites."

Chris put his hand on Jason's shoulder. "Please let me go with you."

"No, I can't risk anything happening to her. The note is very clear. Somebody will be watching. The minute they see me with another person, it's all over."

"But the chances of them actually dognapping her are—"

"Doesn't matter. I'm not gonna risk it." Jason stopped counting the bills, having lost count. He stacked them together to start again, saying, "Wait a minute…why couldn't you be there ahead of me? Watch what goes on? Then I leave, and you wait for them to show up. Maybe then we could get them."

"I'll do it," Chris agreed. "I'd like to get my hands on the bastard. Twist his balls off. Slowly."

"Unless he doesn't have any." Jason mouthed the numbers as he counted the hundreds, dealing them to the table.

"Come on…you don't think it's a woman, do you? If it's not that bitch upstairs, I wouldn't believe it. A woman isn't capable of being so vicious."

"Eighty-seven, eighty-eight," Jason said out loud to keep his pace.

"And that Pedersen, I swear, Jase, she does have 'em. Only they're brass."

"I can't imagine anyone with such a sick mind, threatening to do such a thing."

Chris watched him put the 10,000 dollars in an envelope, make a new fold in the flap to stretch over the thickness, and tape it down. His love for Jason suddenly wrenched his heart; his respect for Jason's determination tugged at his loins.

Chapter 72

Dr. Pomalee's crepe soles cushioned his footsteps. When he spoke, Laurie jumped and squealed in fright. "You scared me," she said, leaning into the computer, blocking his view.

He shook his head as he read the papers in his hand. "Don't you ever get tired of sitting at that damned computer?"

"I love it. You will too when you see everything it can do. When will you be ready for your demonstration?"

"Not now. Too busy. But I will. Promise."

"How'd the tooth extraction go?"

Dr. Pomalee had to stoop his six-foot-four frame to lean on his hands on the back of her chair. "Patient's fine. Mistress is a wreck. She'll probably ask about getting a set of false teeth. Canine Caps—that'd be a good business name."

Laurie laughed, and he swatted her with his folder. "Be back later if you need me for anything."

She nodded. Once Dr. Pomalee was gone, she turned back to the computer screen to continue what she'd been reading:

"The roughly 78 million dogs in the country produce about 10 million tons of poop. One and a half million pets live in the city of New York."

Laurie reached for her calculator to figure out how much waste that would be.

If I need him for anything? she thought suddenly, and she felt her cheeks burn.

"Slightly more than half are licensed."

Boy, he would blush too if he knew what I was thinking!

And what I need him for.

They produce about seventy-five tons of waste per day.

I'd love to tell him.

Twenty-five thousand to thirty thousand tons a year.

Someday, I will.

A lot of shit. She smiled.

Chapter 73

A strand of Rosa's long gray hair fell on her shoulder. She deftly wound it around her finger, took an oversized hairpin out of her bun, and used it to work it back inside and smooth it down. The salesman waited for her to finish and return her attention to the showcase.

"Now this camera has both the automatic focus and automatic exposure. You don't have to do anything. It thinks for you."

"Still so confusing. I don't know. Don't you have—"

"And the beauty of it is"—he bounced it in his palm—"it weighs practically nothing. Here—feel."

"Nah. Don't they still make those simple ones? You know? That's all I need."

"Simple? Can't get more simple than this. All you gotta do it aim and shoot. And look at this." He unscrewed the lens. "You don't want thirty-five millimeter, although that's your most popular. You want close-ups; we put in a different lens—one, two, three."

"Uh-uh. Really. How much is it anyway?"

"It lists for $379, but I tell you what—you're such a nice lady, I'm going to give it to you for $299 if you buy it now. And I'll throw in a leather case. How's that?"

"What?" Rosa didn't try to hide her surprise. "No, no, I only want a little thing, I don't wanna spend more than twenty or twenty-five dollars. Oh, no, sorry." She bent over and scooped up Princess. "Three hundred dollars! You crazy. No way." She hurried toward the door, afraid to look back at him, at all the cameras that had to be replaced in their plastic bags and refit into the boxes. On her way out, she knew the foreign jabber behind her was the salesman complaining about her. *They don't look like they have anything to do anyway*, she thought, *always lounging against the counters*. You could see them through the windows as you walked by. "It's his own fault," Rosa told Princess when they got out to the street. "I tell him I want a Brownie when I walk in."

Chapter 74

Eileen moved the bud vase with the silk rose off the mahogany drop-leaf table, turned the rag bond paper at the proper angle for writing, and placed her fountain pen, reserved for important signatures, next to it. The stage was set. A ballpoint on the kitchen table was good enough for paying bills, for keeping her ledger up-to-date, for correspondence, but solemn documents required a ceremonial ritual. Sitting at the old-fashioned secretary gave the sense of formality and dignity that her letter needed to make it official. The old piece of furniture, which had been her mother's, her grandfather's, and her great-grandfather's, added a feeling of continuity, a connection to her past generations, a family authorization to whatever she wrote while sitting there.

I, Eileen Hargan, wish to add the following to my Last Will and Testament. If I should die before my beloved pet, Fibber McGee, I want him to live with my good friend and neighbor, Rosa Bassetti, 335 East 83rd Street, New York, NY 10028. In order for her to provide for him comfortably, I leave her the sum of…

She twisted the cap around on the back of the pen while she considered the amount. If she made it too much, Charlene would probably drag Danny into court to contest it. If it wasn't enough…if it wasn't enough, Rosa would take good care of him anyway. As good as Eileen did. Well, almost as good.

Now that they had vowed to do this for each other, Eileen was very happy, relieved to have such a great weight of worry lifted. If they had been any more serious—or drunk—she was sure they would have cut their wrists and mingled their blood in an oath. As it was, she was as giddy as a teenager about having a new friend. Somebody she could really talk to and share secrets with. They should spend more time with each other to give their dogs a chance to get used to them, just in case. She would suggest that. Maybe when she helped Rosa write her letter, because her English wasn't so good. Rosa didn't think she needed a letter. She had no money to leave, and nobody who would want her Princess. Still, as Eileen told her, it's always best to put everything in writing.

Chapter 75

Ken Hollis ordered fish and a draft beer. Bernie Petris's thick eyebrows arched into question marks; he asked for a steak, closed the menu, and handed it back to the waiter. "What's with you? On a diet?"

"No. Just trying to cut down on the bad stuff." He stroked his chest. "All the animal fat, cholesterol, you know—things like that. Me? No, I'm not worried about my weight."

"You're lucky. You don't have to be," Bernie pushed back from the table to demonstrate his paunch. "That's what I oughta be doing. My wife's always after me. And now my kids're nagging me to quit." He patted the pack of cigarettes in his breast pocket. "So where are we?"

"Nowhere. Well, I shouldn't say nowhere. A little closer than we were before. Talk, talk, talk, but to get these guys—your office included; your office *especially*—to do anything is like pulling teeth."

"I know. But having the mayor admit there's a problem and that we're the ones who need to solve it, having him discuss it with the commissioner, actually call a meeting—"

"It would help a lot more if he *attended* the meeting."

"I know, but look—do you have any idea what's going on right now in the city? The threatened transit walkout, the highest crime rate we've ever had, Sanitation's contract coming up, the Planning Commission scandal, and—"

"Whaddya think? I live on Mars? Of course I know." Ken sucked the head off his beer. "Listen, know when they'll do something? When somebody's grandfather gets murdered on the way to his doctor's office, or a poor old lady gets killed on her way to the incinerator with her garbage."

"You're probably right," Bernie admitted, "but in a city like this, it's hard enough taking care of the shit we have, much less finding the manpower—and the money—for shit before it even happens. Speaking of little old ladies, whatever happened with that woman in the bank? You know who I mean? The teller who called my office about the old lady making a large withdrawal?"

Ken watched the waiter put the steak, still sizzling in a metal platter, in front of Bernie. "Ah, that looks good." He bent his head and took an audible sniff of his own lunch. "This, on the other hand, does not." After tasting it, he said, "Healthy? Yes. Satisfying? Definitely not. Yes, Miss Hargan. A sweet old lady. Retired teacher. Typical spinster type. Very prim."

"There's an old-fashioned word."

"Prim? Or Spinster? Yeah, but they're just the right words to describe her. Old-fashioned. A real schoolmarm. And so…so sweet. Even while she was upset, you know, she offered me tea. She seemed so fragile. A tiny person. Prettiest blue eyes you've ever seen. You can tell she was beautiful when she was young. Girl in the bank was right." Ken Hollis put his fork down and tried to grasp the fine bone stuck between his front teeth.

"Old scam? 'We found this money on the street; you put up some of yours to show good faith, so we can share it!'"

"Um-um," he mumbled. "Worse, much worse. She's got a dog. Damn." He gave up on the bone. "I'm never ordering fish again. I hate it anyway. No, it was extortion of the worst kind. Threatened to steal the dog. Kill it. You can tell she lives frugally, probably saved every penny she ever earned; neat apartment. She has to pay 10,000 dollars. She loves that dog. It's her whole life. Ugly little thing, if you ask me. One of those Boston Bulldogs or Terriers or whatever you call them. Looks almost as old as she does. So what can she do? She's scared to death. And while she's trying to make up her mind if she should give her life's savings, the bastards send her an ear. No, no, not her dog's but somebody else's dog's. With a warning that if there's any more delay, they'll mutilate it. So of course she pays up."

"Pricks!"

"The thing is, she did pay." Ken moved his plate back and crumbled his napkin on top of it. "It was easy. You think they're going to retire? On 10,000 dollars? Uh-uh. They're going to do it again. And when they find out how many little old ladies who love their pets live in New York, how many elderly people on Social Security who never touch their real money because they're afraid to…shit, there's an inexhaustible supply of victims for them. Know what makes it even harder?" Ken stopped talking while the waiter cleared the table. "That we'll never know. Who are they going to report it to? The local precinct? You said it yourself—the crime rate is higher than ever. The drug problem. So a senior citizen calls and says that she just got a letter asking for money. On a scale of one to ten, how do you think they're going to prioritize it?" He looked at the waiter. "Just coffee, please. Decaf."

Bernie grimaced at Ken. "You're so good. I have to cut down on the caffeine too. But I'm not starting today. I'll have regular," he told the waiter. "You know, this might be a case for the NYPD, instead of some powerless committee about the elderly," Bernie continued. "Starting last January, the ASPCA closed its investigative unit, and the police department now responds to all animal cruelty complaints. Luckily, Bill Bratton is an animal lover and since he took over the department, there's been a 160-percent increase in animal rescues and arrests. 'Course the ASPCA still assists them in forensic investigation, field assistance, and training. Stuff like that."

Ken tore open a packet of Sweet 'N Low, waiting for his coffee. "Don't know if it's animal cruelty or people cruelty. I was reading a dog magazine, and they had an article about this kind of swindle. In the Midwest, mostly. People put ads in the paper about their lost dogs. They get a call from somebody in the next state or somewhere saying they found the dog. Wire money so they can ship it back or escort it on a plane. But that's small potatoes and, besides, the dog is already gone. It takes real New Yorkers to think up a variation like this."

"What d'ya think we can do? Quickly? Without funds?" Bernie pushed back to make room for the waiter to place his coffee.

"What's going on. It wouldn't have to cost a lot of money. Just give lectures at community centers, neighborhood places where old people go, those small freebie newspapers."

"Trouble is, Ken, the kind of old people they prey on don't go anywhere. You post signs for a meeting, a lecture, you know how many show up?"

"I guess so. But it would be a start. Nothing's foolproof. Nothing is going to reach everybody."

"Tell you what." Bernie shifted to get his wallet out of his pants pocket. He held up his hand, indicating that he was paying. "Why don't you write up a proposal, nothing elaborate, maybe even an informal letter to me. Something I can show the Comish." Bernie raised his credit card to call the waiter back with the check. "You don't even have a dog. Since when you reading magazines about them?"

"Since I have a friend with a dog." Ken put his hand in front of his mouth to cough and cover his grin.

Chapter 76

A two-day growth of fuzz spread across his face like a stain. His thin, tawny hair separated from the oil that had not been washed out and hung in clumps over his eyes. His jeans were so worn at the knees that there was no trace of blue or denim thread. His sneakers were filthy, and bare skin showed through the large hole in the canvas of the right one. He crouched against the back of the newsstand. His sign, printed with a heavy marker on the bottom of a carton and leaning against his legs—I AM HOMELESS. PLEASE HELP—hadn't encouraged any more than the six quarters and five nickels he occasionally jingled in the coffee container, most of which he had contributed himself. He tried to keep his hands tucked in his armpits behind the sign, so they wouldn't give him away.

Christopher Barrett never took his eyes off the street, off the doors of the supermarket just down the block. He was glad he had saved his "painting pants." He had rolled them up and put them into the garbage when they were finished with the apartment. Then, impulsively, he had taken them out again and stuffed them between the broom and mop handles in the small closet in the kitchen. Jason had yelled, "Don't be ridiculous! They stink and have spots all over them. By the time we're ready for another paint job, you'll have another pair of pants ready to donate to the cause."

It must be a good half hour since Jason had come out of the store and another half hour since Chris had posted himself here. After being chased from his ideal vantage point in the recessed garage entrance directly across the street from Gristede's by the doorman of the adjoining apartment house, he had squatted in front of the TD bank center, until the guard came out and swaggered in front of him menacingly. He had deliberately left his watch at home, to fit with his disguise. But now he wished he knew how long he had been here. His behind hurt from sitting in one position for so long; his cheeks started to tingle from numbness.

His original plan had been to wait inside the supermarket where he'd have a perfect view. He had even brought all their empty bottles with him, so he could stand in front of the redemption machine. But whether the machine was legitimately out of order, or they had turned it off to discourage that clientele, or they just didn't allow that on the Upper East Side, he didn't know. The manager counted his stash, gave him a credit to bring to the cash register, and then escorted him out.

A truck pulled into the service area right next to Gristede's. The driver and his helper began stacking plastic crates, obstructing Christopher's view. As he stood to peer over them, remembering to stoop slightly, someone stopped at the newsstand just behind him to buy cigarettes. He thought he recognized one of his writers. His stomach tightened. "See what happens," he wanted to shout, "to editors whose authors don't meet their deadlines?"

Chapter 77

Kola lay on her side, her paw resting across Clifford's shoulder. His arm stretched over her, fingers caressing her. "He doesn't even come home every night anymore," he whispered to Kola. "It's better when he's not here anyhow. 'Member all the fighting? They kept yelling at each other. 'Member? Now when he's here, they don't fight. They don't do nothin'. Not even talk. I liked it better when they made a lot of noise. Didn't you? What if he never comes back? Oh, Kola, what'll we do? Maybe they'll get divorced, and I'll never see him again. Or they'll make me go live with him half the time. We'll have to leave here and go to a new place. What if they don't have TV? What if there's no video games? What if I can't carry all my things? Or they won't let me take my cowboy hat?"

He moved closer until their bellies were touching, pressing, arms and paws and legs entwined. Their bodies were braided like lovers. Clifford wept into her chest. "I hate him. Why can't they just be like always? Suppose when I start school, I come home one day, and she's not here? Maybe if I have to go live with him sometimes, he won't let you come." Clifford raised his head, startled at the thought. "He didn't really want you in the beginning. Did you know that?" He lay down again and hugged her tighter. "But don't worry, Kola. I won't go without you. Never. We'll go away somewhere. Just the two of us. So we can always be together. And I'll take care of you. Forever and ever."

Kola's thick fur muffled his sobs, her whimpers harmonizing with his.

Chapter 78

Every day, 9,000 healthy dogs and cats are put to death. A great reduction from the 45,000 it was thirty years ago. Estimates are that eight to ten million dogs are destroyed annually, three to five million cats. Less than ten percent of the dogs get adopted, five percent of the cats:

- *9,000 killed every day, three-and-a-quarter million every year*
- *500 million dollars, in private and public funds, is spent on animal control*
- *But nobody has an accurate record of the number of killings*
- *9,000 killed every day*

Animal Care & Control in New York City is only one of almost 14,000 shelters in the country. It gets around 30,000 animals a year. Just about half are adopted. The other half are destroyed.

9,000 are killed every day.

The cursor throbbed on the screen. It seemed to beat faster, as if in a frenzy of perverted excitement, keeping in time to the bile-filled balloon floating up and down Laurie's esophagus.

Chapter 79

Louise shoved the night table closer to her bed to make more room on the floor. She hated to exercise. Walking was one thing but now that she stopped doing it every morning because of the heat, she was afraid she'd get lazy and her body soft if she didn't do something. It was difficult with Honda standing over her, poking his face between her up-and-down strokes, wanting her to stop or make him part of the game.

"And four and five." She raised and lowered her legs, grunting between the numbers. "So what do you want from him?" she asked herself, in response to her decision not to see Ken so much because it was getting serious. "Here you are, like everyone else, on the lookout for a guy you can have a future with. You find a perfectly sensible man you really might make it with. And what do you want to do? Give him up. Fourteen, fifteen. Because you like him. I ask you, girl, are you crazy? Nineteen, twenty." She turned on her side, reaching her right toe to her outstretched left arm. "So you're afraid to get hurt. Why do you think you're going to get hurt? Six, seven. Because, sooner or later, he'll dump you. Why will he dump you? Who knows? So, suppose he does? What's the worst that could happen? You'll be upset. But you'll be upset if you stop seeing him now. So why not enjoy him as long as you can and get upset later? Eleven, twelve. Suppose he doesn't dump you? So? So what? So it will go on. Maybe even marriage and the whole bit. Naw, that's not your thing. Then he'll be the one to get hurt, not you. But you don't want to hurt him. Sixteen. Miss Wonderful, how thoughtful of you. Trying to save him the pain of your leaving him. Twenty!"

She switched sides and rolled over Honda, who had quietly crawled behind her to watch the strange ritual. She screamed, "Hey, you wanna get flattened out, dopey?" Then she hugged him. "Huh? What do you think? Should we keep him? Oh, why am I asking you. If it were up to you, he'd move in tomorrow, wouldn't he?" She scratched the inside of his ear, watching him luxuriate in the sensation from her perch on her elbow. "If only we could find something wrong with him. Besides his long nose. And being so skinny. I don't know any men like that, do you? Maybe he's got his last girlfriend's body buried in the backyard or packed in his trunk. Maybe he's another Norman Bates, and he's got his mother's skeleton all dressed up, sitting in the attic. Or stuffed in a closet." She dropped her voice an octave to imitate Ken Hollis, saying, "Hello. Mom. Look, I've brought you a visitor. Come meet Louise." Then she squeaked his little old mother's reply: "Okay, dear, bring her up to see me."

When Honda started barking at her weird voices, she said, "All right, all right, scaredy-cat. I'll go back to just being me. You know—that's it, Honda. I'm not used to being me. Except with you."

She collapsed flat on her back to think about this revelation. She was always so busy trying to be funny or trying to act like she didn't care that she wasn't used to not doing anything. Not trying. Just being. She curled the fur from the thickness of the dog's neck halfway round her finger. "Suppose I'm not afraid of getting hurt. Maybe what I'm afraid of is that when he sees the real me, he won't want me anymore."

Chapter 80

The old Yellow Pages and White Pages for Manhattan each stood four and seven-eighths inches high and formed the pedestal for Rosa's files. She had to move eight shoe boxes of papers, receipts, and bank statements off the top before she could get them out of the hall closet.

After backing out of the closet on her knees, she smoothed the top of her hair where the plastic bags over her winter clothes had brushed her head and then bent again to pick up the Classified. It weighed five pounds, two ounces. As Rosa carried it into the kitchen and hefted it onto the table, she tried to remember how thin the entire phone directory for her hometown had been. 'Course, in those days, how many people in the Italian countryside even had phones? And now, the Yellow Pages—or YP, as they called it—was not even half the size, so she had thrown it out.

She put on her glasses and unconsciously slid them down on her nose so she could peer over the top of them. Where did she put his card? Why didn't she leave it next to the phone? Finally, she recognized the long listing for Photography under "Equipment & Supplies—Retail."

"If I let my fingers do the walking more often, I be crippled by now," she mumbled as she glanced at the ads for the section. Nothing seemed familiar. Anyway, it was a small place; he probably wouldn't have a big ad. Why hadn't she written it down as soon as he told her? Or put the card in her little leather address book?

She started at the beginning, pushed her glasses up so she could see through the lenses, and went down the list. Damn, it was a weird name; why couldn't she remember? Rosa turned the page angrily, almost pulling it out of the binding. Of course the book was old, and he didn't have the store when it came out. But it had been another camera store, she felt sure. She went to the top again and used a pencil point to guide her eyes down the addresses. She read "461 W. 72" and looked to the left at the name. Clear Shot Camera. That wasn't it, but the address seemed right. *The F-Stop. That's it!* Now it came back to her. When he had told her the name of his shop, she roared and said, "I cannot believe you tella everybody off. You use the 'f-word' in your store. Good; good for you."

He had laughed and explained that the "F" had something to do with light and openings and lenses…things she didn't understand. It was a good thing she remembered.

"Hey, bambina, we find Sabrina's daddy. He help us get a Brownie!"

Chapter 81

The neckline of her dress narrowed to a V, deepening the cleft between her breasts. It would not have been so alluring if it weren't so inconsistent with the very plain style and simple print of the cotton outfit. Or the plain, simple prettiness of her face. It was the surprise that was appealing—lustful naiveté. Jessica turned slightly, knowing the candlelight flickering on her chest would be even more beguiling. Yet why would she want to seduce him?

It was a date, but it wasn't a date. How could desire build up for a man she had listened to gargling every night before he came to bed? Listened to him passing wind that traveled like a muffled echo from his side of the mattress to hers; listened to his coughing mucous out of his throat every morning and cracking his knuckles in front of the TV? Of course she couldn't have been much of a bargain either over the past fifteen years—the periods when she wore her hair very long and slept in rollers; when her skin would break out every month and she'd paste brown gobs of Clearasil on her pimples. Then there was the afternoon he came home early and walked in on her douching. God, he must have been turned off a million times too.

"It's just that I've been unhappy for a long time." Lenny's words squirmed out of his mouth.

"I know you have," Jessica responded, "but I have too."

"It's not the same."

"Oh? Why?"

"Because you're his *mother*."

"Yes, but you're his father."

"It's different, Jess. It's like…like you're an animal when it comes—"

"An animal?"

"Lemme finish. I mean a jungle animal, doing anything to protect her young. I meant it nice. Like you'd do anything, lay down your life. That's the way it is with mothers. Your devotion was—I don't know—fulfilling to you. It was like having a cause or a career."

"That's what you think? That I got all my satisfaction from having a handicapped child?" Jessica's voice screeched. She glanced at the next table, defying the couple sitting there to listen. They ignored her, but she moved the candle away from the center of the table so she could lean over anyway. Lenny automatically bent his head toward her. "You think I *enjoyed* it?" Her whisper was like a hiss.

"No, no. Don't be ridiculous. I don't mean that. It's like he was yours. I was just an outsider. Taking care of him kept you busy. No, I don't mean it was fulfilling, maybe just filling. It occupied you. Your life revolved around him. I think I…I don't know what I think."

"C'mon, tell me. It's about time you opened up and said. I thought that was the whole point of this." Jessica motioned to their drinks, reminding him that he had suggested the cocktails—to talk. "You're finally getting it off your chest. Don't stop now."

"Okay. What I was going to say, what just came to my mind was that, well, that I felt left out. That's right—left out. Like I wasn't part of my own family. I was a bystander." Saying it aloud, finally, voicing it, made him acknowledge it.

His declaration unlocked all the thoughts he could not think before, the feelings he dared not feel. He sniveled as he revealed them to his wife and to himself.

Jessica was relieved by his outburst, at his trying, as Dr. Kravitz would say, to be in touch with himself. She was also angry at him, at his self-pity—a luxury she could never afford. Then, as she listened to him struggling with his emotions, an incredible tenderness softened her. She reached for his hand and held it; it pulled her heart. Maybe it was sexy to know somebody so well. To be witness to all the worst in a person you've been with for a long time.

"You didn't include me," Lenny went on. "It was you and Clifford. You taking Clifford to this doctor; you trying a new medicine on Clifford or Dr. Kravitz suggesting different therapy for Clifford; you deciding to do this or that for Clifford…put him in a school, take him out of the school, change doctors, get a dog. And what was I? I was only good to work and bring home the money to pay for it. I missed having a son I could do things with, take to a ballgame now and then, have a pizza with while you were cleaning house. Oh, what the hell difference does it make now? What I'm saying is you wanted to be the one in charge of what happened to Clifford, to us."

"Well, you didn't participate, so I had to do it myself. Don't you realize how immature you're being? You resent that your son isn't normal enough to be pals with, to show off to the guys. I can understand that you were jealous—"

"What? Oh, come on."

"Yes, jealous. That's what you're really saying. I spent all my time with Clifford and didn't save any for you. You're right about that. Maybe I was over-zealous. I was disappointed too, you know, that he wasn't what I wanted. Oh, God, forgive me for saying that. He was what I wanted, but maybe not what I expected."

"You never asked me. You made the decisions and then told me about them. You never wanted my opinion, never asked for it. You never gave me any responsibility in his life, in our lives."

"Don't you see? Responsibility wasn't—isn't—mine to give you. To dole out. It's something you have to have on your own. It's like freedom, Len. You have it or you don't have it. You can't ask somebody for it. It's not somebody else's to give you. It's within you."

"How'd you know that was going to be next, Jess?"

"What?"

"Asking you for my freedom."

Chapter 82

That summer replacement show was stupid, Laurie thought as she clicked the television off. She brought her laptop to the couch, folded her legs under her, and scrolled through her e-mails. After deleting the junk ones, there were just a few from e-pals. Funny how that worked. People from your past who you really wouldn't want to talk to on the phone or see in person became important enough to trade niceties with and have a digital conversation with. At least it was more personal than Facebook and having the whole Eastern Seaboard know your business.

On an impulse, she went to the site. She wanted to scream, *"Hey, don't you know the horrible things going on out there? Don't you know how animals are suffering? Don't you care about helping them? Can't you try to do something about cruelty?"* That's what she wanted to write, but instead, on an impulse, she typed in "Hey, guys, did you know 9,000 healthy dogs and cats are put to sleep every day?"

Chapter 83

Elena's toes touched the treetops. Her legs tapered to points as she stretched her feet straighter, reaching for the branches. They sliced through the air with a hum, engulfing her in the wind she created. Upside down, the sun, the leaves, the building spires streaked across the expanse of sky in a blur. Her legs thrust down, abruptly changing direction, like a rudder turning suddenly, skidding on the water. She was drowning in the dizzy froth. She screamed.

She relaxed her legs and as her speed slowed, the metal web of monkey bars, the silver chute, toddlers in the sandbox, and the slats of wooden benches converged on her, following her in reverse. Nausea surged in her chest. She came to a stop, slightly tilted in her seat. "Did you see how high I went? That was the highest I ever went…the highest anybody ever went," Elena said excitedly.

"Yes, you were pretty high. Now start me." Elena's friend Diana held the chains of Elena's swing steady.

"You can do it yourself. I did."

"No, I need a good push. Come on, you promised."

"I don't feel like it," Elena said. "Let's go back."

"That's not fair. You went for a long time."

"I did, didn't I? Can you believe how high I got?"

"C'mon, please," Diana whined, unimpressed.

"Okay, I'll give you a push, but then let's go back to my house. This is baby stuff."

"There's nothing to do," Diana insisted. "You get any new clothes for Isabelle?"

"No." Elena stood up and held the swing from behind. "Get on if you want me to push." When Diana climbed on the swing, Elena walked backwards as far as she could, pulling the swing with her. "There's things we could do. Like dress up, or we could play on the Xbox or something."

"What's Xbox?" Diana asked.

"It's a TV game thing. I'll show you. My brother got it." Elena pushed and then let go, raising her hands higher, ready to push again when Diana swung back to her. "It's fun."

"Your brother lets you use it?" Diana's voice trailed off as she gained momentum.

"No, not really. But it's okay. He won't know."

"Harder, harder. What about your señora?"

"Oh, Señora Sanchez doesn't pay attention. She does whatever I say."

"What?" Diana shrieked.

"Never mind. When you come down, that's what we'll do." Elena's words rose and fell to the tempo of her friend's swinging.

"Push me harder—harder!"

Their happy squeals filled the playground.

Chapter 84

"Ready, little girl?" Sabrina's tail was so short it was hardly noticeable under her long fur, but there was no mistaking her answer to Jason's question as her backside swayed with its vigorous wagging.

"Don't you think you're overreacting a little?"

Jason followed the sound of Chris's voice to the open bathroom door and told his reflection, "I'm not taking any chances. Better safe than sorry."

"That sounds like one of your AIDS group's slogans," Chris said.

"As an editor, don't you think it's a bit trite?"

"To say the least." Chris twisted his mouth to the side, stretching his skin taut. He made short, scratchy strokes down his cheek with the razor.

"I'd worry all day. This way, she's right there, where I can see her. Besides, she's not at all in the way. And since your stakeout didn't work—"

"I wasn't even thinking about that," Chris insisted. He held the razor under the faucet, shook the water off, and spoke to Jason through the mirror. "You're probably confusing her. She's used to being home. After all, the store is a strange place to her."

"Wrong. She knows it's mine. Everything there must smell of me. She made herself right at home after the first day. She doesn't even bother getting up anymore every time the door opens and someone comes in."

"Probably because it's too hard for her to get up with her arthritis."

"Oh, come on, she's still young. Everybody has a little arthritis. She's only seven. In dog years, she's even younger than I am."

"All I'm saying is that you're changing her whole routine. She'll get used to it, having company all day long. Then, at some point, you'll stop taking her every day, and she'll be miserable staying alone in the apartment."

"You're making a big to-do. She's safer with me. I feel safer."

"Well, if it's safety you're thinking about"—Chris examined up close a nick he'd made with the razor—"it seems to me that nobody can actually get in here. But anybody can walk into the store and hold you up or threaten you."

"Well, I'm sorry. I want her with me." Jason went into the foyer, picked up his keys, and bent to clip the leash onto Sabrina's collar. "C'mon. Daddy's gonna be late."

"Je-sus," Chris muttered.

"You're forgetting one thing!" Jason yelled down the hallway before he stormed out. "She's *my* dog." On the other side of the door, he added quietly, "And it's my life, goddammit."

Chapter 85

Ken blackened the rules on his yellow pad and used a ruler to draw vertical lines, making a chart. He inserted a few numbers and then doodled a stick flower in the margin, turning the petals into ears, adding a body and a tail. He still couldn't believe the figures. There must be an error.

Bernie had agreed with him when Ken called him from the lobby of One Police Plaza. Now, Ken replayed the morning's conversation in his head while he filled a crude ceramic mug with his potent brew.

"You musta read it wrong," Bernie had said.

"No, I looked it up twice. In the stats. And then in the Crime Comparison Report."

"It doesn't seem possible."

"That's what it said. A seventy percent increase in animals stolen in the country every year. But nobody has the exact number. How come we don't hear about them? They don't even make the papers."

"Eh." Bernie had seemed to shrug through the phone. "Penny-ante stuff. They sell 'em for twenty, twenty-five bucks to laboratories, research centers. Sometimes the owners are lucky. They post little signs in the neighborhood and offer a reward. If the guy can make more returning the dog before he sells it, he does."

"But Christ, what's worse? They use 'em as bait to train fighting dogs. Or sell them to puppy mills to be breeders. If they look like pedigreeds—"

"I didn't realize it was such a big business," Bernie had said. "You sure?"

"Must be. The records don't lie. Hell, the records don't exist. They don't even have a handle on the ones that are reported. What about all the ones that *weren't* reported? You know what's so terrible about it? It's, like, the six million dead. The number is too big. You can't fathom it. Or think of them as six million individual lives. It's incomprehensible. We're talking here about thousands of broken hearts. People looking for their pets, not knowing their fate. Little children crying for their dogs."

"C'mon, in a city this size, with the crime rate we have, who you think's gonna worry about some kid missing his dog?"

"That's one thing. Stealing it to sell it, as if it's a gold chain or a hubcap or a car radio. But the old lady thing, that's different."

"Why?"

"Taking it for ransom," Ken had explained. "They play on a person's grief. Especially an old one."

"Aw, buddy, sure. But there's not much you can do about it, so don't get an ulcer over it."

"I'll only get an ulcer if I *don't* do anything about it."

Chapter 86

It was 7:25 when Laurie got home. "Everybody alive?" She tentatively opened the bathroom door where she had locked up Megabyte to separate her new boarder from the other two. An orange flurry streaked past her. She went inside and sat on the edge of the bed, untied her sneakers, threw her socks into the corner, and stroked Oscar absentmindedly. She leaned back on her elbows, stretched her legs off the mattress, and flexed her ankles. She was exhausted and weak from the heat. Felix seemed to fall out of the ceiling, he pounced on her leg with such force. "And where have you been hiding, love?" She wiggled her toes, teasing him as he walked down her shin to swipe at them. He dug into her skin like a tiger clutching a tree limb. Then Megabyte came to the doorway and Felix hissed angrily at her—and at Laurie for bringing the intruder home. He crouched menacingly.

She took off her dress and then hurled her bra after her socks. "Ooh, that feels good." She raised her breasts and patted the dampness where the stiff underwire had confined her. She changed into a long T-shirt. "Who's hungry?" She walked into the kitchen, barefoot, and poured herself a glass of Malbec from the bottle she had left standing on the counter. Felix slithered against her, the caress thrusting his back to a peak. He meowed loudly. Laurie liked to believe he was showing his contentment and affection, but she knew better—he was whining his impatience because she was taking so long with his dinner. She mixed some canned food, disguised as tuna fish, into the healthy brand.

She made a face as she took a sip of the wine. She swished it around her mouth before forcing it down, the bitterness stinging her tongue and cheeks. "Yuck." She shook her head. "Too hot to leave out in this weather."

The three plastic bowls clattered on the linoleum when she put them down on the floor. Laurie went into the living room, relieved that there'd be no fighting for a while, at least until they finished dinner. She struggled with the window latch and then pushed the rough frame up, holding her hand in front of it to test for a breeze. She stretched out on the couch with the mail. *What a life. I must be doing something wrong,* she thought absently. She fell fast asleep.

The ripples of the East River vibrated with silver spangles where the sun touched the water. The background din of rubber chafing concrete and engines droning under hoods grew loud as the thin but steady stream of cars on the FDR Drive seemed to rush toward them as they jogged along the promenade.

"I gotta stop for a minute." Ken dropped onto the bench and wiped his face with a handkerchief. Perspiration glued little commas of hair to his temples. "Whew, you're gonna kill me."

"Uh-uh." Louise faced him, jogging in place. "Just the opposite. I'm gonna save your life. It's good for you."

"What is? Getting thrown out of bed at the crack of dawn and then working up a sweat? Not to mention an appetite?"

"You're lucky I let you sleep so late. It's 6:30 already!" Louise laughed between pants. "By the way, I hope the noise didn't keep you up last night."

"That's not what kept me up," he said with a smirk. "What noise?"

"Just the sounds of the city. That sometimes happens. People who come in once in a while are not used to the traffic, talking on the street, sirens. It was like that when I first moved here."

"You don't say?" he teased.

"Took some getting used to. Then, the first time I went back home after that, I couldn't sleep because of the quiet."

"I didn't mind it at all. It was nice staying in, nice not having to travel to get here this morning." Ken reached for her hand. She hesitated because it was clammy with sweat. She wiped it on her spandex pants and then gave it to him. "And it was nice spending the night with you." His voice turned gravelly as he put his arms around her waist to pull her closer to the bench. He let his head rest on her chest for an instant. The softness of her breast against his cheek jerked a nerve in his groin. He jumped up. "Now that I have my second wind, you're in trouble, lady," he said and sprinted down the walkway.

"Why you can't take a ride? I pay the bus." Rosa rested the broom on a parked car so she could use her hands to express her exasperation with Eileen.

"I told you. It's not that I don't want to keep you company. I hate leaving him. And if I did go, I'd pay my own way."

"You can't stay locked up with him forever."

"No, no, I'm too afraid."

"They not going to bother you again."

"How do you know?"

"It wouldn't make sense, getting you mad. Maybe you go to the police."

Eileen looked around to make sure no one was listening and lowered her voice to a husky whisper. "But they know I paid once. They could think I'd pay again."

"No, they probably think you have no more money. They try somebody else first. It would do you good. Then we could go out for lunch. Wouldn't that be nice?"

"Yes, it would. But I would be too nervous to eat. I'd be thinking all the time, suppose something happens to him because I went out? If I came home, and he was gone, or hurt, oh God, I'd kill myself. Honest, I would. I'd never forgive myself for going out. No, I'm too nervous."

"Ah, I think, I plan how we make this a good day. We go to the West Side. We buy a camera. We coulda take a walk in the park, maybe. Then eat in a restaurant." Rosa's disappointment was obvious.

"Don't be angry. I just don't want to let him out of my sight."

"What happen if you have to go someplace and you can't take him?"

"Like where?"

"I don't know. Maybe the doctor."

"Why, then, I guess I'd just ask you to come over and babysit. Yes, that's what I'd do. Would you?"

"Who knows? I may not even be alive next week."

"Well, maybe I won't be either. But if you were alive, would you?"

"Maybe."

"See, you *are* angry that I won't go."

"No, no. I told you, I'm not angry. Maybe sorry that you so scared. It's a disappointment, that's all. And yes, I would do it."

"I knew you would. You know what? I'd never ask anybody else. 'Cause I wouldn't trust anybody else with him. Just you."

"*Grazie.* I wouldn't ask anyone else either. Only you."

"Good. I tell you—let's have lunch anyway. I'll make a cool salad, maybe tuna or salmon, and you come up. Okay? You can go to the West Side another day."

"Ah, but I need the camera."

"Why do you need it today?"

"You know."

"Come on. I'm going to make lunch. You can start being a detective tomorrow."

Pets are a 58-billion-dollar industry. Laurie shook her head at the staggering amounts spent yearly by those who love their pets:

$21.6 billion on food

$10,000,000 on dog apparel

$920,000,000 on animal-health products

$418,000,000 on grooming and boarding

$14.4 billion on veterinarians

$242,700,000 on medicine

It's estimated that 100,000,000 animals die in laboratories every year worldwide, 20,000,000 in the United States. There are 1,200 registered research facilities—government and commercial ones—in hospitals and universities. Nobody knows the number of unregistered facilities. Three animals die every second, 900 every five minutes. Horribly. Dogs, cats, primates, rabbits, guinea pigs, fish, birds.

Laurie squeezed her eyes shut to block out the images of dogs being cut open without anesthesia, their vocal cords cut so they can't bark or cry. But the pictures scrolled around her insides, icy fingers clenching her colon.

Kola rested her head on her two large front paws and without moving, she stretched her eyes to follow Clifford. She watched him roll his old jeans and stuff them into the shopping bag. Socks. His windbreaker. Without understanding what it was, she was saddened by his sadness. A sense of gloom hovered over them both, like the darkness of clouds heavy with rain. The anxiety of waiting for the thunderstorm to explode made her uneasy.

Kola lifted her head and stared at the bag as she saw her knotted rawhide bone disappear inside it.

THREE

LABOR DAY

Chapter 87

"You sure you want to?" Chris's tone intimated he didn't really think so.

"Yeah, I'm sure," Jason answered in between his rhythmic licking of envelopes after he folded and stuffed them with the meeting announcements. "I'm nervous, but I'm excited about it."

"Why don't you use a sponge before you cut yourself?"

"Nah, saliva's better. And faster."

"How do you think they'll react?"

"Who knows? But don't you think it's about time I did it, actually told my folks?"

"I guess. But I'm scared."

"What are *you* scared of? It won't matter. Worst that can happen is they never want to see you again."

"I'm scared for you." Christopher walked up behind the desk and bent to wrap himself around Jason. "I just don't want you to be disappointed."

Jason paused in his routine to embrace the arms twisted across his chest. He had always *felt* smaller than Christopher, wanted to be smaller. But now, sitting down, he pressed his head back, his thick salt-and-pepper waves leaning on Chris's midriff, and stretched to his full emotional height. "I won't be disappointed. I just want them to love you, because I do."

Christopher rocked him in an affectionate hug and then broke away. He came back from the kitchen with two beers and held an ice-cold glass against Jason's bare back before setting it down on the desk for him. Jason bit off some of the head. Licking his foamy mustache, he spun around on his chair, his feet lifting off the floor. "Whee, I'm a free man, a free man who has finally grown up," he sang.

Christopher laughed out loud. "What a great caption!"

"For what?"

"For the picture."

"What picture?"

"The one of you I'm going to take right now with my phone… you, personifying maturity, with the milky mustache, legs in the air, whirling in a chair."

Sabrina ran to Christopher and from where she sat in the secure shadow between his legs, she howled at Jason.

"See?" Chris said. "You're even scaring the hell out of her."

"C'mere, girl, it's okay. C'mon." Jason stopped the chair and slapped his thighs. She made a running leap into his lap, licking his face and crying with relief that he was still the same master.

"Seriously, when are you going to tell them?" Chris asked.

"I don't know. I haven't planned it out that carefully yet. I think I have to play it by ear. I want to wait until we get there, though, so I can do it in person. Maybe introduce you to them, let you charm them first."

"Jase, your parents are old. You're going out to your sister's alone when they first arrive. That's when you should break it to them gently. When it's just a few family. Then, by the time Labor Day rolls around, it won't be such a shock. They'll have a little while to get used to the idea."

"Nah. They'll be nervous from the plane trip. They have to get organized and unpacked, and all my sisters' kids will be coming over to visit them. They haven't even seen their first great-grandchild yet. It will be too hectic. I figured by the time we have the party, they'll be relaxed. And with the excitement of seeing everyone, and opening their presents, and the barbecue, they wouldn't dare cause a scene. Especially in front of company."

"There will be other people there too, besides family, won't there? I mean, I'm not going to be the only outsider, am I?"

"Knowing my sister, she probably invited the world. After all, it's not every day you can celebrate your parents' sixty-second anniversary."

"Jason, at their age, it just might be better to talk to them privately. I mean, I'd go with you when you first go out to see them. I could wait in another room or something until you tell them. Give them a chance to adjust before throwing it in their faces."

"Hey, what's going on here? You're the one who always thought I was being dishonest by not telling them. You're the one who has urged me for the past four years—ever since we've been together—to tell my family. Convinced me that I'm my own person, and they'll accept me, whoever I am. Whatever I am. Now…now that I finally feel comfortable about it—no, not comfortable—anxious to bare my soul, to share this with my mother and father, now you're the one who's hesitating. Christopher Barrett, you're a big talker."

"Uh-uh. It's just that you're so optimistic about how they're going to accept me as your lover, for Chrissake, and I don't think it's going to be so easy. They might be so horrified…Jesus, Jason, just think what it'll do to them, finding out that their son, who for fifty-four years they thought they knew, is gay! They might go crazy. Or have a heart attack!"

"C'mon. This is the twenty-first century, not the Dark Ages. They're pretty with-it people."

"I hope so. I wouldn't want to be the cause of ruining the big Labor Day weekend for everybody, not to mention the anniversary celebration."

"Yeah? Are you sure that's it?"

Chris spun around on his way to the kitchen for another beer. "What'dya mean?"

"Maybe you're afraid of bringing it all back."

"Bringing what back?"

"Your own hurt."

"What are you talking about?"

"Isn't that what happened with your folks?" Jason asked gently. "Isn't that why you never see them, why you practically never hear from them? Why you never talk about them?"

"Come on, where'd you get that idea?"

"Oh, shit, look." Jason took his finger out of his mouth, dripping with blood.

"What happened?"

"You were right. I got a paper cut."

"Lemme see." Christopher walked toward him. He cleared his throat and blinked to stop the stinging in his eyes.

Jason stuck his finger out and as Chris came close to examine it, Jason held his arms out to him. Christopher gasped and then fell against him, sobbing.

Chapter 88

Louise speared her salad with a plastic fork and shoved a straw through the lid on her diet soda.

She glanced at her calendar, still open to Friday and the list of calls she hadn't been able to complete. A strand of soggy lettuce clung to her chin as she ripped off the Friday page, folded it in half, and tacked it to her bulletin board where the telephone numbers could nag her.

She couldn't believe it was the second week of August already—summer was almost over. Although she certainly wouldn't think so with the sidewalks steaming from the humidity, and the office freezing from the air conditioning, the grinding of its antiquated machinery grating on both her ears and her nerves.

No, she wouldn't believe it, unless she looked at this season's wardrobe…the tan insoles of her sandals now black from where her feet had stuck to them and the straps raw where the leather had worn—and her two white T-shirts graying, with loose threads at the neck showing where the fine ribbing was starting to split.

Summer might not be officially over for a few weeks yet but, as a state of mind, it was done. The first liberation of short sleeves and bare toes…of waking up when it was light and coming out of the subway at the end of day, thinking it still was day…of scrawny little trees and ivy blossoming over their metal bars…of beaches and barbecues, parks and picnics…of strangers who'd never seen each other stepping onto the street and discovering neighbors…of the country coming to the city… of freedom… and love—all of it was done.

Louise threw away the remnants of her lunch, blotted the oil on her chin, wiped the desk with the same napkin, and moved her pile of folders back to the center. As she went through the top case file, she suddenly felt the sadness of an ending. She hoped it was the ending only of summer.

Chapter 89

The crosstown bus jerked to a stop, and even though Rosa leaned against the back door with all her weight, she couldn't open it. "Getting off! Getting off!" she yelled to the driver frantically. A teenage boy reached over her shoulders and touched the yellow strips to unlock the automatic doors. "*Grazie*," she muttered as she stepped off the bus. She walked back to the corner to get the downtown bus, with the transfer almost shredded in her fist. She wouldn't have needed it if she had one of those cards to pay the fare. But she'd never figure out how to use it anyway. Just as easy to get a roll of quarters every time she went to the bank.

She had used the slow, fourteen-block ride to 72nd Street to practice the phone call she was going to make to the Transit Authority about the awful doors on the busses and having to be Arnold Schwarzen-somebody to open them. Now, still rehearsing her complaint—her lips moved in silent dialogue—she walked right past Jason's shop. When she realized she had missed it, she backtracked and finally burst into the store, breathlessly calling, "Allo, allo?"

Suzanne looked up from sorting the morning's delivery of developed pictures. Before she had a chance to even look confused, Sabrina came to the doorway of the back room, her head tilted, her right ear poking straight up. She stood, poised in anticipation, like a marcher waiting for the drum roll to start the parade. "Ah, there's the little girl; there she is." A big smile was in Rosa's voice. The dog bounded around the far counter and frantically hopped across the floor, her front legs jumping together, her hind legs together.

Rosa bent as far down as she could, her arms out, delighted at the ecstatic yelps. "Come on, you silly bunny, come on to Mama," she urged her. She caught her on her last long spring and held her tight.

Jason strode out, hugging his upper arms in paternal pleasure. "God, somebody would think you were killing her," he laughed.

"If this is the noise she make when she happy, can you imagine if she sad?" Rosa rocked the little Yorkie, who weighed even less than Princess, against her cushioned chest and kissed her. Each smacking of Rosa's lips on her face pulled a shrill whine of unbearable pleasure from Sabrina.

"Nice to see you here, Ms.…."

"Bassetti. Rosa Bassetti. Just Rosa."

"Rosa, right! What brings you to this side of town?"

"You. I mean, you store. I come for a camera."

"Ah, you must be getting a visit from the grandchildren or something."

"Uh-uh. Don't have any." Rosa looked out of the sides of her eyes, exaggerating the need for secrecy.

"Tell you what," Jason said, humoring her. "Got some time?"

She nodded.

"Come in the back. I have a hot plate with a kettle. We'll sit down and have a cup o' tea, and you can tell me all about it."

"Good." Rosa followed Jason behind the counter to the back room. "It will give me a chance to rest. Wait 'til you hear about my bus ride over here." She nuzzled Sabrina. "What a nice surprise she's here with you. You always bring her to work with you?"

"No," Jason answered. Caught up in the conspiratorial mood, he held his finger to his mouth and pointed his eyebrows to Suzanne. "It's a long story. I'll tell you about it when we sit."

Chapter 90

"There are more than three hundred breeds of dog. They come in a wide assortment, from a record two-pound Chihuahua to a three-hundred-pound Mastiff.

"Their occupations range from shepherding farm animals to rescuing victims, to guiding the blind, to fighting wars, to aiding the deaf, to detecting drugs and weapons, to assisting the handicapped, to protecting property, to accepting the mentally handicapped. All in the service of their human owners. All without pay.

"Of the eighty million lucky dogs in this country who have good homes"—Laurie paused a moment and then typed the rest of the sentence in caps—"ABOUT TWO MILLION OF THEM ARE STOLEN EVERY YEAR."

Chapter 91

Lenny stood with one foot off the curb, trying to hail a cab. He wondered if Jessica's call was some kind of ploy to get him to come over. No, it would be pretty stupid, since he'd find out as soon as he got there if it wasn't true. If it was, then it would be the final irony. Just when Clifford was becoming more normal, enjoying his boyhood, he'd get kidnapped.

He pulled back his arm as a truck nearly hit him as it tried to make the intersection before the light changed. No, the irony would be that just when Lenny was beginning to enjoy a son, he'd lose him. Like his wife.

Lenny Marcus was one of those men whose coarse black whiskers start bristling on his cheeks and throat by noon. He knew it made him look unkempt, so he always kept an electric razor in his briefcase and tried to mow his face before going to lunch. A shave was the last thing he'd have time for today, what with Jessica's phone call, having to break his appointment with a client, and cleaning up his desk since he didn't know how long he'd be gone. With the humidity at 88 percent, the sweat trickled down from his scalp, cutting wet swatches through the dark fuzz and leaving white creases across his neck. His straight hair parted in greasy clumps and hung above the scowl of frustration at not being able to find a taxi. He looked angry and sloppy.

And nervous. Another nut case walking around the streets. People moved out of his way as he hurried across 57th Street, resigned to taking the Third Avenue bus, fumbling in his pocket for his MetroCard as he went.

He hadn't taken his house keys to the office with him, so when he got to the apartment, he had to ring the bell. Dr. Michelle Kravitz opened the door. "Hi," she said quietly, standing sideways so he could pass.

"Hi," he mumbled back, furious.

"She's in the bedroom. On the phone."

I'll just be calm, he thought, willing the pulse in his neck to slow. So what if she called her first? So what if he was an outsider? If that was what Jessica wanted, that's what he'd be—a rational, objective outsider who wasn't so emotionally involved that he couldn't sort things out. He stood his briefcase on the floor, threw his suit jacket over the back of the couch, and was about to go to the bedroom when Jessica came out.

"Oh, Lenny," she came to him, obviously relieved to see him. Without thinking, he put his arms out. She came into them spontaneously, curling her body to be enfolded. He held her for a while, patting her back and relishing the comfort of their touching.

He broke the embrace, pushing her away so he could look at her. "Okay, tell me."

She wasn't crying, but she looked so sad. Lines of defeat corrugated her forehead and fanned out from her eyes. "He's just…gone. The Center called. They wanted to know if I picked him up."

"You did bring him this morning?"

"Of course. We got there at 8:30. Then I went to the dentist—I had a 9:30 appointment—and did a few errands. I had just gotten home when they called."

"When? What time?"

"Right before I called you—11:15, 11:30."

"Did they call as soon as they noticed Clifford was gone? Or did they try finding him first?"

"I don't know. Why?"

Lenny shrugged. "I don't know. But maybe it would help to know if he disappeared at 8:45 or 11:00—how much time he had to get away."

"Get away?" Jessica's voice became shrill. "What are you talking about? Somebody must have taken him."

"Where's Kola?"

"What?"

"The dog? Where is she? She didn't come out when I rang. Don't tell me she's gone too?"

Jessica's mouth dropped open, and she turned to run through the apartment, frantically calling out, "Kola, here girl. Come on, Kola" as she peered into rooms and looked under the beds, in back of doors, and behind the shower curtain.

When Dr. Kravitz's eyes met Lenny's, they both recognized the truth and accepted a truce in the hostility between them.

"Oh, my God, I never realized." Jessica clapped her hand over her mouth.

"Let's just sit down and try to figure out how many places he'd be able to get to by himself, okay?" Dr. Kravitz suggested.

"She's right, Jess," Lenny agreed. "We have to just be logical."

Jessica shook her head. "Call 911. Call the police. They have to start looking for Clifford and Kola right away."

"Before we do that," Dr. Kravitz said calmly, "let's work on our list of places so we can give them proper information. And figure out how Clifford got Kola with him."

"Oh, shut up, Michelle," Jessica snapped. "I don't want to hear about the proper information. This is my son you're talking about. Our son. Not an experiment. His life could be in danger, and you want to sit and make a list? Tell her, Lenny."

Lenny pulled Jessica to the couch and put his arm around her shoulder, rocking with her. "It's okay, Jess. Dr. Kravitz is right. We have to be as systematic and thorough as we can be. Otherwise, the police won't be able to help us. Come on, honey; snap out of it," Lenny Marcus said with gentle authority.

He went to the intercom, called the lobby, and spoke with the doorman. He walked back to Jessica and Michelle with a grim expression. "The doorman unlocked the apartment door for Clifford because he said he forgot something. Then he left with Kola."

Chapter 92

"I'm going to send you all the papers to fill out for the Housing Authority," Louise said. "And if you need help with any questions, just call me, and we'll go over them on the phone."

"Ah, but I wish you would come here," Yolanda responded. "I'd love to make dinner for you. I make a mean paella."

"Yolanda, I just can't. I've been so busy, you wouldn't believe."

"But it's been so long since you were here. And the kids would love to see you. Especially Elena. She's always asking when you're gonna come visit, when she can call you."

Louise winced. "I know, I know. Listen, it's just that…that I've been involved in all sorts of things, and I haven't had a second. Personal things. In a few weeks, I'll definitely make a date with you. But we don't want to hold up the application. It would be silly. The waiting list is so long, the sooner you get on it, the sooner they might find something for you."

Yolanda's voice betrayed her disappointment. "When you think that will be? When I'm old and gray?"

"Not that long. Five years. Three, if you're lucky."

"Ay!"

"It won't be so bad. Look, five years will come and go anyway. This way, you'll have something to look forward to. And, who knows? They already broke the ground for a new project going up in the Bronx. It could even be ready by the time you're at the top of the list. Just think:

you might even be the first person to live in it—a brand-new kitchen and bathroom, clean hallways, fresh paint…and best of all, at least three bedrooms.”

“You really think so?”

“Yes.”

“But if it takes so long, Ricky will be out of college already and working, and if we have two incomes, we’ll be making too much money.”

“Yolanda, you’ll still be eligible. Honest.”

“Okay, but I wish you could come.”

“I know. I do too. Listen, here’s what we’ll do. I’ll send the papers. You sit down and fill out all the questions you know how to answer. Then we’ll go over the rest on the phone, and you’ll send them back to me. Then, the first weekend after Labor Day, I promise, I’ll come over. Maybe not for dinner, but I will visit.”

“Okay, okay.”

“And in the meantime, you start putting the extra money Ricky’s giving you someplace safe, so when the city finds you that apartment, you’ll be able to buy some nice things for it. Okay?”

“Sí, sí, señorita.” Yolanda’s playful reply showed her enthusiasm about the future. “I guess I’m pretty lucky, huh? Having you to help me. And having a son like my Ricky. Ricardo Jr. Did you ever hear of a boy giving his mama almost his whole salary?”

“No, you have good children, Yolanda. Just like you. That’s why I’m downloading the application as we speak and putting it in the mail right away. Because I want to help you get out of there.”

Chapter 93

Laurie didn't know what to do about the comments posted on her Wall. Some were stupid, asking why she would be spoiling someone's appetite by saying what she had, but most were sympathetic. She'd been announcing one fact a day—not elaborating, just giving the basic, stomach-turning details. Now there were 143 "likes" on her page. Names she didn't know; "friends" who were friends with a friend. What had she started here? More important, how would it end? Would it help the animals at all? It already helped Laurie because the sickening feeling that invaded her every time she read something about animal misery turned into a hint of excitement. Excitement that she could influence friends, even if they were just Facebook friends, to share her outrage about mistreated animals.

Laurie's spirits were suddenly buoyed, even as she reported that 11.5 million unnecessary tests are performed by the cosmetic and personal-care industry every year in this country. Causing eleven-and-a-half million animals to suffer horribly, until they eventually die. That's when she had a brainstorm. She typed a little heading for today's fact: PET-ICULAR.

Chapter 94

Ken Hollis squirmed in the low couch, waiting for Rosa to come back. He stared at the little dog standing guard outside the bathroom door, trying to protect her mistress from the stranger in the house. As if the frail little thing with the balding back and glazed eyes could do anything. *She probably doesn't even have any teeth*, Ken thought. He heard the toilet flush and then settled back, trying to look comfortable.

It was a funny thing about older people. They seemed to forget that everybody else was busy. That working people had to travel to and fro, had jobs to perform, with pressures and personal chores to take care of. They didn't understand—or didn't want to understand—that not everybody was retired and had nothing to do and unlimited time to do it. His grandparents had been like that, before his grandmother died. Now, his grandfather was bad enough for the two of them—he turned getting out of bed, washing, putting on clothes, making a cup of instant coffee and a slice of white toast into such a major production that by the time he got ready for the day, it was over.

As Rosa scooped up her pathetic Poodle and bounced onto the chair opposite him, Ken felt guilty. He was just antsy because he had a lot of things to tend to today and the last thing he needed was to sit here pretending to be relaxed.

Finding three messages on his cell phone—and running low on his battery listening to them—did not start his afternoon well. Rosa certainly didn't look frantic now, at least not the way she had sounded when he'd called her back.

"So what's the scoop?" Ken asked.

"It's a whole ring of them. She wasn't the only one. It's like a serial-killer thing. They doing it all over. See? I told you it wasn't anybody she knows and…" Her words tumbled out at the same speed as her excitement, amplifying the volume and her accent.

"Whoa, take it easy," Ken interrupted.

Rosa, sitting on the edge of the cushion, held her hand flat over her breast, as if trying to slow down each deep breath. "Okay, okay, I tell you from the beginning. There's this man, used to live around here, but he move away. He's queer. That has nothing to do with the story, I just telling you. Gay, they call it now. I meet him in the park once, and he give me his card, for a camera store, on the West Side it is, and I wanted to buy one so I could help you—you know, in case I see something suspicious. I take a picture and show you. Okay?"

She wanted to make sure he was following her but didn't wait for an answer. "Okay, so he has a dog—that's how I know him, I know everyone who has a dog. Right, bambina?" She automatically stroked the dog lying along the crevice between her thighs. "So I go there finally, and his dog, she's there in the store. And I ask him how come he brings the dog to work. Okay, you got it so far? So he takes me in the back—he has a little room there—and we have a cup of tea, and I play with Sabrina—her name is Sabrina. That's a pretty name, don't you think? Especially for a Yorkie— and he tells me…"

Rosa gulped some air and moved back in the chair, pausing for suspense.

"So what did he tell you?" Ken asked. "Don't leave me hanging now."

"He got the same letter that Eileen Hargan got. Same thing. So it's not just one time, one person, one dog. It's a whole crime wave. I tell him what happen here. He say he's going to send me a copy of the letter so I can show you. He has it at home. Well?"

"Well, well, well." Ken crossed his arms and rocked slightly, digesting the implications of the story. "That really changes things."

"Didn't I tell you?"

"You sure did. This is very interesting…very." Ken stood up and shook out the cramp in his right leg. Then he paced in front of the couch. "Now you'll really have to help me think this out."

"Sure. Let's have some Chianti. We put our glasses together. Then we put our heads together."

Chapter 95

The basement of the Presbyterian church was crowded and noisy with people greeting each other and scraping bridge chairs on the tile floor. Jason tapped his already neat notes into a neater pile on the podium and tried to avoid looking at the large crucifix staring down at him from high on the opposite wall. The only other time in his life he'd been in a church had been for the wedding of his previous boss's daughter and somehow, because the church was filled with flowers and a bride and attendants in pastel dresses, it hadn't seemed so religious. But now, in the stark room below the chapel, with the crosses and paintings of Christ as the only decorations, Jason felt like a foreigner. His mother would probably answer that he'd be a foreigner in a synagogue too, for as often as he'd been in one in the past thirty years. Even so, when he did attend something—a bar mitzvah or a funeral or a wedding—he felt comfortable, on familiar ground. He wished the school was still open and available for community meetings.

When he looked up, his eyes instantly fell on Christopher, finding each other in the mass of faces like emotional magnets. All the times that Chris had asked him to go with him to church and Jason had shrugged off the invitation without explanation now rushed to his thoughts. But Chris's look was so tender and so understanding that Jason wanted to weep. He cleared his throat a few times and called the meeting to order.

After the guest speaker, Bertram Burroughs, the first of the tenants' rights attorneys they would interview over the next two months, finished his lecture on procedures, rights, and options and explained the no-buy pledges that Jason handed out, a noisy question-and-answer period followed. When several arguments erupted, Mr. Burroughs suggested that the tenants settle their disagreements privately and prepare a list of specific topics requiring his legal advice. With a final look at his watch, he snapped his attaché case shut, nodded to Jason, and left.

"Can I have the floor, please? I'd like the floor." Nettie Pedersen's voice reached over the commotion, and her request for permission to speak restored order to the room. "I want to know," she said, enunciating slowly and waiting for the last of the talking to stop, "what we're going to do about people with pets. I don't think we should allow any pets at all in the building." She had to talk louder to override the murmuring that was beginning to grow in volume. "They soil the elevator and the hallways, and pee on our canopy legs, and mess on the sidewalk in front, and we shouldn't allow them at 407 West End Avenue."

"Ah, quiet," a disgusted voice shouted out. But it didn't stop the barrage of comments from other tenants.

"Well, maybe we should have a rule about new people moving in, certainly not people already living here."

"What've you got against animals, lady?"

"She's right. I can hear meowing out in the back courtyard when some people's cats get out. It's very annoying." A young woman stood up so her complaint could be heard over the others.

"Yes, and what about that horrible stain right in the middle of the rug in the lobby? Where some mutt had an accident."

"You can't ask people to get rid of a pet they've had for years."

"Who says? If we're going to plunk down a few hundred thousand dollars to buy our apartments, we're entitled to live the way we want, make any rules we want."

"Please, please, folks." Jason used his pen as a gavel. "Let's simmer down. Please, let's be orderly."

Nettie stood up to point at Jason. "And having a chairman who's the biggest offender doesn't help. How can he be objective when he has a dog? It's not fair. I say let's get rid of the chairman, and his dog!"

Jason silently appealed to Christopher for help. And he wondered just how vicious Ms. Pedersen's self-righteousness was.

Chapter 96

The sun squeezed through the narrow cracks between the wooden planks of the benches, painting white stripes on the ground. The geometric precision was interrupted where they curved over the sleeping bodies in crooked bands. Iridescent bubbles of dew pulsed on the limbs of trees and blades of grass, poised in the glow of dawn in the park.

A scratching of leaves as a gray squirrel raked them with his paw alerted Kola to morning. She crawled flat on her belly from the cramped hideout under the bench. She stood and slowly stretched her shoulders and back and then squatted down and urinated in the dirt.

With the warmth of the dog's body gone, the light chill from the night and the dampness woke Clifford. He struggled out after Kola and hugged himself warm. "Hey, girl," he whispered, bending on his knees and holding out his arms to her. "Sleep good, huh?" They nuzzled. He slid his knapsack out, dented from where it had pillowed his head, and then the beach towel he'd used to cover himself. He packed it away and then walked over to a tree, looked around before opening his fly, and squirted against its corrugated trunk.

He found the dinner roll in the bottom of the bag, broke it in half, and shared it with Kola. "Might be a while before the hot-dog men come to work," he explained. After splashing water from a stone fountain on his face, Clifford filled his cupped hand with water so Kola could drink. Then they walked eastward. He tried not to look at the lumpy hill behind the Hecksher playing fields, littered with bodies of people and their belongings, hanging from the tops of Duane

Reade shopping bags and overflowing shopping carts. But they were all over, strewn on the terrace circling the game building, where later in the day, men would face each other over the chiseled checkerboard tables; wedged in the crevices between large boulders; lying on the old benches (even those mottled with pigeon droppings); and picking their breakfast out of the garbage pails.

The first night, Clifford had been scared of being too far away from people, but he was more scared of getting too close to the dirty, smelly vagrants. He understood they were homeless; news reports had talked about them on TV once. Not like him. He had a home; he just didn't want to go there anymore. He would rather stay by himself. Besides, with Kola here, he wasn't by himself. And wasn't afraid. As soon as the army of orange-vested maintenance men would begin their day's mission of trying to restore the park, the homeless would scatter, mingling with the strollers and sunbathers and joggers and bicyclists and athletes, as well as the sitters, just relaxing on a summer morning.

Clifford walked by the pond, landscaped with overgrown weeds, its water a dark khaki with sludge. A few brave ducks floated by. Clifford looked at the apartment buildings towering behind the trees. He liked to start the day here. The buildings reminded him of his own house. He longed to go home. Sleep in his bed. But he couldn't, because he didn't want to see his mother and father the way they had become. No, he wouldn't go back. He took one more wistful look at the skyline, scalloped with leaves, and then turned into the vast interior of Central Park.

Chapter 97

Laurie was greeted by a soft breeze as she climbed up from the 77th Street station. The early morning air was a refreshing reminder that fall was only a few weeks away. But it was still early. By lunchtime, when she went out to pick up a sandwich or a yogurt to bring back to the office, it would be hazy, hot, and humid, just as the weather report threatened. Some things they got right.

While she stood at the counter waiting for her muffin to be toasted, she looked through the window of the coffee shop at the Upper East Siders on their way downtown. From where she changed from the Flushing line at Grand Central, she sometimes took the express to 86th Street and then walked back to 74th. She was always early, so she didn't have to rush, and she enjoyed the exercise. This morning, she was even half an hour earlier than usual, having gotten up long before her alarm went off.

"Where's my English down?" the counterman shouted into the kitchen as he continued to fill containers of regular coffee.

Laurie could see two torsos through the cut-out in the wall. Two very hairy chests and four furry arms sticking out of white uniforms, already stained with blotches of oil and grease, moved in and out of view. She watched the frame like a marionette stage, amazed at the irony of places like this, keeping the counters looking clean, the bubble domes over the Danish looking spotless, the stainless steel looking polished…and keeping help that always looked greasy.

Laurie walked down Lexington, holding the white bag of breakfast in her left hand. Since she was going against the crowd headed to the subway station, she liked to pretend she lived here in the city and was just walking to her apartment, that she didn't have to travel to it via two subway lines. She hated commuting. If she lived in a real suburb, she wouldn't mind, but Queens was just as much city as Manhattan was, only without the excitement and sophistication. Or convenience. Someday, she dreamed, they'd get married and move to the country, raise a few large dogs, and have a menagerie of animals roaming around. They could keep his apartment in town for those times when they would come in for the theater or an affair or dinner in a special restaurant. Felix and Oscar would hate it, having other animals around. Well, she wouldn't let them spoil her fantasy. She wouldn't worry about them until she had to face the decision. Laurie enjoyed being "Mrs. Pomalee" as she turned down 74th Street and continued to walk east toward York. She unlocked the door to the office and entered, setting her paper bag down on the corner table that held the magazines, and went in the back to turn on the air conditioner. She put all her things on the reception desk and then sat down, breathing hard, trying not to move too much until it cooled off a bit. She took her shoes out of her tote bag and exchanged them for the sneakers she'd been wearing. She unpacked her breakfast, threw away the skimpy, damp napkins, went to the sink in the nearest examining room and pulled two paper towels from the dispenser to use as a placemat.

Just as she crunched into the English muffin, she thought she heard a door upstairs click softly. She stopped in mid-bite, straining to listen. Since Dr. Pomalee's apartment was high on the fourth floor and completely sound-proof, it was impossible to hear anything up there. It sounded almost like it came from her own office, two stories above where she sat now. She went to the foot of the staircase and yelled, "Hello? Anyone there?"

The dogs on the floor beneath her started howling and barking. She couldn't hear anything more, so she shrugged to herself and went back to the desk, where she ate her muffin. She made a mental note to leave a memo for Stacy to straighten out the magazines in the waiting room.

The aluminum foil made a tinny squeak as she crumbled it up. At the same time she thought she felt, more than heard, a muffled creak, like a step on a wooden floorboard covered with carpet. Even though the air conditioner was droning steadily, the temperature hadn't dropped enough to cool off the office. But goose pimples sprouted up and down Laurie's arms.

Chapter 98

Rosa pushed the handle of the leash all the way up her arm to free her hand. She closed her left eye and screwed up her cheeks so tightly that she could hardly see out of the right eye. She took a step back, her mouth open, grimacing in concentration. Her finger finally pressed the camera's button down, and her whole body jumped as the shutter sprang open. "Got it!"

"You better do it again," Hector said, relaxing his smile.

"Why? You look-a great."

"Yes, but I think you had your finger over the lens."

"Oy!" Rosa stretched her hands out to look at them still holding the camera in the same position. "Ay-yi-yi, I did. Okay, again. Move the broom more. I can see the handle. That's it." Her face resumed its distorted expression as she dug the camera into the bridge of her nose and moved it a fraction in each direction. "Okay, ready? I'm gonna snap. Hold still now. Keep smiling."

"Take it already," the super urged, just as Rosa clicked.

"You moved. You shouldn'ta talk."

"That's because you take so damn long. Now I know why them models get so much for posing all day. It's hard work, standing still."

"Oh, stop. If it come out good, I give it to you."

"Okay. Now you mind if I go back to work?" He winked and touched the visor of his mesh cap in salute; then he turned back to the high-rise to finish sweeping.

"Yes, you can go. If you so anxious to work!"

Rosa strolled up 83rd Street, appraising the trees and buildings and pedestrians for their photographic possibilities. She stopped to consider the flower box on the first floor of a brownstone, the pansies brightening up the metal security gates in front of the open window. Out of the corner of her eye, she saw an SUV slow down and double-park. She raised the camera in front of her face and peered over the top of it to watch the Puerto Rican driver get out. He was carrying a large manila envelope. He checked the number of the nearest house and started to walk in Rosa's direction. She slowly aimed the camera at the flower box, stepped back as if to frame the shot but then quickly turned around and snapped the messenger's picture. She picked up Princess, holding her in her left arm while her right hand steadied the camera thumping against her breasts from the end of the strap around her neck. She walked as fast as she could toward First Avenue and only when she turned the corner did she dare to look back to see if the messenger was running after her.

She hid in the doorway of a boutique, pretending to admire the clothes in the window. When she saw the vehicle pass the intersection a few minutes later, she exhaled loudly and went back down her block. "Are we lucky, bambina." She squeezed Princess. "Ah, look, there he is, you boyfriend." Rosa waved to Eileen as she came out and stood on her stoop, checking the street in both directions before going down the steps.

When they met midway, Princess squirmed in Rosa's arms to greet Fibber McGee. She put her gently on the sidewalk, patted the camera, and excitedly told Eileen about the picture she had managed to get.

"But he was probably just an innocent bystander."

"Maybe. But suppose he wasn't? And anyway, who gets envelopes delivered by messenger around here?"

Eileen shrugged. "I don't know."

"As soon as I get the pictures developed, I'll show you. You can see if he looks familiar, if you ever saw him before."

"And if I did?"

"Well, we can go to the police or that nice Mr. Hollis and have real evidence to show them. A face. A possible suspect."

"Well…"

"In the meantime, here—hold this." Rosa took her leash and handed it to Eileen so she could walk to the curb. "I gonna take pictures of the dogs."

"What for?"

"In case…" Rosa didn't finish her thought: in case they end up missing. Instead, she said, "In case we have nothing to do some night. We drink a little vino, we look at the pictures. I show you an old family album. You show me. We get sentimental from the pictures. Good idea, hah?"

Chapter 99

Louise stood in front of the window, spreading her arms out like wings and then clutching her hands together, weaving her fingers tight. When she stretched her arms above her head in luxurious abandonment, her long T-shirt rode up her hips, exposing the cheeks sticking out from the band of her underpants.

Ken was watching her from the dining room table, which was covered with his notes and a pile of half-used legal pads. He'd been trying to write, but he couldn't help looking up again and again to stare at her. He thought she was sexier in her oversized shirt and naked legs, her inner thighs scraping together, her bare feet suctioned to the dusty wood floor, than some women he'd seen in satin baby-dolls and high-heeled pom-pom slippers. "You know, you're beautiful," he said spontaneously to her back, his feelings warming his voice and his insides.

"You're the first guy who ever said that." Louise used her position to sway her torso a few times in mock gyrations. "Cute, maybe. Independent, definitely. Attractive, sometimes. But beautiful? Uh-uh."

"What'd they know?" He came up to her, hugging her from behind, his forearms locked across her chest. "And for that matter, what do you know? Always trying to play yourself down. Minimize your femininity."

She leaned against him, but her weight was rooted to the floor. "No, I don't."

"Yes, you do."

"Don't."

"Do."

"Don't."

"Do." He rocked with her until the game made them both laugh, and in the fun, she finally relaxed her body on his.

Honda stood on his hind legs, yelping, and tried to squeeze between them.

"Okay, okay, I can take a hint, fella. But you'll have to fight me for her." Ken started wrestling with the dog.

"I guess it's women and children to the kitchen," Louise complained good-naturedly.

Ken rolled on the floor with Honda, enjoying the background clatter of dishes, until Louise came back in and swept the books and pads to the end of the table. Ken washed up in the kitchen before he sat down. "He really has sharp teeth," he said, examining the red marks on the back of his hands as he sat down.

"I know. Can you imagine if he didn't *like* you?"

"Not now, Honda. Go lie down," Ken ordered as the dog's muzzle searched for a comfortable spot on his knees.

"He really adores you." Louise watched her dog obediently curl up under the table. "And I adore him," she added, looking at the big eyes staring back at her, his ears twitching as he listened. "He knows we're talking about him."

"I know. Don't forget; I'm a dog person too. This makes me realize how much I miss having one."

"Isn't it sickening that some people could mistreat them, be so cruel to them?"

"Yes, I can't believe what I've been reading. About the torture in the research labs. About the people who run the puppy mills, who manufacture dogs just to sell them to laboratories. Breed them, bring their young into the world only to live in the worst pain and fear and then die. Without ever having a chance to live. Without ever having someone pet them or feed them."

"Yuck. You know what's even worse? Those poor things don't know any better. They don't miss what they never had. But take a pet, take even Honda, having been loved and cared for all his life. If he was stolen and suddenly put into one of those places…hundreds of them dumped into a cage, piled so deep that the ones on the bottom suffocate or get crushed to death, starving, afraid, wondering where his mother—I mean, where I am. God, I get nauseated thinking about it. I would die if something like that ever happened to him." Her voice faded as she disappeared into the kitchen.

"Well, it happens to some pets. And just the threat of it is enough for people like you, who love their dogs, to cough up whatever the dognappers ask for," Ken called in to her. "I wanna show you some of the leaflets I got. You wouldn't believe the pictures."

"No way. I don't want to see. I don't want to know." Louise put the mugs of coffee down and went back in the kitchen, continuing the chatter. "Ever since you told me about that poor old lady, I haven't been sleeping so good, worrying about Honda."

Even though Honda was tired from playing and his eyes were half closed, he struggled to keep them open as he tried to follow the conversation.

"Let's not talk about it anymore," Louise said, bringing in the basket of rolls and bagels. "I don't want to spoil my appetite."

"Okay. Let's change the subject. See, I told you—you don't have to worry about meeting my parents on Labor Day. I'll tell 'em you make breakfast just like a Jewish mother. But you have to learn one thing."

"What's that?"

"Never do that in front of them." He pointed to her plate. "Do what?"

"Put American cheese on a bagel."

Chapter 100

Clifford's image gaped at Jessica from posters on the sidewalk. The photograph was muddy, the enlargement too grainy. The space where the head should have sloped down to the neck was filled in, the contour of the face lost in dark blotches of toner. The wavy blond hair was inked into a black hat sliding onto the forehead. Crude shadings formed a barely recognizable nose and chin. Lids and lashes were washed away, yet the eyes that stared from the middle of the hazy features were haunting. The slightly open mouth was bisected by the thin twine tied around a bundle of printed posters, as if gagging a scream.

Jessica tore off a long piece of masking tape, slid a poster from under the twine, and taped it to the lamppost. She pushed her supplies ahead of her to the next pole, which was a NO PARKING sign. She looked across the street and noticed that Lenny was already at the corner, taping a poster to the traffic light. He crossed over and started on her side, working back until they met each other.

"Which way should we go—68th or 70th?" Jessica asked, looking around her, trying to decide.

"Doesn't matter. Let's go down and then we can stop over there and have a cup of coffee first." Lenny pointed to the luncheonette sign.

"Let's not waste time."

"In this heat, preventing a heart attack or sunstroke is not a waste of time. I have to sit inside for a few minutes. Cool off."

She reluctantly put everything into her shopping cart. "Okay."

As soon as they spread out in a booth at the luncheonette, Lenny blotted his face and the back of his neck with a paper napkin. "Whew, it's hot out there."

Jessica didn't answer. She took a poster out of her tote bag and stood it at the end of the table, propped against the wall. "It doesn't even look like him. I hate it."

Lenny adjusted the picture slightly so he could face it directly. "Yes, it does. Granted, it's a lousy copy, but that's how he looks."

"No, he doesn't."

"You just still see him the way he used to be. With that emptiness. The vacant stare."

"No. It's just that…I don't know…that expression on his face is…"

"What?"

Jessica shrugged. "Pathetic? Pitiful. Something. Something I don't like."

"Nah, not pathetic. Sad, maybe. Yeah, the little guy looks sad. Lonely."

"But that can't be. He's not sad, and he's not lonely. That's why I hate it."

Lenny didn't even glance at the waitress when he said, "I'll have fried eggs, up, and bacon and rye toast. And an iced coffee." He looked at Jessica. "You?"

Jessica didn't speak.

"Give her the same—no, wait, how about an order of French toast? French toast and another iced coffee. Thanks."

He nodded to the waitress, who scribbled on her pad and then waved her pencil at Lenny in acknowledgment. And sympathy.

"We should've taken one of him with Kola," Jessica said. "Somebody might recognize the dog."

"Yes, too bad we don't have one like that," Lenny agreed. "But it's okay. The sign says he might be with a dog. And it's a good description of her."

The coffees came, and Jessica occupied herself with stirring hers with the straw. "Maybe we should have looked for a better picture. Full view. To give a feeling of his size."

"There was no time, Jess. You know that. The police needed it right away. Besides, it says he's eleven years old. How big could he be? People can tell. If they see him, they'll know it's him."

"Oh, my baby." Jessica rummaged in her pocketbook as the tears started flowing. When she couldn't find a tissue, she pulled a napkin out of the old-fashioned dispenser, held it over both of her eyes, and sobbed into her palm.

Lenny grabbed her wrist and held it until she quieted. "They're gonna find him. I promise you. Kola will protect him. You know that. And you know, he's a pretty smart little kid, our Clifford. He can take care of himself."

"No, no, he can't. He's so helpless."

"Not anymore." It occurred to Lenny as he listened to Jessica cry and moan that maybe she wasn't happy with the way Clifford had gotten better. Her whole life had been wrapped around him, taking care of him, escorting him from doctor to clinic to specialist to therapy. For almost a decade. Was it possible that she resented that she could no longer be his keeper, no longer be a martyr, with everybody saying, "Poor Jessica; she can't let that child out of her sight for a second." Could she miss the old Clifford? Could she be just a little scared of her freedom now? It was something to bring up. Later. When Clifford was back home. And wouldn't that be a real pisser? Lenny's being jealous that his son was dependent on Jessica when maybe it was the other way around—the mother dependent on the son.

He furiously shook pepper onto his eggs.

Jessica wailed "No-o-o!" just as the waitress placed her order in front of her.

"Was he wrong?" the waitress asked. "You don't like French toast?" She quickly withdrew the plate.

"No, no, I'm sorry. I love French toast."

The waitress replaced the plate and left. Jessica started giggling through her sobs.

"Thatta girl," Lenny encouraged her. "Give the poor woman an inferiority complex. Rejecting her French toast!" He smiled as Jessica started to eat.

"Why'd you think he looked lonely?" Jessica asked as she poured maple syrup over the French toast.

Lenny shrugged. "I dunno. He does. At least in the picture. Maybe he reminded me of…"

"Of what?"

Lenny shrugged again and turned slightly to look at the photo. He tried to avoid the eyes appealing to him but was held by them. He saw not Clifford but Leonard Marcus as a boy. And for the first time, he shared a secret with his son.

Chapter 101

Christopher Barrett rubbed his thumb along the binding of the *Publishers Weekly* that was opened across his thighs. He rolled his head a few times to loosen his neck muscles and stretched his legs out in front of him. He didn't even realize that his eyes were closed until the crinkling of the magazine jolted him as Sabrina jumped into his lap. Her paws slid on the glossy pages as she crawled onto his chest. He pretended she knocked him over and as he lay back, loudly exaggerating his wounds and fending her off, the periodical fell onto the floor. "Sure. I don't blame you. It's only the Fall Announcement issue anyway."

"Hah, you've been reading that for weeks. Atta-girl, go get him," Jason cheered from the sidelines, swiveling around in the desk chair to watch the wrestling match. "He doesn't like dogs, Sabrina, so get him good."

"Hey, don't tell her that."

"Well, it's true. You told me that."

"When?"

"When we first met. And she was still a puppy, practically. Remember? You said you were a cat person, and you didn't think you'd ever be able to live with a dog!"

"Maybe I was talking about you." Christopher's laugh turned into a shout as he pushed Sabrina away. "Hey, cut it out! For a little girl, you play rough!"

"See, she still listens to me. And she probably remembers that you didn't like her back then."

"Sure, I did. I was just a little afraid."

"Come on; she was young. And she was so tiny."

"I know. But I had never had a dog. Maybe I was afraid of getting involved with her, which would mean getting really involved with you. That was a long time ago." Chris hugged Sabrina with his arms and hugged Jason with his eyes. "Almost finished?"

"Naw." Jason slapped the pile of papers he had been working on. "I guess I should send out a reminder to all the tenants that they should sign the no-buy pledges even if they're going to buy."

"No matter how many times you tell them, they don't understand."

"I know. And I hate to leave this." Jason pointed to the stack of letter-size folders with correspondence and notes on recruiting new volunteers for SAVE. "The building conversion seems so insignificant when people are suffering and dying."

"Don't start getting depressed now. You're doing more than your share. You can't help everyone."

"I know, but I wish I could."

"And look what you're doing for that old Italian dame."

"Miss Bassetti? What am I doing for her?"

"That's what I'd like to know," Chris teased. "Just what are you doing for her?"

"Wouldn't you like to know." Jason stood up and tucked his shirt tighter into his chinos, brightening up. "In fact, you would know if you would come with me."

"Not on your life."

"Why? She's really terrific. I'm surprised you don't remember her. She was always out on the street, walking her Poodle. Talking to everyone. She's not an old-lady type. She's funny, smart. She knows the score."

"You trying to score with her?"

"C'mon, Chris." Jason picked up a folder to swat him, but Sabrina curled her lips over her teeth and yelped softly.

"See? You're upsetting her. She doesn't want to have to bite you, but she's telling you she will if she has to, to protect me."

"Okay. No more teasing. Sabrina, it's all right. I'm not going to hit him. And if I did, you wouldn't dare bite me, would you?" Jason cooed to her.

Sabrina leaped from Christopher's chest to Jason's outstretched hands.

"Really, Chris, if we could get to the bottom of this thing about her, the blackmail or extortion or whatever you want to call it, I'd feel better."

"Do you really think the old lady can help?"

"Well, I told you, she's smart. And she's in touch with some guy who's involved. He's not with the police department, but he has some connection with them or the mayor."

"How'd he get into it?"

"He's doing a study or something about scams against the elderly. That's how it started. The one victim was seventy-five or eighty years old—Miss Bassetti's friend—so the police thought it was a scam against old people, because it was easy. Miss Bassetti was going to call the guy at the department and tell him about Sabrina. Anyway, I'm curious about the pictures she took."

"You don't really expect to recognize anybody, do you?"

"Ya never know. It should be interesting. And she promised a bowl of spaghetti with homemade sauce. Please."

"Well…but what about her?" Chris pointed his chin at Sabrina. "I thought we agreed not to leave her alone anymore. Just in case."

"She was invited too, so if you come with me, we'll take her."

"Okay, give me a minute to change. Besides, I wanna meet the new Alfred Stieglitz. Alfreda."

Chapter 102

Twilight sifted down through the trees, covering the ground in a gauze of deepening purple. The heaviness of the heat had evaporated with the sun's sinking behind the Hudson, and a ripple of air moved through the branches now, the leaves fanning their cracked limbs. Blackness settled like dust, ending the brief transition from day to night.

Kola watched the stragglers of homeless who had claimed the plot between the northern end of the reservoir and the tennis courts, just before the 97th Street Transverse. They came from their doorways and railroad terminals and street corners and subway stations to spend the night with comrades who shared their fate, secure in the safety of their numbers from the muggers and perverts who were said to roam the park, looking for victims. They parked their sacks of belongings and their shopping carts of goods and old baby carriages teeming with clothes and, like birds building nests, constructed tents and beds from cartons and bags and newspapers and discarded coats.

Kola didn't know any one of them, but she knew all of them, by the foul cloud of stale urine and stale breath and stale sweat that hung over them. By the slow gaits that brought them at dusk. By the backs crooked from the bundles they dragged with then.

They didn't speak to each other as they entered the colony, claimed their reserved spaces, and busied themselves preparing for the night. But once they were comfortably organized, they acknowledged a neighbor with a nod, or offered a bottle, or an extra shoe, or a smoothed-out cigarette butt—like cowboys sitting around a campfire during a cattle drive in the Old West, swapping stories and smokes and songs.

After Clifford's scare the other night—a teenager had ridden across his towel and tried to swipe his bag—he had decided it would be better to be near other people. When he wandered into the camp early the next day and hesitantly stretched out, a grisly-looking figure had appeared from behind a boulder to yell at him that it was his spot. Clifford had found a different spot. And because the others didn't mind his being there, and even had offered him food and tips on surviving on the streets, he returned. But whenever that crusty man ambled in, which hadn't been often, he grumbled that no boys or dogs should be allowed. Clifford learned to ignore him, as the rest of them did.

"Hey, Kola, look what I got." She moved closer, sat next to him on the towel striped with a narrow band of tire dirt, and watched him unwrap the large rawhide bone he had been saving until the old one was chewed up. Her thick tail twitched steadily under her as he finally broke the packaging and tried to pull the hard plastic off. Kola couldn't contain her eagerness; she stood, her tail plumed straight above her like a rich, full feather. Once the bone was in her mouth, she lay down, contentedly exercising her gums and sharpening her teeth, as her master's body leaned against her reassuringly.

"You and your damn mutt!" The raised foot high over Clifford's head was as much a surprise as the shrill war cry. More than the weapon, more than the venom in his shriek, maybe more than the threat to her beloved companion, the words "Damn Mutt" stirred a memory deep in Kola. A memory of her terrible life between being the happy Beauty and the trustworthy Rowan, a life of fear and hunger and anger, when "Damn Mutt" was the only name she was called. A time of hatred for the owner of an appliance store in White Plains.

Before Clifford could react by rolling out of the way, before the foot, momentum gathered behind it, could even start its descent, Kola had sprung. In one dazzling bolt of lightning, a streak so fast her tan spots ran into her white fur, in one graceful movement, Kola knocked him down and clamped her jaws around his neck.

Chapter 103

Felix was cornered. His spine stretched like a rubber band, and just before it could snap, it pulled up into a perfect arch, his back suspended in an inverted V. As he raised his paw to box, a raspy warning hissed from his throat.

"Gotcha!" Laurie picked him up and put him in the bedroom, closing the door quickly so he couldn't get out. "You big phony! You wouldn't dare scratch me." She stomped around the apartment looking for Oscar. "Oscar, here we go. Come on out, wherever you are." Laurie couldn't find her. She peeked in the closet, in back of the couch, under the chair, and behind the toilet, calling to her. "I'm just trying to help you guys. Come on out." She finally found Oscar wedged between the top of the refrigerator and the cabinet over it. She scooped her up and opened the bedroom door just enough to shove her in.

As soon as the carrier came out, they always hid. She should have corralled them first but hadn't thought of it. She only wanted to get Megabyte into it and take her back to the office. Nobody could say she hadn't tried. But it just wasn't working. The constant fighting was too much for her. She remembered how Felix and Oscar had been in the beginning. At each other's throats. Everybody had told her to wait it out; they would get used to each other. She would never have believed that they'd be friends, yet here they were, almost inseparable. They wouldn't admit it, but they were.

Given enough time, they'd probably accept Megabyte too, but Laurie decided she either was getting too old or too involved with the computer or her job. She just didn't have the patience to come home every night and try to keep three cats separated. Besides, Megabyte had been perfectly content in the office. She should have left well enough alone. Her nerves were on edge, and they'd all be better off if she brought Megabyte back.

It wasn't hard to catch her then, meowing against the crack of the bedroom door. The answering wails sounded like they were from long-lost lovers rather than rivals, so Laurie had a second's hesitation about her decision. But she grabbed her, pushed her into the carrier, and stuck her fingers in the holes to reassure her—of what she didn't know, but it made her feel more two-faced.

Once on Queens Boulevard, the long staircase up to the elevated subway looked especially high in the 88-degree heat with 73-percent humidity. On the spur of the moment, when a cab stopped for the light right in front of her as she waited to cross, Laurie decided to splurge. Besides, traffic going into the city at this hour on a weeknight shouldn't be too heavy or too expensive.

She composed the notice for the bulletin board as she settled back in her seat. "Adorable feline needs loving home." But maybe Megabyte would be better off at the office. She wasn't one of the half a million pet cats estimated to be living in New York City—Laurie recalled her latest entry—but Megabyte was doing okay. Who was to say that she needed to live in a regular home with regular people? She had a roof over her head, food, water, plenty of animals to play with or tease, and enough part-time affection from the staff to be okay. She wasn't one of the twenty thousand strays that would be picked up by Animal Care & Control this year. No matter what Dr. P. threatened, she knew he'd never turn an unwanted animal over to them. She kept trying to convince herself that this was the right thing to do, but every time the wet little nose filled one of the holes in the carrier, Laurie winced with guilt.

Before she unlocked the door of Manhattan Veterinary Associates, the clamor of shrill barking and howling made Megabyte stoop in the carrier, alert and ready to stalk her attackers, even though she was unable to pace back and forth. Laurie stopped to listen, her key poised in front of the lock. The commotion could not be from her arrival; they couldn't have even heard her yet. The dogs boarded in the basement were trying to defend themselves against an intruder.

Chapter 104

Ken concentrated on sponging up the egg yolk with his whole-wheat toast, obviously savoring every morsel.

Rosa surveyed the moms sitting around her at the outdoor tables, some of them rocking baby carriages with one hand while eating with the other. Every time she passed Gracie Mews, it was mobbed, and there always seemed to be people waiting in the doorway for openings to be seated. But she had never been here herself. She was tickled when Ken led her here. She felt very special, eating at such a popular restaurant, even though it was just around the corner from her apartment.

"What'samatt…she doesn't make-a you breakfast?" Rosa couldn't help asking.

"Who?" His tongue reached for his chin to taste the last spot that had slid off the bread.

"Who? You know who. You girlfriend, who."

"Who said I have a girlfriend?" He hid his smirk in the coffee cup.

"I can tell. What you think? I don't know what'sa going on?"

"What do you think is going on?"

"Ah, c'mon." Rosa slapped the table. "You think I'm dumb? You live all the way out on Long Island. You work downtown. You teach. So how come when I say I come to you office or come to you school, you gonna be in this neighborhood at this hour? She lives around here. And"—she pointed an accusatory finger at Ken—"you stayed there last night. Now, where does she live?"

"I'm surprised you don't know."

"How's that?"

"Well, you traipse all over town taking pictures of shady-looking characters and local dogs. You run across the city and back to check out leads, and now you bring me this evidence," Ken tapped the edge of the envelope on the table. "So if you're such a super detective, so you should have detected where she lives."

"Hah! I was right, see? There is a girl. You admitted it. Finding out where she lives is easy. I just follow you."

"You better not!" Ken's boyish grin spread from his lips across his cheeks, wrinkling his eyes, making his nose look longer.

"I won't…if you tell me about her." Rosa reached over the dirty plates and playfully scratched Ken's scalp, her fingers denting the hair between his curls.

"Okay, I'll tell you all about Louise, but first"—he turned serious— "let's talk about the letter."

"Nice boys they are; he bring-a his boyfriend over. They act just like two people. I cook them spaghetti." Rosa leaned closer, looked sideways around the coffee shop to make sure no one could hear her. She whispered, "Same instructions, practically. Same drop-off. Same MF."

"MO," he corrected, "modus operandi."

"MF. Mother-effer. Must be somebody who knows that supermarket good. Maybe works there."

Ken tried to suppress his smile. He'd have to tell Bernie that one: MF. "The other thing is, it knocks our theory about the elderly. 'Cause these two gays, they might be old, but they're definitely not elderly."

"Old? They're about fifty-two, fifty-five."

"Well, that's old."

"Ach. Not to me."

"What'd you call old?"

"Someone older'n me, that's sure. And don't ask how old that is, 'cause a lady, she doesn't have to tell."

"Okay. Well, let's call them middle-aged. So we got two victims now—"

"Two we know about," Rosa interrupted.

"Right. Two we know about. One is middle-aged; one is elderly. One is homosexual. No connection so far. They both have older dogs they're nuts about."

"Doesn't count."

"Why?"

"You could say that 'bout everybody who has a dog for a pet. At least everybody I know."

"Maybe. One is a shop owner who looks like a good mark; the other's a retired schoolteacher, living on a fixed income. Both live uptown, one on the East Side, one on the West Side. They both have to leave the money in the same supermarket."

"What else?"

Ken shrugged and tilted his cup, waiting to catch the waitress's attention as she hurried through the door to the outside seating area with a tray held high with one hand.

"I'm trying to think. We have to find something they have in common."

"So, what about Louise?"

"What about her?"

"You really involved, like they say, or you just sleeping with her?"

Chapter 105

Eileen entered her Social Security and pension deposits in the ledger book in the column marked INTEREST. Even though she had changed the title in the top margin from NAME OF STOCK to MONTHLY INCOME, it bothered her that the form was still not correct. She was premature in entering September's credits, but she had the book out to record some dividends, so she got a little ahead of herself. Anyway, it wasn't as if she couldn't count on the checks being sent to the bank on time, and if the United States government or the New York City Board of Education went bankrupt and couldn't pay her, whiting out the figures and correcting the total would be the least of her problems.

She went back through the pages and tallied up August. In pencil. All the dividends were in, but she'd still have another grocery bill, possibly something at the hardware store, so she couldn't finish all her expenses or balance them against her income. But she knew what the final amount would be, almost to the dollar. And it was ten thousand dollars less than it used to be. Eileen's sigh was broken by a groan. How long did it take to save ten thousand dollars when you didn't have anything extra to save? Which is why she couldn't understand how Rosa Bassetti was off buying cameras and developing pictures. Eileen was sure she had no extra income. And probably no savings to speak of. If she was living on Social Security, how could she risk spending that kind of money? Eileen might be able to cut a little more off her food, but that would only come to pennies, nickels. It took a lot of nickels to make ten thousand dollars. She had to face it; she'd never be able to make it up, and she should just stop thinking about it. Because whenever she did think about it, she got a pain in her heart. If Rosa ever knew how much money Eileen really had, she'd probably yell at her for living the way she did. Like Patsy McQuinlan always did. Or she'd laugh. *Well, it takes all kinds,* Eileen lectured herself, *and if she wants to live from hand-to-mouth, that's her problem!*

She pushed her book away and fanned herself with her bank statement. She took a long pull of iced tea, enjoying the shock as it cooled the inside of her chest. Mr. McGee lumbered through the kitchen door and sat next to her chair, panting. "You hot too?" She stroked his head. "I know, but we can't put the air conditioner on 'til after five. Understand?" His tongue drooped sideways. His soulful eyes seemed to follow Eileen's words as they left her mouth. "It's just too expensive during the day when all the offices have theirs on. See?" She turned sideways at the table and fanned his face hard. "Better? Poor Fibber."

Looking at him now, old, lethargic from the heat, his breathing straining his lungs, Eileen remembered how easily she had given up the ten thousand dollars when she thought Fibber McGee's life was at stake. And she remembered how much she loved that dog. She glanced at the clock over the stove and suddenly pushed herself back from the table. "The heck with it. C'mon. Or as Rosa would say, 'Who else but yourself should you treat good?'" She tried to mimic the Italian accent as she went into the bedroom, but it came out more of an Irish brogue. Once Fibber was inside with her, Eileen closed the door. She pushed in the LOW COOL button and as the motor spun to life, she lifted him onto the bed.

"In just a second it will be cool." She hugged him. "And just think," she gloated as she defended her extravagance out loud, "it will mean that much less money for Charlene!"

Chapter 106

The last of the water swirled around the recess, slowed to a thin stream, and gurgled down the drain in the floor, leaving a few opaque bubbles of ammonia on the stainless steel rim. The scrawny figure walked on the sides of his feet, close to the edge of the concrete, to avoid the puddles, winding the hose in large circles around his arm as he went. He stood by the entrance and inspected the long room and the open doors to its fourteen rooms, eight on one side, six on the other. He put the hose down, took the rag hanging out of his back pocket, sprayed some Fantastik on it, and scrubbed the smudge on the wall next to the light switch.

He stepped into the hallway, hung the hose in a closet, opened the double-louvered doors concealing a built-in sink, and filled the bucket. He went to the next room, which he had cleaned earlier, and double-checked the typewritten instructions Scotch-taped to the little table just inside to make sure he hadn't overlooked any details. It was quiet. The four were either drugged, still under anesthesia, or just too weak to cry. An occasional twitch of a leg or flutter of an eyelid was the only sign of life. Besides the level of liquid receding in the intravenous tubes. He reread the list to make sure he had given them the proper medication, prying their teeth open and pushing the pills back to their throats, forcing them to swallow in reflex.

He peeked back into the larger room to see if the floor had dried. He replaced all the bowls he had washed, carried his bucket from cubicle to cubicle. Everything was immaculate, ready for the day, ready for the boarders to return from their outing. He touched his chin to see if the pimple he detected under his skin this morning had grown.

Chapter 107

The triage nurse in the Emergency Room at Metropolitan Hospital looked in her desk for a treat to give the four-year-old whose broken leg was being set in the trauma room. She pulled the drawer out farther and looked in the back. The REPORT OF A DOG BITE that she had thrown in there the night before slid forward. She took it out, along with an aging yellow lollipop that had melted onto its cellophane wrapper.

She licked the sticky lemon flavor off her finger and hurried to meet a heart-attack victim. After that, it was a whirlwind of attending to patients, prying information out of new arrivals, and calling for specialists. When she came back to her desk, she collapsed in her chair for a two-minute break. She slipped off her left shoe to massage the throbbing callous, stretched her arms, and rotated her shoulders. Then, energy renewed, she resumed the midnight-to-eight.

Toward the end of her shift, she called her husband at his all-night gas station in Brooklyn to tell him what time she'd be ready to come home and started cleaning up for the replacement team. As she sat at her desk to freshen her makeup, she noticed the lollipop and realized she had never had time to give it to the little girl, who was probably fast asleep in her own bed by now. She stuck it back in the drawer. She saw the card with the report of a dog bite and knew she might get into trouble for not mailing it on time. She considered just dumping it. What good would it do the Bureau of Animal Affairs anyway, when the victim didn't even have an address. That's why they'd had to admit him, just to watch him in case of rabies. She flipped the card over. It was postpaid by the Department of Health. She could just drop it in a mailbox, when she passed one. She put it in her bag and waited in the doorway, hoping the day nurse would be on time. She could always blame the delay on the post office. They deserved it.

Chapter 108

Honda waited on the worn welcome mat, a spasm of shakes and shudders spraying water and hair in the hallway. As soon as Louise came back with the old bath towel, he offered his front paw, his ears flat back as if admitting some guilt. "It's okay; it's not your fault it rained." She rubbed him vigorously. "But did you have to jump into the puddle?" When she was finished with all four feet, she massaged his body dry and twisted the towel into a terry-cloth rope. The air cracked as she slashed it toward him. She screamed in fright as she let him chase her through the apartment and eventually grab the end of the rope. They both grunted and growled during a fierce tug-of-war and then tumbled to the floor so the victor could administer his customary licks of consolation to the loser. That was the best part of the game.

Louise relaxed flat on her back, with Honda's head resting on her shoulder, one front paw across her chest. Warmth and affection spread through her. She wondered if the bonding between a mother and a newborn baby on her breast could be any stronger. "You're my guy, aren'tcha?" She kissed the silver triangle between his eyes and held him tighter to her. She relished the feeling and worried that she would never be able to share it with another human being. Even Ken, although each time she was with him, she felt closer to experiencing it—abandon with someone. The ultimate freedom. Like she felt with her dog. For a minute, she wanted to shrug off the intimacy that she was ashamed must hint of perversion.

Honda's brows were lost in his thick fur but the shaggy ridge shirred in concentration as his eyes tried to follow Louise's mood, able to distinguish every nuance of her expression. "Don't worry," she reassured him, "there's no way you're going to be boarded. Not for Labor Day, not next Christmas, not even for the apocalypse. Uh-uh." She had told Ken she would consider it. Well, she just had. She could never enjoy the weekend, worrying about Honda being in a cage. Not that he would be mistreated. But her soul lurched at the thought of Honda crying for her, wondering why he was being punished. You couldn't explain to a dog that it was only for a few days. That she couldn't bring him to a stranger's house and even though Ken's parents might love animals, she couldn't ask them. She couldn't explain to Honda that he'd be better off in a kennel than at home all alone.

Look how he was now, at the end of a long day. She knew that he knew what time it was. No matter what anybody said, he knew. And he waited at the door so he could hear her coming in downstairs. Unable to contain himself. Then anxiously watching her change into a pair of jeans, eager to go. Not only because his bladder was probably bursting, but because his heart was bursting with the joy of being with her, the anticipation of coming home from their walk and spending time together with her. No, she just couldn't put him in a kennel.

The fleeting possibility that Ken would give her a hard time about it tugged in her chest. That he would make her choose between them. But as soon as the thought took form, it evaporated. That was one of the endearing things about Ken. He respected her feelings, no matter what they were. Respected them and accepted them. Something that nobody had ever done before. Or to be honest, maybe it was because she had never let anyone know what her feelings were before. No, it was going to be all right. At least she hoped it was, because if there was any doubt, if Louise were ever forced to make a decision, she knew who she'd give up. *God knows, I've done it before.*

"You're my guy," she said out loud and clutched Honda, "my main squeeze."

Chris Barrett could hardly bear the excitement stirring in his gut. He knew, after the first page, that this was going to be it. Now, more than a third into the story, he was sure of it. He got up to mix himself a scotch and soda. He set a coaster on the cocktail table for his drink, lit a cigarette, and stretched out on the couch, inhaling the first deep drag. He reached behind to turn the lamp higher, as the rain had brought dusk early. That, of course, was the test—not reading at the desk. The fact that Jason's files were all over it didn't have anything to do with it. Work-reading was done at the desk, pleasure-reading on the couch.

Sabrina stood on the fanned-out pages he had been turning face down on the floor as he finished them. The hell with electronic submissions and squinting at a screen. Chris always had the manuscripts printed out. And he favored the loose sheets over ones that came in some fancy spiral fasteners or glued bindings that were so heavy to hold. "Uh-uh, little girl, careful." Chris picked her up with one hand and moved the box with the rest of the pages from his stomach to make room for her. "Careful, careful, that's our fortune there." He took a long sip of his drink and blotted his hand, wet from the frosty glass, on Sabrina's belly.

"So whaddya think? We're going to be rich and famous, you lucky dog you." Chris scratched the spot under her neck that she loved, the one Jason always said gave her a canine orgasm. "After all these years, reading all that crap—I must've read a thousand novels—I finally have a best-seller. Yup, and we're going to be able to write our own ticket from now on. Because I discovered it." His explanation to the Yorkie became a singsong tale. "Would you believe…I selected this old bond-paper box out of the mountain of other old bond-paper boxes and manila envelopes? They don't even get read anymore, just returned with a form letter saying we don't accept unsolicited manuscripts. It's our lucky day, girl. Can you imagine? I just felt like thumbing through anything, just for something to do instead of watching TV. That's fate. Maybe we'll get a big enough bonus, with the small advance I'm going to offer, to quit. That's right, quit. Say 'screw you' and walk out."

Chris thought of all the encouragement he had given to Jason to start his own business, to open the store, and take the risk, when deep down Chris had always been afraid to do that himself. If he could build up just a little more of a nest egg, he would do it. Become a literary agent, like he'd wanted to for the past twenty years. The luster that had attracted the young Christopher Barrett, just out of college, to the prestigious world of publishing had long ago tarnished. Words like scholarly, erudite, letters, intellectual, and classics had been replaced with terms like mass-market, paperbacks, promotions, author tours, packaging, acquisitions, marketing, floor bids. And most recently, digital. Old, respected publishing houses were being swallowed up by communications conglomerates, and authors who couldn't write an English sentence were getting advances the size of movie-star salaries. The intellectual quest had gotten lost somewhere in the drudgery. The literary aura had faded. And so had Christopher Barrett's dreams.

But now, discovering a new talent, a real writer, immersing himself in the eloquently told story, Chris's youthful enthusiasm came back. "Know what?" he said softly to Sabrina. "We could get a little house in the country. We'd keep the apartment for as long as Jason had the store. Just the three of us. Wouldn't you like that?"

Chris made another drink and curled up to finish the manuscript, with Sabrina fast asleep in the crook of his left arm. His old passion for books swelled in his brain; his eagerness to celebrate it with Jason throbbed in his groin.

Lenny unpacked his duffel bag. He put his dirty laundry in the hamper, his shirts on top of Jessica's dress on the vanity shelf, where she would automatically sort Chinese laundry and dry cleaners, and his toiletries in the medicine chest. He didn't feel like talking to anyone so when the phone rang, he let the answering machine pick it up.

He recognized Dr. Kravitz's voice before she left her name. Lenny unpacked his clean underwear while he listened to her breathless message. "Great," he said out loud and then clamped his hand over his mouth, as if she could hear him. "Great," he repeated in a whisper, patting the boxer shorts as he put them on top of the neat pile in his drawer.

Almost all of the files were now in the database. Certainly there were enough for Laurie to finally demonstrate the new procedure. Early this morning, she had entered all the names scheduled in the appointment book for the day and had given Dr. Pomalee a printout for each patient, an entire medical history on a single sheet. Only one history was not available—a German Shepherd who had not been in for two years— and she put his folder on the bottom. By November, she expected to have the previous two years' records input. She was very pleased with the doctor's reaction…his astonishment was still glowing on her cheeks. Right after Labor Day, she was going to get a temp in so Stacy could sit with her all day and learn the system. Then she'd be able to do the same thing at the terminal on her desk, automatically printing a bill at the end of an office visit.

Her watch, which she kept fifteen minutes fast, showed five thirty. Storage cabinets blocked the view, so she couldn't see out, but she could hear the rain hitting the window panes and thrumming the air conditioner. Time to call it a day, if you counted coming in at eight and gobbling lunch at her desk "a day." Which reminded her that there was still some of lunch left. Laurie retrieved the plastic container from the refrigerator and held it open so Megabyte could lick the remnants. "What? You don't like homemade tuna salad? Okay with me if you'd rather have cat food than the real thing! Crazy cat." She left the container on the floor in case the cat changed her mind. Before she went home, she'd go downstairs for a can of food. There was no point getting drenched. She might as well stay until the rain let up. Besides, she'd been so busy lately that she hadn't had time to work on her own project.

She folded back her spiral notebook cover, turning the pages to find where she had left off. The keys on her computer clicked slowly at first, and then she increased her speed as her fingers found the rhythm and the melody of rain.

Chapter 109

A printout of the form reporting an animal bite made its way through the proper channels and finally ended up on the desk of the secretary to the deputy commissioner at the Bureau of Animal Affairs. She asked the deputy commissioner what to do with it and, when he read the severity of the wound and the number of stitches it required, he had her call Metropolitan Hospital for more details. By that time, Alex Petrowicz, the forty-eight-year-old homeless victim, had vanished. The 19th Precinct had notified the Central Park Precinct, because the incident occurred in its jurisdiction, and they, in turn, briefed their officers to be on the lookout for a large white dog with tan spots, with a young, blond male, probably a runaway.

Chapter 110

Dr. Pomalee clicked the switch on the wall intercom above the little sink. "Attendant, please," he said into the round plate dotted with holes while he massaged the soap into his hands. Behind him, a Mrs. Fleischenbaum was reassuring her black Cocker Spaniel that nobody was going to hurt him. His nails kept scraping on the stainless steel as he tried to stand on the examining table, but Mrs. Fleischenbaum held him down with her torso stretched across his back. She murmured in his ear, "It's okay. I'm not going to let him hurt you. It's okay, baby."

"Everything else seems fine." Dr. Pomalee turned to face her, pulling rubber gloves over his fingers. "His heart's good, as well as his eyes, ears, and teeth. We'll just clean out those anal glands so Pepper here can move his bowels more easily."

"Oh, thank you. I'm so glad, Doctor. Hear that? You're fine."

The door to the examining room moved quietly and a lanky young boy seemed to slide sideways through the opening. Pepper's paws scrambled in fear as he tried to get away from this new arrival, and Mrs. Fleischenbaum was doubtful that the puny young man would be able to hold him down.

"All right, now, you can either wait outside or just stand over there in the corner, so you don't distract him."

"But Dr. Pomalee, maybe it would be better if I tried to hold him myself. He'd be less scared." To demonstrate, she lay across the Spaniel, flattening his body so he couldn't move.

"C'mon, he'll be fine." Dr. Pomalee nodded to the boy, who deftly raised the dog to a standing position and held him motionless. "Just remember: it hurts you more than it hurts him."

Pepper let out one shrill yelp as the first swollen gland burst between the doctor's fingers and the foul, fecal pus oozed out, filling the small examining room with a putrid smell. The attendant tried not to let them see that he was about to gag from the odor that dizzied his senses from the force of its repulsiveness. He thought about squeezing his pimple like that. He shrugged nonchalantly. The gray smock, which looked more like a smoking jacket than a medical uniform, was much too big for him. It shifted across his shoulders and hung toward his back. He tried breathing through his mouth. Even the dog's owner, pushing herself further into the wall, gasped and held a tissue over her face like a mask.

He waited until Dr. Pomalee was ready to squeeze the second gland. As the dog yelped again, he kept his arms, as strong as lead pipes, wrapped around the dog and dug his thumbnail into the animal's soft belly.

Chapter 111

Louise put the coffee cups, still warm from the dinner dishes, in the sudsy water. After she rinsed them, she started scrubbing the broiler she had left soaking in the bottom of the sink. She was mad at herself. She hadn't told Ken about next weekend. The longer she waited, the harder it would be. She tried to figure out what Dr. Matthews would suggest if she were still in therapy. *"Are you sure it's really the dog?"*

"Of course I'm sure."

She played a conversation in her head, adding the right scenery to make it more authentic. She was sitting in the velour recliner that she had accused him of buying so his patients could return to their wombs in its protective comfort. He was in the club chair opposite, his feet on the ottoman, looking as if he were relaxing in his study rather than working in his office, a luxury she always resented him for.…

"But don't you find it strange that it always happens that as soon as you get a little close to someone, your dog interferes?"

"He does not."

"No, I guess he doesn't. I should say, you blame your dog for getting in the way."

"I do not."

"Think back. Stop being defensive and just think about some of the things you've told me. 'This guy wouldn't have worked out because he didn't like my dog.' 'That guy wouldn't have lasted anyway because my dog didn't like him.' 'It would never have worked with so-and-so because he tried to

make me feel guilty for taking good care of my dog.' Or 'he tried to come between us' or 'he resented my feelings for the dog' or 'he expected me to choose between them,' or 'he didn't like the dog enough,' or 'the dog didn't like him enough.' Haven't you said all those things at one time or another?"

"Maybe."

"And now you're having a real relationship with someone. Not a one-night stand or a one-week stand. It's lasted a few weeks, and you seem to like him as much as he likes you. And he doesn't just like your dog; he's crazy about Honda, and Honda is crazy about him. So your dog can't be your scapegoat this time. You either have to decide you want the relationship to continue—wherever it goes—and make some kind of commitment. Or you have to end it. Instead, you're trying to bring the dog into it, using him as an excuse. To do nothing."

"I'm not. It's just that I can't put him in a kennel. He would die. Maybe I feel more responsible for him than I should. But, after my parents died, after that terrible period, the moving, the readjustment, I can't let him think that he's lost me too. I just can't do it to him. And don't tell me he's just a dog and plenty of people board their dogs for vacations and everything. I know they do. But I don't. And I don't see what's wrong with that."

"There's nothing wrong with that. But this Ken has made a big commitment to you, I think. And by arranging to bring you home to meet his folks, it seems to be the next step in a relationship that is going somewhere. And now you want to abort that plan by saying you can't go to Connecticut because of your dog. How do you think that's going to make him feel?"

"I don't care."

"Well, if you don't care, I guess none of this matters. But just consider that maybe it's not that you don't care. Maybe you care too much. And you're afraid."

"What would I be afraid of?"

"I don't know. I'm not a mind reader. I try to be a mind healer. You have to figure out what it is you're afraid of. Maybe that he won't like you. Maybe that you'll be a disappointment to him, and then he won't want you anymore. Sometimes, Louise, it's easier to dismiss something, give it up, than it is to take the risk of being rejected…."

"Hey, what are you so intent on in here?" She hadn't heard Ken come into the kitchen, and his breath against the back of her neck startled her. "What that needs is some elbow grease." He gently pushed her aside, grabbed the worn Brillo pad and started scouring. Maybe Dr. Matthews was right. She'd have to be out of her mind to give up a guy like this. She might be crazy, but she wasn't stupid.

She wiped her hands on a paper towel and impulsively hugged him from behind, laying her head between his shoulder blades. Louise had never had a problem with sex, only with affection. So she was very much aware that the casual squeeze she had just given him was a major emotional outburst for her.

Ken turned around and looked down at her with that tender expression that always melted her, much as her father's loving look used to do. His hands, still foamy with soap, flattened against hers in a patty-cake touch. Then their fingers plaited together and a current of excitement charged through them, from one to the other. Louise pressed into him, her pelvis grinding against him, bone chafing bone, honing the eroticism of devotion turned to desire. Her voice was hoarse when she said, "Let's go inside."

On the way to the bedroom, they stripped off most of their clothes. Louise fell onto the bed on her stomach, her breasts rubbing the stitching of her summer quilt, the coarse thread brushing her nipples as she squirmed. Ken straddled the back of her thighs. He clutched her buttocks through the bikini panties she still had on and moved up so the tip of his penis touched the silk crotch. Her hips began to rotate slowly, and he timed his movements to pick up her rhythm and swing his erection to meet her behind as it rose up and came down. He kneaded her cheeks with his hands, pulling them apart, mesmerized by the sliver of fabric narrowing and disappearing into the widening cleavage. He stood on his knees finally and pulled her panties down to her ankles, where they bound her feet together. He pushed her up to a crouch in front of him. He held one hand across the fissure, using his fingers to spread her two fleshy halves. His other hand guided his penis from the back of her waist along the cleft to its end in the recesses of her vaginal lips, where he lubricated it, and let it slide back along the same route.

Louise groaned and pushed her weight against his arms, flexing her elbows straighter, so they could hold her bent in position. Ken moved down to the edge of the bed and rolled her panties over her feet. When he gently held her thighs, her knees automatically moved apart, her body rocked backward, exposing the source of all her passion. Ken bent his face and saw her insides quiver from the closeness of his breath. Louise gasped, the air stopped in her chest. Ken plunged his tongue inside and drank the liquid satin.

Chapter 112

Laurie's stomach twisted as she approached the cage. The thought of this adorable little creature being sent to a shelter, longing for attention and affection, only to be euthanized after a few days, made her feel like retching. Megabyte stood, her ears back, a pathetic longing in her eyes. Laurie pulled the lever back, released the lock, and picked her up. Megabyte rubbed her face into the nest between Laurie's neck and shoulder, and whimpered. "I wouldn't have left you here, baby," she cooed to her. She gently pulled her away from her chest and placed her in the nylon Sherpa bag. Megabyte lay down and purred, as if she knew she was going back home.

"They're just going to have to suck it up and realize you're part of the household too, and you're not leaving," she promised.

When she got home and set the carrier on the floor, Felix and Oscar stopped in their tracks on the way to greet Laurie.

"You guys are just going to have to fight it out, 'cause nobody's leaving here. Understand?" Megabyte's back arched into a bow when she stepped out of the carrier, staring at them. But they both just looked at her without hissing or crouching into attack mode. Until the newcomer headed for the kitchen and their water bowl. Laurie rushed to put a second water bowl in the corner of the bedroom, crossing her fingers that Megabyte would claim it without any competition. So far, there was peace and quiet.

Laurie checked her Facebook page and saw 783 "likes." That meant that 783 people had read her PET-ICULAR, and even though they called it a "like," she knew they didn't like what they read but were affected by the information. Maybe their awareness would lead them to speak out or donate or adopt or write their congressmen. Maybe, maybe…

Chapter 113

"Pretty good. I like how you did this—bulleting the solution points so they follow your overview."

"Thanks."

"I'll send a copy to Commissioner Cooker and one to the mayor, although you could probably set up most of it yourself, without the city's help. Unless, of course, you want to get paid." Bernie Petris took the lids off the two containers and passed one over to Ken. "Thought you were taking it black."

"I am." Ken broke a packet of Sweet 'N Low over the steaming coffee. "Except when I'm out. Then I treat myself to a regular."

Bernie leaned all the way back in his chair and put his feet up on the edge of the desk, which was government-issue, old, and scratched. "Then how often do you actually drink it black?"

"Hm." Ken Hollis pretended to concentrate on his answer. "Once, maybe twice a month I make a cup at home. And it's much easier, since I usually don't remember to buy milk anyway."

"Big shot!" Bernie took a long swallow. "Ah, that hits the spot. But maybe iced woulda been better on a day like today. Boy, it's sweltering."

"Yeah, but it has been all summer."

"Can you believe it's almost over? Labor Day already. Weekend after this one."

"Yeah. Time flies when you're having fun."

"Or getting old. However you look at it."

"Thing is, Bernie, I'd like to get this organized as soon as possible. Once school starts, I won't have much time to give it."

"I realize. You know I'll give it my best push. How much we talking about? Ballpark."

"Oh, not much. As you said, we can get a local school or church to give us a room. There are always volunteers around to do the typing and copying and envelopes. Stuff like that. In fact, I had a brainstorm the other night. Thought I'd run it by you."

"What's that?" Bernie smacked the last of the coffee off his lips and tossed the container into the pail in the corner.

"I was thinking of changing one of my courses, community issues and services, to what we're talking about—growing crimes connected with the elderly. And having field-work requirements. That way, I could get the students out there for hands-on studying. Who knows? Maybe somebody can think of something better than I have so far." Ken handed his coffee container to Bernie to throw out. "Even if it's too late for this semester, I could certainly do it for spring. I'm sure we'll still have a problem then. Or a worse one."

"Not a bad idea. Well, you have an appointment scheduled with the mayor and the whole committee right after Labor Day. Why not bring it up? By then, he will have read your report"—Bernie tapped the folder on the wood—"and he'll be more informed. Oh, that reminds me, talking about 'informed.' Heard something you might wanna check. Cooker was telling me about the Central Park Precinct looking for a young boy. With a big dog. Assumed he was just another runaway. Routine investigation. Until a bum showed up in the hospital with his neck practically perforated by this dog biting him. They link it to the missing persons they have out and talk to the parents. Still routine. Until the mother and father have a big fight in front of the detectives, and something comes out about a payoff the woman made for the dog. I didn't get the whole thing, but now they suspect maybe the kid was really kidnapped. By the people who threatened the dog. Probably nothing to it, but hey, I don't know. I thought maybe you'd be interested in the dog thing."

"I'm sure it has nothing to do with my old lady." Ken had become possessive of Eileen Hargan. "But I guess I could give them a call. Have the number?"

"Sure, buddy." Bernie sifted some of his papers around and finding his notation on a scratch pad, he copied it down for Ken.

Chapter 114

As soon as Yolanda Santiago came home, she sat down, untied her laces, and pushed her shoes off. She stood up, reached under the white skirt, and yanked down her pantyhose. Then, with a loud "Dios," she pulled them off and flexed her toes. Señora Sanchez offered to bring her a cold papaya juice, but Yolanda was too tired and too hot to decide if she wanted one. The overtime for doing a double-shift went right into her furniture fund for when they moved—if they moved—but it was hell on her feet. And her back, which ached constantly; the tip of her spine was sore even when she got out of bed in the morning.

Staying for the last meal at Mount Sinai meant she got home just after her own kids' supper, although it was a relief sometimes to miss the clamor of chattering and squabbling at the table. And the dishes. Yolanda tried to fix dinner before she left at 4:30 a.m., but it was hard to think of meat and rice before she ate breakfast. Fortunately, Señora Sanchez didn't mind cooking and had even taken to sleeping on the couch on those nights that Yolanda was going to be late, because it was easier for her than going home and coming back.

Yolanda finally got up and went to her bedroom. The side of the double bed that Maria shared with Elena was mussed up, but six-year-old Maria was sitting on the floor between it and the twin bed Yolanda slept in, coloring. "Mama! Mama!" She jumped up, arms open for a hug.

Yolanda picked her up and kissed her cheek loudly. "Why aren't you asleep, mija?"

"I wanted to finish. Put me down." Maria rushed to hold up her coloring book. "Look at Cinderella, Mama. Isn't she beautiful?"

Yolanda was hanging up her uniform but turned absently, and trying to sound enthusiastic, she complimented Maria on the colors of the gown and the neatness of the strokes inside the black outline. She put on her nightgown and slippers and asked, "Where's everybody?"

"They're playing a game on the Wii."

"Oh, your brother's going to kill them."

"Uh. Ah." She shook her head once to each side as she enunciated two distinct words in her favorite expression.

"How d'ya know?"

"'Cause he's in the bedroom too."

"Ricky's home tonight?"

"Uh-ha-ah." Maria used her second favorite expression.

"Okay, that's enough for you. Into bed. Hurry." She patted her behind and slipped on a housecoat. The buttons on the housecoat had long ago fallen off, and Yolanda held it closed with her hand. She bent to tuck in Maria, switched on the nightlight in the floor socket so she and Elena would be able to find their way to bed, turned off the overhead fixture, and blew a kiss to Maria before she slipped out.

She hesitated outside the smaller bedroom, on the other side of the kitchen, her hand on the knob, listening. There was a lot of noise from mechanical television voices and those of children, all talking at the same time.

"No, stop, ooh, don't." As soon as she heard Elena wail, her maternal instinct made her open the door quickly. Her oldest daughter was sitting on the foot of the bed, her eyes closed, rocking sideways.

Yolanda breathed a sigh of relief. Whatever it was, it wasn't as bad as her imagination, as her worst fear. Having a son with no father around, a teenager who was always testing his manhood and trying to prove to his friends how macho he was, as well as having a young daughter… Dios, she didn't know how she'd survive until they were adults. When the twins were small and slept with her, there was no choice but for Elena and Ricardo Jr. to share a room. But they were much younger then, anyway. Some of her friends thought she was lucky; some of them didn't have two bedrooms. But she thought she'd be better off if they'd all had to be in the same room. At least she'd be able to watch everything that was going on. She was so glad when the little ones were old enough and she could split them up and put the two boys together and the girls in with her. But even that didn't stop her from worrying. Señora Sanchez was too old, too deaf, maybe even too naïve to ever be able to notice something fishy going on.

"What's wrong?" Yolanda asked, stepping into the room. She felt guilty at her relief, at her lack of real concern for whatever had happened, as long as it wasn't that. God forgive her for even thinking it.

"Hi, Mama." Elena came over to her and stood on her toes to plant a kiss on her mother's lips.

"Ricky's scaring us," Michael said. He was on the floor in front of the TV, concentrating on a Mr. Potato Head in the circle of his crossed legs.

"Don't I get a kiss hello?" She smiled at Maria's twin, knowing he couldn't have cared less who had come in, as long as it was somebody he could report his brother to.

"In a minute," Michael answered. "Ricky's trying to give us nightmares again. After you told him not to."

Ricky clicked the remote control and the sound abruptly stopped. "Hi, Ma. Don't listen to them."

"You're not scaring them, are you? You know how easily you frighten them with your horror stories."

"Yeah, he does it on purpose," Michael reported.

"C'mon. Nuthin' like that." Her firstborn lounged on his pillow in a T-shirt and jockey shorts.

Elena shouted. "Gross! It's worse than monsters and ghosts. He was making up these things, Mama." She scrunched up her face in disgust.

"I was only telling 'em about—"

Elena covered her ears with her hands. "No, no, don't say it again. Mama, tell him not to."

"Ma, honest," Ricky insisted. "I was telling them about work—that's all."

Chapter 115

The sun squeezed through the tightly shut blinds and like a shiny scythe, it left a swatch of light in the darkness. It cut across Laurie's face, waking her. She didn't move, because Oscar was fast asleep, burrowed into her armpit, and half of Felix's body was over her chest, his head just touching Oscar's side. She tried not to disturb them as she reached her hand over and pulled the shorter cord on the blinds to angle the slats. Her bedroom brightened with morning.

From where she lay, the branch of the tree in front of her building waved in and out of her view. A breeze. She moved gently, and the two cats did their wake-up exercises, stretching their backs and their paws to their very ends, pleasure rattling in their rib cages and echoing against her. She turned off the air conditioner and switched on the radio. She listened to the end of a song and part of the news, waiting to hear the weather forecast. The humidity had dropped to 30 percent and it was only 68 degrees outside. The forecast was for a pleasant day with a high in the eighties. Laurie nuzzled her furry friends for a few minutes and then got up. She struggled with the window and once it opened, she stuck her head out to breathe the fresh air and feel its current on her skin. Then she closed it all but a few inches so the cats couldn't fall out.

She quickly washed up and put on a pair of old jeans and a one-size-fits-all shirt that tented her figure. She went out to pick up a coffee at Dunkin' Donuts and the newspaper. Once on the street, she was invigorated by the gentle wind that carried a promise of autumn. She gulped its freshness and decided the weather was too beautiful to go right back. She walked down Woodhaven to the corner where it met Queens Boulevard and, on the spur of the moment, she went into the diner to have her breakfast instead of heading to Dunkin' Donuts. She skimmed the *News*, read the picture captions, and headed back to her apartment.

As she casually strolled home, looking at seemingly abandoned apartment houses, she tried to decide what she could do with a day as perfect as this one. She wished she had a car so she could take a ride to the country and just drive on narrow roads, smell the grass, and watch the trees whiz past. She could always take a bus to the beach. But she hated the beach. She could catch up on her housework, a word she associated with her grandmother, but the weather was too wonderful to stay indoors. No matter what, she would not—absolutely not—go to the office. Lightning should strike her dead if she broke her oath. Laurie smiled to herself, imagining a bolt of electricity leaving the summer sky to hit her and the headlines announcing FREAK STORM IN ELMHURST KILLS 1.

Surely she could find something to do with herself. Or with someone. She had neglected her old friends in the past few years. Except for holidays and birthdays, she hardly bothered with anyone. Maybe nobody would want to see her anymore. If she was having this much trouble deciding what to do with herself today, what would she do next weekend when she had three days off? Then everything would surely be deserted, everybody away for Labor Day. It was depressing to think of the end of summer, even though she didn't care about it very much. It was more like she hadn't noticed its coming. And now it was leaving, closing…her final chance to enjoy the season.

She hadn't even been on a real vacation in…she strained her memory… probably six or seven years. Not counting the week she took off when she moved from her last apartment in Brooklyn. Or when she flew to Scottsdale, Arizona, right after her parents retired. Before she had the fight with them. And now all the time was lost. Of course, if she really needed the time off or wanted it for a special trip, she was sure Dr. Pomalee would let her take some of it and add it on to the current three weeks she was entitled to. But she never would ask or want it.

The sun was getting stronger and it beat on her shoulders and the back of her neck as she walked. Even with her dark glasses, she squinted against the white glare. The breeze had long since evaporated, and she was uncomfortably hot. She walked as if on an endless desert, toward a mirage. She checked her wallet, just in case a bus came along, to make sure her MetroCard was there. Her lips puckered into a scowl, and she quickened her pace, anxious now to return to…she didn't know.

When Laurie finally got home, she rushed past Felix, waiting by the door to be greeted, to throw herself across her bed. She grabbed the pillow as she fell and let her grief explode in sobs.

Chapter 116

Children of all sizes and ethnic backgrounds clustered outside the entrance to the zoo, in groups according to age and the bright matching shirts with the name of the day care or community center or church they belonged to ironed onto both the front and back. They darted in and out between the same color-coded adults. Some wandered off and intermingled, so one blue shirt stood out in a mass of orange; two red shirts were spotted in the green group. Their escorts shouted at them and chased them, sounding more like drill sergeants than day-camp counselors. It was virtually impossible for a child to get lost, but there was always one, sometimes two, who found a way—especially the youngest, who were easily distracted by a balloon, a squirrel, a pigeon, or a paralyzing fullness in the bladder.

So they were lined up by the counselors and counted and re-counted to make sure no one was missing. This was the first time since the subway platform when they got off the train, before walking hand in hand up Fifth Avenue to 64th Street where, still attached to each other, they undulated down the wide stairs like a gaudy Oriental paper snake.

Clifford watched casually as some of them scrambled to find room on the long wooden benches while their leftover mates talked and laughed and played silly tricks on each other. Each day the children were different; the shirts were different, as were the organizations and the leaders. What remained the same was some kind of roll call and a consultation by the sergeants to plan their strategy for maneuvers inside. Since the Central Park Zoo had been redesigned long ago, and the big animals moved to more humane habitats in the Bronx, the zoo seemed much smaller. And, except for the youngest visitors, who were fascinated by everything, the older kids seemed disappointed by not seeing elephants and tigers and giraffes. That was on the way out. On the way in, they were excited and hyper and eager to get on with their day trip. This was the time they started munching their snacks.

Clifford had become adept at his scam. He nonchalantly wandered toward the kids about his height so that even though his shirt didn't match, he wouldn't be very noticeable. Most days, he'd see an occasional white shirt like his on somebody whose mother had forgotten it was the trip day. Of course, all the kids made a fuss over Kola, pushing one another to get close enough to pet her. And Clifford, between answering what her name was and what kind of dog she was and how old she was, would point to the kids' snacks and blatantly ask, "Can I have a few of those?" The kids were eager to exchange a few pretzels or Goldfish or a cookie or popcorn for an extra chance to touch the massive dog—the first real animal they'd seen since arriving at the zoo. Clifford usually mooched enough to satisfy his mid-morning hunger, and sometimes he was even offered a whole bag to take with him for later.

Now, as the counselors urged the children to assemble, Clifford walked over to the iron railing opposite them and wiped his hands on his denim-clad thighs. "Good girl," he told Kola, as she sat on her waving tail. They watched the assorted children pounce through the turnstile, shouting happily.

Clifford imagined them going home and chattering to their parents about everything they'd done and seen, about the big, beautiful white dog with golden spots who licked their hands. Maybe their parents would tell them to sit down and eat or get into their pajamas or wash up or brush their teeth, before being snuggled into bed. Clifford missed his bed. He missed home. And he missed his mother more than anything. But he could never go back, and he would probably never see her again. As long as he lived. He didn't have to worry anymore about being asked to choose between his parents, or about living with his father, or about Kola being sent away. Since she'd bitten that man, he knew that if they ever found her, they'd take her away. Kill her. Maybe even arrest him! No, they'd have to hide forever.

"C'mon, Kola. Let's go, girl." Clifford swiped his nose with the back of his hand and led his dog back into the depths of the park.

Chapter 117

Louise usually ate at her desk. It was too hot to wander around or sit outside on a bench or a step or a ledge, like all the other clerical picnickers. The streets were a smorgasbord of vendors, and it was more comfortable to pick up something and come back to the air conditioning, even if the office was noisy and distracting. It gave her a chance to catch up on a few personal chores, like writing a long overdue e-mail to her aunt and reading a few pages of a magazine while she nibbled at her salad.

Ken had surprised her the other day when he was downtown for a meeting by calling her for lunch. He'd insisted on picking her up in her office, even after she'd suggested meeting in a restaurant or in her lobby. She'd acted like an adolescent, blushing when the receptionist escorted him down the maze of hallways to point out the doorway of her cubicle and then waited to see how they greeted each other. Louise showed him around a little, trying to disregard the questioning looks from coworkers as she took him on a tour. When she'd occasionally had to make an introduction, she'd felt awkward. She didn't know what to call him—my friend, my boyfriend. My lover. Silly. She had shared some very personal moments with this man, and she was afraid, she realized now, she might embarrass him by calling him her boyfriend. Didn't want to make him feel that she had assumed they had a thing going. She must really need to have her head examined.

Louise opened the right-hand middle drawer enough to use as a footrest and pushed her chair back to a reclining position. She took a sip of soda and draped the *People* open across her thighs. She wasn't going to answer the phone until her lunch hour was over, but the ringing was annoying, so she looked at the caller ID and picked it up. It was Ken, and he was very excited. He'd just spoken to the father of a runaway boy and even though the man wouldn't talk about it, Ken knew he had also received a ransom note about their dog. Seemed to be a sore point between the man and his wife, and the man didn't want to have anything to do with it. But he did tell Ken he could call back when she was home and discuss it with her.

"I feel I'm on to something. Something bigger than a scheme against the old lady. Maybe more widespread."

"Nobody would ever believe it of you. You're so…deceiving. A nice, kind, gentle man. A nice, kind, Jewish man. They don't go in for cops-and-robbers things."

"You haven't seen the rest of my wardrobe."

"What d'ya mean?"

"You've only known me in mild weather. You don't know…I have a rumpled-up dirty trench coat. Like Colombo's."

"See, you're in the wrong profession. You oughta become a detective."

"Wouldn't work. Wanna hear the story of my life? Perry Mason had Della Street. Superman had Lois Lane. James Bond had…a whole menagerie. All the great investigators have beautiful secretaries or assistants. With my record, I'd come home to my beautiful, bachelor penthouse, with its high-tech electronic marvels and latest seduction equipment, and turn the light on over my circular, rotating mirrored bed with the built-in bar and movie screen in the footboard. I'd pull back the exotic silk sheets and find—ta-da—someone like Rosa Bassetti waiting for me in her flannel nightie."

Louise howled. "C'mon, it could be worse."

"How could it be worse?"

"I don't know. I suppose what would be worse would be finding Rosa Bassetti *without* her flannel nightgown."

This time Ken laughed loudly. "She's not really that bad, you know. In fact, I kinda think you'd like her. Maybe when I visit her this week, you'd like to meet her."

"I think I would. I wanna make sure you're not pulling my leg, and she's not some gorgeous blonde."

"With a name like Bassetti? A blonde Italian?"

"Oh, right. Let me rephrase that. I meant some gorgeous lady… with blonde hair under her arms." Louise couldn't believe she'd said that. Blurted her idiotic response as if she were talking to a teenage girlfriend or trying to get laughs from her coworkers, as she often did. She tried too hard. The silence stung her. Oh, God, she was really a jerk.

Then Ken guffawed and it was all right. "I'm going to give her a call today, because I want to see her before Labor Day. Matter of fact, I'd like to get the whole thing resolved before the weekend."

A whoosh of air rushed into Louise's lungs, inflated them, pushed them against her ribs. "Ken…"

"What? What's the matter? Louise, are you there?"

"Yes. I didn't know how to tell you."

"Tell me what? Hey, don't do this to me. Tell me."

"I can't go to Connecticut."

"What? I don't believe it! Why in hell not? What happened?" Ken's voice was more disappointed than angry.

"I want to meet your parents, honest. It's just that ever since you asked me, as much as I want to go, I'm sick—just sick—about having to put Honda somewhere for three days. I'm sorry. I know it's foolish, but I can't help it. I love that dog, and I die, thinking of what it would do to him, being in a cage. I'd have to take him on Thursday night so we could leave on Friday, and I wouldn't be able to pick him up until Tuesday because they'd be closed Monday night—and I've been nauseated with the worry and—"

"It's okay."

"What?" The last of her words had sucked the air out, leaving a hollowness in her chest.

Ken's voice was as soft and sweet as the look Louise tried to envision. "I know how you feel. I'm just surprised you didn't decide before now."

"Actually I did. I just didn't know how to tell you."

"Please don't ever be afraid to tell me anything. That's what it's all about, isn't it?"

"Yes," Louise answered almost shyly.

"There's no way I'm going to tell my mother, though. She'd kill me. And probably you too. She's been planning this, you know, for a few weeks, and she's really excited about meeting you. Tell you what. Let's leave early Saturday morning, spend the day up there, have dinner with them, come back to the city, pick up the dog, drive out to my house, and stay there on Sunday. Then, Monday morning, we can drop Honda back at home and go back to my parents again. I think they're planning a barbecue party on Labor Day. How's that sound?"

"Oh, Ken, it sounds fantastic. But what about all the driving? I'm sure it's at least two hours each way. You won't mind?"

"Of course I'll mind. But not as much as I'd mind not being with you."

Tears trickled down Louise's cheek.

"Hey, you there?" he asked.

"Yes." Her voice cracked with static.

"You crying?"

"Yes, of course I'm crying."

"But I thought you *liked* my idea."

"I do."

"Then why are you crying, for Chrissake?"

"That's why. Because I like your idea. And because"—she blew her nose loudly into the receiver—"you're so wonderful."

"Are all women as crazy as you?"

"Who knows? I just know I'm crazy about you." There.

She'd said it.

Chapter 118

Jason taped a sign announcing, in bright orange letters, COPIES MADE—ONLY 11 CENTS to the inside of the F-Stop's window. The tenant association needed a copier machine for all the literature they were sending out, but even though members were willing to chip in for the balance that the operating fund couldn't pay in order to purchase one, there was no place to put it. Jason's offer to keep it in the store, charge for copies, and turn the money over to SAVE had been met with suspicion and all sorts of questions about the legality of it. In the end, he decided it was a good business investment and tax deduction, so he leased one himself. His biggest customers in the week he'd had it had been people copying their Medicare statements; it would take a lot of doctor bills to pay for it.

But Jason himself was making good use out of it. Now, he fed in the two-page meeting notice for the next tenants' meeting, outlining the agenda and reminding everyone to bring their signed no-buy pledges with them. There were plenty of volunteers who would type and Xerox and put notices under doors. But not today and probably too busy tomorrow, but gladly next week. As Jason unconsciously nodded to the loud digestive noises the copier made in spitting out the papers, he thought about the enthusiasm that quickly had waned, the way it did with the general participation. No matter how interested everyone seemed to be in the future of their building and their individual apartments, attendance stank. They could rarely vote on anything, because they never had enough people present. Except for Miss Personality Pedersen, who could be relied on not to miss anything, especially a chance to start a good fight. The most opinionated people would shout their views, argue, and then not come back the next time to help make a decision about them. Jason found it all very frustrating.

He took the copies out of the sorter and checked each set to make sure it was collated properly. *Jason Ruderman,* he thought, *chairman of the 407 West End Avenue Tenants Association, secretary of the Support for AIDS Victims Everywhere organization. Jason Ruderman, whose high school yearbook might have said "least likely to do anything that matters" and whose many résumé versions omitted headings like "extracurricular" or "interests" or "affiliations." Jason Ruderman, the lost cause, now has a cause. Two of them.*

Chapter 119

The narrow counter on the side of the dispensary cabinet was a perfect place. It was hidden from the doorway so if people did suddenly appear, they wouldn't see him; even if they did, they wouldn't be able to see what he was doing there. There wasn't much room for the pad, since the thin ledge was really only meant for filling pill bottles or sorting the little sample tubes of ointment the pharmaceutical companies sent. But it served his purpose.

He meticulously printed the message, his left hand awkwardly outlining the block letters, his right toe simultaneously tracing the same crude shapes on the vinyl floor. It took a long time this way, sometimes several sessions to complete one set of instructions. But he couldn't take a chance by using his right hand. He didn't know if handwriting experts could trace printing. It would probably never come to that anyway. He wasn't being real greedy. Sure, if he asked for 25,000 dollars or 40,000, people would call the police. But ten thousand bucks or fifteen wasn't that much to them. It was easier to pay it than to take the chance. He never expected it to be so simple, but it was. So far. All he had to do was send the letter and then pick up the money. One, two. If he had known, he would have started off with 15,000 dollars, but he was too nervous in the beginning. The old lady and the gay paid the 10,000 thousand quickly.

So he upped the next one. But that was the limit. No more than 15,000. He already had 35,000 dollars, spread out in six different banks. He promised himself he'd stop when he had 50,000. Just one more.

He wondered what he'd do if somebody didn't pay. If he'd really go through with what he threatened. Or if he'd just skip that person and go on to the next. He probably would do it, just to teach them a lesson. Like they deserved. In fact, he had a funny feeling last time, when he watched the Marcus bitch nervously going into the Laundromat. There was that queasy mixture of exhilaration and fear in his belly and, at the same time, a slight sense of disappointment. Because it was all too easy. He wondered if he missed the electrifying tension of violence about to be committed. Or missed having his rage explode in a vicious, bloody, disgusting act. Now that he thought about it, he knew that was it. As the fantasy of his fury filled his brain, his stomach turned in revulsion. And his sphincter muscle clenched in excitement.

Chapter 120

Rosa didn't try to hide her surprise when she opened the door and saw Louise Sidway. Ken cleared his throat and introduced her. Rosa had expected Louise to be tall and thin, like Ken was, and pretty. But she wasn't. She looked hard, especially with her shoulders thrust forward in a permanent hunch. And the way her lower jaw was. Her red hair, squared around her face, made her look geometric, almost like a mechanical doll with a wind-up screw on her sloped back. Rosa decided all Louise needed was large hoop earrings and a little brighter lipstick, and she could stand on the corner of 42nd Street and Eighth Avenue. Because even in Rosa's day, when she was the busiest hat-check in town, she saw hookers who looked better than Louise did. She was disappointed; Ken Hollis could do better than that.

She stood aside to let them in. From behind, Rosa realized that Louise *was* tall—she towered over Rosa anyway. But her hips, heavy and low, detracted from her height and pulled her down.

Louise looked quietly around the room, as if waiting for a formal invitation to sit down. Then she noticed the hairless bundle standing on the cushion of the easy chair, her stump of a tail erect, waiting for someone to tell her what was going on, who was there, what the sudden flurry of movement meant. "Well, hel-lo," she said, going right to Princess. When she realized the dog's eyes were sightless with a milky film, Louise put the back of her hand against her snout so Princess could smell her. She dropped her pocketbook on the floor and, ignoring the unsightly lumps and fuzzy skin, gently lifted up Princess and sat down, cradling the dog like a baby. "Aren't you a cutie?" she murmured. Princess couldn't hear, but the vibrations of the tender tone, together with the gentle touch, told her she was in safe hands. She spread her front paws open in Louise's lap so the stroking fingers could find her chest and, when they did, she moaned with pleasure.

Well, beauty isn't everything, Rosa thought, pushing her step stool in front of a kitchen cabinet and standing on its bottom rung. She reached for three wine goblets with the navy Chambord crest, a souvenir of the elegant restaurant where she started her hat-check career, before landing the great one at the Rainbow Room, where she worked for twenty years—before it went out of business and she did too, taking an early retirement. Had she known they were going to reopen a few years later, maybe she would have gone back. But by then, they wouldn't have wanted someone her age. And it was all different. Different from the days you could walk around to the tables with your case of cigarettes or maybe bring a white phone to one of the booths for an important customer getting a call to the restaurant.

She poured burgundy from the gallon bottle stored in the space between the refrigerator and sink and carefully carried two glasses into the living room. When she came back with the third, she dragged a wooden kitchen chair with her other hand and parked it opposite Louise. Ken was to Louise's side, comfortable on the couch, holding his drink on the arm, the stem of his glass toying with the spot where the nap of velvet, stringy with age, showed through the worn slipcover.

"That you real color?" Rosa asked bluntly, pointing to Louise's hair as she sat down.

"Of course. Would anyone pay for a color like this?" Louise laughed, patting her hair.

When she laugh, Rosa thought, *her whole face, it lights up. Then, she look pretty. Well, almost pretty.* She nodded her approval to Ken.

He winked at Louise as if to say, *"Didn't I tell you she was a case?"* Then he asked out loud, "So, any more news?"

"Nah. Just some ideas. You?"

"Well, as a matter of fact, I did find out something. There was another one."

"No!" Rosa inched her buttocks forward. The back of her dress remained stuck to the chair, the front riding up over her thighs. From where Louise sat, she could see the brown band of Rosa's stocking stretched into the clasp of an old-fashioned garter. It reminded her of her grandmother. "Who? Just tell me—they hurt the dog?"

"No. This one would be a hard one to hurt. He's huge."

"She," Louise interrupted.

"'Scuse me—she. Whatever it is, it's big. And ferocious."

Louise looked directly at Rosa. "You ever notice how people who aren't dog people get their sexes mixed up?"

"Yes," Rosa said, nodding knowingly. "Anyone who calls my little girl a boy has to answer to me! It's an insult!"

"Ah, who could mistake this dainty little thing for a boy?" Louise tickled Princess's belly. "On the other hand, my big lug of a male is so gentle and sweet, if you didn't know, you'd think he was a female. Only you'd better not say that to him!"

"What kind he is?" Rosa asked.

"Macho. Mucho macho." Louise's laugh was infectious, and Rosa joined her. "He's your basic mutt. But he's mostly Lab. Black Labrador, and he has this silver triangle right here." Louise drew one on her forehead with her finger. "He's gorgeous. Isn't he gorgeous, Ken?"

"It doesn't seem like my opinion would count for much around here, all of a sudden being a non-dog person, but yes, he is gorgeous."

Louise ignored him to continue on her favorite subject. "And really very masculine. If anybody ever called him a girl, he'd know it, believe me, and would probably rip that person apart. Like he would anybody who didn't treat me right. Are you listening over there?" she asked Ken with a big smile.

"He must love you a lot," Rosa commented.

"I do." Ken said it without thinking, and Louise, stunned, grinned and looked down.

"We talkin' about the dog." Rosa slapped her thigh jovially but then impulsively went over and held Ken's face in both her hands. "My children, my children, you make-a nice couple." She left him and stood in front of Louise, forcing her to lift her head to look at her. When she did, the blush spread from her neck to her cheeks, glowing on her fair skin. Rosa bent over and gave Louise an awkward half-hug, her large bosom brushing Louise's chin. "Now, that's settled," she said authoritatively, her blessing obviously final. "We have a toast to you." She saluted them with her wine. "Okay, now, back to business. But first, we fill up the glasses." She retrieved the jug and brought it into the living room. As she poured, she asked, "What happen? With this new one?"

"Marcus family," Ken answered. "Couple in their mid-thirties, give or take a few years. They have an eleven-year-old son who used to be—I don't know, not exactly autistic but had some development problems. They adopted a dog from the ASPCA. She's big." He turned to Louise, saying, "I saw her picture; you'd love her. She and the boy are very attached. Since they got her, kid has done a 100 percent turnaround. Anyway, they got a note a few weeks ago. Almost the same as the others." Ken took a wad of papers out of his breast pocket and sifted through them. "The woman made the payoff. Husband didn't want to give in, didn't want to have anything to do with it. The mother was afraid to risk anything happening to the dog and the son then regressing. Here—this is a copy of the letter she got." He handed it to Rosa. "But listen to the kicker—the boy ran away from home with the dog."

"What? You mean because he's afraid they kidnap the dog?" Rosa asked.

"No, the mother, Mrs. Marcus, doesn't think he even knew about the note or the threat. Seems she and her husband are having some marital problems, and she thinks the kid might've been unhappy about that. Anyway, he's only eleven; he can't have gone too far. Trouble is, in this city, you don't have to go too far to lose yourself. Anyway, they were evidently hiding out in Central Park, sticking close to a group of homeless men. Maybe the kid felt safer with a bunch of people around. One of them hated the dog and picked on the kid. One night, who knows what this guy did—nobody knows—but the dog went for him. Bit him badly. So bad he was taken to the hospital and had enough stitches in his neck to look like his head was zippered on. But before they could do anything more, the guy ran away."

"What guy?" Rosa looked confused.

"The guy in the hospital. The victim. He probably had his own reasons for not wanting to be found or identified. Maybe he's an escaped convict or something or owes five years' alimony. Whatever reason he has for becoming homeless is likely the same reason he doesn't want to talk to the police. And he knows the dog bite will be reported, and the police will come. That's how I found out, by the way. There was a missing-person file on the boy, and the homeless man described the kid at the hospital. Some very smart cop linked them up."

"So what happens then?" Rosa leaned forward, all ears.

"Nothing. Looks like the kid is still hiding, probably more afraid for his dog than he was before. Of course, the guy isn't going to be around to press charges, but the kid doesn't know that. The Marcuses are frantic about their son. At this point, they certainly don't want to pursue the blackmailer. The police were worried about the guy—about rabies, about the guy getting it, foaming at the mouth and ranting and raving through the streets, maybe committing some heinous crimes. But now that they've located the Marcuses, who think it was their dog, at least the cops are pretty sure it wasn't a stray. In fact, the mother just went to their vet to get a statement that the dog has had all its shots." Ken shuffled through the papers still in his hand. "Here's a copy of that."

As he passed it over, the letterhead caught Rosa's eye and she shouted excitedly, "Hey, that's my doctor too."

"Really?" Ken tilted his head. "That's a coincidence."

"Manhattan Vet'anry Associates," Rosa announced and skipped right to the bottom. "See, it's signed by him—Dr. Pomalee."

Louise jumped up. "Dr. Pomalee! I don't believe it. That's my dog's doctor. Let me see that." She took the letter from Rosa, scanned it, and handed it back. "Why do you go to 74th Street from here?"

"He used to be closer, but it's like anything else. I like him, he knows me, and he treats my dog good."

"That's why I go to him," Louise agreed. "He's actually not very pleasant to me, but he's wonderful to my dog."

Ken stood up to retrieve his papers. "Well, ladies, it's very nice that you two have something in common—" He stopped short, and all three of them simultaneously opened their mouths in amazement.

Louise was the first to recover. "Do you suppose…?" Rosa slapped her forehead. "How stupid we don't think of it."

Ken nodded. "The most simple, the most obvious. But wait—you think that guy…what's his name? Justin Ruderman?"

"Jason," Rosa corrected.

"Right, Jason Ruderman. He's all the way over on the West Side. You don't think…"

Rosa was already at her desk, pulling out drawers. She turned a manila envelope over, emptying it, and photographs and bits of papers covered the surface of the drop-leaf. She found the card right away. "Here—the F'n Stop. You call. I no speak too good English when I'm nervous."

Chapter 121

Laurie couldn't sleep. She rolled onto her stomach, burying her face in her pillow, dislodging Felix, who wheezed his anger at her and then pompously strutted out of the bedroom, like a tap dancer strutting off stage. She turned onto her back, clutching the pillow over her. But she couldn't block out the frenzy of eyes spinning in her brain, circling, darting. Pleading for help. Calling Laurie Jensen to rescue them.

Eyes of dogs hanging upside down by their paws in Philippine meat markets; eyes of chimpanzees visible between electrodes dangling from their heads; eyes of mother seals watching their babies skinned alive, tears melting into their fur; eyes of rabbits taped open and coated with detergent; eyes of wolves chewing their legs off in traps; eyes of dolphins still strangling as steel nets sliced their necks. Eyes of animals being gassed, trapped, burned, electrocuted.

Her own eyes could not shut them out. They haunted her—with the agony of their torture, with the gruesome slowness of their dying, with their aloneness and pain. She could see nothing else except millions of eyes and their grisly suffering. They blinded her.

Her belly churned bile to her throat. She gagged on its sourness and ran to the bathroom, heaving over the toilet.

She slapped cold water on her cheeks and then braced herself on the edge of the sink. Her arms wobbled.

She went into the kitchen and poured a glass of red wine, which she brought into the living room with her. She sat on the couch, waiting for her body to stop shaking, and then sipped her drink in the dark.

A set of iridescent amber disks beamed on both sides of the room, an occasional flicker reminding her that she was being watched. "Over here, guys, c'mere." She patted the couch, but they didn't come. No matter how enchanting they could be, they still weren't dogs. "You're wondering what I'm doing, huh? Well, so am I. What am I doing here?" she asked out loud. "What am I doing with my life?"

Laurie rubbed the light condensation on her glass and wondered if she was becoming an alcoholic. It seemed that she was doing this a lot lately—coming home, tired, depressed, and having one or two drinks to relax her. It was only wine, but she read somewhere that it was just as bad as liquor. It's not like she had to have it. Except, even when she promised herself on the subway or walking to her apartment that she would not have a drink tonight, she came in and had one anyway. More like three. Sometimes she just wanted to have one to help her calm down. Like now. A few minutes ago, she was ready to puke her guts out, and now she felt fine.

"Hey, wanna cuddle?" A current of air announced a cat streaking by. "Even you don't want me anymore. Thanks, loads." Laurie's voice was slightly slurred. *Maybe nobody wants me,* she thought, *because I'm not very worth wanting.* She had to do something because she couldn't go on like this. She was almost finished with her project, but then what? Anyway, what good would it do anyone—especially the animals—when it was done? Maybe the whole thing was for nothing. It's not like she had something better to do. But she should. That was her problem. Wasting her time on a cause that she couldn't help, wasting her life on a man she couldn't have.

Laurie refilled her glass, curled her legs under her, and tried to drown her despair. The wine was warm and thick as syrup as it slid down her throat. For a moment, she dreamed of her mother's embrace, and she sniveled loudly.

She swiped her finger across her nose as Felix jumped into her lap, followed by Oscar, who gently touched her face with a paw before curling up against her leg. They both lifted their heads and glared as Megabyte tentatively climbed onto the couch and got comfortable in the corner. Then they circled their faces into their butts in secure mode, which Laurie called sleeping inside out. Three cats on the couch. An omen, for sure.

Chapter 122

Fibber McGee lifted his leg against the giant concrete banister and dribbled on the bottom step.

"Aw, Miss Hargan, look what he done." Wally Schilder's loud whine came from two doors away, where he was hosing the sidewalk.

Eileen looked down and saw the urine spots darkening the stone. She tugged the leash, scolding her dog with a "naughty, naughty," which Wally knew was half-hearted for his sake. So did Fibber. "Sorry," she called back to him. "Do it quick so it won't stain." She watched him drag the hose and stepped back to the curb so she wouldn't get sprinkled.

"'I's okay. Whatcha doin' out here so early?"

"I haven't been sleeping. So I thought I'd catch Miss Bassetti; she goes out early." Eileen would never have referred to her as Rosa to someone like Wally Schilder. A worker. Just like she never referred to another teacher by her first name to a student or even a parent. It wouldn't be proper. "And how are you, Wally? When are you leaving for vacation?"

"I'm fine. You know me, Ms. Hargan. Comes Labor Day, I take off for my month. This is my last day."

"I didn't realize. Where are you going this year?"

"Europe. Promised the wife I'd take her to Germany. She still has people there. Some first cousins, an uncle. So, as long as we're there, we're doing the grand tour. London, Paris, Rome. Then the Rhineland."

"That's wonderful, Wally. When do you leave?"

"Today at four o'clock. Soon as my day's over. Going to spend the weekend with the grandchildren in New Jersey first. Then Monday, we'll get ready and leave on Tuesday. Didn't want to travel on Labor Day anyway."

"Well, good for you. I hope you have a good time."

"Thanks, Ms. Hargan. I'm sure we will." As he turned to talk to her, the hand holding the hose followed, and Eileen did a two-step out of its reach. "G'won, I'm not going to get you." Wally released his thumb, controlling the water, and went back to where he'd been working. "You take care."

"Thank you. You too. And have a good time." *Think of that,* Eileen said to herself. *A part-time superintendent is off to Europe, and I've never been.* She laughed at her own silliness. "How do you like that, Mr. McGee?" The dog cocked his head in her direction, but she didn't elaborate. It's not like she couldn't afford to go. If she wanted. She just never wanted. She preferred knowing the money was safe in the bank, rather than using it for something as frivolous as a trip. But more and more lately, it had seemed increasingly frivolous not to spend it. Look how easy she'd withdrawn the 10,000 dollars.

Only that was different. That was almost a necessity. But as her friend said, "If you can find it for something like that, you can find it for pleasure."

It wasn't too late. She wouldn't go to Europe—not that far—but maybe someplace closer. The Caribbean. Florida. Maybe she'd even invite Rosa to go with her. If she had a companion, it would be easier. Not that she hadn't had her choice of companions before, but maybe there just hadn't been anybody with whom she would consider spending several weeks traveling. It seemed like a shame that Eileen would die without having been farther than Los Angeles—and that had been in 1972. Why should Danny and his wife inherit the money? Charlene was really nothing to her and would probably get a three-week, expenses-paid trip to the other side of the world when Eileen died. *The hell she will!* Eileen thought. She pulled Fibber McGee closer to her. "Over my dead body," she said out loud to him.

"Over you dead body what?"

Even though she knew it wasn't Fibber McGee answering her, the timing was so startling that she jumped. "Rosa, you scared me."

"I see. You gotta be paying attention more. I tol' you. Anybody could come behind you and grab the leash." Rosa demonstrated by pulling it away from Eileen. Then she bent over to say a personal greeting to Fibber McGee. "Now, what you tellin' him?"

"Well, get this, Rosa Bassetti. I was thinking of taking a real vacation. And taking you with me."

"G'won."

"Yes. What would you say to going to Paris? Or London? Or both?" It came out before she had a chance to think. What had happened to the Caribbean or Florida?

"I'da say…ho-ly shit."

"Rosa!"

"But I say in Italian so you wouldn'ta be upset."

Eileen laughed. "Of course, we can't go until"—she moved her gaze downward to Fibber and Princess, prancing around each other—"until they're gone." Her pointed look at Rosa warned her not to repeat the words out loud, not to scare the two dogs.

"Of course. And I hope they both be around for a long, long time. But how wonderful to look forward. You really wanna take me?"

"Better you than that Charlene." As soon as Eileen said it, she knew she would do it. If she lived that long. And she damn well intended to.

Not that she'd run out of horrors in this country, but Laurie was so overwhelmed by the animal cruelty she came across that she had to start a new page for international obscenities.

Two million dogs a year killed in the South Korean meat market. Hung, live, upside down by their rear legs where housewives and chefs could examine what kind of meal they'd make.

Canned hunts in Africa where lions that were raised in captivity, in parks, interacting with people, got too big and were sold to a different business, where so-called hunters paid to shoot them dead. Targets confined to a small enclosure.

In the last two years, more than 70,000 elephants—majestic animals with strong emotions and family bonds—have been slaughtered. Their tusks savagely cut out of their flesh, leaving them to bleed to death in excruciating pain.

Next, she would report on the farming industry and the eight billion animals raised in factory-like environments and subjected to torturous lives.

As she typed, her stomach twisted, and she started to gag on the vomit threatening to churn up her guts.

Chapter 123

Yolanda tapped the hard-boiled egg on the table and peeled the shell back as she half listened to Señora Sanchez's commentary on their neighborhood, her children in Colombia, her children in New York, the state of the city, and the plight of poor people everywhere. Without a pause in her monologue, Señora got up from the kitchen chair, opened the refrigerator, took out the jar of mayonnaise, and placed it next to Yolanda. "You making too much," she told Yolanda in Spanish.

"Not the way those kids eat. And it's more fun when they're out… gives them a bigger appetite. This is going to be a real picnic. They have the tables and benches all set up. I wish you'd come with us."

Señora Sanchez waved her hand. "I'm too old for that."

"Nobody's too old. The bus is comfortable, air conditioned, and we'll leave you somewhere in the shade while we go off exploring. Please. The children would love it."

"Nah. I'll just stay home, like I do every holiday, and wait for someone to visit me. You'd think one of my daughters or my granddaughters could find time to stop by and just say hello." She switched to English. "How you doin'?"

"You'll just be disappointed, like always," Yolanda responded, ignoring the question. "That's why you should come with us. So you won't be alone."

"It's not the kind of holiday that you can't be alone. Not like Easter or Christmas. It's okay. Ricardo going?"

"Are you kidding? You know he wouldn't do a family thing, like go to Bear Mountain with us. What would his friends say? Anyway, I think he has to work."

"On Labor Day?"

"Labor Day isn't 'til Monday. It's just a regular Saturday for him."

"You think he's going to stay there when school starts?"

Yolanda cut the eggs into a big soup bowl, chopped some onions, and added salt and pepper and the mayo. She mixed the ingredients hard with a wooden spoon. "I hope so, I hope so. They asked him to. Oh, wouldn't it be wonderful if he stayed 'til he was finished with school and then went on to college? And then—who knows? He might go to medical school or whatever you have to do to become a vet himself: Dr. Ricardo Santiago Jr. Sometimes I dream about it, Señora, walking down the aisle for my son's graduation from college. Oh, if my mother, poor soul, could have lived to see it—he was her favorite, you know."

"He's everybody's favorite. *El joven es encantador.* A charmer. If I had a young daughter around his age, I'd lock her up. Soon as his face clears up, he's going to be a real lady-killer, that one."

"Don't tell him that. His head is big enough as it is. Yes, he knows how to be charming, but the real reason he's so appealing is that he's…I don't know…caring. *Sensitive.* That's it, sensitive."

"Could this be the mother speaking? Of course she has no prejudice about her son." Señora Sanchez laughed and reached over to run her finger along the rim of the bowl to scoop a taste of egg salad. "The bread will get soggy."

"Don't worry. I'm not going to make the sandwiches 'til the morning, just before we leave. Tell me—good?"

"Of course it's good. Needs a little more salt, though."

"I was talking about Ricky," Yolanda said, sprinkling more salt into the bowl. "He's a good boy, isn't he?"

"Of course he's a good boy. You worry too much. About all of them. They're good children. You did a good job bringing them up."

"Well, I had lots of help. I don't know what I would have done without you."

Señora Sanchez beamed. "It was good to have a tough old bird around, hah? Someone with the exact right mixture of discipline and love."

"Now look who's not at all prejudiced."

Wordlessly, the señora stood up and held the plastic container steady on the table, while Yolanda tilted the bowl over it. "So then," Yolanda asked, shoveling the egg salad into it with the wooden spoon, "how come I always worry?"

"How come? Because you are a mother; that's how come."

Chapter 124

Jason Ruderman looked around the living room, his eyes examining everything to make sure it was all right. As if whatever was wrong would be noticeable now and not after they came back. The windows were all closed, the lights all turned off, except for the lamp in the bedroom, which faced the street.

Chris walked into the foyer and pointed to the carrier, open on the floor, airing out. "I'll take that."

Jason nodded and called out, "Now, don't start hiding, Sabrina. We're going on a fun trip. You don't even have to get in your carrier yet." He went into the kitchen and came back with a small rawhide bone and a rubber hamburger, which he put into the carrier. "And if you're real good and quiet, we may be able to let you sit on Daddy's lap on the choo-choo."

"Don't count on it," Chris told him. "The train will probably be mobbed; somebody's bound to complain."

"It'll be just our luck that somebody like Nettie Pedersen will go all the way to Amagansett on the same train."

"No, that would be the good news. The bad news would be if Nettie Pedersen herself was on the train. 'Oh, Conductor. Conductor.'" Chris pursed his lips in a prudish pout. "'There is a loose ani-mule in this car, and I must insist that it be crated immediately.'"

Jason laughed, and Sabrina cocked her head at the shrill imitation.

"'And furthermore, Conductor,'" Chris continued, "'the two gentlemen escorting her are not gentlemen at all. They are of a homosexual persuasion, and I must request that they not be permitted to sit together. In fact, they should be crated too. They should not be allowed to ride next to decent people.'"

"'Well, miss,'" Jason said, taking the conductor's part and deepening his voice as low as he could while making a stern face, "'I quite agree. The Long Island Rail Road rules and regulations do not permit any lewd or lascivious behavior, so…I demand that you stop drooling over my sexy body at once. Or I shall force you'"—Jason opened his fly, pulled out his penis, and shook it back and forth at the imaginary Ms. Pedersen—"'to take this and this and this.'"

When they finished roaring with laughter, Christopher followed Jason into the kitchen, and watched him push each knob on the stove to make sure the jets were closed all the way.

"Let me just double-check the bathroom," Jason said.

"I already did."

"Doesn't hurt to look again. Did you look in the tub too?"

"Jason, for Chrissake, we never ever leave water dripping. Why would we now, just when we're going away?"

"Who knows why? Because I'm a nut." Jason's voice faded as he went to check. Moments later, he came back, picked up Sabrina's leash, and then stood for a moment, looking to Chris like a little boy about to go away to camp for the first time.

"You okay?" Chris asked.

Jason continued to stare at Christopher Barrett—his friend, his lover, his life companion. His eyes softened with his love. And deep within him, he felt serene in the knowledge that his mother and father would understand that and even be glad for him. That his whole family would embrace him and Chris. Jason hugged Chris close and patted his back emotionally before pulling away. As Jason hooked the leash onto the dog's collar, he hid a tear on his cheek. Then, silently, they took their bags and the carrier, locked the door, and walked down the hall toward the elevator, with Sabrina waddling between them. *Yes,* Jason thought, *I feel serene. And giddy.*

Chapter 125

Jessica paced back and forth in the police station while her husband sat on the edge of a wooden bench and cracked his knuckles. The desk sergeant hung up the phone. "Mr. Marcus? Ma'am?" As they approached the desk, Jessica fumbled for Lenny's hand and squeezed it. "They're bringing 'im right down," the sergeant said kindly. "Detective's gone to get him. He'll be coming through that door there." He pointed to the far end of the lobby-like hall.

"Is the dog still with him?" Jessica's voice was shaky with fear. "They didn't send her to the ASPCA, did they?"

"No, we're not monsters. From the way I hear it, the little fella survived so well because of that dog. Anyways, he put up a big fight when they tried to take them in separate cars. No, they're still together. But you're going to have to have her examined and…well, the detective will explain everything to you."

They nodded their thanks, walked back to the bench, and stared at the door. Where the paint wasn't peeled, it was black with fingerprints. Lenny took his hand away, pulled his fingers for a few faint cracks of his knuckles, and then slipped it back in Jessica's.

"Oh, God, I'm so nervous," she whispered.

"Why? He's all right."

"Because. Because I'm afraid he hates us now, hates me. That's why he did it. I don't know how to act."

"Don't act, Jess, just be yourself. He loves you. It's going to be okay."

"Don't yell at him," she instructed. "Whatever you do, don't yell."

"Come on. What do you take me for? And I've never yelled at him in his life."

"You don't have to raise your voice to be yelling. It's like my father always did to me. It's the tone of disapproval. Sorry. I know you don't yell. I just don't want to scare him away."

"I think he's had enough," Lenny said. "I don't think he's going to run away again."

"I didn't mean run away. I meant retreat. Inside himself. Go back to the way he was."

"He's not going to do that. He's come a long way. He's grown up fast—eleven years in the past one. He's not going to go…backward now."

"Len, I want him to continue therapy. Please don't interfere with that. If you dislike Michelle so much, we'll take him somewhere else. But it's important for him. Promise you'll let him continue, without fighting about it."

"Jess, Jess, I don't object to his going to Dr. Kravitz. Or anybody else. But stop trying to plan everything every second. Let him be just a little boy for a change. He's entitled to—"

The door opened. The same electric impulse jumped through both their hands; the air hung suspended in their lungs. Clifford and Kola followed a burly man through the door and then stopped to look around. Jessica exhaled so quickly that a whistle rode her breath. Kola's tail stiffened. Even matted with dirt, the white fur that hung from her tail created a feathery bow, arched in attention. The luxuriant plume swayed once, poised as she turned her head in their direction, her eyes fixing on theirs. Then it fanned wildly in recognition before she yowled her happy surprise. In three great leaps, she was dancing on her hind legs with Jessica.

Jessica tried to open her arms to Clifford, who just had started toward them, but Kola kept coming into them. She could not stop yelping and smothering Jessica with sloppy licks. Clifford watched as he came closer, stopped, and waited, trying to gauge his father's response. Then Leonard Marcus was down on his knees, his hands pleading. Clifford dropped the canvas knapsack he was carrying and ran the last few steps into his father's hug. A lump clogged Lenny's throat. He swallowed hard, forcing it down. "Welcome home," he whispered against Clifford's ear. The small body fit comfortably against his chest and Lenny held him there tightly, bosom to bosom. "We were worried about you, son." His words came out gravelly.

Then suddenly, they were exchanging partners in an orgy of kissing, hugging, howling, licking, and crying. The desk sergeant swiped the back of his hand across his nose. "Somethin' bothering you?" the detective asked.

"Naw, why'd you ask?" They frowned at each other for a few seconds and then broke into broad smiles and gave each other a high-five.

Chapter 126

The ends of the shoelaces were open, the white tongues sticking out of his high-tops. Although he was thin, his feet were an E-wide and gave him an athletic look. The thick rubber soles of his sneakers padded his footsteps as he walked around the office, making sure no one had come in yet. He peeked through the window at the waiting room, straining his neck to look as far as he could toward both corners, since she had a tendency to come in early. He tried, but he just couldn't have gotten here any sooner, what with waiting for his mother to get out of the bathroom this morning and the delay on the A train. It had to be today, so they'd get it right after Labor Day. Otherwise, he'd only be working on Saturdays, and it would have to wait another whole week.

The coast was clear. He went to the four-drawer cabinet in the receptionist's cubicle and crouched in front of the bottom drawer marked S-Z CURRENT. The ones above it had already been emptied out, the files transferred to the computer upstairs. He was excited about starting school on Tuesday; he was taking a computer class for one of his sciences. He knew he was going to be a whiz at it—he loved mechanical things. Maybe he would go to college for it. But first, he needed just a little more money to pay for his education. *And theirs,* he thought, snickering silently. Not that they'd learn their lesson.

How dare they—how fucking dare they—come in with their spoiled little pets and make such a fuss over them? Spend all that money on injections and pills and medicated baths, and X-rays, not to mention operations and pulling teeth and…jeez, imagine pulling a dog's teeth, giving it anesthesia and all! He noticed the folder for "Sidway, Louise," pulled it out, and read the medical history of her dog, Honda. Of course he would never do anything to her—especially since she was the one who got him the job in the first place. He was just curious. No, she was an okay lady. It was the rest of them. The middle-aged women fawning, pampering, cooing. Writing out checks. Whipping out credit cards. No matter how much it cost. Young girls with their kittens, talking to them through the holes in the carriers, apologizing to them for bringing them. God, it sucked! Didn't they know there were poor people out there, little kids with no food? While they were buying gourmet cat foods and rhinestone leashes, there were babies practically dying of starvation. People who couldn't even afford to go to a doctor. Yet here they were, bringing their animals to a hospital.

And what about decent people who just couldn't get it together? They didn't offer to help *them*, give them rent money or send their children to college. For their pets, they had it, not for other human beings. Look at his father, running out on them. He knew why—his father couldn't cope. No matter how hard his father worked, it never got better, never got easier. Well, he wasn't going to let that happen to his mother or to the rest of his family. He already had enough to take care of them. It was just too bad he couldn't use it yet. It was too soon. Only if there was an emergency.

Every day was an emergency for some of his friends. Trying to scrape together enough for the next meal. Life sure wasn't fair. Not when these jerks could take care of dogs and cats, and there was nobody to take care of the people.

Ah, there it is. He held the chart in one hand and copied down the address with his other. It was the least they could do. Give up some more money. It was for a much better cause than their pets. He admitted, though, that he got a great deal of pleasure from imagining their absolute terror, knowing their fear. They deserved to suffer.

His skin tingled when he thought about the old lady opening the envelope with the ear. Even as he cut it off the dead mutt in the plastic bin, waiting to be picked up by the crematorium, he thought he would've enjoyed it much more cutting it off a live dog, hearing it scream. No, he didn't really want to hurt an animal; he wanted to hear its owner scream in horror.

Chapter 127

It was a delightful 68 degrees and even though the forecast was for highs in the mid-80s, the early morning breeze smelled like autumn. The last day of August would be remembered for its clear skies and bright sun. But not for long. Tomorrow, the skies might be the same blue and the sun as hot, but they would belong to September and the promise of a spectacular season of crunchy leaves and bracing air and old cardigans.

Rosa opened her mouth and inhaled deeply, enjoying the freshness in her chest. There was nobody around. Few cars lined the curb but she still would not let Princess squat in an empty parking space. She remembered a dog back in 1976, whose owner had let her pee in the gutter. Someone in the car right behind her had turned on the ignition, and the loud noise had startled the dog, causing a heart attack. The dog collapsed and died in the puddle of urine. Right in front of her owner.

The old man Wally Schilder had hired to clean the street and carry the garbage out during Wally's vacation was nowhere around, even though big black plastic bags leaned against each other in front of every brownstone. If she stood in a line straight and bent a little, they almost looked like mountains. Rosa checked her watch so she could write down the time when she went back upstairs to show Wally how many days the man was late. She did that every year.

She strolled to the corner, enjoying the emptiness of the block, but feeling a little like the only person left on earth after a bomb fell.

Everybody was on their way somewhere for the weekend, but it was just like any other Saturday to her. Any other weekend. If she could go anywhere, where would she go? She shrugged. "I'd go back-a home," she said out loud. "To Italy." It was nice of Eileen Hargan to invite her on a trip. But they'd never do it. By the time both their dogs were dead and they were free to travel, they'd probably be too old or too sick. Besides, Eileen's intentions might be good, but that woman would never part with her money. *Must be the Irish in her,* Rosa thought. It didn't matter. It was nice to think about going somewhere.

She hoped the kids would have a nice time over the Labor Day weekend. Well, they were in their thirties, so they really weren't kids anymore—except to her. They made a good-looking couple. Rosa pictured them as bride and groom, walking down the aisle in a fancy synagogue. Louise was Christian, but Rosa was sure she'd convert if she and Ken got married. "Do Jewish people walk down the aisle?" she asked Princess.

Not knowing, she pictured them walking down the aisle of a church, everybody nodding to the beautiful maid of honor in her long blue gown. Rosa twirled around in the street, pretending to show it off. Blue was her best color.

They said they'd call her on Tuesday to let her know how it went—if his parents liked her. Anyway, Ken also promised to tell her every single detail, give her a blow-by-blow description of the police investigation, and let her know if it was the guy in the vet's office. The guy for whom Louise got the job. Rosa had seen him there last time she went to the vet. She didn't like his looks, and she wouldn't let him hold Princess on the table. The way he came in and out of the room, so quiet—there was something sneaky about him. She knew it then. Maybe they wouldn't be able to catch him without her.

She picked Princess up and nuzzled her. "You tired already? Mama carry you. They going to need my help. Because it's really me who figure it out, bambina. And me who knows all the stories. Me who find out about that Jason, and me who think to call him and ask if he still go to his old vet from when he live on the East Side. Sí, they need me to tell them everything."

An old man came up the block, walking slowly. He went into the six-story building near the corner, and Rosa strolled in that direction, waiting for him. She knew who he was. A cranky old Kraut who lived on 80th Street off York. He came out with a big broom and started sweeping the sidewalk.

"You late," she announced. When he didn't answer, she repeated it.

"Says who?" He glared at her, pointing the broom like a weapon.

"Says me."

"And who're you?"

"Me, I'm Rosa Bassetti, and I live on this street."

"So? I don't have to answer to you."

"No?"

"No. I don't have to talk to a crazy old lady talking to herself on the street."

"I was not-a talking to myself. I was talking to my dog!" she shrieked at him, holding Princess's head.

The man sneered, confirming that she was even crazier than he thought.

"Hey, you *capice*?" She put Princess down so she could use both her arms to give him the old Italian salute.

"Can you believe that little shit?" Louise complained to Honda. "After going out on a limb to get him the job, after helping his mother and his sister, the little prick does something like that?" Louise slammed the stainless steel bowl on the floor with such venom that part of the wet food jumped over the top and onto the floor. Honda's ears went back and his tail dropped between his back legs. He sat in front of his dinner, his head slightly cocked to ask what he had done wrong.

"And I had such hopes for him too. For after graduation, for his future. He certainly fucked up his life. And mine too." Louise held onto the rim of the kitchen sink, slightly bent to gulp some deep breaths. "It's okay; you're a good boy. I'm not mad at you." She crouched on the floor, and Honda slithered toward her, still acting guilty. "It's okay, big guy. I'm sorry I scared you." She opened her arms, and Honda rubbed his head against her chest with a little whimper. "You silly boy, you didn't do anything wrong. Mama did. Trusting that asshole." What a jerk he was. He probably didn't even know that the New York State criminal justice system considered sixteen- and seventeen-year-olds as adults.

Calmer now, cooing apologies to Honda, she knew no matter how pissed off she was at Rick, she would never let Yolanda down. She'd stand by her when they arraigned him, help her bail him out, and maybe try to sway the court to give him another chance.

And she would not let this ruin her weekend. Let *his* be ruined, thinking about spending a few nights in a jail cell.

Laurie left to get the newspaper and a bagel for her breakfast. It was too pleasant out to sit in her cramped, windowless kitchen, so without making the conscious decision to do so, she kept on walking. There weren't many people around—they all had somewhere to go—and when she came to a tiny coffee shop that looked empty, she was sure it was closed for the holiday weekend. But she peered in the window anyway and saw lights on and silhouetted movements in the back. She went in and took a booth, tentatively waiting to be told to move. The unwritten law that only three or more can sit at a table for four is so ingrained in New Yorkers that Laurie, even though she had checked first to make sure there were plenty of other tables, felt guilty. As she watched the waitress coming toward her with a coffeepot, she gratefully pushed her cup over. After she ordered the number three—two eggs and bacon, home fries, and toast—she spread the *News* open and sat back comfortably, relishing the forbidden space.

She ate her breakfast, read most of the paper, except for the sports section, and had two refills of coffee, which were not responsible for her feeling so stimulated. The first day of September carried an expectancy in its breeze, a joyful eagerness to meet the coming season. Laurie Jensen's spirit was invigorated. She suddenly felt an urge deep in her being to not only accept her future but to steer its course. A small stretch of her arms as she leaned against the vinyl back of the seat seemed to loosen her body. But it was her soul, yawning widely to engulf life itself, that energized her. She was now up to 2,347 "likes" on her Posts and encouraging outrage on her Wall, and she knew something positive was going to come of it all.

Embarrassed to dawdle any longer, she nodded her head to the waitress and pointed to her cup. "Last one, thanks," she said as the young girl, probably with the least seniority to get stuck working this Saturday, poured more coffee from the glass pot.

Laurie turned the pages backward to find the one with the horoscope column. There it was: "Your new beginnings start with healing old wounds. Contact a long-lost friend or relative today." A mild sadness crept into her excitement and by the time she had left a dollar tip, rolled up the newspaper, and brought the check to the register behind the takeout sign at the counter, her mood had changed.

Outside, her forehead gathered into pleats from the brightness of the sun…and from salt stinging her eyes. Maybe she'd go home and call her mother. Talk to her; tell her she was coming for a visit. Whether her father liked it or not. It was too late to go this weekend; no, it didn't pay, not with the airfares what they were. But if she spoke to her mother now, she could make a reservation for Thanksgiving. That was so far away; maybe Columbus Day. Why not? If she went in to the office later today and again on Monday and next weekend, she'd have everything finished by October 12th. So Dr. Pomalee wouldn't mind if she took more time off, maybe a whole week. *If* her mother wanted her to come home. Of course she would. Mothers were like that.

Laurie hurried along Woodhaven Boulevard, intent on thoughts of what she'd say to her mother after all this time.

The traffic light blinked an amber warning, but she stepped off the curb anyway. A horn startled her, and the driver screamed out the window, "Where the hell you going, lady? Dincha see the light?"

Where the hell was she going? She snapped back to her surroundings and rushed to the safety of the opposite sidewalk. She looked around, once again aware of the glorious day. She inhaled deeply. Of course! She'd write the dialogue with her mother on the computer and then rehearse her part before she called. Why hadn't she thought of that before? She headed home, a girlish skip in her walk.

Kola lay coiled around herself on the bed, her nose snuggled to her rear, her tail a canopy over her. An occasional current of air from the open window stirred the hairs in its path. Suddenly, her ear twitched, and her body heaved with a strangled yelp and then jerked awkwardly. Clifford left the desk where he was examining his new pencil box and notebook, preparing for Tuesday. He brought a large brush with him and sat on the bed, gently stroking her forehead with his hand. Without opening her eyes, she uncurled herself and burrowed backward into his thigh. Clifford dug the metal bristles into her and with long, steady strokes, he massaged her skin, soothed her nerves, and obliterated her past.

He watched her face, the nostrils of the shiny black nose pulsing. "It'll be okay, girl. I'll only be gone part of the day. I'm gonna come home every day. And if I have to be late, Mom promised to keep you company. She's gonna be studying anyway. You'll never be alone 'slong as I'm here. We gotta stick together, forever." He stretched out, facing her, and rested his head in her neck. His blond hair and her white fur wove together. He put his arm around her side and let his lids, heavy with tiredness, close. Her unconscious groan of pleasure was more a cat's purr. In her sleep, Kola Marcus, née Kid-Beauty-Damn Mutt-Rowan, lifted a heavy paw and held it to Clifford's shoulder.

The hair on men's legs didn't seem to have any relation to the hair on their heads. There was the long and straight kind that completely covered the flesh in a soft down; the curly, kinky kind that looked like fuzzy coils; and then there was an in-between kind like Ken's, Louise thought, rich and thick and smooth, with spots of tan showing through, more heavily in the thighs where the growth wasn't so generous. She watched Ken, bent over the car trunk, rearranging a beach chair and toolbox and some small cartons to accommodate their bags. In his khaki shorts and sandals, his legs were long and sinewy and as he hefted a snow tire out of the way, the muscle in the back of his shin moved, slithering under his skin.

Somebody ought to do a study, Louise decided, comparing chest and leg hair with head hair. Research on why guys with straight, thinning hair always seem to have excessive, gorilla-type body hair. And why guys like Ken Hollis, whose hair was so thick and curly, like she wished hers was, had the opposite kind on his legs and almost none at all in the cleft between his nipples. From the way he was stooped away from her, Louise noticed that the white disk of baldness in the center of the whorls at the back of his skull had grown larger. Not that she minded. She liked it. As much as she liked the gray highlights in the blond, which gave him that ashy aura of maturity she found so attractive.

"Christ, what do you have in here?" He pushed her bag in next to the chair.

"Just a bathing suit for when it warms up and a pair of nice pants for tonight."

"I know for sure it can't be a bikini. It weighs a ton." He patted everything down and slammed the trunk.

"Well, I had to bring my hair dryer, and my curling iron, and another pair of shoes."

"My mother will take one look and think you're staying for a month!"

"I just might."

Ken walked around and opened the passenger door for her, gesturing chivalrously for her to get in. "It's no threat. She'd be delighted."

"Sure! Just wait 'til she finds out her son is bringing home a shicker."

"Shiksa, shiksa," he corrected her. "How many times do I have to tell you? A shicker is a drunk. A shiksa is a Gentile." Ken smoothed the hem of her skirt inside, then closed the door. He walked around to his side and got in the car, smiling affectionately at her.

"Well then, I have the perfect name for Louise Sidway," she said seriously.

"Buckle up." Ken Hollis clicked his seat belt. "What?"

Louise pulled her belt across her shoulders, down to the hasp at her waist. "Know what they ought to call a non-Jewish female who is drunk with love? A shicker-shiksa. Or on days you want a little variety, a shiksa-shicker."

As he turned the key and the motor sputtered, Ken Hollis's roar of laughter was lost in the roar of the engine. He pulled away. A few blocks further, he waited in the access lane, the smile still broadening his face. Looking out the right window for a hole in the steady line of oncoming vehicles, his eyes couldn't help but fall on the girl sitting beside him. The one who made him laugh. And sometimes cry. He wanted her to be there when he was driving, when he was waking, or working, or relaxing, or eating, or thinking, or sleeping. Especially when he was sleeping, when he could reach out to touch a dream. He wanted her to be there always. Somehow, he knew she would be.

With a tenderness that made his chest full, he pulled onto the FDR Drive.

Laurie's Posts

PET-ICULAR

Six to eight million cats and dogs are brought to shelters every year.

Three to four million of them are euthanized.

That's an improvement over the 20 million from thirty or forty years ago.

It's better, but not good enough.

PET-ICULAR

The US military chops off the legs of live goats and pigs to understand war wounds. They stuff tubes down cats' throats, and they crush mice into cylinders. More than ten thousand living, breathing, suffering creatures are shot, mutilated, and killed by them—our government—every year.

PET-ICULAR

Who cries for the animals used in research? Between 70 and 100 million animals in the United States are maimed, blinded, scalded, force-fed chemicals, genetically manipulated, hurt, and killed each year—all in the name of science—by private institutions, household product and cosmetics companies, government agencies, educational institutions, and scientific centers. Maybe you don't care so much about the 20 million rats and mice, but what about the sixty thousand dogs, the twenty-six thousand cats, and the thirty thousand primates? Who cries for them, too weak and hurting too much to cry for themselves?

PET-ICULAR

In a landmark ruling, a ring of eight perpetrators were recently sentenced to short prison terms for injuring or killing 500 to 640 dogs in their dog-fighting operation. How many other rings are operating out there?

PET-ICULAR

The tobacco industry is still using animals to experiment, forcing them to breathe cigarette smoke six hours straight every day for up to three years. Or apply tar to their skin to cause tumors to grow. They already know smoking is bad for you. What are they trying to prove?

PET-ICULAR

The US exports almost 12 million pelts a year to service the 500-million-dollar global fur industry. Foxes, mink, lynx, born and nursed in suffocating crowds, only to be killed and skinned, some of them while alive.

PET-ICULAR

The Dallas Safari Club auctioned a permit to shoot a black rhino in the name of conservation. It went to a bidder for $350,000. The government of Namibia, which issued the permit, allowed this to "cull" the species. Even though in the past fifty years, the number of black rhinos has dwindled from seventy thousand to five thousand. A man with $350,000 could do so much to save wildlife.

PET-ICULAR

More than sixty-four thousand dogs—our best friends—were used in research as recently as 2012. More than 98 percent of schools have stopped using animals, but what about the other 2 percent, including the University of Mississippi Medical School, Wayne Medical School, two other universities, and twenty scientific facilities? The National Institutes of Health had given the University of Wisconsin $3 million to conduct sickening experiments on cats. Luckily, the laboratory was closed down in January 2015.

PET-ICULAR

An estimated 100 million sharks are killed for their fins every year. Or for sport. Their fins are chopped off. Then the sharks are thrown back into the ocean, alive, where they struggle to breathe, suffocating or bleeding to death. I hate sharks, but I hate people who do this to living creatures more.

PET-ICULAR

During the 2009 recession, 500,000 to 1,000,000 dogs and cats were given up to shelters.

PET-ICULAR

The ten-billion-dollar illegal wildlife trade is fourth—after drugs, arms, and human trafficking—in profit. Rhino horns sell for $35,000 a pound, more than the price of gold.

PET-ICULAR

Of the ten thousand puppy mills in the country, only two thousand are licensed, giving them the authority to cage, torture, and abuse dogs so they can breed two million puppies. Dogs who never know the touch of a human hand, whose paws never know the feel of grass. Missouri gets the star for the most.

PET-ICULAR

It took the international outrage over the murder of Cecil the lion to expose trophy hunters for the barbaric human beings they are. Worse than indifferent to the lives of animals, they revel in the pleasure of killing them. And pay big bucks, in this case $55,000, to do it. What is the sport in having someone lure an animal close enough to shoot it?

PET-ICULAR

Baby monkeys are torn away from their mothers at birth and subjected to terrifying experiments. Why? To measure their emotional pain. The National Institutes of Health is actually breeding monkeys so they have more babies to subject to psychological torture. Then they kill and dissect most of them before they're eight years old. How can they endure eight years of cruelty and horror?